THE HOLLOW OF HER HAND

"The black pile is mine, the gay pile is yours," she went
on, turning toward the sleeping girl

(*Page 47*)

THE HOLLOW
OF HER HAND

By

GEORGE BARR McCUTCHEON

AUTHOR OF
GRAUSTARK, TRUXTON KING, ETC.

WITH ILLUSTRATIONS BY
A. I. KELLER

GROSSET & DUNLAP
PUBLISHERS :: :: NEW YORK

CONTENTS

THE HOLLOW OF HER HAND

CHAPTER I

THE train, which had roared through a withering gale of sleet all the way up from New York, came to a standstill, with many an ear-splitting sigh, alongside the little station, and a reluctant porter opened his vestibule door to descend to the snow-swept platform: a solitary passenger had reached the journey's end. The swirl of snow and sleet screaming out of the blackness at the end of the station-building enveloped the porter in an instant, and cut his ears and neck with stinging force as he turned his back against the gale. A pair of lonely, half-obscured platform lights gleamed fatuously at the top of their icy posts at each end of the station; two or three frost-encrusted windows glowed dully in the side of the building, while one shone brightly where the operator sat waiting for the passing of No. 33.

The train itself was dark. Frosty windows, pelted for miles by the furious gale, white outside but black within, protected the snug travellers who slept the sleep of the hurried and thought not of the storm that beat about their ears nor wondered at the stopping of the fast express at a place where it had never stopped before. Far ahead the panting engine shed from its open fire-box an aureole of glaring red as the stoker fed coal into its rapacious maw. The unblinking head-light threw its rays into the thick of the blinding snow storm, fruitlessly searching for the rails through drifts denser than fog and filled with strange, half-visible shapes.

An order had been issued for the stopping of the fast express at B——, a noteworthy concession in these

days of premeditated haste.   Not in the previous career
of flying 33 had it even so much as slowed down for the
insignificant little station, through which it swooped at
midnight the whole year round.   Just before pulling
out of New York on this eventful night the conductor
received a command to stop 33 at B—— and let down
a single passenger, a circumstance which meant trouble
for every despatcher along the line.

The woman who got down at B—— in the wake of
the shivering but deferential porter, and who passed by
the conductors without lifting her face, was without
hand luggage of any description.   She was heavily
veiled, and warmly clad in furs.   At eleven o'clock that
night she had entered the compartment in New York.
Throughout the thirty miles or more, she had sat alone
and inert beside the snow-clogged window, peering
through veil and frost into the night that whizzed past
the pane, seeing nothing yet apparently intent on all
that stretched beyond.   As still, as immobile as death
itself she had held herself from the moment of departure
to the instant that brought the porter with the word
that they were whistling for B——.   Without a word
she arose and followed him to the vestibule, where she
watched him as he unfastened the outer door and lifted
the trap.   A single word escaped her lips and he held out
his hand to receive the crumpled bill she clutched in her
gloved fingers.   He did not look at it.   He knew that it
would amply reward him for the brief exposure he endured on the lonely, wind-swept platform of a station,
the name of which he did not know.

She took several uncertain steps in the direction of
the station windows and stopped, as if bewildered.   Already the engine was pounding the air with quick,
vicious snorts in the effort to get under way; the vesti-

bule trap and door closed with a bang; the wheels were creaking. A bitter wind smote her in the face; the wet, hurtling sleet crashed against the thin veil, blinding her.

The door of the waiting-room across the platform opened and a man rushed toward her.

"Mrs. Wrandall?" he called above the roar of the wind.

She advanced quickly.

"Yes."

"What a night!" he said, as much to himself as to her. "I'm sorry you would insist on coming tonight. To-morrow morning would have satisfied the —"

"Is this Mr. Drake?"

They were being blown through the door into the waiting-room as she put the question. Her voice was muffled. The man in the great fur coat put his weight against the door to close it.

"Yes, Mrs. Wrandall. I have done all that could be done under the circumstances. I am sorry to tell you that we still have two miles to go by motor before we reach the inn. My car is open,— I don't possess a limousine,— but if you will lie down in the tonneau you will find some protection from —"

She broke in sharply, impatiently. "Pray do not consider me, Mr. Drake. I am not afraid of the blizzard."

"Then we'd better be off," said he, a note of anxiety in his voice,— a certain touch of nervousness. "I drive my own car. The road is good, but I shall drive cautiously. Ten minutes, perhaps. I — I am sorry you thought best to brave this wretched —"

"I am not sorry for myself, Mr. Drake, but for you.

You have been most kind. I did not expect you to meet me."

"I took the liberty of telephoning to you. It was well that I did it early in the evening. The wires are down now, I fear." He hesitated for a moment, staring at her as if trying to penetrate the thick, wet veil. "I may have brought you on a fool's errand. You see, I — I have seen Mr. Wrandall but once, in town somewhere, and I may be wrong. Still, the coroner, — and the sheriff,— seemed to think you should be notified,— I might say questioned. That is why I called you up. I trust, madam, that I *am* mistaken."

"Yes," she said shrilly, betraying the intensity of her emotion. It was as if she lacked the power to utter more than a single word, which signified neither acquiescence nor approval.

He was ill-at-ease, distressed. "I have engaged a room for you at the inn, Mrs. Wrandall. You did not bring a maid, I see. My wife will come over from our place to stay with you if you —"

She shook her head. "Thank you, Mr. Drake. It will not be necessary. I came alone by choice. I shall return to New York to-night."

"But you — why, you can't do that," he cried, holding back as they started toward the door. "No trains stop here after ten o'clock. The locals begin running at seven in the morning. Besides —"

She interrupted him. "May we not start now, Mr. Drake? I am — well, you must see that I am suffering. I must see, I must know. The suspense —" She did not complete the sentence, but hurried past him to the door, throwing it open and bending her body to the gust that burst in upon them.

He sprang after her, grasping her arm to lead her

across the icy platform to the automobile that stood in the lee of the building.

Disdaining his command to enter the tonneau, she stood beside the car and waited until he cranked it and took his place at the wheel. Then she took her seat beside him and permitted him to tuck the great buffalo robe about her. No word was spoken. The man was a stranger to her. She forgot his presence in the car.

Into the thick of the storm the motor chugged. Grim and silent, the man at the wheel, ungoggled and tense, sent the whirring thing swiftly over the trackless village street and out upon the open country road. The woman closed her eyes and waited.

You would know the month was March. He said: " It comes in like a lion," but apparently the storm swallowed the words for she made no response to them.

They crossed the valley and crept up the tree-covered hill, where the force of the gale was broken. If she heard him say: " Fierce, wasn't it? " she gave no sign, but sat hunched forward, peering ahead through the snow at the blurred lights that seemed so far away and yet were close at hand.

" Is that the inn? " she asked as he swerved from the road a few moments later.

" Yes, Mrs. Wrandall. We're here."

" Is — is he in there? "

" Where you see that lighted window upstairs." He tooted the horn vigorously as he drew up to the long, low porch. Two men dashed out from the doorway and clumsily assisted her from the car.

" Go right in, Mrs. Wrandall," said Drake. " I will join you in a jiffy."

She walked between the two men into the feebly

lighted office of the inn. The keeper of the place, a
dreary looking person with dread in his eyes, hurried
forward. She stopped stock-still. Some one was
brushing the stubborn, thickly caked snow from her
long chinchilla coat.

"You must let me get you something hot to drink,
madam," the landlord was saying dolorously.

She struggled with her veil, finally tearing it away
from her face. Then she took in the rather bare,
cheerless room with a slow, puzzled sweep of her eyes.

"No, thank you," she replied.

"It won't be any trouble, madam," urged the other.
"It's right here. The sheriff says it's all right to serve
it, although it is after hours. I run a respectable, law-
abiding house. I wouldn't think of offering it to any-
one if it was in violation —"

"Never mind, Burton," interposed a big man, approaching. "Let the lady choose for herself. If she
wants it, she'll say so. I am the sheriff, madam. This
gentleman is the coroner, Dr. Sheef. We waited up
for you after Mr. Drake said you'd got the fast train
to stop for you. To-morrow morning would have done
quite as well. I'm sorry you came to-night in all this
blizzard."

He was staring as if fascinated at the white, colourless face of the woman who with nervous fingers unfastened the heavy coat that enveloped her slender figure. She was young and strikingly beautiful, despite
the intense pallor that overspread her face. Her
dark, questioning, dreading eyes looked up into his with
an expression he was never to forget. It combined
dread, horror, doubt and a smouldering anger that
seemed to overcast all other emotions that lay revealed
to him.

"This is a — what is commonly called a 'road-house'?" she asked dully, her eyes narrowing suddenly as if in pain.

The inn-keeper made haste to resent the implied criticism.

"My place is a respectable, law-abiding —"

The sheriff waved him aside.

"It is an inn during the winter, Mrs. Wrandall, and a road-house in the summer, if that makes it plain to you. I will say, however, that Burton has always kept well within the law. This is the first — er — real bit of trouble he's had, and I won't say it's his fault. Keep quiet, Burton. No one is accusing you of anything wrong. Don't whine about it."

"But my place is ruined," groaned the doleful one. "It's got a black eye now. Not that I blame you, madam, but you can see how —"

He quailed before the steady look in her eyes, and turned away mumbling.

There were half a dozen men in the room, besides the speakers, sober-faced fellows who conversed in undertones and studiously kept their backs to the woman who had just come among them. They were grouped about the roaring fireplace in the lower end of the room. Steam arose from their heavy winters garments. Their caps were still drawn far down over their ears. These were men who had been out in the night.

"There is a fire in the reception-room, madam," said the coroner; "and the proprietor's wife to look out for you if you should require anything. Will you go in there and compose yourself before going upstairs? Or, if you would prefer waiting until morning, I shall not insist on the — er — ordeal to-night."

"I prefer going up there to-night," said she steadily.

The men looked at each other, and the sheriff spoke. "Mr. Drake is quite confident the — the man is your husband. It's an ugly affair, Mrs. Wrandall. We had no means of identifying him until Drake came in this evening, out of curiosity you might say. For your sake, I hope he is mistaken."

"Would you mind telling me something about it before I go upstairs? I am quite calm. I am prepared for anything. You need not hesitate."

"As you wish, madam. You will go into the reception-room, if you please. Burton, is Mrs. Wrandall's room quite ready for her?"

"I shall not stay here to-night," interposed Mrs. Wrandall. "You need not keep the room for me."

"But, my dear Mrs. Wrandall —"

"I shall wait in the railway station until morning if necessary. But not here."

The coroner led the way to the cosy little room off the office. She followed with the sheriff. The men looked worn and haggard in the bright light that met them, as if they had not known sleep or rest for many hours.

"The assistant district attorney was here until eleven, but went home to get a little rest. It's been a hard case for all of us — a nasty one," explained the sheriff, as he placed a chair in front of the fire for her. She sank into it limply.

"Go on, please," she murmured, and shook her head at the nervous little woman who bustled up and inquired if she could do anything to make her more comfortable.

The sheriff cleared his throat. "Well, it happened last night. All day long we've been trying to find out who he is, and ever since eight o'clock this morning we've been searching for the woman who came here with him.

She has disappeared as completely as if swallowed by
the earth. Not a sign of a clew — not a shred.
There's nothing to show when she left the inn or by
what means. All we know is that the door to that room
up there was standing half open when Burton passed
by it at seven o'clock this morning — that is to say, yesterday morning, for this is now Wednesday. It is
quite clear, from this, that she neglected to close the
door tightly when she came out, probably through
haste or fear, and the draft in the hall blew it wider
open during the night. Burton says the inn was closed
for the night at half-past ten. He went to bed. She
must have slipped out after every one was sound asleep.
There were no other guests on that floor. Burton and
his wife sleep on this floor, and the servants are at the
top of the house and in a wing. No one heard a
sound. We have not the remotest idea when the
thing happened, or when she left the place. Dr.
Sheef says the man had been dead for six or eight hours
when he first saw him, and that was very soon after
Burton's discovery. Burton, on finding the door open,
naturally suspected that his guests had skipped out
during the night to avoid paying the bill, and lost no
time in entering the room.

"He found the man lying on the bed, sprawled out,
face upward and as dead as a mack — I should say,
quite dead. He was partly dressed. His coat and
vest hung over the back of a chair. A small service
carving knife, belonging to the inn, had been driven
squarely into his heart and was found sticking there.
Burton says that the man, on their arrival at the inn,
about nine o'clock at night, ordered supper sent up to
the room. The tray of dishes, with most of the food
untouched, and an empty champagne bottle, was found

on the service table near the bed. One of the chairs
was overturned. The servant who took the meal to the
room says that the woman was sitting at the window
with her wraps on, motor veil and all, just as she was
when she came into the place. The man gave all the
directions, the woman apparently paying no attention
to what was going on. The waitress left the room
without seeing her face. She had instructions not to
come for the tray until morning.

"That was the last time the man was seen alive.
No one has seen the woman since the door closed after
the servant, who distinctly remembers hearing the key
turn in the lock as she went down the hall. It seems
pretty clear that the man ate and drank but not the
woman. Her food remained untouched on the plate
and her glass was full. 'Gad, it must have been a
merry feast! I beg your pardon, Mrs. Wrandall!"

"Go on, please," said she levelly.

"That's all there is to say so far as the actual
crime is concerned. There were signs of a struggle,—
but it isn't necessary to go into that. Now, as to
their arrival at the inn. The blizzard had not set in.
Last night was dark, of course, as there is no moon,
but it was clear and rather warm for the time of year.
The couple came here about nine o'clock in a high
power runabout machine, which the man drove. They
had no hand-baggage and apparently had run out from
New York. Burton says he was on the point of refusing them accommodations when the man handed him a
hundred dollar bill. It was more than Burton's cupidity could withstand. They did not register. The
state license numbers had been removed from the automobile, which was of foreign make. Of course, it was
only a question of time until we could have found out

who the car belonged to. It is perfectly obvious why
he removed the numbers."

At this juncture Drake entered the room. Mrs.
Wrandall did not at first recognise him.

"It has stopped snowing," announced the new-
comer.

"Oh, it is Mr. Drake," she murmured. "We have
a little French car, painted red," she announced to the
sheriff without giving Drake another thought.

"And this one is red, madam," said the sheriff, with
a glance at the coroner. Drake nodded his head.
Mrs. Wrandall's body stiffened perceptibly, as if de-
flecting a blow. "It is still standing in the garage,
where he left it on his arrival."

"Did no one see the face of — of the woman? " asked
Mrs. Wrandall, rather querulously. "It seems odd
that no one should have seen her face," she went on
without waiting for an answer.

"It's not strange, madam, when you consider *all* the
circumstances. She was very careful not to remove
her veil or her coat until the door was locked. That
proves that she was not the sort of woman we usually
find gallavanting around with men regardless of —
ahem, I beg your pardon. This must be very distressing to you."

"I am not sure, Mr. Sheriff, that it *is* my husband
who lies up there. Please remember that," she said
steadily. "It is easier to hear the details now, before
I *know*, than it will be afterward if it should turn out
to be as Mr. Drake declares."

"I see," said the sheriff, marvelling.

"Besides, Mr. Drake is not *positive*," put in the
coroner hopefully.

"I am reasonably certain," said Drake.

"Then all the more reason why I should have the story first," said she, with a shiver that no one failed to observe.

The sheriff resumed his conclusions. "Women of the kind I referred to a moment ago don't care whether they're seen or not. In fact, they're rather brazen about it. But this one was different. She was as far from that as it was possible for her to be. We haven't been able to find any one who saw her face or who can give the least idea as to what she looks like, excepting a general description of her figure, her carriage, and the out-door garments she wore. We have reason to believe she was young. She was modestly dressed. Her coat was one of those heavy ulster affairs, such as a woman uses in motoring or on a sea-voyage. There was a small sable stole about her neck. The skirt was short, and she wore high black shoes of the thick walking type. Judging from Burton's description she must have been about your size and figure, Mrs. Wrandall. Isn't that so, Mrs. Burton?"

The inn-keeper's wife spoke. "Yes, Mr. Harben, I'd say so myself. About five feet six, I'd judge; rather slim and graceful-like, in spite of the big coat."

Mrs. Wrandall was watching the woman's face. "I am five feet six," she said, as if answering a question.

The sheriff cleared his throat somewhat needlessly.

"Burton says she acted as if she were a lady," he went on. "Not the kind that usually comes out here on such expeditions, he admits. She did not speak to any one, except once in very low tones to the man she was with, and then she was standing by the fireplace out in the main office, quite a distance from the desk. She went upstairs alone, and he gave some orders to Burton before following her. That was the last time

Burton saw her. The waitress went up with a specially prepared supper about half an hour later."

"It seems quite clear, Mrs. Wrandall, that she robbed the man after stabbing him," said the coroner.

Mrs. Wrandall started. "Then she was *not* a lady, after all," she said quickly. There was a note of relief in her voice. It was as if she had put aside a half-formed conclusion.

"His pockets were empty. Not a penny had been left. Watch, cuff-links, scarf pin, cigarette case, purse and bill folder,— all gone. Burton had seen most of these articles in the office."

"Isn't it — but no! Why should I be the one to offer a suggestion that might be construed as a defence for this woman?"

"You were about to suggest, madam, that some one else might have taken the valuables — is that it?" cried the sheriff.

"Had you thought of it, Mr. Sheriff?"

"I had not. It isn't reasonable. No one about this place is suspected. We have thought of this, however: the murderess may have taken all of these things away with her in order to prevent immediate identification of her victim. She may have been clever enough for that. It would give her a start."

"Not an unreasonable conclusion, when you stop to consider, Mr. Sheriff, that the man took the initiative in that very particular," said Mrs. Wrandall in such a self-contained way that the three men looked at her in wonder. Then she came abruptly to her feet. "It is very late, gentlemen. I am ready to go upstairs, Mr. Sheriff."

"I must warn you, madam, that Mr. Drake is reasonably certain that it *is* your husband," said the coroner uncomfortably. "You may not be prepared fot the shock that —"

"I shall not faint, Dr. Sheef. If it *is* my husband I shall ask you to leave me alone in the room with him for a little while." The final word trailed out into a long, tremulous wail, showing how near she was to the breaking point in her wonderful effort at self-control. The men looked away hastily. They heard her draw two or three deep, quavering breaths; they could almost feel the tension that she was exercising over herself.

The doctor turned after a moment and spoke very gently, but with professional firmness. "You must not think of venturing out in this wretched night, madam. It would be the worst kind of folly. Surely you will be guided by me — by your own common sense. Mrs. Burton will be with you —"

"Thank you, Dr. Sheef," she interposed calmly. "If what we all fear should turn out to be the truth, I could not stay here. I could not breathe. I could not live. If, on the other hand, Mr. Drake is mistaken, I shall stay. But if it *is* my husband, I cannot remain under the same roof with him, even though he be dead. I do not expect you to understand my feelings. It would be asking too much of men,— too much."

"I think I understand," murmured Drake.

"Come," said the sheriff, arousing himself with an effort.

She moved swiftly after him. Drake and the coroner, following close behind with Mrs. Burton, could not take their eyes from the slender, graceful figure. She was a revelation to them. Feeling as they did that she was about to be confronted by the most appalling crisis

imaginable, they could not but marvel at her composure. Drake's mind dwelt on the stories of the guillo-
tine and the heroines who went up to it in those bloody
days without so much as a quiver of dread. Somehow,
to him, this woman was a heroine.

They passed into the hall and mounted the stairs.
At the far end of the corridor, a man was seated in
front of a closed door. He arose as the party approached. The sheriff signed for him to open the
door he guarded. As he did so, a chilly blast of air
blew upon the faces of those in the hall. The curtains
in the window of the room were flapping and whipping
in the wind. Mrs. Wrandall caught her breath. For
the briefest instant, it seemed as though she was on the
point of faltering. She dropped farther behind the
sheriff, her limbs suddenly stiff, her hand going out to
the wall as if for support. The next moment she was
moving forward resolutely into the icy, dimly lighted
room.

A single electric light gleamed in the corner beside
the bureau. Near the window stood the bed. She
went swiftly toward it, her eyes fastened upon the
ridge that ran through the centre of it: a still, white
ridge that seemed without beginning or end.

With nervous fingers, the attendant lifted the sheet
at the head of the bed and turned it back. As he let
it fall across the chest of the dead man, he drew back
and turned his face away.

She bent forward and then straightened her figure
to its full height, without for an instant removing her
gaze from the face of the man who lay before her: a
dark-haired man grey in death, who must have been
beautiful to look upon in the flush of life.

For a long time she stood there looking, as motion-

less as the object on which she gazed.   Behind her were
the tense, keen-eyed men, not one of whom seemed to
breathe during the grim minutes that passed.   The
wind howled about the corners of the inn, but no one
heard it.   They heard the beating of their hearts,
even the ticking of their watches, but not the wail of
the wind.

At last her hands, claw-like in their tenseness, went
slowly to her temples.   Her head drooped slightly
forward, and a great shudder ran through her body.
The coroner started forward, expecting her to collapse.

"Please go away," she was saying in an absolutely
emotionless voice.   "Let me stay here alone for a
little while."

That was all.   The men relaxed.   They looked at
each other with a single question in their eyes.   Was
it quite safe to leave her alone with her dead?   They
hesitated.

She turned on them suddenly, spreading her arms
in a wide gesture of self-absolution.   Her sombre eyes
swept the group.

"I can do no harm.   This man is mine.   I want to
look at him for the last time — alone.   Will you go?"

"Do you mean, madam, that you intend to —" began the coroner in alarm.

She clasped her hands.   "I mean that I shall take
my last look at him now — and here.   Then you may
do what you like with him.   He is your dead — not
mine.   I do not want him.   Can you understand?   *I
do not want this dead thing*.   But there is something
I would say to him, something that I must say.   Something that no one must hear but the good God who
knows how much he has hurt me.   I want to say it

close to those grey, horrid ears. Who knows? He
may hear me!"

Wondering, the others backed from the room. She
watched them until they closed the door.

.   .   .   .   .   .

Listening, they heard her lower the window. It
squealed like a thing in fear.

.   .   .   .   .   .

Ten minutes passed. The group in the hall conversed in whispers.

"Why did she put the window down?" asked the
wife of the inn-keeper, crossing herself.

Drake shook his head. "I wonder what she is saying to him," he muttered.

"A wonderful nerve," said Dr. Sheef. "Positively
wonderful. I've never seen anything like it."

"Her own husband, too," said Mrs. Burton.
"Why, I — I should have said she'd go into hysterics.
Such a handsome man he was."

"I guess, from what I've heard of this fellow, Wrandall, he's not been an angel," volunteered the sheriff.

Drake shook his head once more.

"He ain't one now, I'll bet on that," said the man
who stood guard. "He's in hell if ever a man —"

"Sh!" whispered the woman in horror. "God forgive you for uttering words like that!"

"Every one in the city knows what sort of a man
he's been," said Drake.

"He comes of a fine family," said the coroner.
"One of the best in New York. I guess he's never been
much of a credit to it, however."

"They say he ran after chorus girls," said Mrs.
Burton. The men grinned.

"I've an idea she's had the devil's own time with

him," mused the sheriff, with a jerk of his head in the direction of the door.

"Poor thing," said the inn-keeper's wife.

"Well," said Drake, taking a deep breath, "she won't have to worry any more about his not coming home nights. I say, this business will create a fearful sensation, sheriff. The Four Hundred will have a conniption fit."

"We've got to land that girl, whoever she is," grated the official. "Now that we know who he is, it shouldn't be hard to pick out the women he's been trailing with lately. Then we can sift 'em down until the right one is left. It ought to be easy."

"I'm not so sure of it," said the coroner, shaking his head. "I have a feeling that she isn't one of the ordinary type. It wouldn't surprise me if she belongs to — well, you might say, the upper ten. Somebody's wife, don't you see. That will make it rather difficult, especially as her tracks have been pretty well covered."

"It beats me, how she got away without leaving a single sign behind her," acknowledged the sheriff. "She's a wonder, that's all I've got to say."

At that instant the door opened and Mrs. Wrandall appeared. She stopped short, confronting the huddled group, dry-eyed but as pallid as a ghost. Her eyes were wide, apparently unseeing; her colourless lips were parted in the drawn rigidity that suggested but one thing to the professional man who looks: the *risis sardonicus* of the strychnæ victim. With a low cry, the doctor started forward, fully convinced that she had swallowed the deadly drug.

"For God's sake, madam," he began. But as he spoke, her expression changed; she seemed to be aware

of their presence for the first time. Her eyes narrowed in a curious manner, and the rigid lips seemed to
surge with blood, presenting the effect of a queer,
swift-fading smile that lingered long after her face
was set and serious.

"I neglected to raise the window, Dr. Sheef," she
said in a low voice. "It was very cold in there."
She shivered slightly. "Will you be so kind as to
tell me what I am to do now? What formalities remain for me —"

The coroner was at her side. "Time enough for
that, Mrs. Wrandall. The first thing you are to do is
to take something warm to drink, and pull yourself together a bit —"

She drew herself up coldly. "I am quite myself,
Dr. Sheef. Pray do not alarm yourself on my account.
I shall be obliged to you, however, if you will tell me
what I am to do as speedily as possible, and let me do
it so that I may leave this — this unhappy place without delay. No! I mean it, sir. I am going to-night
— unless, of course," she said, with a quick look at the
sheriff, "the law stands in the way."

"You are at liberty to come and go as you please,
Mrs. Wrandall," said the sheriff, "but it is most fool-
hardy to think of —"

"Thank you, Mr. Sheriff," she said, "for letting
me go. I thought perhaps there might be legal restraint." She sent a swift glance over her shoulder,
and then spoke in a high, shrill voice, indicative of extreme dread and uneasiness:

"Close the door to that room!"

The door was standing wide open, just as she had
left it. Startled, the coroner's deputy sprang forward
to close it. Involuntarily, all of her listeners looked

in the direction of the room, as if expecting to see the form of the murdered man advancing upon them. The feeling, swiftly gone, was most uncanny.

"Close it from the *inside*," commanded the coroner, with unmistakable emphasis. The man hesitated, and then did as he was ordered, but not without a curious look at the wife of the dead man, whose back was toward him.

"He will not find anything disturbed, doctor," said she, divining his thought. "I had the feeling that something was creeping toward us out of that room."

"You have every reason to be nervous, madam. The situation has been most extraordinary,— most trying," said the coroner. "I beg of you to come downstairs, where we may attend to a few necessary details without delay. It has been a most fatiguing matter for all of us. Hours without sleep, and such wretched weather."

They descended to the warm little reception-room. She sent at once for the inn-keeper, who came in and glowered at her as if she were wholly responsible for the blight that had been put upon his place.

"Will you be good enough to send some one to the station with me in your depot wagon?" she demanded without hesitation.

He stared. "We don't run a 'bus in the winter time," he said gruffly.

She opened the little chatelaine bag that hung from her wrist and abstracted a card which she submitted to the coroner.

"You will find, Dr. Sheef, that the car my husband came up here in belongs to me. This is the card issued by the State. It is in my name. The factory number is there. You may compare it with the one on the car. My husband took the car without obtaining my consent."

" Joy riding," said Burton, with an ugly laugh. Then he quailed before the look she gave him.

" If no other means is offered, Dr. Sheef, I shall ask you to let me take the car. I am perfectly capable of driving. I have driven it in the country for two seasons. All I ask is that some one be directed to go with me to the station. No! Better than that, if there is some one here who is willing to accompany me to the city, he shall be handsomely paid for going. It is but little more than thirty miles. I refuse to spend the night in this house. That is final."

They drew apart to confer, leaving her sitting before the fire, a stark figure that seemed to detach itself entirely from its surroundings and their companionship. At last, the coroner came to her side and touched her arm.

" I don't know what the district attorney and the police will say to it, Mrs. Wrandall, but I shall take it upon myself to deliver the car to you. The sheriff has gone out to compare the numbers. If he finds that the car is yours, he will see to it, with Mr. Drake, that it is made ready for you. I take it that we will have no difficulty in —" He hesitated, at a loss for words.

" In finding it again in case you need it for evidence? " she supplied. He nodded. " I shall make it a point, Dr. Sheef, to present the car to the State after it has served my purpose to-night. I shall not ride in it again."

" The sheriff has a man who will ride with you to the station or the city, whichever you may elect. Now, may I trouble you to make answer to certain questions I shall write out for you at once? The man is

Challis Wrandall, your husband? You are positive? "

"I am positive. He is — or was — Challis Wrandall."

Half an hour later, she was ready for the trip to New York City. The clock in the office marked the hour as one. A toddied individual in a great buffalo coat waited for her outside, hiccoughing and bandying jest with the half-frozen men who had spent the night with him in the forlorn hope of finding *the girl.*

Mrs. Wrandall gave final instructions to the coroner and his deputy, who happened to be the undertaker's assistant. She had answered all the questions that had been put to her, and had signed the document with a firm, untrembling hand. Her veil had been lowered since the beginning of the examination. They did not see her face; they only heard the calm, low voice, sweet with fatigue and dread.

"I shall notify my brother-in-law as soon as I reach the city," she said. "He will attend to everything. Mr. Leslie Wrandall, I mean. My husband's only brother. He will be here in the morning, Dr. Sheef. My own apartment is not open. I have been staying in a hotel since my return from Europe two days ago. But I shall attend to the opening of the place to-morrow. You will find me there."

The coroner hesitated a moment before putting the question that had come to his mind as she spoke.

"Two days ago, madam? May I inquire where your husband has been living during your absence abroad? When did you last see him alive? "

' She did not reply for many seconds, and then it was with a perceptible effort.

"I have not seen him since my return until — to-night," she replied, a hoarse note creeping into her voice. " He did not meet me on my return. His brother Leslie came to the dock. He — he said that Challis, who came back from Europe two weeks ahead of me, had been called to St. Louis on very important business. My husband had been living at his club, I understand. That is all I can tell you, sir."

" I see," said the coroner gently.

He opened the door for her and she passed out. A number of men were grouped about the throbbing motor-car. They fell away as she approached, silently fading into the shadows like so many vast, unwholesome ghosts. The sheriff and Drake came forward.

" This man will go with you, madam," said the sheriff, pointing to an unsteady figure beside the machine. " He is the only one who will undertake it. They're all played out, you see. He has been drinking, but only on account of the hardships he has undergone to-night. You will be quite safe with Morley."

No snow was falling, but a bleak wind blew meanly. The air was free from particles of sleet; wetly the fall of the night clung to the earth where it had fallen.

" If he will guide me to the Post-road, that is all I ask," said she hurriedly. Involuntarily she glanced upward. The curtains in an upstairs window were blowing inward and a dim light shone out upon the roof of the porch. She shuddered and then climbed up to the seat and took her place at the wheel.

A few moments later, the three men standing in the middle of the road watched the car as it rushed away.

" By George, she's a wonder! " said the sheriff.

CHAPTER II

THE sheriff was right. Sara Wrandall was an extraordinary woman, if I may be permitted to modify his rather crude estimate of her. It is difficult to understand, much less to describe a nature like hers. Fine-minded, gently bred women who can go through an ordeal such as she experienced without breaking under the strain are rare indeed. They must be wonderful. It is hard to imagine a more heart-breaking crisis in life than the one which confronted her on this dreadful night, and yet she had faced it with a fortitude that seems almost unholy.

She had loved her handsome, wayward husband. He had hurt her deeply more times than she chose to remember during the six years of their married life, but she had loved him in spite of the wounds up to the instant when she stood beside his dead body in the cold little room at Burton's Inn. She went there loving him as he had lived, yet prepared, almost foresworn, to loathe him as he had died, and she left him lying there alone in that dreary room without a spark of the old affection in her soul. Her love for him died in giving birth to the hatred that now possessed her. While he lived it was not in her power to control the unreasoning resistless thing that stands for love in woman: he *was* her love, the master of her impulses. Dead, he was an unwholesome, unlovely clod, a pallid thing to be scorned, a hulk of worthless clay. His blood was cold. He could no longer warm her with it; it could no longer kill the chill that his misdeeds cast about her tender

sensitiveness; his lips and eyes never more could smile
and conquer. He was a dead thing. Her love was a
dead thing. They lay separate and apart. The tie
was broken. With love died the final spark of respect
she had left for him in her tired, loyal, betrayed heart.
He was at last a thing to be despised, even by her.
She despised him.

She sent the car down the slope and across the moon-
less valley with small regard for her own or her companion's safety. It swerved from side to side, skidded
and leaped with terrifying suddenness, but held its way
as straight as the bird that flies, driven by a steady
hand and a mind that had no thought for peril. A sober man at her side would have been afraid; this man
swayed mildly to and fro and chuckled with drunken
glee.

Her bitter thoughts were not of the dead man back
there, but of the live years that she was to bury with
him: years that would never pass beyond her ken, that
would never die. He had loved her in his wild, ruthless
way. He had left her times without number in the
years gone by, but he had always come back, gaily un-
chastened, to remould the love that waited with dog-
like fidelity for the touch of his cunning hand. But
he had taken his last flight. He would not come back
again. It was all over. Once too often he had tried
his reckless wings. She would not have to forgive
him again. Uppermost in her mind was the curiously
restful thought that his troubles were over, and with
them her own. A hand less forgiving than hers had
struck him dead.

Somehow, she envied the woman to whom that hand
belonged. It had been her divine right to kill, and yet
another took it from her.

Back there at the inn she had said to the astonished sheriff:

"Poor thing, if she can escape punishment for this, let it be so. I shall not help the law to kill her simply, because she took it in her own hands to pay that man what she owed him. I shall not be the one to say that he did not deserve death at her hands, whoever she may be. No, I shall offer no reward. If you catch her, I shall be sorry for her, Mr. Sheriff. Believe me, I bear her no grudge."

"But she robbed him," the sheriff had cried.

"From my point of view, Mr. Sheriff, that hasn't anything to do with the case," was her significant reply.

"Of course, I am not defending *him*."

"Nor am I defending her," she had retorted. "It would appear that she is able to defend herself."

Now, on the cold, trackless road, she was saying to herself that she did have a grudge against the woman who had destroyed the life that belonged to her, who had killed the thing that was hers to kill. She could not mourn for him. She could only wonder what the poor, hunted terrified creature would do when taken and made to pay for the thing she had done.

Once, in the course of her bitter reflections, she spoke aloud in a shrill, tense voice, forgetful of the presence of the man beside her:

"Thank God, they will see him now as I have seen him all these years. They will know him as they have never known him. Thank God for that!"

The man looked at her stupidly and muttered something under his breath. She heard him, and recalling her wits, asked which turn she was to take for the station. The fellow lopped back in the seat, too drunk to reply.

For a moment she was dismayed, frightened. Then she resolutely reached out and shook him by the shoulder. She had brought the car to a full stop.

" Arouse yourself, man! " she cried. " Do you want to freeze to death? Where is the station? "

He straightened up with an effort, and, after vainly seeking light in the darkness, fell back again with a grunt, but managed to wave his hand toward the left. She took the chance. In five minutes she brought the car to a standstill beside the station. Through the window she saw a man with his feet cocked high, reading. He leaped to his feet in amazement as she entered the waiting-room.

" Are you the agent? " she demanded.

" No, ma'am. I'm simply stayin' here for the sheriff. We're lookin' for a woman — Say! " He stopped short and stared at the veiled face with wide, excited eyes. " Gee whiz! Maybe you —"

" No, I am not the woman you want. Do you know anything about the trains? "

" I guess I'll telephone to the sheriff before I —"

" If you will step outside you will find one of the sheriff's deputies in my automobile, helplessly intoxicated. I am Mrs. Wrandall."

" Oh," he gasped. " I heard 'em say you were coming up to-night. Well, say! What do you think of —"

" Is there a train in before morning? "

" No ma'am. Seven-forty is the first."

She waited a moment. " Then I shall have to ask you to come out and get your fellow-deputy. He is useless to me. I mean to go on in the machine. The sheriff understands."

The fellow hesitated.

"I cannot take him with me, and he will freeze to death if I leave him in the road. Will you come?"

The man stared at her.

"Say, *is* it your husband?" he asked agape.

She nodded her head.

"Well, I'll go out and have a look at the fellow you've got with you," said he, still doubtful.

She stood in the door while he crossed over to the car and peered at the face of the sleeper.

"Steve Morley," he said. "Fuller'n a goat."

"Please remove him from the car," she directed.

Later on, as he stood looking down at the inert figure in the big rocking chair, and panting from his labours, he heard her say patiently:

"And now will you be so good as to direct me to the Post-road."

He scratched his head. "This is mighty queer, the whole business," he declared, assailed by doubts. "Suppose you are *not* Mrs. Wrandall, but — the other one. What then?"

As if in answer to his question, the man Morley opened his blear-eyes and tried to get to his feet.

"Wha — what are we doin' here, Mis' Wran'all? Wha's up?"

"Stay where you are, Steve," said the other. "It's all right." Then he went forth and pointed the way to her. "It's a long ways to Columbus Circle," he said. "I don't envy you the trip. Keep straight ahead after you hit the Post-road." He stood there listening until the whir of the motor was lost in the distance. "She'll never make it," he said to himself. "It's more than a

strong man could do on roads like these.   She must be
crazy."

Coming to the Post-road, she increased the speed of
the car, with the sharp wind behind her, her eyes intent
on the white stretch that leaped up in front of the lamps
like a blank wall beyond which there was nothing but
dense oblivion.   But for the fact that she knew that this'
road ran straight and unobstructed into the outskirts
of New York, she might have lost courage and decision.
The natural confidence of an experienced driver was
hers.   She had the daring of one who has never met
with an accident, and who trusts to the instincts rather
than to an actual understanding of conditions.   With
her, it was not a question of her own capacity and
strength, but a belief in the fidelity of the engine that
carried her forward.   It had not occurred to her that
the task of guiding that heavy, swerving thing through
the unbroken road was something beyond her powers
of endurance.   She often had driven it a hundred miles
and more without resting, or without losing zest in the
enterprise: then why should she fear the small matter
of thirty miles, even under the most trying of conditions?

The restless, driving desire to be as far as possible
from that horrid sight at the inn, with all that went to
make it repellant, put strength into her arms.   The
car swung from one side of the road to the other, picking its way through the opaque desert, reeling from·
rut to rut past hideous shadows and deeper into the
black abyss that lay ahead.   No friendly light gleamed
by the wayside; the world was black and cold and dead.
She alone was on the highway, the only human creature
who defied the night.   Off there on either side people
lived, and slept, and were in darkness just as she was,

but not in dreadful darkness. They were not pursued
by ghosts; they were not running away from a Thing!
They slept and were at peace, and their lights were
out for they were not afraid in the dark. She thought
of it: she was alone! No other creature was abroad —
not one!

Sharply there came to her mind the question: was
she the only one abroad in this black little world?
What of the other woman? The one who was being
hunted? Where was she? And what of the ghost at
her heels?

The car bounded over a railroad crossing. She
recalled the directions given by the man at the station
and hastily applied the brake. There was another
and more dangerous crossing a hundred yards ahead.
She had been warned particularly to take it carefully,
as there was a sharp curve in the road beyond.

Suddenly she jammed down the emergency brake, a
startled exclamation falling from her lips. Not twenty
feet ahead, in the middle of the road and directly in
line with the light of the lamps, stood a black, motionless figure — the figure of a woman whose head was
lowered and whose arms hung limply at her sides.

The woman in the car bent forward over the wheel,
staring hard. Many seconds passed. At last the forlorn object in the roadway lifted her face and looked
vacantly into the glare of the lamps. Her eyes were
wide-open, her face a ghastly white.

" God in heaven! " struggled from the stiffening lips
of Sara Wrandall. Her fingers tightened on the wheel.

She knew. This was the woman!

The long brown ulster; the limp, fluttering veil!
" A woman about your size and figure," the sheriff had
said.

The figure swayed and then moved a few steps forward. Blinded by the lights, she bent her head and shielded her eyes with her hand the better to glimpse the occupant of the car.

" Are you looking for me? " she cried out shrilly, at the same time spreading her arms as if in surrender. It was almost a wail.

Mrs. Wrandall caught her breath. Her heart began to beat once more.

" Who are you? What do you want? " she cried out, without knowing what she said.

The girl started. She had not expected to hear the voice of a woman. She staggered to the side of the road, out of the line of light.

" I — I beg your pardon," she cried,— it was like a wail of disappointment, — " I am sorry to have stopped you."

" Come here," commanded the other, still staring.

The unsteady figure advanced. Halting beside the car, she leaned across the spare tires and gazed into the eyes of the driver. Their faces were not more than a foot apart, their eyes were narrowed in tense scrutiny.

" What do you want? " repeated Mrs. Wrandall, her voice hoarse and tremulous.

" I am looking for an inn. It must be near by. I do —"

" An inn? " with a start.

" I do not recall the name. It is not far from a village, in the hills."

" Do you mean Burton's? "

" Yes. That's it. Can you direct me? " The voice of the girl was faint; she seemed about to fall.

" It is six or eight miles from here," said Mrs. Wran-

dall, still looking in wonder at the miserable night-
farer.

The girl's head sank; a moan of despair came
through her lips, ending in a sob.

"So far as that?" she murmured. Then she drew
herself up with a fine show of resolution. "But I
must not stop here. Thank you."

"Wait!" cried the other. The girl turned to her
once more. "Is — is it a matter of life or death?"

There was a long silence. "Yes. I must find my
way there. It is — death."

Sara Wrandall laid her heavily gloved hand on the
slim fingers that touched the tire.

"Listen to me," she said, a shrill note of resolve
ringing in her voice. "I am going to New York.
Won't you let me take you with me?"

The girl drew back, wonder and apprehension struggling for the mastery of her eyes.

"But I am bound the other way. To the inn. I
must go on."

"Come with me," said Sara Wrandall firmly. "You
must not go back there. I know what has happened
there. Come! I will take care of you. You must
not go to the inn."

"You know?" faltered the girl.

"Yes. You poor thing!" There was infinite pity
in her voice.

The girl laid her head on her arms.

Mrs. Wrandall sat above her, looking down, held
mute by warring emotions. The impossible had come
to pass. The girl for whom the whole world would
be searching in a day or two, had stepped out of the
unknown and, by the most whimsical jest of fate, into
the custody of the one person most interested of all

in that self-same world. It was unbelievable. She wondered if it were not a dream, or the hallucination of an overwrought mind. Spurred by the sudden doubt as to the reality of the object before her, she stretched out her hand and touched the girl's shoulder.

Instantly she looked up. Her fingers sought the friendly hand and clasped it tightly.

"Oh, if you will only take me to the city with you! If you only give me the chance," she cried hoarsely. "I don't know what impulse was driving me back there. I only know I could not help myself. You really mean it? You *will* take me with you?"

"Yes. Don't be afraid. Come! Get in," said the woman in the car rapidly. "You — you are real?"

The girl did not hear the strange question. She was hurrying around to the opposite side of the car. As she crossed before the lamps, Mrs. Wrandall noticed with dulled interest that her garments were covered with mud; her small, comely hat was in sad disorder; loose wisps of hair fluttered with the unsightly veil. Her hands, she recalled, were clad in thin suede gloves. She would be half-frozen. She had been out in all this terrible weather,— perhaps since the hour of her flight from the inn.

The odd feeling of pity grew stronger within her. She made no effort to analyse it, nor to account for it. Why should she pity the slayer of her husband? It was a question unasked, unconsidered. Afterwards she was to recall this hour and its strange impulses, and to realise that it was not pity, but mercy that moved her to do the extraordinary thing that followed.

Trembling all over, her teeth chattering, her breath coming in short little moans, the girl struggled up beside her and fell back in the seat. Without a word,

Sara Wrandall drew the great buffalo robe over her
and tucked it in about her feet and legs and far up
about her body, which had slumped down in the seat.

"You are very, very good," chattered the girl, almost inaudibly. "I shall never forget —" She did
not complete the sentence, but sat upright and fixed
her gaze on her companion's face. "You — you are
not doing this just to turn me over to — to the police?
They must be searching for me. You are not going to
give me up to them, are you? There will be a reward
I —"

"There is no reward," said Sara Wrandall sharply.
"I do not mean to give you up. I am simply giving
you a chance to get away. I have always felt sorry
for the fox when the time for the kill drew near.
That's the way I feel."

"Oh, thank you! Thank you! But what am I saying? Why should I permit you to do this for me? I
meant to go back there and have it over with. I know
I can't escape. It will have to come, it is bound to
come. Why put it off? Let them take me, let them
do what they will with me. I —"

"Hush! We'll see. First of all, understand me:
I shall not turn you over to the police. I will give you
the chance. I will help you. I can do no more than
that."

"But why should you help me? I — I — Oh, I can't
let you do it! You do not understand. I — have —
committed — a — terrible —" she broke off with a
groan.

"I understand," said the other, something like grimness in her level tones. "I have been tempted more
than once myself." The enigmatic remark made no
impression on the listener.

"I wonder how long ago it was that it all happened," muttered the girl, as if to herself. "It seems ages,— oh, such ages."

"Where have you been hiding since last night?" asked Mrs. Wrandall, throwing in the clutch. The car started forward with a jerk, kicking up the snow behind it.

"Was it only last night? Oh, I've been —" The thought of her sufferings from exposure and dread was too much for the wretched creature. She broke out in a soft wail.

"You've been out in all this weather?" demanded the other.

"I lost my way. In the hills back there. I don't know where I was."

"Had you no place of shelter?"

"Where could I seek shelter? I spent the day in the cellar of a farmer's house. He didn't know I was there. I have had no food."

"Why did you kill that man?"

"There was nothing left for me to do but that."

"And why did you rob him?"

"Ah, I had ample time to think of all that. You may tell the officers they will find everything hidden in that farmhouse cellar. God knows I did not want them. I am not a thief. I'm not so bad as that."

Mrs. Wrandall marvelled. "Not so bad as that!" And she was a murderess, a wanton!

"You are hungry? You must be famished."

"No, I am not hungry. I have not thought of food." She said it in such a way that the other knew what her whole mind had been given over to since the night before.

A fresh impulse seized her. "You shall have food

and a place where you can sleep — and rest," she said.
" Now please don't say anything more. I do not want
to know too much. The least you say to-night, the
better for — for both of us."

With that she devoted all of her attention to the car,
increasing the speed considerably. Far ahead she
could see twinkling, will-o'-the-wisp lights, the first
signs of thickly populated districts. They were still
eight or ten miles from the outskirts of the city and the
way was arduous. She was conscious of a sudden feeling of fatigue. The chill of the night seemed to have
made itself felt with abrupt, almost stupefying force.
She wondered if she could keep her strength, her courage,— her nerves.

The girl was English. Mrs. Wrandall was convinced
of the fact almost immediately. Unmistakably English and apparently of the cultivated type. In fact,
the peculiarities of speech that determines the London
show-girl or music-hall character were wholly lacking.
Her voice, her manner, even under such trying conditions, were characteristic of the English woman of
cultivation. Despite the dreadful strain under which
she laboured, there were evidences of that curious serenity which marks the English woman of the better
classes: an inborn composure, a calm orderliness of
the emotions. Mrs. Wrandall was conscious of a sense
of surprise, of a wonder that increased as her thoughts
resolved themselves into something less chaotic than
they were at the time of contact with this visible condition.

For a mile or more, she sent the car along with
reckless disregard for comfort or safety. Her mind
was groping for something tangible in the way of intentions. What was she to do with this creature?

What was to become of her? At what street corner should she turn her adrift? The idea of handing her over to the police did not enter her thoughts for an instant. Somehow she felt that the girl was a stranger to the city. She could not explain the feeling, yet it was with her and very persistent. Of course, there was a home of some sort, or lodgings, or friends, but would the girl dare show herself in familiar haunts?

She had said to the sheriff that she hoped the slayer of her husband would never be caught. She recalled her words, and she remembered how sincere she had been in uttering them. But she had not figured on herself as an instrument in furthering the hope to the point of actual realisation. What could be more incongruous, more theatric,— yes, more bizarre, than her attitude at this moment? It seemed impossible that this shrinking, inert heap at her side was a living thing; a woman who had slain a fellow creature, and that creature the man who had been her husband for six years. It seemed utterly beyond sense or reason that she should be helping this murderess to escape, that she should be showing her the slightest sign of mercy. And yet, it was all true. She *was* helping her, she was befriending her.

She found herself wondering why the poor wretch had not made way with herself. Escape seemed out of the question. That must have been clear to her from the beginning, else why was she going back there to give herself up? What better way out of it all than self-destruction? Sara Wrandall reached a sudden conclusion. She would advise the girl to leave the car when they reached the centre of a certain bridge that spanned the river! No one would find her . . .

Even as the thought took shape in her mind, she experienced a great sense of awe, so overwhelming that she cried out with the horror of it. She turned her head for a quick glance at the mute, wretched face showing white above the robe, and her heart ached with sudden pity for her. The thought of that slender, alive thing going down to the icy waters — her soul turned sick with the dread of it!

In that instant, Sara Wrandall — no philanthropist, no sentimentalist — made up her mind to give this erring one more than an even chance for salvation. She would see her safely across *that* bridge and many others. God had directed the footsteps of this girl so that she should fall in with the one best qualified to pass judgment on her. It was in that person's power to save her or destroy her. The commandment, " Thou shalt not kill," took on a broader meaning as she considered the power that was hers: the power to kill.

Back of all these finely human impulses was the mysterious arbiter that makes great decisions for all of us, from which there can be no appeal, and which brooks no argument: Self. Self it was that put a single question to her and answered it as well: what personal grievance had she against this unhappy girl? None whatever. Self it was therefore that slyly thanked her for an unspeakable blessing: she had brought to an end not only the life of her husband but the false position she herself had been obliged to maintain through a mistaken sense of duty and self-respect. And who was to say, outside the law, that this frail girl had not just cause to slay?

A great relaxation came over Sara Wrandall. It was as if every nerve, every muscle in her body had reached the snapping point and suddenly had given way. For a moment her hands were weak and powerless; her head fell forward. In an instant she conquered,— but only partially,— the strange feeling of lassitude. Then she realised how tired she was, how fiercely the strain had told on her body and brain, how much she had really suffered.

Her blurred eyes turned once more for a look at the girl, who sat there, just as she had been sitting for miles, her white face standing out with almost unnatural clearness, and as rigid as that of the sphinx.

The girl spoke. "Do they hang women in this country?"

Mrs. Wrandall started. "In some of the States," she replied, and was unable to account for the swift impulse to evade.

"But in this State?" persisted the other, almost without a movement of the lips.

"They send them to the electric chair — sometimes," said Mrs. Wrandall.

There was a long silence between them, broken finally by the girl.

"You have been very kind to me, madam. I have no means of expressing my gratitude. I can only say that I shall bless you to my dying hour. May I trouble you to set me down at the bridge? I remember crossing one. I shall be able to —"

"No!" cried Mrs. Wrandall shrilly, divining the other's intention at once. "You shall not do that. I too thought of that as a way out of it for you, but — no, it must not be that. Give me a few minutes to think. I will find a way."

The girl turned toward her. Her eyes were burning.

"Do you mean that you will help me to get away?"
she cried, slowly, incredulously.

"Let me think!"

"You will lay yourself liable —"

"Let me think, I say."

"But I mean to surrender myself to —"

"An hour ago you meant to do it, but what were you
thinking of ten minutes ago? Not surrender. You
were thinking of the bridge. Listen to me now: I am
sure that I can save you. I do not know all the — all
the circumstances connected with your association with
— with that man back there at the inn. Twenty-four
hours passed before they were able to identify him.
It is not unlikely that to-morrow may put them in
possession of the name of the woman who went with
him to that place. They do not know it to-night, of
that I am positive. You covered your trail too well.
But you must have been seen with him during the day
or the night —"

The other broke in eagerly: "I don't believe any one
knows that I — that I went out there with him. He
arranged it very — carefully. Oh, what a beast he
was!" The bitterness of that wail caused the woman
beside her to cry out as if hurt by a sharp, almost un-
bearable pain. For an instant she seemed about to
lose control of herself. The car swerved and came
dangerously near to leaving the road.

A full minute passed before she could trust herself
to speak. Then it was with a deep hoarseness in her
voice.

"You can tell me about it later on, not now. I
don't want to hear it. Tell me, where do you live?"

. The girl's manner changed so absolutely that there
could be but one inference: she was acutely suspicious.

Her lips tightened and her figure seemed to stiffen in in the seat.

"Where do you live?" repeated the other sharply.

"Why should I tell you that? I do not know you. You —"

"You are afraid of me?"

"Oh, I don't know what to say, or what to do," came from the lips of the hunted one. "I have no friends, no one to turn to, no one to help me. You — you can't be so heartless as to lead me on and then give me up to — God help me, I — I should not be made to suffer for what I have done. If you only knew the circumstances. If you only knew —"

"Stop!" cried the other, in agony.

The girl was bewildered. "You are so strange. I don't understand —"

"We have but two or three miles to go," interrupted Mrs. Wrandall. "We must think hard and — rapidly. Are you willing to come with me to my hotel? You will be safe there for the present. To-morrow we can plan something for the future."

"If I can only find a place to rest for a little while," began the other.

"I shall be busy all day, you will not be disturbed. But leave the rest to me. I shall find a way."

It was nearly three o'clock when she brought the car to a stop in front of a small, exclusive hotel not far from Central Park. The street was dark and the vestibule was but dimly lighted. No attendant was in sight.

"Slip into this," commanded Mrs. Wrandall, beginning to divest herself of her own fur coat. "It will cover your muddy garments. I am quite warmly dressed. Don't worry. Be quick. For the time being

you are my guest here. You will not be questioned.
No one need know who you are. It will not matter if
you look distressed. You have just heard of the
dreadful thing that has happened to me. You —"

"Happened to you?" cried the girl, drawing the
coat about her.

"A member of my family has died. They know
it in the hotel by this time. I was called to the death
bed — to-night. That is all you will have to know."

"Oh, I am sorry —"

"Come, let us go in. When we reach my rooms, you
may order food and drink. You must do it, not I.
Please try to remember that it is I who am suffering,
not you."

A sleepy night watchman took them up in the elevator. He was not even interested. Mrs. Wrandall
did not speak, but leaned rather heavily on the arm of
her companion. The door had no sooner closed behind them when the girl collapsed. She sank to the
floor in a heap.

"Get up!" commanded her hostess sharply. This
was not the time for soft, persuasive words. "Get
up at once. You are young and strong. You must
show the stuff you are made of now if you ever mean to
show it. I cannot help you if you quail."

The girl looked up piteously, and then struggled to
her feet. She stood before her protectress, weaving
like a frail reed in the wind, pallid to the lips.

"I beg your pardon," she murmured. "I will not
give way like that again. I dare say I'm faint. I have
had no food, no rest — but never mind that now. Tell
me what I am to do. I will try to obey."

"First of all, get out of those muddy, frozen things
you have on."

Mrs. Wrandall herself moved stiffly and with unsteady limbs as she began to remove her own outer garments. The girl mechanically followed her example. She was a pitiable object in the strong light of the electrolier. Muddy from head to foot, water-stained and bedraggled, her face streaked with dirt, she was the most unattractive creature one could well imagine.

These women, so strangely thrown together by Fate, maintained an unbroken silence during the long, fumbling process of partial disrobing. They scarcely looked at one another, and yet they were acutely conscious of the interest each felt in the other. The grateful warmth of the room, the abrupt transition from gloom and cheerlessness to comfortable obscurity, had a more pronounced effect on the stranger than on her hostess.

"It is good to feel warm once more," she said, an odd timidness in her manner. "You are very good to me."

They were in Mrs. Wrandall's bed-chamber, just off the little sitting-room. Three or four trunks stood against the walls.

"I dismissed my maid on landing. She robbed me," said Mrs. Wrandall, voicing the relief that was uppermost in her mind. She opened a closet door and took out a thick eider-down robe, which she tossed across a chair. "Now call up the office and say that you are speaking for me. Say to them that I must have something to eat, no matter what the hour may be. I will get out some clean underwear for you, and — Oh, yes; if they ask about me, say that I am cold and ill. That is sufficient. Here is the bath. Please be as quick about it as possible."

Moving as if in a dream, the girl did as she was told. Twenty minutes later there was a knock at the door. A waiter appeared with a tray and service table. He found Mrs. Wrandall lying back in a chair, attended by a slender young woman in a pink eider-down dressing-gown, who gave hesitating directions to him. Then he was dismissed with a handsome tip, produced by the same young woman.

"You are not to return for these things," she said as he went out.

In silence she ate and drank, her hostess looking on with gloomy interest. It was no shock to Mrs. Wran-dall to find that the girl, who was no more than twenty-two or three, possessed unusual beauty. Her great eyes were blue,— the lovely Irish blue,— her skin was fair and smooth, her features regular and of the deli-cate mould that defines the well-bred gentlewoman at a glance. Her hair, now in order, was dark and thick and lay softly about her small ears and neck. She was not surprised, I repeat, for she had never known Challis Wrandall to show interest in any but the most at-tractive of her sex. She found herself smiling bitterly as she looked.

To herself she was saying: "It isn't so hard to bear when I realise that he betrayed me for one who is so much more beautiful than I. He loved me because I am beautiful. His every defection proves it. The oth-ers have all been beautiful. And to think that this gentle, slender creature should have been the one to give him his death-blow. It seems incredible. If it had been struck by some outraged husband, strong of arm and fierce with vengeance, I could understand. But — but this young, pretty, soft-eyed thing!"

But who may know the thoughts of the other occu-

pant of that little sitting-room? Who can put herself in the place of that despairing, hunted creature
who knew that blood was on the hands with which she
ate, and whose eyes were filled with visions of the death-
chair?

So great was her fatigue that long before she finished the meal her tired lids began to droop, her head
to nod in spasmodic surrenders to an overpowering desire for sleep. Suddenly she dropped the fork from
her fingers and sank back in the comfortable chair,
her head resting against the soft, upholstered back.
Her lids fell, her hands dropped to the arms of the
chair. A fine line appeared between her dark eyebrows,— indicative of pain.

For many minutes Sara Wrandall watched the hag-
gardness deepen in the face of the unconscious sleeper.
Then, even as she wondered at the act, she went over
and took up one of the slim hands in her own. The
hand of an aristocrat! It lay limp in hers, and help-
less. Long, tapering fingers and delicately pink with
the return of warmth.

Rousing herself from the mute contemplation of
her charge, she shook the girl's shoulder. Instantly
she was awake and staring, alarm in her dazed, bewildered eyes.

"You must go to bed," said Mrs. Wrandall quietly.
"Don't be afraid. No one will think of coming here."

The girl arose. As she stood before her benefactress,
she heard her murmur as if from afar-off: "Just about
your size and figure," and wondered not a little.

"You may sleep late. I have many things to do
and you will not be disturbed. Come, take off your
clothes and get into my bed. To-morrow we will
plan further —"

"But, madam," cried the girl, "I cannot take your bed. Where are you to —"

"If I feel like lying down, I shall lie there beside you."

The girl stared. "Lie beside *me?*"

"Yes. Oh, I am not afraid of you, child. You are not a monster. You are just a poor, tired —"

"Oh, please don't! Please!" cried the other, tears rushing to her eyes. She raised Mrs. Wrandall's hand to her lips and covered it with kisses.

Long after she went to sleep, Sara Wrandall stood beside the bed, looking down at the pain-stricken face, and tried to solve the problem that suddenly had become a part of her very existence.

"It is not friendship," she argued fiercely. "It is not charity, it is not humanity. It's the debt I owe, that's all. She did the thing for me that I could not have done myself because I loved him. I owe her something for that."

Later on she turned her attention to the trunks. Her decision was made. With ruthless hands she dragged gown after gown from the "innovations" and cast them over chairs, on the floor, across the foot of the bed: smart things from Paris and Vienna; ball gowns, street gowns, tea gowns, lingerie, blouses, hats, gloves and all of the countless things that a woman of fashion and means indulges herself in when she goes abroad for that purpose and no other to speak of. From the closets she drew forth New York "tailor-suits" and other garments.

Until long after six o'clock she busied herself over this huge pile of costly raiment, portions of which she had worn but once or twice, some not at all, selecting certain dresses, hats, stockings, etc., each of which she laid carelessly aside: an imposing pile of many hues, all bright and gay and glittering. In another heap she laid the sombre things of black: a meagre assortment as compared to the other.

Then she stood back and surveyed the two heaps with tired eyes, a curious, almost scornful smile on her lips. "There!" she said with a sigh. "The black pile is mine, the gay pile is yours," she went on, turning toward the sleeping girl. "What a travesty!"

Then she gathered up the soiled garments her charge had worn and cast them into the bottom of a trunk, which she locked. Laying out a carefully selected assortment of her own garments for the girl's use when she arose, Mrs. Wrandall sat down beside the bed and waited, knowing that sleep would not come to her.

CHAPTER III

At half-past six she went to the telephone and called for the morning newspapers. At the same time she asked that a couple of district messenger boys be sent to her room with the least possible delay. The hushed, scared voice of the telephone girl downstairs convinced her that news of the tragedy was abroad; she could imagine the girl looking at the headlines with awed eyes even as she responded to the call from room 416, and her shudder as she realised that it was the wife of the dead man speaking.

One of the night clerks, pale and agitated, came up with the papers. He inquired if there was anything he could do. He tried to tell her that it was a dreadful, sickening thing, but the words stuck in his throat. She stood before him, holding the door open; the light in the hall fell upon her white, haggard face. He began to tremble all over, as if with the ague.

" Will you be good enough to come in? " she inquired, quite steadily. " The newspapers — have they printed the — the details? "

He entered and she closed the door.

" Just the — just the news that it was Mr. Wrandall," he replied jerkily. " Later on they'll have —"

She interrupted him. " Let me have them, please." Without so much as a glance at the headlines, she tossed the papers on the table. " I have sent for two messenger boys. It is too early to accomplish much by telephone, I fear. Will you be so kind as to telephone at seven o'clock or a little after to my apartment? — You will find the number under Mr. Wrandall's name. Please inform the butler or his wife that they may expect me by ten o'clock, and that I shall bring a friend with me — a young lady. Kindly have my motor sent to Haffner's garage, and looked after. When the reporters come, as they will, please say to them that I will see them at my own home at eleven o'clock."

" Can't I — we — I should say, don't you want us to send word to your — your friends, Mrs. Wrandall,— the family, I mean? No trouble to do it, and —"

" Thank you, no. The messengers will attend to all that is necessary. When my lawyer arrives, please send him here to me. Mr. Carroll. Thank you."

The clerk, considerably relieved, took his departure in some haste, and she was left with the morning papers, each of which she scanned rapidly. The details, of course, were meagre. There was a double-leaded account of her visit to the inn and her extraordinary return to the city. Her chief interest, however, did not rest in these particulars, but in the speculations of the authorities as to the identity of the mysterious woman — and her whereabouts. There was the likelihood that she was not the only one who had encountered the girl on the highway or in the neighbourhood of the inn. So far as she could glean from the reports, however, no one had seen the girl, nor was there the slightest hint offered as to her identity. The papers of the previous afternoon had published lurid accounts of the murder, with all of the known details, the name of the victim at that time still being a mystery. She remembered reading the story with no little interest. The only new feature in the case, therefore, was the identification of Challis

Wrandall by his "beautiful wife," and the sensational manner in which it had been brought about. With considerable interest she noted the hour that these despatches had been received from "special correspondents," and wondered where the shrewd, lynx-eyed reporters napped while she was at the inn. All of the despatches were timed three o'clock and each paper characterised its issue as an "Extra," with Challis Wrandall's name in huge type across as many columns as the dignity of the sheet permitted.

Not one word of the girl! Absolute mystery!

Mrs. Wrandall returned to her post beside the bed of the sleeper in the adjoining room. Deliberately she placed the newspapers on a chair near the girl's pillow, and then raised the window shades to let in the hard grey light of early morn.

It was not her present intention to arouse the wan stranger, who slept as one dead. So gentle was her breathing that the watcher stared in some fear at the fair, smooth breast that seemed scarcely to rise and fall. For a long time she stood beside the bed, looking down at the face of the sleeper, a troubled expression in her eyes.

"I wonder how many times you were seen with him, and where, and by whom," were the questions that ran in a single strain through her mind. "Where do you come from? Where did you meet him? Who is there that knows of your acquaintance with him?"

There was no kindly light in her eyes, nor was there the faintest sign of animosity. Merely the look of one who calculates in the interest of a well-shaped purpose. She was estimating the difficulties that were likely to attend the carrying out of a design as yet half-formed and quixotic. There were many things to be considered. At present she was working in utter darkness. What would the light bring forth?

Her lawyer came in great haste and perturbation at eight o'clock, in response to the letter delivered by one of the messengers. A second letter had gone by like means to her husband's brother, Leslie Wrandall, instructing him to break the news to his father and mother and to come to her apartment after he had attended to the removal of the body to the family home near Washington Square. She made it quite plain that she did not want Challis Wrandall's body to lie under the roof that sheltered her.

His family had resented their marriage. Father, mother and sister had objected to her from the beginning, not because she was unworthy, but because her tradespeople ancestry was not so remote as his. She found a curious sense of pleasure in returning to them the thing they prized so highly and surrendered to her with such bitterness of heart. She had not been good enough for him: that was their attitude. Now she was returning him to them, as one would return an article that had been tested and found to be worthless. She would have no more of him!

Leslie, three years younger than Challis, did not hold to the views that actuated the remaining members of the family in opposing her as an addition to the rather close corporation known far and wide as "the Wrandalls." He had stood out for her in a rather mild but none-the-less steadfast manner, blandly informing his mother on more than one occasion that Sara was quite too good for Challis, any way you looked at it: an attitude which provoked sundry caustic references to his own lamentable shortcomings in the matter of family pride and — intelligence.

He and Sara had been good friends after a fashion. He was a bit of a snob but not much of a prig. She had the feeling about him that if he could be weaned away from the family he might stand for something fine in the way of character. But he was an adept at straddling fences, so that he was never fully on one side or the other, no matter which way he leaned.

He had not been deeply attached to his brother. Their ways were wide apart. All his life he had known Challis for what he was; his heart if not his hand was against him. From the first, he had regarded Sara's marriage as a bad bargain· for her, and toward the last bluntly told her so. Not once but many times had he taken it upon himself to inform her that she was a fool to put up with all the beastly things Challis was doing. He characterised as infatuation the emotion she was prone to call love when they met to discuss the escapades of the careless Challis, for she always went to him with her troubles. In direct opposition to his counselling, she invariably forgave the erring lover who was her husband. Once Leslie had said to her, in considerable heat: " You act as if you were his mistress, instead of his wife. Mistresses *have* to forgive; wives don't." And she had replied: " Yes, but I'd much rather have him a lover than a husband." A remark which Leslie never quite fathomed, being somewhat literal himself.

Carroll, her lawyer, an elderly man of vast experience, was not surprised to find her quite calm and reasonable. He had come to know her very well in the past few years. He had been her father's lawyer up to the time of that excellent tradesman's demise, and he had settled the estate with such unusual despatch that the heirs,— there were many of them,— regarded him as an admirable person and — kept him busy ever afterward straightening out their own affairs. Which goes to prove that policy is often better than honesty.

"I quite understand, my dear, that while it is a dreadful shock to you, you are perfectly reconciled to the — er — to the — well, I might say the culmination of his troubles," said Mr. Carroll tactfully, after she had related for his benefit the story of the night's adventure, with reservation concerning the girl who slumbered in the room beyond.

"Hardly that, Mr. Carroll. Resigned, perhaps. I can't say that I am reconciled. All my life I shall feel that I have been cheated," she said.

He looked up sharply. Something in her tone puzzled him. "Cheated, my dear? Oh, I see. Cheated out of years and years of happiness. I see."

She bowed her head. Neither spoke for a full minute.

"It's a horrible thing to say, Sara, but this tragedy does away with another and perhaps more unpleasant alternative: the divorce I have been urging you to consider for so long."

"Yes, we are spared all that," she said. Then she met his gaze with a sudden flash of anger in her eyes. "But I would not have divorced him — never. You understood that, didn't you?"

"You couldn't have gone on for ever, my dear child, enduring the —"

She stopped him with a sharp exclamation. "Why discuss it now? Let the past take care of itself, Mr. Carroll. The past came to an end night before last, so far as I am concerned. I want advice for the future, not for the past."

He drew back, hurt by her manner. She was quick
to see that she had offended him.

"I beg your pardon, my best of friends," she cried
earnestly.

He smiled. "If you will take *present* advice, Sara,
you will let go of yourself for a spell and see if tears
won't relieve the tension under —"

"Tears!" she cried. "Why should I give way to
tears? What have I to weep for? That man up there
in the country? The cold, dead thing that spent its
last living moments without a thought of love for me?
Ah, no, my friend; I shed all my tears while he was
alive. There are none left to be shed for him now. He
exacted his full share of them. It was his pleasure
to wring them from me because he knew I loved him."
She leaned forward and spoke slowly, distinctly, so
that he would never forget the words. "But listen
to me, Mr. Carroll. You also know that I loved him.
Can you believe me when I say to you that I hate that
dead thing up there in Burton's Inn as no one ever
hated before? Can you understand what I mean? I
hate that dead body, Mr. Carroll. I loved the life that
was in it. It was the life of him that I loved, the warm,
appealing life of him. It has gone out. Some one less
amiable than I suffered at his hands and — well, that
is enough. I hate the dead body she left behind her,
Mr. Carroll."

The lawyer wiped the cool moisture from his brow.

"I think I understand," he said, but he was filled
with wonder. "Extraordinary! Ahem! I should
say — Ahem! Dear me! Yes, yes — I've never really
thought of it in that light."

"I dare say you haven't," she said, lying back in
the chair as if suddenly exhausted.

" By the way, my dear, have you breakfasted? "

" No. I hadn't given it a thought. Perhaps it would be better if I had some coffee —"

" I will ring for a waiter," he said, springing to his feet.

" Not now, please. I have a young friend in the other room — a guest who arrived last night. She will attend to it when she awakes. Poor thing, it has been dreadfully trying for her."

" Good heaven, I should think so," said he, with a glance at the closed door. " Is she asleep? "

" Yes. I shall not call her until you have gone."

" May I enquire —"

" A girl I met recently — an English girl," said she succinctly, and forthwith changed the subject. " There are a few necessary details that must be attended to, Mr. Carroll. That is why I sent for you at this early hour. Mr. Leslie Wrandall will take charge — Ah! " she straightened up suddenly. " What a farce it is going to be! "

Half an hour later he departed, to rejoin her at eleven o'clock, when the reporters were to be expected. He was to do the talking for her. While he was there, Leslie Wrandall called her up on the telephone. Hearing but one side of the rather prolonged conversation, he was filled with wonder at the tactful way in which she met and parried the inevitable questions and suggestions coming from her horror-struck brother-in-law. Without the slightest trace of offensiveness in her manner, she gave Leslie to understand that the final obsequies must be conducted in the home of his parents, to whom once more her husband belonged, and that she would abide by all arrangements his family elected to make. Mr. Carroll surmised from the trend of conversation that young Wrandall was about to leave for the scene of the tragedy, and that the house was in a state of unspeakable distress. The lawyer smiled rather grimly to himself as he turned to look out of the window. He did not have to be told that Challis was the idol of the family, and that, so far as they were concerned, he could do no wrong!

After his departure, Mrs. Wrandall gently opened the bedroom door and was surprised to find the girl wide-awake, resting on one elbow, her staring eyes fastened on the newspaper that topped the pile on the chair.

Catching sight of Mrs. Wrandall she pointed to the paper with a trembling hand and cried out, in a voice full of horror:

"Did you place them there for me to read? Who was with you in the other room just now? Was it some one about the — some one looking for me? Speak! Please tell me. I heard a man's voice —"

The other crossed quickly to her side.

"Don't be alarmed. It was my lawyer. There is nothing to fear — at present. Yes, I left the papers there for you to see. You can see what a sensation it has caused. Challis Wrandall was one of the most widely known men in New York. But I suppose you know that without my telling you."

The girl sank back with a groan. "My God, what have I done? What will come of it all?"

"I wish I could answer that question," said the other, taking the girl's hand in hers. Both were trembling. After an instant's hesitation, she laid her other hand on the dark, dishevelled hair of the wild-eyed creature, who still continued to stare at the headlines. "I am quite sure they will not look for you here, or in my home."

" In your home? "

" You are to go with me. I have thought it all over. It is the only way. Come, I must ask you to pull yourself together. Get up at once, and dress. Here are the things you are to wear." She indicated the orderly pile of garments with a wave of her hand.

Slowly the girl crept out of bed, confused, bewildered, stunned.

" Where are my own things? I — I cannot accept these. Pray give me my own —"

Mrs. Wrandall checked her.

" You must obey me, if you expect me to help you. Don't you understand that I have had a — a bereavement? I cannot wear these things now. They are useless to me. But we will speak of all that later on. Come, be quick; I will help you to dress. First, go to the telephone and ask them to send a waiter to — these rooms. We must have something to eat. Please do as I tell you."

Standing before her benefactress, her fingers fumbling impotently at the neck of the night-dress, the girl still continued to stare dumbly into the calm, dark eyes before her.

" You are so good. I — I —"

" Let me help you," interrupted the other, deliberately setting about to remove the night-dress. The girl caught it up as it slipped from her shoulders, a warm flush suffusing her face, a shamed look springing into her eyes.

" Thank you, I can — get on very well. I only wanted to ask you a question. It has been on my mind, waking and sleeping. Can you tell me anything about — do you know his wife? "

The question was so abrupt, so startling that Mrs.

Wrandall uttered a sharp little cry. For a moment she could not reply.

"I am so sorry, so desperately sorry for her," added the girl plaintively.

"I know her," the other managed to say with an effort.

"If I had only known that he had a wife —" began the girl bitterly, almost angrily.

Mrs. Wrandall grasped her by the arm. "You did not know that he had a wife?" she cried.

The girl's eyes flashed with a sudden, fierce fire in their depths.

"God in heaven, no! I did not know it until — Oh, I can't speak of it! Why should I tell you about it? Why should you be interested in hearing it?"

Mrs. Wrandall drew back and regarded the girl's set, unhappy face. There was a curious light in her eyes that escaped the other's notice,— a light that would have puzzled her not a little.

"But you *will* tell me — *everything* — a little later," she said, strangely calm. "Not now, but — before many hours have passed. First of all, you must tell me who you are, where you live,— everything except what happened in Burton's Inn. I don't want to hear that at present — perhaps never. Yes, on second thoughts, I will say *never!* You are never to tell me just what happened up there, or just what led up to it. Do you understand? Never!"

The girl stared at her in amazement. "But I — I must tell some one," she cried vehemently. "I have a right to defend myself —"

"I am not asking you to defend yourself," said Mrs. Wrandall shortly. Then, as if afraid to remain longer, she rushed from the room. In the doorway, she turned

for an instant to say: " Do as I told you. Telephone.
Dress as quickly as you can." She closed the door
swiftly.

Standing in the centre of the room, her hands
clenched until the nails cut the flesh, she said over and
over again to herself: " I don't want to know! I don't
want to *know!* "

A few minutes later she was critically inspecting
the young woman who came from the bedroom attired
in a street dress that neither of them had ever donned
before. The girl, looking fresher, prettier and even
younger than when she had seen her last, was in no way
abashed. She seemed to have accepted the garments
and the situation in the same spirit of resignation and
hope: as if she had decided to make the most of her
slim chance to profit by these amazing circumstances.

They sat opposite each other at the little breakfast
table.

" Please pour the coffee," said Mrs. Wrandall. The
waiter had left the room at her command. The girl's
hand shook, but she complied without a word.

" Now you may tell me who you are and — but
wait! You are not to say anything about what happened at the inn. Guard your words carefully. I
am not asking for a confession. I do not care to know
what happened there. It will make it easier for me to
protect you. You may call it conscience. Keep your
big secret to yourself. *Not one word to me.* Do you
understand? "

" You mean that I am not to reveal, even to you, the
causes which led up to —"

" Nothing — absolutely nothing," said Mrs. Wrandall firmly.

" But I cannot permit you to judge me, to — well,

you might say to acquit me,—without hearing the story. It is so vital to me."

"I can judge you without hearing all of the—the evidence, if that's what you mean. Simply answer the questions I shall ask, and nothing more. There are certain facts I must have from you if I am to shield you. You must tell me the truth. I take it you are an English girl. Where do you live? Who are your friends? Where is your family?"

The girl's face flushed for an instant and then grew pale again.

"I will tell you the truth," she said. "My name is Hetty Castleton. My father is Col. Braid Castleton, of — of the British army. My mother is dead. She was Kitty Glynn, at one time a popular music-hall performer in London. She was Irish. She died two years ago. My father was a gentleman. I do not say he *is* a gentleman, for his treatment of my mother relieves him from that distinction. He is in the Far East, China, I think. I have not seen him in more than five years. He deserted my mother. That's all there is to that side of my story. I appeared in two or three of the musical pieces produced in London two seasons ago, in the chorus. I never got beyond that, for very good reasons. I was known as Hetty Glynn. Three weeks ago I started for New York, sailing from Liverpool. Previously I had served in the capacity of governess in the family of John Budlong, a brewer. They had a son, a young man of twenty. Two months ago I was dismissed. A California lady, Mrs. Holcombe, offered me a situation as governess to her two little girls soon afterward. I was to go to her home in San Francisco. She provided the money necessary for the voyage and for other expenses. She is still in Europe.

I landed in New York a fortnight ago and, following
her directions, presented myself at a certain bank,— I
have the name somewhere — where my railroad tickets
were to be in readiness for me, with further instructions. They were to give me twenty-five pounds on
the presentation of my letter from Mrs. Holcombe.
They gave me the money and then handed me a cablegram from Mrs. Holcombe, notifying me that my services would not be required. There was no explanation.
Just that.

"On the steamer I met — *him*. His deck chair was
next to mine. I noticed that his name was Wrandall —
' C. Wrandall ' the card on the chair informed me.
I —"

"You crossed on the steamer with him?" interrupted
Mrs. Wrandall quickly.

"Yes."

"Had — had you seen him before? In London?"

"Never. Well, we became acquainted, as people do.
He — he was very handsome and agreeable." She
paused for a moment to collect herself.

"Very handsome and agreeable," said the other
slowly.

"We got to be very good friends. There were not
many people on board, and apparently he knew none of
them. It was too cold to stay on deck much of the
time, and it was very rough. He had one of the splendid suites on the —"

"Pray omit unnecessary details. You landed and
went — where?"

"He advised me to go to an hotel — I can't recall the
name. It was rather an unpleasant place. Then I
went to the bank, as I have stated. After that I did
not know what to do. I was stunned, bewildered. I

called him up on the telephone and — he asked me to
meet him for dinner at a queer little café, far down
town. We —"

"And you had no friends, no acquaintances here?"

"No. He suggested that I go into one of the musical shows, saying he thought he could arrange it with
a manager who was a friend. Anything to tide me
over, he said. But I would not consider it, not for
an instant. I had had enough of the stage. I — I
am really not fitted for it. Besides, I *am* qualified —
well qualified — to be governess — but that is neither
here nor there. I had some money — perhaps forty
pounds. I found lodgings with some people in Nineteenth street. He never came there to see me. I can
see plainly now why he argued it would not be — well,
he used the word 'wise.' But we went occasionally to
dine together. We went about in a motor — a little
red one. He — he told me he loved me. That was
one night about a week ago. I —"

"I don't care to hear about it," cried the other.
"No need of that. Spare me the silly side of the
story."

"Silly, madam? In God's name, do you think it
was silly to me? Why — why, I believed him! And,
what is more, I believe that he *did* love me — even now
I believe it."

"I have no doubt of it," said Mrs. Wrandall calmly.
"You are very pretty — and charming."

"I — I did not know that he had a wife until — well,
until —" She could not go on.

"Night before last?"

The girl shuddered. Mrs. Wrandall turned her face
away and waited.

"There is nothing more I can tell you, unless you

permit me to tell *all*," the girl resumed after a moment of hesitation.

Mrs. Wrandall arose.

" I have heard enough.   This afternoon I will send my butler with you to the lodging house in Nineteenth street.   He will attend to the removal of your personal effects to my home, and you will return with him.   It will be testing fate, Miss Castleton, this visit to your former abiding place, but I have decided to give the law its chance.   If you are suspected, a watch will be set over the house in which you lived.   If you are not suspected, if your association with — with Wrandall is quite unknown, you will run no risk in going there openly, nor will I be taking so great a chance as may appear in offering you a home, for the time being at least, as companion — or secretary or whatever we may elect to call it for the benefit of all enquirers.   Are you willing to run the risk — this single risk? "

" Perfectly willing," announced the other without hesitation.   Indeed, her face brightened.   " If they are waiting there for me, I shall go with them without a word.   I have no means of expressing my gratitude to you for —"

" There is time enough for that," said Mrs. Wrandall quickly.   " And if they are not there, you will return to me?   You will not desert me now? "

The girl's eyes grew wide with wonder.   " Desert you?   Why do you put it in that way?   I don't understand."

" You will come back to me? " insisted the other.

" Yes.   Why,— why, it means everything to me. It means life,— more than that, most wonderful friend. Life isn't very sweet to me.   But the joy of giving it to you for ever is the dearest boon I crave.   I *do* give

it to you. It belongs to you. I — I could die for
you."

She dropped to her knees and pressed her lips to
Sara Wrandall's hand; hot tears fell upon it.

Mrs. Wrandall laid her free hand on the dark, glossy
hair and smiled; smiled warmly for the first time in —
well, in years she might have said to herself if she had
stopped to consider.

"Get up, my dear," she said gently. "I shall not
ask you to die for me — if you *do* come back. I may be
sending you to your death, as it is, but it is the chance
we must take. A few hours will tell the tale. Now
listen to what I am about to say,— to propose. I offer
you a home, I offer you friendship and I trust security
from the peril that confronts you. I ask nothing in
return, not even a word of gratitude. You may tell
the people at your lodgings that I have engaged you
as companion and that we are to sail for Europe in a
week's time if possible. Now we must prepare to go
to my own home. You will see to packing my — that
is, *our* trunks —"

"Oh, it — it must be a dream!" cried Hetty Castleton, her eyes swimming. "I can't believe —" Suddenly she caught herself up, and tried to smile. "I
don't see why you do this for me. I do not deserve —"

"You have done me a service," said Mrs. Wrandall,
her manner so peculiar that the girl again assumed the
stare of perplexity and wonder that had been para-
mount since their meeting: as if she were on the verge
of grasping a great truth.

"What *can* you mean?"

Sara laid her hands on the girl's shoulders and looked
steadily into the puzzled eyes for a moment before
speaking.

" My girl," she said, ever so gently, " I shall not ask
what your life has been ; I do not care. I shall not ask
for references. You are alone in the world and you
need a friend. I too am alone. If you will come to me
I will do everything in my power to make you comfortable and — contented. Perhaps it will be impossible
to make you happy. I promise faithfully to help you,
to shield you, to repay you for the thing you have
done for me. You could not have fallen into gentler
hands than mine will prove to be. That much I swear
to you on my soul, which is sacred. I bear you no
ill-will. I have nothing to avenge."

Hetty drew back, completely mystified.

" Who are you? " she murmured, still staring.

" I am Challis Wrandall's wife."

CHAPTER IV

WHILE THE MOB WAITED

THE next day but one, in the huge old-fashioned mansion of the Wrandalls in lower Fifth Avenue, in the drawing-room directly beneath the chamber in which Challis was born, the impressive but grimly conventional funeral services were held.

Contrasting sharply with the sombre, absolutely correct atmosphere of the gloomy interior was the exterior display of joyous curiosity that must have jarred severely on the high-bred sensibilities of the chief mourners, not to speak of the invited guests who had been obliged to pass between rows of gaping bystanders in order to reach the portals of the house of grief, and who must have reckoned with extreme distaste the cost of subsequent departure. A dozen raucous-voiced policemen were employed to keep back the hundreds that thronged the sidewalk and blocked the street. Curiosity was rampant. Ever since the moment that the body of Challis Wrandall was carried into the house of his father, a motley, varying crowd of people shifted restlessly in front of the mansion, filled with gruesome interest in the absolutely unseen, animated by the sly hope that something sensational might happen if they waited long enough.

Men, women, children struggled for places nearest the tall iron fence surrounding the spare yard, and gazed with awed but wistful eyes at the curtained windows and at the huge bow of crepe on the massive portals. In hushed voices they spoke of the murder and expressed a single opinion among them all: the law ought

66

to make short work of her! If this thing had happened
in England, said they who scoff at our own laws, there
wouldn't be any foolishness about the business: the
woman would be buried in quick-lime before you could
know what you were talking about. The law in this
country is a joke, said they, with great irritability.
Why can't we do the business up, sharp and quick, as
they do in England? Get it over with, that's the ticket.
What's the sense of dragging it out for a year? Send
'em to the chair or hang 'em while everybody's interested, not when the thing's half forgotten. Who wants
to see a person hanged after the crime's been forgotten?
And then, think of the saving to the State? Hang 'em,
men or women, and in a couple of years' time there
wouldn't be a tenth part of the murders we have now.
Statistics prove, went on the wise ones, that only one out
of every hundred is hanged. What's that? The jury
system is rotten! No sirree, we are 'way behind England in that respect. Just look at that big murder case
in London last month! Remember it? Murderer was
hanged inside of three weeks after he was caught.
That's the way to do it! And the London police catch
'em too. Our police stand around doing nothing until
the criminal has got a week's start, and then — oh,
well, what can you expect? " Now if I was at the head
of the New York department I'd have that woman behind the bars before night, that's what I'd do. You
bet your life, I would," said more than one. And no
one questioned his ability to do so.

And then all of them would growl at the policemen who pushed them back from the gates, and call
them " scabs " and " mutts " in repressed tones, and
snarl under their breath that they wouldn't be pushing
people around like that if they didn't have stars and

clubs and a great idea of their own importance. "If it wasn't for the family at home dependin' on me for support, I'd take a punch at that stiff, so help me God, even if I went to the Island for it!"

And so it *was* and ever shall be, world without end.

Newsboys, hoarse-voiced and pipe-voiced, mingled with the crowd, and shrieked their extras under the very noses of the always-aloof Wrandalls, who up to this day had turned them up at the sight of a vulgar extra, but who now looked down them with a trembling of the nostrils that left no room for doubt as to their present state of mind.

Up to the very portals these assiduous peddlers yelped for pennies and gave in exchange the latest headlines. "All about Mr. Challis Wran'all's fun'ral!" "Horrible extry!" Ding-donging the thing in the very ears of the dead man himself!

Motor after motor, carriage after carriage, rolled up to the curb and emptied its sober-faced, self-conscious occupants in front of the door with the great black bow; with each arrival the crowd surged forward, and names were muttered in undertones, passing from lip to lip until every one in the street knew that Mr. So-and-So, Mrs. This-or-That, the What-do-you-call-ems and others of the city's most exclusive but most garishly advertised society leaders had entered the house of mourning. It was a great show for the plebeian spectators. Much better than Miss So-and-So's wedding, said one woman who had attended the aforesaid ceremony as a unit in the well-dressed mob that almost wrecked the carriages in the desire to see the terrified bride. Better than a circus, said a man who held his little daughter above the heads of the crowd so that she might see the fine lady in a wild-beast fur.

Swellest funeral New York ever had, remarked another, excepting one 'way back when he was a kid.

At the corner below stood two patrol wagons, also waiting.

Inside the house sat the carefully selected guests, hushed and stiff and gratified. (Not because they were attending a funeral, but because the occasion served to separate them from the chaff: they were the elect.) It would be going too far to intimate that they were proud of themselves, but it is not stretching it very much to say that they counted noses with considerable satisfaction and were glad that they had not been left out. The real, high-water mark in New York society was established at this memorable function. It was quite plain to every one that Mrs. Wrandall,—*the* Mrs. Wrandall,— had made out the list of guests to be invited to the funeral of her son. It was a bluestocking affair. You couldn't imagine anything more so. Afterwards, the two hundred who were there looked with utmost pity and not a little scorn on the other two hundred who failed to get in, notwithstanding there was ample room in the spacious house for all of them. There wasn't a questionable guest in the house, unless one were to question the right of the dead man's widow to be there — and, after all, she was upstairs with the family. Even so, she was a Wrandall — remotely, of course, but recognisable.   ✦

Yes, they counted noses, so to say. As one after the other arrived and was ushered into the huge drawing-room, he or she was accorded a congratulatory look from those already assembled, a tribute returned with equal amiability. Each one noted who else was there, and each one said to himself that at last they really had something all to themselves. It was truly a pleas-

ure, a relief, to be able to do something without being
pushed about by people who didn't belong but thought
they did. They sat back,— stiffly, of course,— and
in utter stillness confessed that there could be such a
thing as the survival of the fittest. Yes, there wasn't
a nose there that couldn't be counted with perfect
serenity. It was a notable occasion.

Mrs. Wrandall, the elder, had made out the list.
She did not consult her daughter-in-law in the matter.
It is true that Sara forestalled her in a way by sending word, through Leslie, that she would be pleased
if Mrs. Wrandall would issue invitations to as many of
Challis's friends as she deemed *advisable*. As for herself, she had no wish in the matter; she would be satisfied with whatever arrangements the family cared to
make.

It is not to be supposed, from the foregoing, that
Mrs. Wrandall, the elder, was not stricken to the heart
by the lamentable death of her idol. He *was* her idol.
He was her first-born, he was her love-born. He came
to her in the days when she loved her husband without
much thought of respecting him. She was beginning
to regard him as something more than a lover when
Leslie came, so it was different. When their daughter
Vivian was born, she was plainly annoyed but wholly
respectful. Mr. Wrandall was no longer the lover;
he was her lord and master. The head of the house
of Wrandall was a person to be looked up to, to be
respected and admired by her, for he was a very great
man, but he was dear to her only because he was the
father of Challis, the first-born.

In the order of her nature, Challis therefore was her
most dearly beloved, Vivian the least desired and last
in her affections as well as in sequence.

Strangely enough, the three of them perfected a curiously significant record of conjugal endowments. Challis had always been the wild, wayward, unrestrained one, and by far the most lovable; Leslie, almost as good looking but with scarcely a noticeable trace of the charm that made his brother attractive; Vivian, handsome, selfish and as cheerless as the wind that blows across the icebergs in the north. Challis had been born with a widely enveloping heart and an elastic conscience; Leslie with a brain and a soul and not much of a heart, as things go; Vivian with a soul alone, which belonged to God, after all, and not to her. Of course she had a heart, but it was only for the purpose of pumping blood to remote extremities, and had nothing whatever to do with anything so unutterably extraneous as love, charity or self-sacrifice.

As for Mr. Redmond Wrandall he was a very proper and dignified gentleman, and old for his years.

Secretly, Vivian was his favourite. Moreover, possessing the usual contrariness of man, and having been at one time or other, a hot-blooded lover, he professed — also in secret — a certain admiration for the beautiful, warm-hearted wife of his eldest son. He looked upon her from a man's point of view. He couldn't help that. Not once, but many times, had he said to himself that perhaps Challis was lucky to have got her instead of one of the girls his mother had chosen for him out of the minute elect.

It may be seen, or rather surmised, that if the house of Wrandall had not been so admirably centred under its own vine and fig tree, it might have become divided against itself without much of an effort.

Mrs. Redmond Wrandall was the vine and fig tree.

And now they had brought her dearly beloved son

home to her, murdered and — disgraced. If it had been either of the others, she could have said: "God's will be done." Instead, she cried out that God had turned against her.

Leslie had had the bad taste — or perhaps it was misfortune — to blurt out an agonised "I told you so" at a time when the family was sitting numb and hushed under the blight of the first horrid blow. He did not mean to be unfeeling. It was the truth bursting from his unhappy lips.

"I knew Chal would come to this — I knew it," he had said. His arm was about the quivering shoulders of his mother as he said it.

She looked up, a sob breaking in her throat. For a long time she looked into the face of her second son.

"How can you — how dare you say such a thing as that?" she cried, aghast.

He coloured, and drew her closer to him.

"I — I didn't mean it," he faltered.

"You have always taken sides against him," began his mother.

"Please, mother," he cried miserably.

"You say this to me *now*," she went on. "You who are left to take his place in my affection.— Why, Leslie, I — I —"

Vivian interposed. "Les is upset, mamma darling. You know he loved Challis as deeply as any of us loved him."

Afterwards the girl said to Leslie when they were quite alone: "She will never forgive you for that, Les. It was a beastly thing to say."

He bit his lip, which trembled. "She's never cared for me as she cared for Chal. I'm sorry if I've made it worse."

"See here, Leslie, was Chal so — so —"

"Yes. I meant what I said a while ago. It was sure to happen to him one time or another. Sara's had a lot to put up with."

"Sara! If she had been the right sort of a wife, this never would have happened."

"After all is said and done, Vivie, Sara's in a position to rub it in on us if she's of a mind to do so. She won't do it, of course, but — I wonder if she isn't gloating, just the same."

"Haven't we treated her as one of us?" demanded she, dabbing her handkerchief in her eyes. "Since the wedding, I mean. Haven't we been kind to her?"

"Oh, I think she understands us perfectly," said her brother.

"I wonder what she will do now?" mused Vivian, in that speech casting her sister-in law out of her narrow little world as one would throw aside a burnt-out match.

"She will profit by experience," said he, with some pleasure in a superior wisdom.

.   .   .   .

In Mrs. Wrandall's sitting-room at the top of the broad stairway, sat the family,— that is to say, the *immediate* family,— a solemn-faced footman in front of the door that stood fully ajar so that the occupants might hear the words of the minister as they ascended, sonorous and precise, from the hall below. A minister was he who knew the buttered side of his bread. His discourse was to be a beautiful one. He stood at the front of the stairs and faced the assembled listeners in the hall, the drawing-room and the entresol, but his infinitely touching words went up one flight and lodged.

Sara Wrandall sat a little to the left of and behind

Mrs. Redmond Wrandall, about whom were grouped
the three remaining Wrandalls, father, son and daughter, closely drawn together. Well to the fore were
Wrandall uncles and cousins and aunts, and one or two
carefully chosen blood-relations to the mistress of the
house, whose hand had long been set against kinsmen
of less exalted promise.

The room was dark. A forgotten French clock
ticked madly and tinkled its quarter-hours with surpassing sprightliness. Time went on regardless. One
of the Wrandall uncles, obeying a look from his wife,
tiptoed across the room and tried to find a way to
subdue the jingling disturber. But it chimed in his
face, and he put his black kid glove over his lips. The
floor creaked horribly as he went back to his chair.

Beside Sara Wrandall, on the small pink divan, sat
a stranger in this sombre company: a young woman
in black, whose pale face was uncovered, and whose
lashes were lifted so rarely that one could not know of
the deep, real pain that lay behind them, in her Irish
blue eyes.

She had arrived at the house an hour or two before
the time set for the ceremony, in company with the
widow. True to her resolution, the widow of Challis
Wrandall had remained away from the home of his
people until the last hour. She had been consulted,
to be sure, in regard to the final arrangements, but the
meetings had taken place in her own apartment, many
blocks distant from the house in lower Fifth Avenue.
The afternoon before she had received Redmond Wrandall and Leslie, his son. She had not sent for them.
They came perfunctorily and not through any sense
of obligation. These two at least knew that sympathy was not what she wanted, but peace. Twice dur-

ing the two trying days, Leslie had come to see her.
Vivian telephoned.

On the occasion of his first visit, Leslie had met the
guest in the house. The second time he called, he made
it a point to ask Sara all about her.

It was he who gently closed the door after the two
women when, on the morning of the funeral, they entered the dark, flower-laden room in which stood the
casket containing the body of his brother. He left
them alone together in that room for half an hour or
more, and it was he who went forward to meet them
when they came forth. Sara leaned on his arm as
she ascended the stairs to the room where the others
were waiting. The ashen-faced girl followed, her eyes
lowered, her gloved hands clenched.

Mrs. Wrandall, the elder, kissed Sara and drew her
down beside her on the couch. To her own surprise,
as well as that of the others, Sara broke down and wept
bitterly. After all, she was sorry for Challis's mother.
It was the human instinct; she could not hold out
against it. And the older woman put away the ancient
grudge she held against this mortal enemy and dis-
solved into tears of real compassion.

A little later she whispered brokenly in Sara's ear:
" My dear, my dear, this has brought us together. I
hope you will learn to love me."

Sara caught her breath, but uttered no word. She
looked into her mother-in-law's eyes, and smiled through
her tears. The Wrandalls, looking on in amaze,
saw the smile reflected in the face of the older woman.
Then it was that Vivian crossed quickly and put her
arms about the shoulders of her sister-in-law. The
white flag on both sides.

Hetty Castleton stood alone and wavering, just inside the door. No stranger situation could be imagined than the one in which this unfortunate girl found herself at the present moment. She was virtually in the hands of those who would destroy her; she was in the house of those who most deeply were affected by her act on that fatal night. Among them all she stood, facing them, listening to the moans and sobs, and yet her limbs did not give way beneath her. . . .

Some one gently touched her arm. It was Leslie. She shrank back, a fearful look in her eyes. In the semi-darkness he failed to note the expression.

"Won't you sit here?" he asked, indicating the little pink divan against the wall. "Forgive me for letting you stand so long."

She looked about her, the wild light still in her eyes. She was like a rat in a trap.

Her lips parted, but the word of thanks did not come forth. A strange, inarticulate sound, almost a gasp, came instead. Pallid as a ghost, she dropped limply to the divan, and dug her fingers into the satiny seat. As if fascinated, she stared over the black heads of the three women immediately in front of her at the full length portrait hanging where the light from the hall fell full upon it: the portrait of a dashing youth in riding togs.

A moment later Sara Wrandall came over and sat beside her. The girl shivered as with a mighty chill when the warm hand of her friend fell upon hers and enveloped it in a firm clasp.

"His mother kissed me," whispered Sara. "Did you see?"

The girl could not reply. She could only stare at the open door. A small, hatchet-faced man had come up from below and was nodding his head to Leslie

Wrandall,— a man with short side whiskers, and a
sepulchral look in his eyes. Then, having received a
sign from Leslie, he tiptoed away. Almost instantly
the voices of people singing softly came from some
distant, remote part of the house.

And then, a little later, the perfectly modulated
voice of a man in prayer.

Back of her, Wrandalls; beside her, Wrandalls; beneath her, friends of the Wrandalls; outside, the rab-
ble, those who would join with these black, raven-like
spectres in tearing her to pieces if they but knew!

Sitting, with his hand to his head, Leslie Wrandall
found himself staring at the face of this stranger
among them; not with any definable interest, but because she happened to be in his line of vision and her
face was so singularly white that it stood out in cameo-
like relief against all this ebony setting.

The droning voice came up from below, each well-
chosen word distinct and clear: tribute beautiful to the
irreproachable character of the deceased. Leslie
watched the face of the girl, curiously fascinated by
the set, emotionless features, and yet without a conscious interest in her. He was dully sensible to the
fact that she was beautiful, uncommonly beautiful. It
did not occur to him to feel that she was out of place
among them, that she belonged downstairs. Somehow
she was a part of the surroundings, like the spectre at
the feast.

If he could have witnessed all that transpired while
Sara was in the room below with her guest — her
companion, as he had come to regard her without having in fact been told as much,— he would have been
lost in a maze of the most overwhelming emotions.

To go back: The door had barely closed behind

the two women when Hetty's trembling knees gave way beneath her. With a low moan of horror, she slipped to the floor, covering her face with her hands.

Sara knelt beside her.

" Come," she said gently, but firmly; " I must exact this much of you. If we are to go on together, as we have planned, you must stand beside me at his bier. Together we must look upon him for the last time. You must see him as I saw him up there in the country. I had my cruel blow that night. It is your turn now. I will not blame you for what you did. But if you expect me to go on believing that you did a brave thing that night, you must convince me that you are not a coward now. It is the only test I shall put you to. Come; I know it is hard, I know it is terrible, but it is the true test of your ability to go through with it to the end. I shall know then that you have the courage to face anything that may come up."

She waited a long time, her hand on the girl's shoulder. At last Hetty arose.

" You are right," she said hoarsely. " I should not be afraid."

Later on, they sat over against the wall beyond the casket, into which they had peered with widely varying emotions. Sara had said:

" You know that I loved him."

The girl put her hands to her eyes and bowed her head.

" Oh, how can you be so merciful to me? "

" Because he was not," said Sara, white-lipped. Hetty glanced at the half-averted face with queer, indescribable expression in her eyes.

Then her nerves gave way. She shrank away from the casket, whimpering like a frightened child, muttering, almost gibbering in the extremity of despair. She had lived in dread of this ordeal; it had been promised the day before by Sara Wrandall, whose will was law to her. Now she had come to the very apex of realisation. She felt that her mind was going, that her blood was freezing. In response to a sudden impulse she sprang up and ran, blindly and without thought, bringing up against the wall with such force that she dropped to the floor, quite insensible.

When she regained her senses, she was lying back in Sara Wrandall's arms, and a soft faraway voice was pleading with her to wake, to say something, to open her eyes.

If Leslie Wrandall could have looked in upon them at that moment, or at any time during the half an hour that followed, he would have known who was the slayer of his brother, but it is doubtful if he could have had the heart to denounce her to the world.

When they were ready to leave the room, Hetty had regained control of her nerves to a most surprising extent, a condition unmistakably due to the influence of the older woman.

" I can trust myself now, Mrs. Wrandall," said Hetty steadily as they hesitated for an instant before turning the knob of the door.

" Then, I shall ask *you* to open the door," said Sara, drawing back.

Without a word or a look, Hetty opened the door and permitted the other to pass out before her. Then she followed, closing it gently, even deliberately, but not without a swift glance over her shoulder into the depths of the room they were leaving.

Of the two, Sara Wrandall was the paler as they went up the broad staircase with Leslie.

The funeral oration by the Rev. Dr. Maltby dragged on.   Among all his hearers there was but one who believed the things he said of Challis Wrandall, and she was one of two persons who, so the saying goes, are the last to find a man out; his mother and his sister.   But in this instance the mother was alone.   The silent, attentive guests on the lower floor listened in grim approval: Dr. Maltby was doing himself proud.   Not one but all of them knew that Maltby *knew*.   And yet how soothing he was.

Thus afterwards, to his wife, on the way home after a fruitful silence, spoke Colonel Berkimer, well known to the Tenderloin:

" When I die, my dear, I want you to be sure to have Maltby in for the sermon.   He's really wonderful."

" You don't mean to say you *believed* all that he said," cried his wife.

" Certainly *not*," he snapped.   " That's the point."

Once at the end of a beautifully worded sentence, eulogistic of the dead man's character as a son and husband, the tense silence of the room upstairs was shattered by the utterance of a single, poignant word:

" God ! "

It was so expressive of surprise, of scorn, of contempt, although spoken in little more than a whisper, that every one in the room caught his or her breath in a sharp little gasp, as if cringing from the effect of an unexpected shock to a sensitive nerve.

Each looked at his neighbour and then in a shocked sort of way at every one else, for no one could quite make out who had uttered the word, and each wondered if, in a fit of abstraction, he could have done it himself.   It unmistakably had been the voice of a woman, but whose?   Hetty knew, but not by the slightest sign

did she betray the fact that the woman who sat beside
her was the one to utter the brief but scathing estimate
of the minister's eulogy.

The hatchet-faced little undertaker stood in the open
door again and solemnly bowed his head to Leslie, lifting his dolorous eyebrows in lieu of the verbal question.
Receiving a simple nod in reply, he announced that as
soon as the guests had departed he would be pleased to
have the family descend to the carriages.

Outside, the shivering, half-frozen multitude edged
its way up to the line of blue-coats and again whispered the names of the departing guests, and every neck
was craned in the effort to secure the first view of the
casket, the silk-hatted pall-bearers and the weeping
members of the family.

"They'll be out with 'im in a minute now," said a
hoarse-voiced man who clung to the ornamental face
of the tall gate and passed back the word, for he could
see beyond the stream of guests into the hallway of
the house.

"Git down out o' that," commanded a policeman
tapping him sharply with his night-stick.

"Aw, I ain't botherin' anybody —"

"Git down, I say!"

Grumbling, the man slunk back, and a woman took
his place. This was better for the crowd, as her voice
was shriller and she had less compunction about making herself heard.

A small boy crept beyond the line and peered, round-
eyed, up the carpeted steps. He received a sharp
push from a night-stick and went blubbering back into
the crowd.

And all through the eager, seething mob went sharp-
eyed men in plain clothes, searching each face with

crafty eyes, looking for the sign that might betray the woman who had brought all this about. They were men from the central office. Another of their ilk had the freedom of the house in the guise of an undertaker's assistant. He watched the favoured few!

There is a saying that a strange, mysterious force drags the murderer to the scene of his crime, whether he will or no, to look with others upon the havoc he has wrought. He has been known to sit beside the bier of his victim; he has been known to follow him to the tomb; he has been known to betray himself at the very edge of the grave. A grim, fantastic thing is conscience!

At last the crowd gave out a deep, hissing breath and surged forward. They were bearing Challis Wrandall down the steps. The wall of policemen held firm; the morbid hundreds fell back and glared with unblinking eyes at the black thing that slowly crossed the sidewalk and slid noiselessly into the yawning mouth of the hearse. No man in all that mob uncovered his head, no woman crossed herself. Inwardly they reviled the police who kept them from seeing all that they wanted to see. They were being cheated.

Then there was an eager shout from the foremost in the throng, and the word went singing through the crowd, back to the outer fringe, where men danced like so many jumping-jacks in the effort to see above the heads of those in front.

" Here they come! " went the hoarse whisper, like the swish of the wind.

" Stand back, please! "

" That's his mother! " cried a shrill voice, triumphantly,— even gladly. She was the first to give the news.

"Keep back!" growled the police, lifting their clubs.

"Which one is his wife?"

"Has she come out yet?"

"Get out of my way, damn you!"

"Say, if these cops was doing their duty they'd --"

"That's what I say! No wonder they never ketch anybody."

"Say, they don't seem to be takin' it very hard. I thought they'd be cryin' like --"

"Is that his wife?"

"Poor little thing! Ouch! You big ruffian!"

"Swell business, eh?"

"She won't be sayin' 'Where's my wanderin' boy --'"

"If we had police in this city that could ketch a street car we'd --"

"That's old man Wrandall. I've waited on him dozens o' times."

"Did they have any children?"

Up in the front rank stood a slim little thing with yellow hair and carmined lips, wrapped in costly furs yet shivering as if chilled to the bone. Four plain clothes men were watching her narrowly. She was known to have been one of Challis Wrandall's associates. When she shrank back into the crowd and made her way to the outskirts, hurrying as if pursued by ghosts, two men followed close behind, and kept her in sight for many blocks.

The motors and carriages rolled away, and there was left only the policemen and the unsatiated mob. They watched the undertaker's assistant remove the great bow of black from the door of the house.

By the end of the week the murder of Challis Wrandall was forgotten by all save the police. The inquest was over, the law was baffled, the city was serenely waiting for its next sensation. No one cared.

Leslie Wrandall went down to the steamer to see his sister-in-law off for Europe.

"Good-bye, Miss Castleton," he said, as he shook the hand of the slim young Englishwoman at parting. "Take good care of Sara. She needs a friend, a good friend, now. Keep her over there until she has — forgotten."

CHAPTER V

" You remember my sister-in-law, don't you, Brandy? "
was the question that Leslie Wrandall put to a friend
one afternoon, as they sat drearily in a window of one
of the fashionable up-town clubs, a little more than a
year after the events described in the foregoing chap-
ters. Drearily, I have said, for the reason that it was
Sunday, and raining at that.

" I met Mrs. Wrandall a few years ago in Rome,"
said his companion, renewing interest in a conversation
that had died some time before of its own exhaustion.
" She's most attractive. I saw her but once. I think
it was at somebody's fête."

" She's returning to New York the end of the month,"
said Leslie. " Been abroad for over a year. She had
a villa at Nice this winter."

" I remember her quite well. I was of an age then
to be particularly sensitive to female loveliness. If
I'd been staying on in Rome, I should have screwed up
the courage, I'm sure, to have asked her to sit for me."

" Lord love you, man, she's posed for half the painters in the world, it seems to me. Like the duchesses that
Romney and those old chaps used to paint. It occurs
to me those grand old dames did nothing but sit for
portraits, year in and year out, all their lives. I don't
see where they found time to scratch up the love affairs
they're reported to have had. There always must have
been some painter or other hanging around. I remember reading that the Duchess of — I can't remember the name — posed a hundred and sixty-nine times,

for nearly as many painters. Sara's not so bad as all
that, of course, but I don't exaggerate when I say she's
been painted a dozen times — and hung in twice as
many exhibits."

"I know," said the other with a smile. "I've seen
a few of them."

"The best of them all is hanging in her place up
in the country, old man. It's the one my brother liked.
A Belgian fellow did it a couple of years ago. Never
been exhibited, so of course you haven't seen it. Challis wouldn't consent to its being revealed to the vulgar
gaze, he loved it so much."

"I like that," resented Brandon Booth, with a mild
glare.

"Lot of common, vulgar people do hang about picture galleries, you will have to admit that, Brandy.
They visit 'em in the winter time to get in where it's
warm, and in the summer time they go because it's nice
and shady. That's the sort I mean."

"What do you know about art or the people who —"

"I know all there is to know about it, old chap.
Haven't we got Gainsboroughs, and Turners, and Con-
stables, and Corots hanging all over the place? And
a lot of others, too. Reynolds, Romney and Rae-
burn,— the three R's. And didn't I tag along with
mother to picture dealers' shops and auctions when
every blessed one of 'em was bought? I know *all* about
it, let me tell you. I can tell you what kind of an ' atmosphere ' a painting's got, with my eyes closed; and
as for ' quality ' and ' luminosity ' and ' broadness '
and ' handling,' I know more this minute about such
things than any auctioneer in the world. I am a past
master at it, believe me. One can't go around buying paintings with his mother without getting a liberal

education in art. She began taking me when I was ten years old. Challis wouldn't go, so she *made* me do it. Then I always had to go back with her when she wanted to exchange them for something else the dealer assured her she ought to have in our collection, and which invariably cost three times as much. No, my dear fellow, you are very much mistaken when you say that I don't know anything about art. I am a walking price-list of all the art this side of the Dresden gallery. You should not forget that we are a very old New York family. We've been collecting for over twenty years."

Both laughed. He liked Wrandall best when he affected mockery of this sort, although he was keenly alive to a certain breath of self-glorification in his raillery. Leslie felt a delicious sense of security in railing at family limitations: he knew that no one was likely to take him seriously.

"Nevertheless, your mother has some really fine paintings in the collection," proclaimed Booth amiably, also descending to snobbishness without really meaning to do so. He considered Velasquez to be the superior of all those mentioned by Wrandall, and there was the end to it, so far as he was concerned. It was ever a source of wonder to him that Mrs. Wrandall didn't "trade in" everything else she possessed for a single great Velasquez.

"Getting back to Sara,— my sister-in-law,— why don't you ask her to sit for you this summer? She's not going out, you know, and time will hang so heavily on her hands that she will even welcome another portrait agony."

"I can't ask her to —"

"I'll do the asking, if you say the word."

"Don't be an ass."

"I'm quite willing to be one, if it will help you out, old man," said Leslie cheerfully.

"And make one of me as well, I suppose. She'd think me a frightful cub after all those other fellows. After Sargent, *me!* Ho, ho! She'd laugh in my face."

"If you could paint that smile of hers, Brandy, you'd make Romney look like an amateur. Most wonderful smile. It's a splendid idea. Let her laugh in your face, as you say; then paint like the devil while she's doing it, and your reputation is made for —"

"Will you have another drink?"

"No, thanks. I can change the subject without it. What time is it?"

Both looked at their watches, and put them back again without remark to resume the interrupted contemplation of Fifth Avenue in the waning light of a drab, drizzly day. A man in a shiny "slicker" was pushing a sweep and shovel in the centre of the thoroughfare. They wondered how long it would be before a motor struck him.

Brandon Booth was of an old Philadelphia family: an old and wealthy family. Both views considered, he was qualified to walk hand in glove with the fastidious Wrandalls. Leslie's mother was charmed with him because she was also the mother of Vivian. The fact that he went in for portrait painting and seemed averse to subsisting on the generosity of his father, preferring to live by his talent, in no way operated against him, so far as Mrs. Wrandall was concerned. That was *his* lookout, not hers; if he elected to that sort of thing, all well and good. He could afford to be eccentric; there remained, in the perspective he scorned, the bulk of a huge fortune to offset whatever idiosyncrasies he might choose to cultivate. Some day, in spite of himself, she contended serenely, he would be very, very rich. What could be more desirable than fame, family and fortune all heaped together and thrust upon one exceedingly interesting and handsome young man? For he would be famous, she was sure of it. Every one said that of him, even the critics, although she didn't have much use for critics, retaining opinions of her own that seldom agreed with theirs. It was enough for her that he was a Booth, and knew how to behave in a drawing-room, because he belonged there and was not lugged in by the scruff of an ill-fitting dress-suit to pose as a Bohemian celebrity. Moreover, he was a level-headed, well-balanced fellow in spite of his calling; which was saying a great deal, proclaimed the mother of Vivian in opposition to her own argument that painters never made satisfactory or even satisfying husbands: the artistic temperament and all that sort of thing getting in the way of compatibility.

He had been the pupil of celebrated draughtsmen and painters in Europe, and had exhibited a sincerity of purpose that was surprising, all things considered. The mere fact that he was not obliged to paint in order to obtain a living, was sufficient cause for wonder among the artists he met and studied with or under. At first they regarded him as a youth with a fancy that soon would pass, leaving him high and dry and safe on something steadier than Art. They couldn't understand a rich man's son really having aspirations, although they granted him temperament and ability. But he went about it so earnestly, so systematically, that they were compelled to alter the time-honoured tune and to sing praises instead of whistling their in-

sulting " I-told-you-sos." To the disgust of many, he
had a real purpose supported by talent, and that was
what they couldn't understand in a rich man's son.
They hated to see their traditions spoiled. The only
way in which they could account for it all was that he
was an American, and Americans are always doing
the things one doesn't expect them to do, especially
along grooves that ought to be kept closed by tra-
dition.

When he said good-bye to his European friends and
masters, and set his face toward home, they took off
their hats to him, so to speak, and agreed that he had
a brilliant future, without a thought of the legacy that
one day would be his.

His studio in New York was not a fashionable resting place. It was a work-shop. You could have tea
there, of course, and you were sure to meet people you
knew and liked, but it was quite as much of a work-shop
as any you could mention. He was not a dabbler in
art, not a mere dauber of pigments: he was an *artist*.
People argued that because he was a thoroughbred
and doomed to be rich, his conscious egotism would
show itself at once in the demand for ridiculously high
prices. In that they happily were fooled, not to say
disappointed. He began by painting the portrait of
a well-known society woman of great wealth, who sat
'to him because she wanted to " take him up," and who
was absolutely disconsolate when he announced, at the
end of the sittings, that his price was five hundred dollars. She would not believe her ears.

" Why, my dear Brandon, you will be ruined — utterly ruined — if it becomes known that you ask less
than five thousand," she had cried, almost in tears.
" No one will come to you."

He had smiled. " A master's price is for a master, not for a tyro. If they want to pay five thousand dollars for a portrait, I can recommend a dozen or more gentlemen whose work is worth it. Mine isn't. Some day I hope to be able to say five thousand with a great deal more assurance than I now say five hundred, Mrs. Wheeler, but it won't be until I have courage, not nerve."

" But *nobody* will sit for a five hundred dollar portrait," she expostulated. " Really, Brandon, I prefer to pay five thousand. I can't — I simply cannot tell people that I paid only five —"

" Will you give six hundred? " he asked, his smile broadening.

" Absurd! "

" Seven hundred? "

" Why, it sounds as if you were jewing me up, not I trying to jew you down," she cried, dismayed.

" That's the point," he said, with mock gravity. " If my price isn't what it ought to be in your opinion, it is only fair that I should make concessions. My picture is worth five hundred dollars, but I am willing to do a little better than that by you. I will make it seven-fifty to you, but not a cent more."

" Can't I jew you up any higher, dear boy? "

" No," with a smile; " but if you will consent to sit to me ten years from now, I promise faithfully to ask five thousand of you without a blush."

" Ah, but ten years from now I should blush to even think of having my portrait painted."

" Ten years will make no change in you," said he gallantly, " but I expect them to make quite another artist of me."

And so his price was established for the time being.

He offset the chilling effect of the low figure by deliberately declining commissions to paint women who fell below a rather severe standard of personal attractiveness. Gross women were not allowed to crowd his canvases; ugly ones who succeeded in tempting him were surprised to find how ugly they really were when the portrait was finished. He made it a point never to lie about a woman, not even on canvas. It made him very unpopular with certain ladies who wanted to be lied about — on canvas.

As the result of his rather independent attitude, he had more commissions than he could fill. When it got about that he cared to paint only attractive women, his studio was besieged by ladies of a curious turn of mind. If they discovered that he was willing to paint them, they blissfully dropped the matter and went happily on their way. If they found that his time was so fully occupied that he could not paint them they urged him to reconsider — even offering to quadruple his price if he would only " do " them. One exceedingly plain woman, who couldn't be reconciled to Nature, offered him twenty thousand dollars if he would paint her for the Metropolitan Museum. Another asked him if he was a pupil of Gainsborough. Finding that he was not, she asked *why* not, with all the money he had at his command.

He had been in New York for the better part of two years at the time he is introduced into this narrative. Years of his life had been spent abroad, yet he was not a stranger in a strange land when he took up his residence in Gotham. Society opened its arms to him. It was like a home-coming. Had he been a bridge player, his coronation might have been complete.

Booth was thirty,— perhaps a year or two older;

tall, dark and good-looking. The air of the thoroughbred marked him. He did not affect loose flowing cra-
vats and baggy trousers, nor was he careless about
his finger-nails. He was simply the ordinary, every-
day sort of chap you would meet in Fifth Avenue during parade hours, and you would take a second look
at him because of his face and manner but not on account of his dress. Some of his ancestors came over
ahead of the *Mayflower*, but he did not gloat.

Leslie Wrandall was his closest friend and harshest
critic. It didn't really matter to Booth what Leslie
said of his paintings: he quite understood that he didn't
know anything about them.

" When does Mrs. Wrandall return? " asked the
painter, after a long period of silence spent in contemplation of the gleaming pavement beyond the club's
window.

" That's queer," said Leslie, looking up. " I was
thinking of Sara myself. She sails next week. I've
had a letter asking me to open her house in the country.
Her place is about two miles from father's. It hasn't
been opened in two years. Her father built it fifteen or
twenty years ago, and left it to her when he died. She
and Challis spent several summers there."

" Vivian took me through it one afternoon last summer."

" It must have been quite as much of a novelty to her
as it was to you, old chap," said Leslie gloomily.

" What do you mean? "

" Vivian's a bit of a snob. She never liked the place
because old man Gooch built it out of worsteds. She
never went there."

" But the old man's been dead for years."

" That doesn't matter. The fact is, Vivian didn't

quite take to Sara until after — well, until after Challis died. We're dreadful snobs, Brandy, the whole lot of us. Sara was quite good enough for a much better man than my brother. She really couldn't help the worsteds, you know. I'm very fond of her, and always have been. We're pals. 'Gad, it was a fearful slap at the home folks when Challis justified Sara by getting snuffed out the way he did."

Booth made an attempt to change the subject, but Wrandall got back to it.

" Since then we've all been exceedingly sweet on Sara. Not because we want to be, mind you, but because we're afraid she'll marry some chap who wouldn't be acceptable to us."

" I should consider that a very neat way out of it," said Booth coldly.

" Not at all. You see, Challis was fond of Sara, in spite of everything. He left a will and under it she came in for all he had. As that includes a third interest in our extremely refined and irreproachable business, it would be a deuce of a trick on us if she married one of the common people and set him up amongst us, willy-nilly. We don't want strange bed-fellows. We're too snug — and, I might say, too smug. Down in her heart, mother is saying to herself it would be just like Sara to get even with us by doing just that sort of a trick. Of course, Sara is rich enough without accepting a sou under the will, but she's a canny person. She hasn't handed it back to us on a silver platter, with thanks; still, on the other hand, she refuses to meddle. She makes us feel pretty small. She won't sell out to us. She just sits tight. That's what gets under the skin with mother."

" I wouldn't say that, Les, if I were in your place."

"It is a rather priggish thing to say, isn't it?"

"Rather."

"You see, I'm the only one who really took sides with Sara. I forget myself sometimes. She was such a brick, all those years."

Booth was silent for a moment, noting the reflective look in his companion's eyes.

"I suppose the police haven't given up the hope that sooner or later the — er — the woman will do something to give herself away," said he.

"They don't take any stock in my theory that she made way with herself the same night. I was talking with the chief yesterday. He says that any one who had wit to cover up her tracks as she did, is not the kind to make way with herself. Perhaps he's right. It sounds reasonable. 'Gad, I felt sorry for the poor girl they had up last spring. She went through the third degree, if ever any one did, but, by Jove, she came out of it all right. The Ashtley girl, you remember. I've dreamed about that girl, Brandy, and what they put her through. It's a sort of nightmare to me, even when I'm awake. Oh, they've questioned others as well, but she was the only one to have the screws twisted in just that way."

"Where is she now?"

"She's comfortable enough now. When I wrote to Sara about what she'd been through, she settled a neat bit of money on her, and she'll never want for anything. She's out West somewhere, with her mother and sisters. I tell you, Sara's a wonder. She's got a heart of gold."

"I look forward to meeting her, old man."

"I was with her for a few weeks this winter. In Nice, you know. Vivian stayed on for a week, but

mother had to get to the baths. 'Gad, I believe she
hated to go. Sara's got a most adorable girl staying with her. A daughter of Colonel Castleton, and
she's connected in some way with the Murgatroyds —
old Lord Murgatroyd, you know. I think her mother
was a niece of the old boy. Anyhow, mother and Vivian have taken a great fancy to her. That's proof of
the pudding."

"I think Vivian mentioned a companion of some
sort."

"You wouldn't exactly call her a companion," said
Leslie. "She's got money to burn, I take it. Quite
keeps up with Sara in making it fly, and that's saying
a good deal for her resources. I think it's a pose on
her part, this calling herself a companion. An English
joke, eh? As a matter of fact, she's an old friend of
Sara's and my brother's too. Knew them in England.
Most delightful girl. Oh, I say, old man, *she's* the
one for you to paint." Leslie waxed enthusiastic. "A
type, a positive type. Never saw such eyes in all my
life. Dammit, they haunt you. You dream about
'em."

"You seem to be hard hit," said Booth indifferently.
He was watching the man in the "slicker" through
moody eyes.

"Oh, nothing like that," disclaimed Leslie, with unnecessary promptness. "But if I were given to that
sort of thing, I'd be bowled over in a minute. Positively adorable face. If I thought you had it in you to
paint a thing as it really is, I'd commission you myself
to do a miniature for me, just to have it around where
I could pick it up when I liked and hold it between my
hands, just as I've often wanted to hold the real thing."

"Come, come! You're dotty about her."

" Get Vivian to tell you about her," said Leslie sweepingly.   " Come down and have dinner with me to-night.
She'll bear out —"

" I'll take your word for it.   Thanks for the bid,
but I can't come.   Dining at the Ritz with Joey and
Linda.   I think I'll be off."

He stretched himself, took the final, reluctant look
of the artist at the " slicker " man, and moved away.
Leslie called after him:

" Wait till you see her."

" All right.   I'll wait."

. . . . . .

Sara Wrandall returned to New York at the end of
the month, and Leslie met her at the dock, as he did
on an occasion fourteen months earlier.   Then she
came in on a fierce gale from the wintry Atlantic; this
time the air was soft and balmy and sweet with the
kindness of spring.   It was May and the sea was blue,
the land was green.

Again she went to the small, exclusive hotel near the
Park.   Her apartment was closed, the butler and his
wife and all of their hastily recruited company being
in the country, awaiting her arrival from town.   Leslie attended to everything.   He lent his resourceful
man-servant and his motor to his lovely sister-in-law,
and saw to it that his mother and Vivian sent flowers
to the ship.   Redmond Wrandall called at the hotel
immediately after banking hours, kissed his daughter-
in-law, and delivered an ultimatum second-hand from
the power at home: she was to come to dinner and
bring Miss Castleton.   A little quiet family dinner,
you know, because they were all in mourning, he said in
conclusion, vaguely realising all the while that it really
wasn't necessary to supply the information, but, for

the life of him, unable to think of anything else to say
under the circumstances. Somehow it seemed to him
that while Sara was in black she was not in mourning
in the same sense that the rest of them were. It seemed
only right to acquaint her with the conditions in his
household. And he knew that he deserved the scowl
that Leslie bestowed upon him.

Sara accepted, much to his surprise and gratification.
He had been rather dubious about it. It would not
have surprised him in the least if she had declined the
invitation, feeling, as he did, that he had in a way come
to her with a white flag or an olive branch or whatever
it is that a combative force utilises when it wants to
surrender in the cause of humanity.

Leslie was a very observing person. It might have
been said of him that he was always on the lookout for
the things that most people were unlikely to notice:
the trivial things that really were important. He not
only took in his father's amiable blunder, but caught
the curious expression in Hetty's dark blue eyes, and
the sharp almost inaudible catch of her breath. The
gleam was gone in an instant, but it made an impression on him. He found himself wondering if the girl
was a snob as well as the rest of them. The look in
her eyes betrayed unmistakable surprise and — yes, he
was quite sure of it — dismay when Sara accepted the
invitation to dine. Was it possible that the lovely Miss
Castleton considered herself — but no! Of course it
couldn't be that. The Wrandalls were good enough for
dukes and duchesses. Still he could not get beyond the
fact that he *had* seen the look of disapproval. 'Gad,
thought he, it was almost a look of appeal. He made
up his mind, as he stood there chatting with her, that
he would find out from Vivian what his mother had

done to create an unpleasant estimate of the family in the eyes of this gentle, refined cousin of old Lord Murgatroyd.

He was quite as quick to detect the satirical smile in Sara's frank, amused eyes as she graciously accepted the invitation to the home whose doors had only been half-open to her in the past. It scratched his pride a bit to think of the opinion she must have of the family, and he was inexpressibly glad that she could not consistently class him with the others. He found himself feeling a bit sorry for the old gentleman, and hoped that he missed the touch of irony in Sara's voice.

Old Mr. Wrandall floundered from one invitation to another.

" Of course, Sara, my dear, you will want to go out to the cemetery to-morrow. I shall be only too ready to accompany you. We have erected a splendid —"

" No, thank you, Mr. Wrandall," she interrupted gently. " I shall not go to the cemetery."

Leslie intervened. " You understand, don't you, father? " he said, rather out of patience.

The old gentleman lowered his head. " Yes, yes," he hastened to say. " Quite so, quite so.   Then we may expect you at eight, Sara, and you, Miss Castleton.   Mrs. Wrandall is looking forward to seeing you again. It isn't often she takes a liking to — ahem! I beg your pardon, Leslie? "

" I was just going to suggest that we move along, dad. I fancy you want to get at your trunks, Sara. Smuggled a few things through, eh? Women never miss a chance to get a couple of dozen dresses through, as you'll discover if you become a real American, Miss Castleton. It's in the blood."

Mr. Wrandall fell into another trap. " Now please

remember that we are to dine very informally," he hastened to say, his mind on the smuggled gowns. It was his experience that gowns that escaped duty invariably were " creations."

Leslie got him away.

As soon as they were alone, Hetty turned to her friend.

" Oh, Sara, can't you go without me? Tell them that I am ill — suddenly ill. I — I don't think it right or honourable of me to accept —"

Sara shook her head, and the words died on the girl's lips.

" You must play the game, Hetty."

" It's — very hard," murmured the other, her face very white and bleak.

" I know, my dear," said Sara gently.

" If they should ever find out," gasped the girl, suddenly giving way to the dread that had been lying dormant all these months.

" They will never know the truth unless you choose to enlighten them," said Sara, putting her arm about the girl's shoulders and drawing her close.

" You never cease to be wonderful, Sara,— *so* very wonderful," cried the girl, with a look of worship in her eyes.

Sara regarded her in silence for a moment, reflecting. Then, with a swift rush of tears to her eyes, she cried fiercely :

" You must never, never tell me all that happened, Hetty! You must not speak it with your own lips."

Hetty's eyes grew dark with pain and wonder.

" That is the thing I can't understand in you, Sara," she said slowly.

" We must not speak of it!"

Hetty's bosom heaved. " Speak of it! " she cried, absolute agony in her voice. " Have I not kept it locked in my heart since that awful day —"

" Hush! "

" I shall go mad if I cannot talk with you about —"

" No, no! It is the forbidden subject! I know all that I should know — all that I care to know. We have not said so much as this in months — in ages, it seems. Let sleeping dogs lie. We are better off, my dear. I could not touch your lips again."

" I — I can't bear the thought of that! "

" Kiss me now, Hetty."

" I could die for you, Sara," cried Hetty, as she impulsively obeyed the command.

" I mean that you shall live for me," said Sara, smiling through her tears. " How silly of me to cry. It must be the room we are in. These are the same rooms, dear, that you came to on the night we met. Ah, how old I feel! "

" Old? You say that to me? I am ages and ages older than you," cried Hetty, the colour coming back to her soft cheeks.

" You are twenty-three."

" And you are twenty-eight."

Sara had a far away look in her eyes. " About your size and figure," said she, and Hetty did not comprehend.

CHAPTER VI

SOUTHLOOK

SARA WRANDALL's house in the country stood on a wooded knoll overlooking the Sound. It was rather remotely located, so far as neighbours were concerned. Her father, Sebastian Gooch, shrewdly foresaw the day when land in this particular section of the suburban world would return dollars for the pennies, and wisely bought thousands of acres: woodland, meadowland, beachland and hills, inserted between the environs of New York City and the rich towns up the coast. Years afterward he built a commodious summer home on the choicest point that his property afforded, named it Southlook, and transformed that particular part of his wilderness into a millionaire's paradise, where he could dawdle and putter to his heart's content, where he could spend his time and his money with a prodigality that came so late in life to him that he made waste of both in his haste to live down a rather parsimonious past.

Two miles and a half away, in the heart of a scattered colony of purse-proud New Yorkers, was the country home of the Wrandalls, an imposing place and older by far than Southlook. It had descended from well-worn and time-stained ancestors to Redmond Wrandall, and, with others of its kind, looked with no little scorn upon the modern, mushroom structures that sprouted from the seeds of trade. There was no friendship between the old and the new. Each had recourse to a bitter contempt for the other, though consolation was small in comparison.

It was in the wooded by-ways of this despised do-
main that Challis Wrandall and Sara, the earthly
daughter of Midas, met and loved and defied all things
supernal, for matches are made in heaven. Their marriage did not open the gates of Nineveh. Sebastian
Gooch's paradise was more completely ostracised than
it was before the disaster. The Wrandalls spoke of it
as a disaster.

Clearly the old merchant was not over-pleased with
his daughter's choice, a conclusion permanently established by the alteration he made in his will a year or
two after the marriage. True, he left the vast estate
to his beloved daughter Sara, but he fastened a stout
·string to it, and with this string her hands were tied.
It must have occurred to him that Challis was a prof-
ligate in more ways than one, for he deliberately stip-
ulated in his will that Sara was not to sell a foot of
the ground until a period of twenty years had elapsed.
A very polite way, it would seem, of making his investment safe in the face of considerable odds.

He lived long enough after the making of his will, I
am happy to relate, to find that he had made no mistake.
As he preceded his son-in-law into the Great Beyond by
a scant three years, it readily may be seen that he
wrought too well by far. Seventeen unnecessary years
of proscription remained, and he had not intended them
for Sara *alone*. He was not afraid of Sara, but for
her.

When the will was read and the condition revealed,
Challis Wrandall took it in perfect good humour. He
had the grace to proclaim in the bosom of his father's
family that the old gentleman was a father-in-law to
be proud of. " A canny old boy," he had announced
with his most engaging smile, quite free from rancour

or resentment.   Challis was well acquainted with himself.

, And so the acres were strapped together snugly and
firmly, without so much as a town-lot protruding.

So impressed was Challis by the farsightedness of
his father-in-law that he forthwith sat him down and
made a will of his own.   He would not have it said that
Sara's father did a whit better by her than he would
do.   He left everything he possessed to his wife, but
put no string to it, blandly implying that all danger
would be past when she came into possession.   There
was a sort of grim humour in the way he managed to
present himself to view as the real and ready source of
peril.

Among certain of the Wrandall clan there was serious talk of contesting the will.   It was a distinct
shock to all of them.   Some one made bold to assert that Challis was not in his right mind at the time
it was executed.   For that matter, a couple of uncles
on his mother's side were of the broad opinion that he
never had been mentally adequate.

During a family conference four days after the funeral, Leslie launched forth at some length and with considerable heat, expressing an opinion that met with
small favour at the outset but which had its results
later on.

" Why," he declaimed, standing before the fireplace
with his hands in his pockets, " if Sara dreamed that
we even so much as contemplate making a fuss about
Chal's will, she'd up and chuck the whole blooming
legacy in our faces, and be glad to do it.   She's got
plenty of her own.   She doesn't need the little that
Challis left her.   Then, what would we look like, tell
me that?   What would the world say?   Why, it would

say that she didn't think our money was clean enough
to mix with old man Gooch's. She'd throw it in our
faces and the whole town would snicker."

"Figuratively speaking, young man, figuratively
speaking," said one of the uncles, a stockholder and
director.

"What do you mean by that?"

"That she—ahem! That she couldn't actually
throw it."

"I'm not so literal as you, Uncle George."

"Then why use the word *throw?*"

"Of course, Uncle George, I don't mean to say she'd
have it reduced to gold coin and stand off and take
shots at us. You understand that, don't you?"

"Leslie," put in his father, "you have a most distressing way of — er — putting it. Your Uncle
George is not so dense as all that."

"I didn't use the word ' throw ' in the first place,"
said Leslie, with a shrug. "I said ' chuck.'"

"I distinctly heard you use the word ' throw,'" said
Uncle George, very red in the face.

"It was on the second occasion, George," said Mrs.
Wrandall, loyal to Leslie.

"In either case," said her son, "we'd be made ridiculous. That's the long and short of it. Even if she
handed it to us on a silver plate,— figuratively speaking, Uncle George,— we'd be made to look like thirty
cents."

"Well, I'm damn —" began Uncle George, almost
forgetting where he was, but remembering in time. He
was afraid to utter a word for the next ten minutes, and
Leslie was spared the interruptions.

It was decided that the will should stand. Later
on, the alarming prospect of Sara's perfect right to

marry again came up to mar the peace of mind of all the Wrandalls, and it grew to be horribly real without a single move on her part to warrant the fears they were encouraging.

Sara and Hetty did not stay long in town. The newspapers announced the return of Challis Wrandall's widow and reporters sought her out for interviews. The old interest was revived and columns were printed about the murder at Burton's Inn, with sharp editorial comments on the failure of the police to clear up the mystery.

The woods were green and the earth was redolent of rich spring odours; wild flowers peeped shyly from the leaf-strewn soil in the shadow of the trees; some, more bold than others, came down to the roadway, and from the banks and hedges smiled saucily upon all who passed; the hillsides were like spotless carpets, the meadows a riot of clover hues. The world was light with the life of the new-born year, for who shall say that the year does not begin with the birth of spring? May! May, when the earth begins to bear, not January when it sets out in sorrow to bury its dead. New Year's day it is, when the first tiny flower of spring comes to life and smiles on the face of Mother Earth, and the sun is warm with the love of a gentle father.

"I shall ask Leslie down for the week-end," said Sara, the third day after their arrival in the country. The house was huge and lonely, and time hung rather heavily despite the glorious uplift of spring.

Hetty looked up quickly from her book. A look of dismay flickered in her eyes for an instant and then gave way to the calmness that had come to dwell in their depths of late. Her lips parted in the sudden impulse to cry out against the plan, but she checked the words. For a moment, her dark, questioning eyes studied the face of her benefactress; then, as if nothing had been revealed to her, she allowed her gaze to drift pensively out toward the sunset sea.

They were sitting on the broad verandah overlooking the Sound. The dusk of evening was beginning to steal over the earth. She laid her book aside.

"Will you telephone in to him after dinner, Hetty?" went on Sara, after a long period of silence.

Again Hetty started. This time a look of actual pain flashed in her eyes.

"Would not a note by post be more certain to find him in the —" she began hurriedly.

"I dislike writing notes," said Sara calmly. "Of course, dear, if you feel that you'd rather not telephone to him, I can —"

"I dare say I am finicky, Sara," apologised Hetty in quick contrition. "Of course, he is your brother. I should remem —"

"My brother-in-law, dear," said Sara, a trifle too literally.

"He will come often to your house," went on Hetty rapidly. "I must make the best of it."

"He is your friend, Hetty. He admires you."

"I cannot see him through your eyes, Sara."

"But he *is* charming and agreeable, you'll admit," persisted the other.

"He is very kind, and he is devoted to you. I should like him for that."

"You have no cause for disliking him."

"I do not dislike him. I — I am — Oh, you always have been so thoughtful, so considerate, Sara, I can't understand your failing to see how hard it is for me to — to — well, to endure his open-hearted friendship."

Sara was silent for a moment. "You draw a pretty fine line, Hetty," she said gently.

Hetty flushed. "You mean that there is little to choose between wife and brother? That isn't quite fair. You know everything, he knows nothing. I wear a mask for him; you have seen into the very heart of me. It isn't the same."

Sara came over and stood beside the girl's chair. After a moment of indecision, she laid her hand on Hetty's shoulder. The girl looked up, the ever-recurring question in her eyes.

"We haven't spoken of — of these things in many months, Hetty."

"Not since Mrs. Wrandall and Vivian came to Nice. I was upset — dreadfuly upset then, Sara. I don't know how I managed to get through with it."

"But you managed it," pronounced Sara. Her fingers seemed to tighten suddenly on the girl's shoulder. "I think we were quite wonderful, both of us. It wasn't easy for me."

"Why did we come back to New York, Sara?" burst out Hetty, clasping her friend's hand as if suddenly spurred by terror. "We were happy over there. And free!"

"Listen, my dear," said Sara, a hard note growing in her voice: "this is my home. I do not love it, but I can see no reason for abandoning it. That is why we came back to New York."

Hetty pressed her friend's hand to her lips. "Forgive me," she cried impulsively. "I shouldn't have complained. It was detestable."

"Besides," went on Sara evenly, "you were quite free to remain on the other side. I left it to you."

"You gave me a week to decide," said Hetty, in a

hurried manner of speaking. "I — I took but twenty-four hours — less than that. Over night, you remember. I love you, Sara. I could not leave you. All that night I could feel you pulling at my heart-strings, pulling me closer and closer, and holding me. You were in your room, I in mine, and yet all the time you seemed to be bending over me in the darkness, urging me to stay with you and love you and be loved by you. It couldn't have been a dream."

"It was not a dream," said Sara, with a queer smile.

"You *do* love me?" tensely.

"I *do* love you," was the firm answer. Sara was staring out across the water, her eyes big and as black as night itself. She seemed to be looking far beyond the misty lights that bobbled with nearby schooners, far beyond the yellow mass on the opposite shore where a town lay cradled in the shadows, far into the fast darkening sky that came up like a wall out of the east.

Hetty's fingers tightened in a warmer clasp. Unconsciously perhaps, Sara's grip on the girl's shoulder tightened also: unconsciously, for her thoughts were far away. The younger woman's pensive gaze rested on the peaceful waters below, taking in the slow approach of the fog that was soon to envelop the land. Neither spoke for many minutes: inscrutable thinkers, each a prey to thoughts that leaped backward to the beginning and took up the puzzle at its inception.

"I wonder —" began Hetty, her eyes narrowing with the intensity of thought. She did not complete the sentence.

Sara answered the unspoken question. "It will never be different from what it is now, unless you make it so."

Hetty started. "How could you have known what I was thinking?" she cried in wonder.

"It is what you are always thinking, my dear. You are always asking yourself when will I turn against you."

"Sara!"

"Your own intelligence should supply the answer to all the questions you are asking of yourself. It is too late for me to turn against you." She abruptly removed her hand from Hetty's shoulder and walked to the edge of the verandah. For the first time, the English girl was conscious of pain. She drew her arm up and cringed. She pulled the light scarf about her bare shoulders.

The butler appeared in the doorway.

"The telephone, if you please, Miss Castleton. Mr. Leslie Wrandall is calling."

The girl stared. "For me, Watson?"

"Yes, Miss. I forgot to say that he called up this afternoon while you were out," very apologetically, with a furtive glance at Mrs. Wrandall, who had turned.

"Loss of memory, Watson, is a fatal affliction," she said, with a smile.

"Yes, Mrs. Wrandall. I don't see 'ow it 'appened."

"It is not likely to happen again."

"No, madam."

Hetty had risen, visibly agitated.

"What shall I say to him, Sara?" she cried.

"Apparently it is he who has something to say to you," said the other, still smiling. "Wait and see what it is. Please don't neglect to say that we'd like to have him over Sunday."

"A box of flowers has just come up from the station for you, Miss," said Watson.

Hetty was very white as she passed into the house. Mrs. Wrandall resumed her contemplation of the fog-screened Sound.

" Shall I fetch you a wrap, ma'am? " asked Watson, hesitating.

" I am coming in, Watson. Open the box of flowers for Miss Castleton. Is there a fire in the library? "

" Yes, Mrs. Wrandall."

" Mr. Leslie will be out on Saturday. Tell Mrs. Conkling."

" The evening train, ma'am? "

" No. The eleven-thirty. He will be here for luncheon."

When Hetty hurried into the library a few minutes later, her manner was that of one considerably disturbed by something that has transpired almost on the moment. Her cheeks were flushed and her eyes were reflectors of a no uncertain distress of mind. Mrs. Wrandall was standing before the fireplace, an exquisite figure in the slinky black evening gown which she affected in these days. Her perfectly modelled neck and shoulders gleamed like pink marble in the reflected glow of the burning logs. She wore no jewellery, but there was a single white rose in her dark hair, where it had been placed by the whimsical Hetty an hour earlier as they left the dinner table.

" He is coming out on the eleven-thirty, Sara," said the girl nervously, " unless you will send the motor in for him. The body of his car is being changed and it's in the shop. He must have been jesting when he said he would pay for the petrol — I should have said gasoline."

Sara laughed. " You will know him better, my dear," she said. " Leslie is very light-hearted."

"He suggested bringing a friend," went on Hetty hurriedly. "A Mr. Booth, the portrait painter."

"I met him in Italy. He is charming. You will like *him*, too, Hetty." The emphasis did not escape notice.

"It seems that he is spending a fortnight in the village, this Mr. Booth, painting spring lambs for rest and recreation, Mr. Leslie says."

"Then he is at our very gates," said Sara, looking up suddenly.

"I wonder if he can be the man I saw yesterday at the bridge," mused Hetty. "Is he tall?"

"I really can't say. He's rather vague. It was six or seven years ago."

"It was left that Mr. Wrandall is to come out on the eleven-thirty," explained Hetty. "I thought you wouldn't like sending either of the motors in."

"And Mr. Booth?"

"We are to send for him after Mr. Wrandall arrives. He is stopping at the inn, wherever that may be."

"Poor fellow!" sighed Sara, with a grimace. "I am sure he will like us immensely if he has been stopping at the inn."

Hetty stood staring down at the blazing logs for a full minute before giving expression to the thought that troubled her.

"Sara," she said, meeting her friend's eyes with a steady light in her own, "why did Mr. Wrandall ask for me instead of you? It is you he is coming to visit, not me. It is your house. Why should —"

"My dear," said Sara glibly, "I am merely his sister-in-law. It wouldn't be neecssary to ask me if he should come. He knows he is welcome."

"Then why should he feel called upon to —"

"Some men like to telephone, I suppose," said the other coolly.

"I wonder if you will ever understand how I feel about — about certain things, Sara."

"What, for instance?"

"Well, his very evident interest in me," cried the girl hotly. "He sends me flowers,— this is the second box this week,— and he is so kind, so *very* friendly, Sara, that I can't bear it — I really can't."

Mrs. Wrandall stared at her. "You can't very well send him about his business," she said, "unless he becomes more than friendly. Now, can you?"

"But it seems so — so horrible, so beastly," groaned the girl.

Sara faced her squarely. "See here, Hetty," she said levelly, "we have made our bed, you and I. We must lie in it — together. If Leslie Wrandall chooses to fall in love with you, that is his affair, not ours. We must face every condition. In plain words, we must play the game."

"What could be more appalling than to have him fall in love with me?"

"The other way 'round would be more dramatic, I should say."

"Good God, Sara!" cried the girl in horror. "How can you even speak of such a thing?"

"After all, why shouldn't —" began Sara, but stopped in the middle of her suggestion, with the result that it had its full effect without being uttered in so many cold-blooded words. The girl shuddered.

"I wish, Sara, you would let me unburden myself completely to you," she pleaded, seizing her friend's hands. "You have forbidden me —"

Sara jerked her hands away. Her eyes flashed.

"I do not want to hear it," she cried fiercely. "Never, never! Do you understand? It is your secret. I will not share it with you. I should hate you if I knew everything. As it is, I love you because you are a woman who suffered at the hand of one who made me suffer. There is nothing more to say. Don't bring up the subject again. I want to be your friend for ever, not your confidante. There is a distinction. You may be able to see how very marked it is in our case, Hetty. What one does not know, seldom hurts."

"But I want to justify myself —"

"It isn't necessary," cut in the other so peremptorily that the girl's eyes spread into a look of anger. Whereupon Sara Wrandall threw her arm about her and drew her down beside her on the chaise-longue. "I didn't mean to be harsh," she cried. "We must not speak of the past, that's all. The future is not likely to hurt us, dear. Let us avoid the past."

"The future!" sighed the girl, staring blankly before her.

"To appreciate what it is to be," said the other, "you have but to think of what it might have been."

"I know," said Hetty, in a low voice. "And yet I sometimes wonder if —"

Sara interrupted. "You are paying me, dear, instead of the law," she said gently. "I am not a harsh creditor, am I?"

"My life belongs to you. I give it cheerfully, even gladly."

"So you have said before. Well, if it belongs to me, you might at least permit me to develop it as I would any other possession. I take it as an investment. It will probably fluctuate."

"Now you are jesting!"

" Perhaps," said Sara laconically.

The next morning Hetty set forth for her accustomed tramp over the roads that wound through the estate. Sara, the American, dawdled at home, resenting the chill spring drizzle that did not in the least discourage the Englishwoman. The mistress of the house and of the girl's destiny stood in the broad French window watching her as she strode springily, healthily down the maple lined avenue in the direction of the gates. The gardeners doffed their caps to her as she passed, and also looked after her with surreptitious glances.

There was a queer smile on Sara's lips that remained long after the girl was lost to view beyond the lodge. It was still on her lips but gone from her eyes as she paused beside the old English table to bury her nose in one of the gorgeous roses that Leslie had sent out to Hetty the day before. They were all about the room, dozens of them. The girl had insisted on having them downstairs instead of in her own little sitting-room, for which they plainly were intended.

A nasty sea turn had brought lowering grey skies and a dreary, enveloping mist that never quite assumed the dignity of a drizzle and yet blew wet and cold to the very marrow of the bones. Hetty was used to such weather. Her English blood warmed to it. As she strode briskly across the meadow-land road in the direction of the woods that lay ahead, a soft ruddy glow crept up to her cheeks, and a sparkle of joy into her eyes. She walked strongly, rapidly. Her straight, lithe young figure was a joyous thing to behold. High boots, short skirt, a loose jacket and a broad felt hat made up her costume. She was graceful, adorable; a young, healthy, beautiful creature in whom the blood surged quickly, strongly: the type of woman men are

wont to classify as " ineffably feminine," though why
we should differentiate is no small mystery unless there
really is such a thing as one woman possessing an
adorably feminine quality denied to her sisters. Be
that as it may, there *is* a distinction and men pride
themselves on knowing it. Hetty was alluringly feminine.   Leaving out the matter of morals, whatever they
are, and coming right up to her as an example of her
sex, pure and simple if you please, we are bound to
say that she was perfect.   The best thing we can say of
Challis Wrandall is that he took the same view of her
that we should, and fell in love with her.   He would
have married her if he could, there isn't much doubt as
to that, no matter what she had been before he knew
her or what she was at the time of his discovery.   No
more is it to be considered unique that his brother should
have experienced a similar interest in her, knowing even
less.

She was the sort of girl one falls in love with and
remembers it the rest of his life.

Take her now, for instance, as she swings along the
highway, fresh, trim and graceful, her chin uptilted,
her cheeks warm, her eyes clear and as blue as sapphires,
and we experience the most intense, unreasoning desire
to be near her, at her side, where hands could touch
her and the very spell of her creep out over one to make
a man of him.

The kind of woman one wants to draw close to him
because his heart is sweet.

· She had the blood of a fellow creature on her hands
— the blood of one of us — and yet we men will overlook one commandment for another.   It is a matter of
choice.

What of her present position in the house and in the

heart of the one woman who of all those we know is
abnormally unfeminine in that she subordinates the natural and instinctive animosity of woman toward another who robs her of a husband, no matter how unworthy or how hateful he may have been to her behind
the screen with which she hides her sores from the
world. The answer is ready: Hetty was a slave bound
to an extraordinary condition. There had been no
coercion on the part of Challis Wrandall's wife; no actual restraint had been set upon the girl. The situation was a plain one from every point of view: Hetty
owed her life to Sara, she would have paid with her
life's blood the debt she owed. It had become perfectly natural for her to consider herself a willing,
grateful prisoner — a prisoner on parole. She would
not, could not abuse the parole. She loved her gaoler
with a love that knew no bounds; she loved the walls
Sara had thrown up about her; she was content to live
and die in the luxurious cell, attended by love and kindness and mercy. After all, Hetty was even more feminine than we seem able to convey in words.

Not in that she lacked in pride or sensitiveness, but
that she possessed to a self-satisfying degree the ability
to subordinate both of these to a loyalty that had no
bounds. There were fine feelings in Hetty. She was
honest with herself. She did not look beyond her present horizon for brighter skies. They were as bright
as they could ever be, of that she was sure; her hopes
lay within the small circumference that Sara Wrandall
made possible for her. She knew that her peril, her
ruin lay in the desire to step outside that narrow circle,
for out there the world was cold and merciless.

She lived as one charmed by some powerful influence,
and was content. Not once had the fear entered her

soul that Sara would turn against her. Her trust in Wrandall's wife was infinite. In her simple, devoted heart she could feel no prick of dread so far as the present was concerned. The past was dreadful, but it was the past, and its loathsomeness was moderated by subtle contrast with the present. As for the future, it belonged to Sara Wrandall. It was safe.

If Sara were to decide that she must be given up to the law, all well and good. She could meet her fate with a smile for Sara, and with love in her heart. She could pay in full if the demand was made by the wife of the man she had left in the grim little upstairs room at Burton's Inn on that never-to-be-forgotten night in March.

The one great, inexplicable mystery to her was the heart of Sara Wrandall. She could not fathom it.

She could understand her own utter subjection to the will of the other woman; she could explain it satis- factorily to herself, and she could have explained it to the world. Self-preservation in the beginning, self-sur- render as time went on, self-sacrifice as the preroga- tive.

And so it was, on this grey spring day, that she gazed undaunted at the world, with the shadows all about her, and hummed a sprightly tune through warm red lips that were kissed by the morning mist.

She came to the bridge by the mill, long since deserted and now a thing of ruin and decay. A man in knick- erbockers stood leaning against the rail, idly gazing down at the trickling stream below. The brier pipe that formed the circuit between hand and lips sent up soft blue coils to float away on the drizzle.

She passed behind him, with a single furtive, curious glance at his handsome, undisturbed profile, and in that glance recognised him as the man she had seen the day before.

When she was a dozen rods away, the tall man turned his face from the stream and sent after her the long-restrained look. There was something akin to cautiousness in that look of his, as if he were afraid that she might turn her head suddenly and catch him at it. Something began stirring in his heart, the nameless something that awakens when least expected. He felt the subtle, sweet femininity of her as she passed. It lingered with him as he looked.

She turned the bend in the road a hundred yards away. For many minutes he studied the stream below without really seeing it. Then he straightened up, knocked the ashes from his pipe, and set off slowly in her wake, although he had been walking in quite the opposite direction when he came to the bridge,— and on a mission of some consequence, too.

There was the chance that he would meet her coming back.

CHAPTER VII

A FAITHFUL CRAYON-POINT

LESLIE WRANDALL came out on the eleven-thirty. Hetty was at the station with the motor, a sullen resentment in her heart, but a welcoming smile on her lips. The sun shone brightly. The Sound glared with the white of reflected skies.

"I thought of catching the eight o'clock," he cried enthusiastically, as he dropped his bag beside the motor in order to reach over and shake hands with her. "That would have gotten me here hours earlier. The difficulty was that I didn't think of the eight o'clock until I awoke at nine."

"And then you had the additional task of thinking about breakfast," said Hetty, but without a trace of sarcasm in her manner.

"I never think of breakfast," said he amiably. "I merely eat it. Of course, it's a task to eat it sometimes, but — well, how are you? How do you like it out here?"

He was beside her on the broad seat, his face beaming, his gay little moustache pointing upward at the ends like oblique brown exclamation points, so expansive was his smile.

"I adore it," she replied, her own smile growing in response to his. It was impossible to resist the good nature of him. She could not dislike him, even though she dreaded him deep down in her heart. Her blood was hot and cold by turns when she was with him, as her mind opened and shut to thoughts pleasant and unpleasant with something of the regularity of a fish's gills in breathing.

"I knew you would. It's great. You won't care much for our place, Miss Castleton. Sara's got the pick of the coast in that place of hers. Trust old Sebastian Gooch to get the best of everything. If my dad or my grand-dad had possessed a tenth of the brain that that old chap had, we'd have our own tabernacle up there on the point, instead of sulking at his back gate. That's really where we're located, you know. His back gate opens smack in the face of our front one. I think he did it with malice aforethought, too. His back gate is two miles from the house. It wasn't really necessary to go so far for a back gate as all that, was it? To make it worse, he put a big sign over it for us to read: '*No trespassing. This means you.*' Sara took it down after the old boy died."

"I suppose by that time the desire to trespass was gone," she said. "One doesn't enjoy freedom of that sort."

"I've come to believe that the only free things we really covet are passes to the theatre. We never get over that, I'm sure. I'd rather have a pass to the theatre than a ten dollar bill any time. I say, it was nice of you to come down to meet me. It was more than I — er — expected." He almost said "hoped for."

"Sara was too busy about the house to come," she explained quickly. "And I had a few errands to do in the village."

"Don't spoil it!"

"I am a horribly literal person," she said.

"Better that than literally horrible," he retorted,

rather proud of himself for it. "It's wonderful, the friendship between you two girls — Sara's not much more than a girl, you see. You're so utterly unlike in every way."

"It isn't strange to me," said she simply, but without looking at him.

"Of course, I can understand it," he went on. "I've always liked Sara. She's bully. Much too good for my brother, God rest his soul. He never —"

"Oh, don't utter a thing like that, even in jest," she cried, shocked by his glib remark.

He flushed. "You didn't know Challis," he said almost surlily.

She held her breath.

After a moment, the points of his little moustache went up again in the habitual barometrical smile. Rather a priggish, supercilious smile, she thought, taking a glance at his face.

"I say I can understand it, but mother and Vivian will never be able to get it through those tough skulls of theirs. They really don't like Sara. Snobs, both of 'em — of the worst kind, too. Why, mother has always looked upon Sara as a — er — a sort of brigandess, the kind that steals children and holds them for ransom. Of course, old man Gooch was as common as rags — utterly impossible, you know — but that shouldn't stand against Sara. By the way, her father called her Sallie. Her mother was a very charming woman, they say. We never knew her. For that matter, we never knew the old man until he became prominent as a father-in-law."

The girl was silent. He went on.

"Mother likes you. She doesn't say it in so many words, but I can see that she wonders how you can have anything in common with Sara. She prides herself on being able to distinguish blue blood at a glance. Silly notion she's got, but —"

" Please don't go on, Mr. Wrandall," cried Hetty in distress.

" I'm not saying she isn't friendly to Sara nowadays," he explained. " She's changed a good deal in the last few months. I think she's broadening out a bit. Since that visit to Nice, she's been quite different. As a matter of fact, she expects to see a good bit of Sara and you this summer. It's like a spring thaw, by Jove, it is."

" When does she come to the country? " asked Hetty, bent on breaking his train of confidence.

" In three or four weeks. But, as I was saying, the mater has taken a great fancy to you. She —"

" It's very nice of her."

" She prides herself, as I said before, but she always makes sure by asking questions."

" Questions? "

" Yes. Although she could see through you as if you were plate glass, she made it a point to ask Sara all the questions she could think of. Over in Nice, you know. Of course Sara told her everything, and now she's quite sure she can't be mistaken in people. Really, Miss Castleton, she's very amusing sometimes, mother is."

Hetty was looking straight ahead, her face set.

" What did Sara tell her about me? "

" Oh, all that was necessary to prove to mother that she was right. As if it really made any difference, you know."

" Please explain."

" What is there to explain? She merely gave your

pedigree, as we'd say at the dog show, begging your pardon, ma'am. Pedigrees are a sort of hobby with the mater. She collects 'em wherever she goes."

He gave his moustache a little twist.

" Then my references are satisfactory, so to speak," said she, with a wry little smile.

" Perfectly," said he, with conviction; " if we are to put any dependence in the intelligence office."

" Doesn't it stagger Mrs. Wrandall somewhat to reconcile my pedigree to the position I occupy in Sara's household — that of companion, so to say?" asked Hetty, a slight curl to her lip.

He looked rather blank. " I don't believe she looks at you in just that light," said he uncomfortably.

" I fancy you'd better enlighten her."

" Let well enough alone," quoted he glibly.

" But I *am* a companion," insisted Hetty, a little spot of red in each cheek.

" In a sense, I suppose," said he affably. " Of course, Sara puts you down as a friend."

" I think you'd better understand my real position, Mr. Wrandall," said she firmly.

" I do," said he. " You are Sara's friend. That's enough for me. The fact that your father was or is a distinguished English army officer, and some sort of a cousin to a lord, and that you have the entrée to fashionable London drawing-rooms, is quite enough for mother. That qualifies you to be companion to anybody, she'd say. And there's the end to it."

She was looking at him in amazement. Her lips were slightly parted and her eyes were wide. For a moment she was puzzled. Then a swift smile illumined her face. She understood.

" Of course, in London, it really isn't anything to

boast about, getting into drawing-rooms," she said, vastly amused.

"Well, it is over here," said he promptly.

"And it isn't always open sesame to be related to a peer."

"I suppose not."

"Nevertheless, I am glad that your mother and Miss Vivian take me for what I am. Do you, by any chance, go in for pedigree, Mr. Wrandall?"

The shaft of irony sped over his head.

"Only in dogs and horses," he replied promptly. "It means a lot when it comes to buying a dog or a horse."

"How do you feel when you've been sold?"

"I take my medicine."

"As a good sportsman should."

"I dare say you think I'm a deuce of a prig for saying the things —"

"On the contrary, I appreciate your candour."

"Don't hesitate to say it. I'm used to being called a prig. My brother Challis always considered me one. I think he meant snob. But that was because our ideals weren't the same. By the way, you ought to like Vivian."

"That depends."

"On Vivian, I suppose?"

"Not precisely. I should say it depends on your sister's attitude toward Sara."

"Oh, she likes Sara well enough. Viv's not particularly narrow, Miss Castleton."

Hetty bestowed a smile upon him.

"That's comforting, Mr. Wrandall," she said, and he was silent for a moment, reflecting.

"Do you know," said he, as if a light had suddenly

burst in upon him, " you've got more poise than any, girl I've ever seen? "

" It's my bringing up, sir," she said mockingly.

" Ancestral habit," he explained, with a polite bow.

" Pedigreeable manners, perhaps."

" I wish the mater could have heard you say that," admiringly.

" Don't you adore the country at this time of the year? "

" When I get to heaven I mean to have a place in the country the year round," he said conclusively.

" And if you don't get to heaven? "

" I suppose I'll take a furnished flat somewhere."

Sara was waiting for them at the bottom of the terrace as they drove up. He leaped out and kissed her hand.

" Much obliged," he murmured, with a slight twist of his head in the direction of Hetty, who was giving orders to the chauffeur.

" You're quite welcome," said Sara, with a smile of understanding. " She's lovely, isn't she? "

" Enchanting! " said he, almost too loudly.

Hetty walked up the long ascent ahead of them. She did not have to look back to know that they were watching her with unfaltering interest. She could feel their gaze.

" Absolutely adorable," he added, enlarging his estimate without really being aware that he voiced it.

Sara shot a look at his rapt face, and turned her own away to hide the queer little smile that flickered briefly, and died away.

Hetty, pleading a sudden headache, declined to accompany them later on in the day when they set forth in the car to " pick up " Brandon Booth at the inn.

They were to bring him over, bag and baggage, to stay till Tuesday.

"He will be wild to paint her," declared Leslie when they were out of sight around the bend in the road. He had waved his hat to Hetty just before the trees shut off their view of her. She was standing at the top of the steps beside one of the tall Italian vases.

Sara did not respond.

"By the way, Sara, is she the niece or the grand-daughter of old Lord Murgatroyd? I'm a bit mixed."

"Her father is Colonel Castleton, of the Indian Army, and he is the eldest son of a second son, if you don't find that too difficult to solve. The second son aforesaid mentioned, so to speak, was the brother of Lord Murgatroyd. That would make Colonel Castleton his Lordship's nephew, but utterly without prospects of coming into a title, as there are several healthy British obstacles in the way. I suppose one would call Hetty a grand-niece."

"Mother wasn't quite certain whether you said niece or grand-daughter," explained Leslie. "Her mother's dead, I take it. Who was she?"

"Why are you so curious?"

"Isn't it quite natural?"

"Her mother was a Glynn. You have heard of the Glynns, of course?" She trusted to his vanity and was rewarded. The question was a sort of reproach

"Certainly," he replied, without hesitation. The mere fact that she spoke of them as "_the_ Glynns" was sufficient. It was proof enough that they were people one ought to know, by name at least, if one were to profess intelligence regarding the British aristocracy. As a matter of fact, he had not heard of the Glynns, but that didn't matter. "The Irish Glynns, you mean? " he ventured, taking a chance at hitting the mark. He had a faint recollection of hearing her say that Hetty was part Irish.

" You have only to look into her eyes to know she's Irish," she said diplomatically.

" I've never seen such eyes," he exclaimed.

" She's a darling," said Sara and changed the subject, knowing full well that he would come back to it before long. " Is it true that Vivian and Mr. Booth are interested in each other? "

" Yes and no," he replied, with a profound sigh. " That is to say, she's interested in him and he isn't interested in her — in the way I take you to mean it. I suspect it's an easy matter for a girl to fall in love with Brandy. He's a corking fine chap."

" Then it would be very nice for Vivian, eh? "

" Oh, quite so — quite so. His forbears came over with Noah, according to mother. You know mother, Sara."

" Indeed I do," said she with conviction.

He laughed without restraint. " Mother can rattle off the best families in the Bible without missing a name, beginning with the Honourable Adam. Of course, *she* knows the Glynns and the Castletons and the Murgatroyds, although I dare say they haven't had much to do with the Bible. Come to think of it, she did go to the trouble of looking up the Castleton family in the Debrett."

" She did? " exclaimed Sara, with a slight narrowing of the eyes.

" Yes. She established the connection all right enough. She's keen for Miss Castleton."

" Oh," said she, relieved. After a moment: " And you? "

"I'm mad about her," he said simply, and then, for some unaccountable reason, gave over being loquacious and lapsed into a state of almost lugubrious quiet.

She glanced at his face, furtively at first, as if uncertain of his mood, then with a prolonged stare that was frankly curious and amused.

"Don't lose your head, Leslie," she said softly, almost purringly.

He started. "Oh, I say, Sara, I'm not likely to —"

"Stranger things have happened," she interrupted, with a shake of her head. "I can't afford to have you making love to her and getting tired of the game, as you always do, dear boy, just as soon as you find she's in love with you. She is too dear to be hurt in that way. You mustn't —"

"Good Lord!" he cried; "what a bounder you must take me for! Why, if I thought she'd — But nonsense! Let's talk about something else. Yourself, for instance."

She leaned back with a smile on her lips, but not in her eyes; and drew a long, deep breath. He was hard hit. That was what she wanted to know.

They found Booth at the inn. He was sitting on the old-fashioned porch, surrounded by bags and boys. As he climbed into the car after the bags, the boys grinned and jingled the coins in their pockets and ventured, almost in unison, the intelligence that they would all be there if he ever came back again. Big and little, they had transported his easel and canvases from place to place for three weeks or more and his departure was to be regarded as a financial calamity.

"I could go to ten circuses this summer if that many of 'em was to come to town," said one small citizen as Croesus rode away in a cloud of village dust.

"Gee, I wish to goodness he'd come back," was the soulful cry of another.

"I don't like them pictures he paints, though, do you?" observed another, more critical than avaricious.

"Naw!" was the scornful reply, also in unison.

From which it may be gathered that Mr. Brandon Booth was not cherished for art's sake alone, but for its relation to Mammon.

The object of their comments was making himself agreeable to the lady who was to be his hostess for the next few days. Leslie, perhaps in the desire to be alone with his reflections, sat forward with the chauffeur, and paid little or no heed to that unhappy person's comments on the vile condition of *all* village thoroughfares, New York City included.

"By the way, Sara," he said, suddenly breaking in on the conversation that went on at his back, and thereby betraying a secret wish that was taking shape in his mind, "what have you done with the little red runabout you had a year or two ago?"

She started. "You mean —"

As she hesitated, he went on. "It would come in very handy for twosome tours."

"I disposed of it some time ago, Leslie," said she. "I thought you'd remember."

"Oh,— er — by Jove!" he stammered in confusion.

He remembered that she had *given* it away a day or two after that awful night in March, and he recalled her reason for doing so. He twisted the tiny end of his moustache with unnecessary vigour — I might say fury. It was a most unhappy *faux pas.*

"Softening of the brain," he muttered, in dismal apology to himself.

"And you painted those wretched little boys instead of the beautiful things that Nature provides for us out here, Mr. Booth?" Sara was saying to the artist beside her.

"Of course, I managed to get in a bit of Nature, even at that," said he, with a smile. "Boys are pretty close to earth, you know. To be perfectly honest, I did it in order to get away from the eminently beautiful but unnatural things I'm required to paint at home."

"Your subjects wouldn't care for that," she warned him, in some amusement.

"Oh, as to that, the comments of the boys on the things I did up here weren't altogether flattering to me, so I'm chastened. They were more than frank about them. We live to learn."

"Where are the canvases?"

"I immortalised them, one and all, by destroying them by fire and sword, only the sword happened to be a penknife. They made a most excellent bonfire."

"And so, you've nothing to show for your fortnight?"

"Oh, yes. A most desirable invitation to forget my failures at your expense."

"Poof!"

"I don't blame you. It was inane. Still, I can't help saying, Mrs. Wrandall, that it is a desirable invitation. You won't say 'poof' to that, because I won't listen to it."

"On the other hand, it's very good of you to come."

"It seems to me I'm always in debt to Leslie, with slim prospect of ever squaring accounts," said he whimsically. "But for him, I couldn't have come."

"I suppose we will see you at the Wrandall place this summer."

"I'm coming out to paint Leslie's sister in June, I believe. And that reminds me, I came upon an uncommonly pretty girl not far from your place the other day — and yesterday, as well — some one I've met before, unless I'm vastly mistaken. I wonder if you know your neighbours well enough — by sight, at least — to venture a good guess as to who I mean."

She appeared thoughtful.

"Oh, there are dozens of pretty girls in the neighbourhood. Can't you remember where you met —" She stopped suddenly, a swift look of apprehension in her eyes.

He failed to note the look or the broken sentence. He was searching in his coat pocket for something. Selecting a letter from the middle of a small pocket, he held it out to her.

"I sketched this from memory. She posed all too briefly for me," he said.

On the back of the envelope was a remarkably good likeness of Hetty Castleton, done broadly, sketchily with a crayon point, evidently drawn with haste while the impression was fresh, but long after she had passed out of range of his vision.

"I know her," said Sara quietly. "It's very clever, Mr. Booth."

"There is something hauntingly familiar about it," he went on, looking at the sketch with a frown of perplexity. "I've seen her somewhere, but for the life of me I can't place her. Perhaps in a crowded street, or the theatre, or a railway train — just a fleeting glimpse, you know. But in any event, I got a lasting impression. Queer things like that happen, don't you think so?"

Mrs. Wrandall leaned forward and spoke to Leslie.

As he turned, she handed him the envelope, without comment.

"Great Scott!" he exclaimed.

"Mr. Booth is a mind reader," she explained. "He has been reading your thoughts, dear boy."

Booth understood, and grinned.

"You don't mean to say —" began the dumfounded Leslie, still staring at the sketch. "Upon my word, it's a wonderful likeness, old chap. I didn't know you'd ever met her."

"Met her?" cried Booth, an amiable conspirator. "I've never met her."

"See here, don't try anything like that on me. How could you do this if you've never seen —"

"He *is* a mind reader," cried Sara.

"Haven't you been thinking of her steadily for — well, we'll say ten minutes?" demanded Booth.

Leslie reddened. "Nonsense!"

"That's a mental telepathy sketch," said the artist, complacently.

"When did you do it?"

"This instant, you might say. See! Here is the crayon point. I always carry one around with me for just such —"

"All right," said Leslie blandly, at the same time putting the envelope in his own pocket; "we'll let it go at that. If you're so clever at mind pictures, you can go to work and make another for yourself. I mean to keep this one."

"I say," began Booth, dismayed.

"One's thoughts are his own," said the happy possessor of the sketch. He turned his back on them.

Sara was contrite. "He will never give it up," she lamented.

"Is he really hard hit?" asked Booth in surprise.

"I wonder," mused Sara.

"Of course, he's welcome to the sketch, confound him."

"Would you like to paint her?"

"Is this a commission?"

"Hardly. I know her, that's all. She is a very dear friend."

"My heart is set on painting some one else, Mrs. Wrandall."

"Oh!"

"When I know you better, I'll tell you who she is."

"Could you make a sketch of this other one from memory?" she asked lightly.

"I think so. I'll show you one this evening. I have my trusty crayon about me always, as I said before."

Later in the afternoon Booth came face to face with Hetty. He was descending the stairs and met her coming up. The sun streamed in through the tall windows at the turn in the stairs, shining full in her up-lifted face as she approached him from below. He could not repress the start of amazement. She was carrying a box of roses in her arms — red roses whose stems protruded far beyond the end of the pasteboard box and reeked of a fragrant dampness.

She gave him a shy, startled smile as she passed. He had stopped to make room for her on the turn. Somewhat dazed he continued on his way down the steps, to suddenly remember with a twinge of dismay that he had not returned her polite smile, but had stared at her with most unblinking fervour. In no lit-tle shame and embarrassment, he sent a swift glance over his shoulder. She was walking close to the banister rail on the floor above. As he glanced up their eyes met, for she too had turned to peer.

Leslie Wrandall was standing near the foot of the stairs. There was an eager, exalted look in his face that slowly gave way to well-assumed unconcern as his friend came upon him and grasped his arm.

" I say, Leslie, is — is she staying here? " cried Booth, lowering his voice to an excited half-whisper.

" Who? " demanded Wrandall vacantly. His mind appeared to be elsewhere.

" Why, that's the girl I saw on the road — Wake up! The one on the envelope, you ass. Is she the one you were telling me about in the club — the Miss What's-Her-Name who —"

" Oh, you mean Miss Castleton. She's just gone upstairs. You must have met her on the steps."

" You know I did. So *that* is Miss Castleton."

" Ripping, isn't she? Didn't I tell you so? "

" She's beautiful. She *is* a type, just as you said, old man,— a really wonderful type. I saw her yesterday — and the day before."

" I've been wondering how you managed to get a likeness of her on the back of an envelope," said Leslie sarcastically. " Must have had a good long look at her, my boy. It isn't a snap-shot, you know."

Booth flushed. " It is an impression, that's all. I drew it from memory, 'pon my soul."

" She'll be immensely gratified, I'm sure."

" For heaven's sake, Les, don't be such a fool as to show her the thing," cried Booth in consternation. " She'd never understand."

" Oh, you needn't worry. She has a fine sense of humour."

Booth didn't know whether to laugh or scowl. He

compromised with himself by slipping his arm through
that of his friend and saying heartily:

" I wish you the best of luck, old boy."

" Thanks," said Leslie drily.

CHAPTER VIII

BOOTH and Leslie returned to the city on Tuesday. The artist left behind him a "memory sketch" of Sara Wrandall, done in the solitude of his room long after the rest of the house was wrapped in slumber on the first night of his stay at Southlook. It was as sketchily drawn as the one he had made of Hetty, and quite as wonderful in the matter of faithfulness, but utterly without the subtle something that made the other notable. The craftiness of the artist was there, but the touch of inspiration was lacking.

Sara was delighted. She was flattered, and made no pretence of disguising the fact.

The discussion which followed the exhibition of the sketch at luncheon, was very animated. It served to excite Leslie to such a degree that he brought forth from his pocket the treasured sketch of Hetty, for the purpose of comparison.

The girl who had been genuinely enthusiastic over the picture of Sara, and who had not been by way of knowing that the first sketch existed, was covered with confusion. Embarrassment and a shy sense of gratification were succeeded almost at once by a feeling of keen annoyance. The fact that the sketch was in Leslie's possession — and evidently a thing to be cherished — took away all the pleasure she may have experienced during the first few moments of interest.

Booth caught the angry flash in her eyes, preceding the flush and unaccountable pallor that followed almost immediately. He felt guilty, and at the same time deeply annoyed with Leslie. Later on he tried to explain, but the attempt was a lamentable failure. She laughed, not unkindly, in his face.

Leslie had refused to allow the sketch to leave his hand. If she could have gained possession of it, even for an instant, the thing would have been torn to bits. But it went back into his commodious pocket-book, and she was too proud to demand it of him.

She became oddly sensitive to Booth's persistent though inoffensive scrutiny as time wore on. More than once she had caught him looking at her with a fixedness that betrayed perplexity so plainly that she could not fail to recognise an underlying motive. He was vainly striving to refresh his memory: that was clear to her. There is no mistaking that look in a person's eyes. It cannot be disguised.

He was as deeply perplexed as ever when the time came for him to depart with Leslie. He asked her point blank on the last evening of his stay if they had ever met before, and she frankly confessed to a short memory for faces. It was not unlikely, she said, that he had seen her in London or in Paris, but she had not the faintest recollection of having seen him before their meeting in the road.

Urged by Sara, she had reluctantly consented to sit to him for a portrait during the month of June. He put the request in such terms that it did not sound like a proposition. It was not surprising that he should want her for a subject; in fact, he put it in such a way that she could not but feel that she would be doing him a great and enduring favour. She imposed but one condition: the picture was never to be exhibited. He met that, with bland magnanimity, by proffering the canvas to Mrs. Wrandall, as the subject's " next

best friend," to " have and to hold so long as she might
live," " free gratis," " with the artist's compliments,"
and so on and so forth, in airy good humour.

Leslie's aid had been solicited by both Sara and the
painter in the final effort to overcome the girl's objections. He was rather bored about it, but added his
voice to the general clamour. With half an eye one
could see that he did not relish the idea of Hetty posing
for days to the handsome, agreeable painter. Moreover, it meant that Booth, who could afford to gratify
his own whims, would be obliged to spend a month or
more in the neighbourhood, so that he could devote himself almost entirely to the consummation of this particular undertaking. Moreover, it meant that Vivian's
portrait was to be temporarily disregarded.

Sara Wrandall was quick to recognise the first symptoms of jealousy on the part of her brother-in-law.
She had known him for years. In that time she had
been witness to a dozen of his encounters in the lists of
love, or what he chose to designate as love, and had
seen him emerge from each with an unscarred heart
and a smiling visage. Never before had he shown the
slightest sign of jealousy, even when the affair was at
its rosiest. The excellent ego which mastered him
would not permit him to forget himself so far as to consider any one else worthy of a feeling of jealousy. But
now he was flying an alien flag. He was turning
against himself and his smug convictions. He was at
least annoyed, if not jealous. Doubtless he was surprised at himself; perhaps he wondered what had come
over him.

Sara noted these signs of self-abasement (it could
be nothing else where a Wrandall was concerned), and
smiled inwardly. The new idol of the Wrandalls was

in love, selfishly, insufferably in love as things went
with all the Wrandalls. They hated selfishly, and so
they loved. Her husband had been their king. But
their king was dead, long live the king! Leslie had
put on the family crown,— a little jauntily, perhaps,—
cocked over the eye a bit, so to speak — but it was there
just the same, annoyingly plain to view.

Sara had tried to like him. He had been her friend,
the only one she could claim among them all. And
yet, beneath his genial allegiance, she could detect the
air of condescension, the bland attitude of a superior
who defends another's cause for the reason that it grati-
fies Nero. She experienced a thrill of malicious joy
in contemplating the fall of Nero. He would bring
down his house about his head, and there would be no
Rome to pay the fiddler.

In the train that Tuesday morning, Booth elected
to chaff his friend on the progress of his campaign.
They were seated opposite to each other in the almost
empty parlour-car.

"Buck up, old chap," he counselled scoffingly.
"Don't look so disconsolate. You're coming out again
at the end of the week."

Leslie had been singularly reticent for a matter of
ten miles or more after leaving the little station behind. His attention seemed to be engaged strictly in
the study of objects beyond the car window.

"What's that?" he demanded curtly.

"I say you're lucky enough to be asked again for
the end of the —"

"I've got a standing invitation, if that's what you
mean. Sara gives me a meal ticket, as it were. Nothing extraordinary in my going out whenever I like, is
there?" His manner was a trifle offish.

Booth laughed. " In spite of your disagreeable remark, I wish you good luck, old man."

" What the devil are you driving at, Brandy? "

" I only meant to cheer you up a bit, that's all."

" Thanks ! "

There was another interval of silence. Leslie furtively studied the face of his friend, who had resumed
his dreamy contemplation of the roof of the car, his
hands clasped behind his head, his legs outstretched.

" I say, Brandy," he ventured at last, a trace of embarrassment in his manner, " if you've nothing better
to do, come down and dine with us to-night — *en famille*. Viv said over the 'phone this morning that we
are dining alone in state. Come along, old chap, and
wake us up. What say? "

A clever mind-reader could have laid bare the motive
in this cordial, even eager invitation. He was seeking
to play Vivian against Hetty in the game, which seemed
to have taken on a new turn.

Booth was not a mind-reader, although in jest he
had posed as one. " I'm quite sure I've nothing better
to do," he said. " I'd suggest, however, that you let
the invitation come from some one in authority. Your
mother, for instance."

" Nonsense," cried the other blithely. " You know
you've got a meal ticket at our house, good for a million
punches. Still I'll have Vivian call you up this afternoon."

" If she wants me, I'll come," said Booth in the most
matter-of-fact way.

Leslie settled down with a secret sigh of relief. He
regained his usual loquaciousness. The points of his
little moustache resumed their uprightness.

" How do you like Sara? " he asked. It was a

casual question, with no real meaning behind it as it was uttered. No sooner had it left his lips, however, than a new and rather staggering idea entered his mind,— a small thing at first but one that grew with amazing swiftness.

"She is splendid," said Booth warmly.

"I thought you'd like her," said Leslie, the idea growing apace: It did not occur to him that he might be nurturing disloyalty to the interests of his own sister. Things of that sort never bothered Leslie. When all was said and done, Vivian had but a slim chance at best, so why champion a faint hope? "Why don't you do a portrait of her? It would be a wonderful thing, old chap."

He sat up a trifle straighter in his chair.

"She hasn't asked me to, which is the best reason in the world.

"Oh, I can fix that." His lively imagination was full of it now.

"Thanks. Don't bother."

"And there's this to be said for a portrait of Sara," went on Leslie, rather too eagerly: "she wouldn't object to having it exhibited in the galleries. 'Gad, it would do you a world of good, Brandy."

The other's eyes narrowed. "I suppose I am to infer that Mrs. Wrandall courts publicity."

"Not at all," cried the other impatiently. "What I mean is this: she's taken a fancy to you, and if her portrait could be the means of helping you —"

"Oh, cut that out, Les,— cut it out," growled Booth coldly.

"Well, in any event, if you want to paint her, I can fix it for you," announced his companion.

"If you don't mind, old chap, I'll tackle Miss Cas-

tleton first," said Booth, dismissing the matter with a
yawn.

"I hate the word tackle," said Leslie.

On a bright, sunny afternoon two weeks later, Mrs.
Redmond Wrandall received her most intimate friend
in her boudoir. They were both in ample black. Mrs.
Rowe-Martin, it seems, had suffered a recent bereavement — with an aspect of permanency,— in the loss of
a four thousand dollar Airdale who had stopped traffic
in Fifth Avenue for twenty minutes while a sympathetic
crowd viewed his gory remains, and an unhappy but
garrulous taxi-cab driver tried to account for his
crime. He never even thought of the insanity dodge.
The Airdale was given a most impressive funeral and
was buried in pomp with all his medals, ribbons, tags,
collars and platinum leashes, but minus a few of the
uncollected parts of his anatomy. While it had been a
complete catastrophe, he was by no means a complete
carcass.

Be that as it may, his mistress went into mourning,
denying herself so many diversions that not a few of
her friends became alarmed and advised her husband
to put her in a sanitarium. He was willing, poor chap,
but not she. She couldn't see the sense of confining
her grief to the four walls of a sanitarium while the
four winds of heaven were at her disposal.

The most distressing feature of the great Airdale's
taking-off lay in the fact that his descendants — he
had several sets of great-grandchildren —appeared to
be uncommonly ordinary brutes, without a symptom of
good breeding in the lot of them. They were so unde-
viatingly *gauche* and middle-class, that already the
spiteful tongues of envy had begun to question his
right to the medals and ribbons acquired at the bench

shows, where Mrs. Rowe-Martin was considered one of
the immortals.   She could have got a blue ribbon on a
yellow dog any time.   Of course, in defence of her
exotic Airdale, she unblinkingly fell back on the para-
phrase: " It's a wise father that knows his own son ";
or the other way round, just as you please.

Mrs. Rowe-Martin professedly was middle-aged —
that is to say, just rounding fifty.   As a woman is always fifty until she is sixty, just as it is nine o'clock
until the stroke of ten, there may be some question as
to which end of the middle-aged period she was rounding, but as that isn't material to the development of this
story, we will give her the benefit of the doubt and
merely say that sensibly she dressed in black.

She was Mrs. Wrandall's closest friend and confidante.   It was Mrs. Rowe-Martin who rushed over and
gave the smelling salts to Mrs. Wrandall when that excellent lady collapsed on hearing that her son Challis
was going to marry the daughter of old Sebastian
Gooch.   It was she who acted as spokeswoman for the
distressed mother and told the world — that is to say,
their world — that Sara was a scheming, designing
creature, whose sole aim in life was to get into the smart
set by the easiest way.   It was she who comforted Mrs.
Wrandall, after the lamentable deed was done, by pro-
claiming from the house-tops that old man Gooch's
daughter should never enter society if she could prevent
it, and went so far as to invite Challis to all of her
affairs without asking his wife to accompany him, quite
as if she didn't know that he had a wife.   (In speaking
of her to Challis, she invariably alluded to Sara as
Miss Gooch, for something over a year after the wedding — and might have gone on for ever had not Mrs.
Wrandall, senior, upset everything by giving a recep-

tion in honour of her daughter-in-law: a bolt from a clear sky, you may be sure, that left Mrs. Rowe-Martin stunned and bleeding on the battlefield of a mistaken cause.) She never quite got over that bit of treachery on the part of her very best friend, although she made the best of it by slyly confiding to other stupefied persons that Challis's father had taken the bit in his mouth,— God knows why! — and that Mrs. Wrandall thought best to humour him for the time being, at least. And it was she who came to Mrs. Wrandall in her greatest trial and performed the gentlest deeds that one woman can do for another when all the world has gone black and hateful to her. When you put her to the real test, a woman will always rise above herself, no matter how lofty she may have considered herself beforehand.

They were drinking tea, with the lemon left out.

" My dear," said Mrs. Rowe-Martin, " I quite agree with you. Leslie should be thinking of it."

" It means so much to me, Harriet, his getting the right sort of girl. I feel confident that he is interested — very deeply interested in Miss Castleton."

" I am *so* glad you like her."

" She is a dear."

" My sister has met her in London, and at one or two of the country places. I was inquiring only yesterday. When I mentioned that she is related to Lord Murgatroyd, Frances remembered her quite well. She sees a lot of them, you know, during the season," explained Mrs. Rowe-Martin affably.

Mrs. Wrandall concealed her curiosity. In the most casual way she remarked:

" I must ask Miss Castleton if she remembers Mrs. Roodleigh."

"Oh, I fancy she won't recall her," her friend made
haste to say. "Young girls are not likely to remember
elderly persons whom they meet — Oh, you might say
in passing, for that's what it really is, you know."

"Still, if Frances knows the Murgatroyds so intimately it isn't likely —"

"Did I say she knew them intimately?" protested
the other, somewhat plaintively. "How like me! So
stupid! As a matter of fact, my dear, I don't believe
Frances knows them at all — except as one knows people in a general sort of way. Drawing-rooms, you
know, and all that sort of thing. Of course, every one
knows Lord and Lady Murgatroyd. Just as they
might know the Duke of — well any one of the great
dukes, for that matter."

"Or King George," added Mrs. Wrandall softly,
without a perceptible trace of spite.

"She has met them, of course," said Mrs. Rowe-
Martin defensively. Somehow, a defence was called
for; she couldn't sit there and say nothing.

Mrs. Wrandall changed the subject, or at least divided it. She put the chaff aside, for that was what
Mrs. Rowe-Martin's revelations amounted to.

"Leslie is such a steady, unimpressionable boy, you
see," she said, apropos of nothing.

"And so good looking," added her friend beamingly.

"It wouldn't be like him to make a mistake where
his own happiness and welfare are concerned," said the
subject's mother, speaking more truth than she knew,
but not more than Mrs. Rowe-Martin knew. That lady
knew Leslie like a book.

"And he is really devoted to her?"

"I fear so," said her hostess, with a faint sigh. The
other sighed also.

"My dear, it would be perfectly lovely. Why do you say that?"

"I suppose it's the way all mothers feel. Of course, I want to be sure that he is to be very, very happy."

"That is perfectly natural. And he *will* be happy."

If either of them recalled the strenuous efforts Mrs. Wrandall had made a couple of years before to get her only daughter married off to a degenerate young English duke, the thought was submerged in the present sea of sentimentality. It speaks well for Vivian's character that she flatly refused to be given in marriage, although it appeared to be the fashion at the time. It was the year of the coronation.

"Miss Castleton is a most uncommon girl," said Mrs. Wrandall, again apropos of nothing that had gone before.

"Most English girls are," agreed her friend, scenting something.

"I mean to say, she is so unlike the girls one sees in society. My husband says she's level-headed. Sound as a rivet, he also says. Nothing silly or flip about her, he adds when he is particularly enthusiastic, and he knows I hate the word 'flip.' Of course he means flippant. He is very much taken with her."

Mrs. Rowe-Martin pondered a moment before risking her next remark.

"I can't quite understand her taking up with Sara Gooch in this fashion. You know what I mean. Sara is the last person in the world you'd think a gently bred person would—" Here she pulled herself up with a jerk. "I mean, of course, a gently bred girl. Naturally she would appeal to men — and gently bred men, at that. But this present intimacy — well, isn't it rather extraordinary?"

Mrs. Wrandall drained her cup, without taking her eyes from the face of her friend.

" You must remember, my dear Harriet, that Miss Castleton looks upon Sara as a Wrandall, not a Gooch. She was the wife of a Wrandall. That covers everything so far as the girl is concerned. I dare say she finds Sara amusing, interesting, and we all know she is kindness itself. It doesn't surprise me that Miss Castleton admires her, or that she loves her. Sara has improved in the last seven or eight years." She said this somewhat loftily.

Mrs. Rowe-Martin was most amiable. " She has, indeed, thanks to propinquity."

" And her own splendid intelligence," added Mrs. Wrandall.

" Isn't it wonderful how superior they are when it comes to intelligence? " cried her friend, almost plaintively. " I've noticed it in shop-girls and manicures, over and over again."

" Perhaps you got the effect by contrast," said Mrs. Wrandall, pouring a little more tea into her friend's cup. Mrs. Rowe-Martin was silent. " Sara deserves a lot of credit. She has made a position for herself, a very decided position. We are all quite proud of her."

Mrs. Rowe-Martin was on very intimate terms with the Wrandall family skeleton. She could afford to be plain spoken.

" It is hard to reconcile your present attitude, my dear, to the position you held a few years ago. Heaven knows you weren't proud of her then. She was dirt beneath your feet."

" My dear Harriet," said Mrs. Wrandall, without so much as the flutter of an eyelid, " I am not saying that

I would select her as a daughter-in-law, even to-day.
Don't misunderstand me."

" I am not underestimating her splendid intelligence,"
said Mrs. Rowe-Martin sharply, and her hostess was
so long in working it out that it was allowed to pass
unresented. " I dare say she will marry again," went
on the speaker blandly.

Sara's mother-in-law was startled.

" It's rather early to suggest such a thing, isn't it? "
she asked reproachfully.

" Forgive me," cried Mrs. Rowe-Martin, but she did
not attempt to unsay the words. She meant them to
sink in when she uttered them. It was commonly predicted in society that Challis Wrandall's wife would
further elevate herself by wedding the most dependable
nobleman who came along, and without any appreciable
consideration for the feelings of her late husband's family.

" It is quite natural — and right — that she should
marry," said Mrs. Wrandall, after a moment's deliber-
ation. " She is young and beautiful and we sincerely
hope she will find some one — But, my dear, aren't we
drifting? We were speaking of Leslie."

" And Miss Castleton. You are quite satisfied, then?
You don't feel that he would be making a mistake? "

Mrs. Wrandall touched her handkerchief to the corners of her eyes.

" We could not possibly raise any objection to Miss
Castleton, if that is what you mean, Harriet," she said.

" I am so glad you feel that way about it, my dear,"
said her friend, touching her handkerchief to her lips.
" It would grieve me more than I can tell you if I
thought you would have to go through with another
experience like that of — Forgive me! I won't distress

you by recalling those awful days. Poor, susceptible Challis ! "

"No," said Mrs. Wrandall firmly; "Leslie is safe. We feel quite sure of him."

The visitor was reflective. "I suppose there is no doubt that Miss Castleton will accept him," she mused aloud.

"We are assuming, of course, that Leslie means to ask her," said Leslie's mother, with infinite patience.

"I only mentioned it because it is barely possible she may have other fish to fry."

"Fish? "

"A figure of speech, my dear."

And it set Mrs. Wrandall to thinking.

CHAPTER IX

BRANDON BOOTH took a small cottage on the upper road, half way between the village and the home of Sara Wrandall, and not far from the abhorred " back gate " that swung in the teeth of her connections by marriage. He set up his establishment in half a day and, being settled, betook himself off to dine with Sara and Hetty. All his household cares, like the world, rested snugly on the shoulders of an Atlas named Pat, than whom there was no more faithful servitor in all the earth, nor in the heavens, for that matter, if we are to accept his own estimate of himself. In any event, he was a treasure. Booth's house was always in order. Try as he would, he couldn't get it out of order. Pat's wife saw to that. She was the cook, housekeeper, steward, seamstress, nurse and everything else except the laundress, and she would have been that if Booth hadn't put his foot down on it. He was rather finicky about his bosoms, it seems — and his cuffs, as well.

Pat and Mary had been in the Booth family since the flood, so to speak. As far back as Brandon could remember, the quaint Irishman had been the same wrinkled, nut-brown, merry-eyed comedian that he was to-day, and Mary the same serene, blarneying wife of the man. They were not a day older than they were in the beginning. He used to wonder if Methuselah knew them. When he set up bachelor quarters for himself in New York, his mother bestowed these priceless domestic treasures upon him. They journeyed up from Philadelphia and complacently took charge of his destinies;

no matter which way they led or how diversified they may have been in conception, Brandon's destinies always came safely around the circle to the starting point with Pat and Mary atop of them, as chipper as you please and none the worse for erosion.

They stoutly maintained that one never gets too old to learn, a conclusion that Brandon sometimes resented.

He had been obliged to discharge three chauffeurs because Pat did not get on well with them, and he had found it quite impossible to keep a dog for the simple reason that Mary insisted on keeping a cat — a most unamiable, belligerent cat at that. He would have made home a hell for any well-connected dog.

As he swung jauntily down the tree-lined road that led to Sara's portals, Booth was full of the joy of living. Dusk was falling. A soft bronze glowed in the western sky. Over the earth lay the tranquil purple of spent refulgence, the after-glow of a red day, for the sun had shone hot since early morn through a queer, smoky screen of haze. There was a deep stillness over everything. Indolent Nature slept in the shadows, as if at rest after the weary day, with scarcely a leaf stirring. And yet there was a subtle coolness in the air, the feel of a storm that was yet unborn — the imperceptible shudder of a tempest that was drawing its first breath.

Before the night was half gone, the storm would be upon them, to revel for a while and then pass on, leaving behind it the dank smell of a grateful earth.

But Booth had no thought for the thing that was afar off. He was thinking of the quarter-of-an-hour that came next in the wheel of time, whose minutes were to check off the results of a fortnight's anticipation. He had not seen either of the ladies of Southlook in the past two weeks, but he had been under the spell of them so sharply that they were seldom out of his thoughts.

Sara was at the bottom of the terrace, moving among the flower beds in the formal garden. He distinguished her from a distance: a slender, graceful figure in black. A black scarf edged with maribou covered her shoulders, the line of a white neck separating it from the raven hue of her hair. He paused at the lower gate to look. Then his gaze was drawn to the gleaming white figure at the top of the terrace, outlined distinctly against the blue-black sky that hung over the Sound. Hetty stood there, straight and motionless, looking out over the water. So still was the evening wind that not a flutter of her soft gown was noticeable. She was like a statue.

At the sound of his footsteps on the gravel, Sara looked up and instantly smiled her welcome. When Sara smiled the heart of man responded, long in advance of his lips. Hers was the inviting, mysterious smile of the Orient, with the eyes half shaded by drooping, languorous lids: dusky, shadowy eyes that looked at you as through a veil, and yet were as clear as crystal once you lost the illusion.

" It is so nice to see you again," she said, giving him her hand.

" ' My heart's in the highlands,' " he quoted, waving a vague tribute to the heavens. " And it's nice of you to see me," he added gracefully. Then he pointed up the terrace. " Isn't she a picture? 'Gad, it's lovely — the whole effect. That picture against the sky —"

He stopped short, and the sentence was never finished, although she waited for him to complete it before remarking:

" Her heart is not in the highlands."

"You mean — something's gone wrong —"

"Oh, no," she said, still smiling; "nothing like that. Her heart is in the lowlands. You would consider Washington Square to be in the lowlands, wouldn't you?"

"Oh, I see," he said slowly. "You mean she's think- 'ing of Leslie."

"Who knows? It was a venture on my part, that's all. She may be thinking of you, Mr. Booth."

"Or some chap in old England, that's more like it," he retorted. "She can't be thinking of me, you know. No one ever thinks of me when I'm out of view. Out of sight, out of mind. No; she's thinking of something a long way off — or some one, if you choose to have it that way."

"In that case, it isn't good for her to be thinking of things so remote. Shall we shout ' halloa the house '? "

He shot a glance at her and responded gallantly: "If she isn't thinking of us, why should we be thinking of her? Is it too near the dinner hour for you to let me sit here and rest before attempting to climb all those steps? And will you sit beside me, as the good Omar might have said?" He was fanning himself with his straw hat.

She searched his face for a second, a smiling but inscrutable expression in her eyes, and then sat down on the rustic bench at the foot of the terrace.

"Why didn't you let me send the motor for you?" she asked, as he took his place beside her.

"I mean to have an appetite in the country," he said, taking a deep, full breath. "Motors don't aid the appetite. Aeroplanes are better. I had a flight with a friend up in Westchester last week. I was very hungry when I came down."

"We'll all be flying before we really know it," said she. "Hetty tried it in France this spring. Have you seen Leslie this week?"

"I've been in Philadelphia for a few days. Is he coming out on Friday?"

"Oh, yes. He comes so often nowadays that we call him a commuter."

"Attractive spot, this," said he, with a significant glance up the terrace.

"So it would appear."

"He's really keen about her?"

She did not reply, but her smile meant more than words.

"I am eager to get at the portrait," said he, after a moment.

"Leslie tells me that you want to do me also," said she carelessly.

He flushed. "Confound him! I suppose it annoys you, Mrs. Wrandall. He shouldn't carry tales."

"But do you?"

"I should say I do," he cried warmly. "For my own pleasure and satisfaction, you understand. There's nothing I'd like better."

"We'll see how successfully you flatter Hetty," said she. "If it is possible to make her prettier than she really is, you may paint me. I shall be the first to fall at your feet and implore you to make me beautiful."

His eyes gleamed. "If I fail in that," said he warmly, "it will be because I am without i..tegrity."

Again she smiled upon him with half-closed, shadowy eyes, and shook her head. Then she arose.

"Let us go in. Hetty is eager to see you again."

They started up the terrace. His face clouded.

"I have had a feeling all along that she'd rather

not have this portrait painted, Mrs. Wrandall. A queer sort of feeling that she doesn't just like the idea of being put on canvas."

"Nonsense," she said, without looking at him.

"Of course, I could understand her not caring to give up the time to it. It's a nuisance, I know. But it isn't that sort of feeling I have about her attitude. There's something else. Doesn't she like me?"

"Of course she does," she exclaimed. "How ridiculous. She will love it, once the picture is under way. It is the beginning of it that disturbs her. Isn't that always the way?"

"I am afraid you don't know women," said he banteringly.

"By the way, have you been able to recall where you first saw her, or is your memory still a blank?" she asked suddenly.

"I can't think where it was or when," said he, "but I am absolutely positive I've seen her before. Her face is not the kind one forgets, you know."

"It may come to you unexpectedly."

"It's maddening, not to be able to remember."

The dusk of night hid the look of relief that came into her eyes.

Hetty met them at the top of the steps. The electric porch lights had just been turned on by the butler. The girl stood in the path of the light. Booth was never to forget the loveliness of her in that moment. He carried the image with him on the long walk home through the black night. (He declined Sara's offer to send him over in the car for the very reason that he wanted the half-hour of solitude in which to concentrate all the impressions she had made on his fancy.)

The three of them stood there for a few minutes,

awaiting the butler's announcement. Sara's arm was about Hetty's shoulders. He was so taken up with the picture they presented that he scarcely heard their light chatter. They were types of loveliness so full of contrast that he marvelled at the power of Nature to create women in the same mould and yet to model so differently.

They were as near alike in height, figure and carriage as two women could be, and yet there was a subtle distinction that left him conscious of the fact that two vastly different strains of blood ran through their veins. Apart, he would not have perceived this marked difference in them. Hetty represented the violet, Sara the pansy. The distinction may be subtle. However, it was the estimate he formed in that moment of comparison.

The English girl's soft white gown was cut low in the neck, her shapely arms were bare. Sara's black covered her arms and shoulders, even to the slender throat. The hair of both was black and rich and alive with the gloss of health. The eyes of one were blue and velvety, even in the glare of light that fell from above; those of the other were black, Oriental, mysterious.

As they entered the vestibule, a servant came up with the word that Miss Castleton was wanted at the telephone, "long distance from New York."

The girl stopped in her tracks. Booth looked at her in mild surprise, a condition which gave way an instant later to perplexity. The look of annoyance in her eyes could not be disguised or mistaken.

"Ask him to call me up later, Watson," she said quietly.

"This is the third time he has called, Miss Castleton," said the man. "You were dressing, if you please, ma'am, the first time —"

" I will come," she interrupted sharply, with a curious glance at Sara, who for some reason avoided meeting Booth's gaze.

" Tell him we shall expect him on Friday," said Mrs.
Wrandall.

" By George!" thought Booth, as she left them.
" I wonder if it can be Leslie. If it *is* — well, he
wouldn't be flattered if he could have seen the look in
her eyes."

Later on, he had no trouble in gathering that it *was*
Leslie Wrandall who called, but he was very much in the
dark as to the meaning of that expressive look. He
only knew that she was in the telephone room for ten
minutes or longer, and that all trace of emotion was
gone from her face when she rejoined them with a brief
apology for keeping them waiting.

He left at ten-thirty, saying good-night to them on
the terrace. Sara walked to the steps with him.

" Don't you think her voice is lovely?" she asked.
Hetty had sung for them.

" I dare say," he responded absently. " Give you
my word, though, I wasn't thinking of her voice. *She*
is lovely."

He walked home as if in a dream. The spell was
on him.

Far in the night, he started up from the easy chair
in which he had been smoking and dreaming and racking
his brain by turns.

" By Jove!" he exclaimed aloud. " I remember! I've
got it! And to-morrow I'll prove it."

Then he went to bed, with the storm from the sea
pounding about the house, and slept serenely until Pat
and Mary wondered whether he meant to get up at all.

" Pat," said he at breakfast, " I want you to go to

the city this morning and fetch out all of the *Studios*
you can find about the place. The old ones are in that
Italian hall seat and the late ones are in the studio.
Bring all of them."

"There's a divvil of a bunch of thim," said Pat rue-
fully.

He was not to begin sketching the figure until the
following day. After luncheon, however, he had an appointment to inspect Hetty's wardrobe, ostensibly for
the purpose of picking out a gown for the picture.
As a matter of fact, he had decided the point to his own
satisfaction the night before. She should pose for him
in the dainty white dress she had worn on that occasion.

While they were going over the extensive assortment of gowns, with Sara as the judge from whom there
seemed to be no appeal, he casually inquired if she had
ever posed before.

Two ladies' maids were engaged in flinging the costly
garments about as if they represented so much rubbish.
The floor was littered with silks and satins and laces.
He was accustomed to this ruthless handling of exquisite
fabrics by eager ladies of wealth: it was one way these
pampered women had of showing their contempt for
possession. Gowns came from everywhere by the arm-
load; from closets, presses and trunks, ultimately landing in a conglomerate heap on the floor when cast aside
as undesirable by the artist, the model and the censor.

He watched her closely as he put the question. She
was holding up a beautiful point lace creation for his
inspection, and there was a pleading smile on her lips.
It must have been her favourite gown. The smile faded
away. The hand that dangled the garment before his
eyes suddenly became motionless, as if paralysed. In
the next instant, she recovered herself, and, giving the

lace a quick fillip that sent its odour of sachet leaping to his nostrils, responded with perfect composure.

" Isn't there a distinction between posing for an artist, and sitting for one's portrait? " she asked.

He was silent. The fact that he did not respond seemed to disturb her after a moment or two. She made the common mistake of pressing the question.

" Why do you ask? " was her inquiry. When it was too late she wished she had not uttered the words. He had caught the somewhat anxious note in her voice.

" We always ask that, I think," he said. " It's a habit."

" Oh," she said doubtfully.

" And by the way, you haven't answered."

She was busy with the gown for a time. At last she looked him full in the face.

" That's true," she agreed; " I haven't answered, have I? No, Mr. Booth, I've never posed for a portrait. It is a new experience for me. You will have to contend with a great deal of stupidity on my part. But I shall try to be plastic."

He uttered a polite protest, and pursued the question no farther. Her answer had been so palpably evasive that it struck him as bald, even awkward.

Pat, disgruntled and irritable to the point of profanity,— he was a privileged character and might have sworn if he felt like it without receiving notice,— came shambling up the cottage walk late that afternoon, bearing two large, shoulder-sagging bundles. He had walked from the station,— a matter of half-a-mile,— and it was hot. His employer sat in the shady porch, viewing his approach.

" Have you got them? " he inquired.

Pat dropped the bundles on the lower step and stared,

speechless. Then he mopped his drenched, turkey-red face with his handkerchief. He got his breath after a spell of contemptuous snorting.

"Have I got what?" he demanded sarcastically. "The measles?"

"The *Studios*, Patrick," said Booth reprovingly.

"No, sor," said Pat; "I came absolutely empty-handed, as you may have seen, sor."

"I knew I couldn't be mistaken. I was confident I saw nothing in your hands."

"I kept thim closed, sor, so's you couldn't see what was r'ally in thim. I've been wid you long enough, sor, to know how you hate the sight av blisthers."

"They must be quite a novelty to you, Patrick. I should think you'd be proud of them."

"Where am I to put them, sor?"

"The blisters?"

"Yis, sor."

"On this table, if you please. And you might cut the strings while you're about it."

Pat put the bundles on the wicker table and cut the heavy twine in dignified silence. Carefully rolling it up in a neat ball, he stuck it in his pocket. Then he faced his employer.

"Is there annyt'ing else, sor?"

"I think not, at present."

"Not aven a cup av tea, sor?"

"No, thanks."

"Thin, if you will excuse me, I'll go about me work. I've had a pleasant day off, sor, thanks to ye. It's hard to go back to work afther such a splindid spell of idleness. Heigho! I'd like to be a gintleman av leisure all the time, that I would, sor. The touch I've had av it to-day may be the sp'iling av me. If you're a smart man, Mr. Brandon Booth, ye'll not be letting me off for a holiday like this again very soon."

Booth laughed outright. Pat's face wrinkled into a slow, forgiving grin.

"I love you, Pat," cried the painter, "in spite of the way you bark at me."

"It's a poor dog that don't know his own master," said Pat magnanimously. "Whin you're t'rough wid the magazines, I'll carry thim down to the cellar, sor."

"What's the matter with the attic?"

"Nothing at all, at all. I was only t'inking they'd be handier for you to get at in the cellar. And it's a dom sight cooler down there."

With that he departed, blinking slyly.

The young man drew a chair up to the table and began the task of working out the puzzle that now seemed more or less near to solution. He had a pretty clear idea as to the period he wanted to investigate. To the best of his recollection, the *Studios* published three or four years back held the key. He selected the numbers and began to run through them. One after another they were cast aside without result. In any other cause he would have tired of the quest, but in this his curiosity was so commanding that he stuck to the task without complaint. He was positive in his mind that what he desired was to be found inside the covers of one of these magazines. He was searching for a vaguely remembered article on one of the lesser-known English painters who had given great promise at the time it was published but who dropped completely out of notice soon afterward because of a mistaken notion of his own importance. If Booth's memory served him right, the fellow came a cropper, so to speak, in trying to ride rough shod over public opinion, and went to the dogs. He had been painting sensibly up to that time, but suddenly went in for the most violent style of impressionism. That was the end of him.

There had been reproductions of his principal canvases, with sketches and studies in charcoal. One of these pictures had made a lasting impression on Booth: the figure of a young woman in deep meditation standing in the shadow of a window casement from which she looked out upon the world apparently without a thought of it. A slender young woman in vague reds and browns, whose shadowy face was positively illuminated by a pair of wonderful blue eyes.

He came upon it at last. For a long time he sat there gazing at the face of Hetty Castleton, a look of half-wonder, half-triumph in his eyes. There could be no doubt as to the identity of the subject. The face was hers, the lovely eyes were hers: the velvety, dreamy, soulful eyes that had haunted him for years, as he now believed. In no sense could the picture be described as a portrait. It was a study, deliberately arranged and deliberately posed for in the artist's studio. He was mystified. Why should she, the daughter of Colonel Castleton, the grand-niece of an earl, be engaged in posing for what evidently was meant to be a commercial product of this whilom artist?

He remembered the painting itself as he had seen it in the exhibition at the National Academy when this fellow — Hawkright was his name — was at the top of his promise as a painter. He remembered going back to it again and again and marvelling at the subtle, delicate beauty of the thing. Now he knew that it was the face, and not the art of the painter that had affected him so enduringly. The fellow had shown other paintings, but he recalled that none of them struck him save this one.   After all, it *was* the face that made the picture memorable.

Turning from this skilfully coloured full page reproduction, he glanced at first casually over the dozen or more sketches and studies on the succeeding pages. Many of them represented studies of women's heads and figures, with little or no attempt to obtain a likeness. Some were half-draped, showing in a sketchy way the long graceful lines of the half-nude figure, of bare shoulders and breasts, of gauze-like fabrics that but illy concealed impressive charms.   Suddenly his eyes narrowed and a sharp exclamation fell from his lips.   He bent closer to the pages and studied the drawings with redoubled interest.

Then he whistled softly to himself, a token of simple amazement.   The head of each of these remarkable studies suggested in outline the head and features of Hetty Castleton!   She had been Hawkright's model!

.   .   .   .   .   .

The next morning at ten he was at Southlook, arranging his easel and canvas in the north end of the long living-room, where the light from the tall French windows afforded abundant and well-distributed light for the enterprise in hand.   Hetty had not yet appeared.   Sara, attired in a loose morning gown, was watching him from a comfortable chair in the corner, one shapely bare arm behind her head; the free hand was gracefully employed in managing a cigarette.   He was conscious of the fact that her lazy, half-alert gaze was upon him all the time, although she pretended to be entirely indifferent to the preparations.   Dimly he could see the faint smile of interest on her lips.

" By Jove," he exclaimed with sudden fervour, " I wish I could get you just as you are, Mrs. Wrandall.

Do you mind if I sketch you in — just to preserve the pose for the future —"

"Never!" she cried and forthwith changed her position. She laughed at the look of disappointment in his face.

"You've no idea how — er — attractive —" he began confusedly, but broke off with a laugh. "I beg your pardon. I couldn't help it."

"The potent appeal of a cigarette," she surmised shrewdly.

"Not at all," he said promptly. He was a bit red in the face as he turned to busy himself with the tubes and brushes. When he glanced at her again, he found that she had resumed her former attitude.

Hetty came in at that moment, calm, serene and lovelier than ever in the clear morning light. She was wearing the simple white gown he had chosen the day before. If she was conscious of the rather intense scrutiny he bestowed upon her as she gave him her hand in greeting, she did not appear to be in the least disturbed.

"You may go away, Sara," she said firmly. "I shall be too dreadfully self-conscious if you are looking on."

Booth looked at her rather sharply. Sara indolently abandoned her comfortable chair and left them alone in the room.

"Shall we try a few effects, Miss Castleton?" he inquired, after a period of constraint that had its effect on both of them.

"I am in your hands," she said simply.

He made suggestions. She fell into the positions so easily, so naturally, so effectively, that he put aside all previous doubts and blurted out:

"You *have* posed before, Miss Castleton."

She smiled frankly. "But not for a really truly portrait," she said. "Such as this is to be."

He hesitated an instant. "I think I recall a canvas by Maurice Hawkright," he said, and at once experienced a curious sense of perturbation. It was not unlike fear.

Instead of betraying the confusion or surprise he expected, Miss Castleton merely raised her eyebrows inquiringly.

"What has that to do with me, Mr. Booth?" she asked.

He laughed awkwardly.

"Don't you know his work?" he inquired, with a slight twist of his lip.

"I may have seen his pictures," she replied, puckering her brow as if in reflection.

He stared for a second.

"Why do you look at me in that way, Mr. Booth?" she cried, with a nervous little laugh.

"Do you mean to say you — er — that is, you don't know Hawkright's work?"

"Is that so very strange?" she inquired plaintively.

"By Jove," he muttered, quite taken aback. "I don't understand. I'm flabbergasted."

"Please explain yourself," she said stiffly.

"You must have a double somewhere, Miss Castleton," said he, still staring. "Some one who looks enough like you to be —"

"Oh," she cried, with a bright smile of understanding. "I see! Yes, I have a double — a really remarkable double. Have you never seen Hetty Glynn, the actress?"

"I am sure I have not," he said, taking a long breath. It was one of relief, he remembered afterward.

" If she is so like you as all that, I *couldn't* have forgotten her."

" She is quite unknown, I believe," she went on, ignoring the implied compliment. " A chorus-girl, or something like that. They say she is wonderfully like me — or was, at least, a few years ago."

He was silent for a few minutes, studying her face and figure with the critical eye of the artist. As he turned to the canvas with his crayon point, he remarked, with an unmistakable note of relief in his voice:

" That explains everything. It must have been Hetty Glynn who posed for all those things of Hawkright's."

" I dare say," said she indifferently.

CHAPTER X

THE next day he appeared bright and early with his copy of the *Studio*.

"There," he said, holding it before her eyes. She took it from his hands and stared long and earnestly at the reproduction.

"Do you think it like me?" she inquired innocently.

"Amazingly like you," he declared with conviction.

She turned the page. He was watching her closely. As she looked upon the sketches of the half-nude figure a warm blush covered her face and neck. She did not speak for a full minute, and he was positive that her fingers tightened their grasp on the magazine.

"The same model," he said quietly.

She nodded her head.

"Hetty Glynn, I am sure," she said, after a pause, without lifting her eyes. Her voice was low, the words not very distinct.

He drew a long breath, and she looked up quickly. What he saw in her honest blue eyes convicted her.

Sara Wrandall came into the room at that moment. Hetty hastily closed the magazine and held it behind her. Booth had intended to show the reproduction to Mrs. Wrandall, but the girl's behaviour caused him to change his mind. He felt that he possessed a secret that could not be shared with Sara Wrandall, then or afterward. Moreover, he decided that he would not refer to the Hawkright picture again unless the girl herself brought up the subject. All this flashed through his mind as he stepped forward to greet the new-comer.

When he turned again to Hetty, the magazine had disappeared. He never saw it afterward, and, what is more to the point, he never asked her to produce it.

There was a marked change in Hetty's manner after that when they were left alone together. She seemed inert, distrait and at times almost unfriendly. There were occasions, however, when she went to the other extreme in trying to be at ease with him. These transitions were singularly marked. He could not fail to notice them. As for himself, he was uncomfortable, ill-at-ease. An obvious barrier had sprung up between them.

When Sara was present, the girl seemed to be her old self, but at no other time. Frequently during the sittings of the next few days he caught her looking at him without apparently being aware of the intensity of her gaze. He had the feeling that she was trying to read his thoughts, but what impressed him more than anything else was the increasing look of wonder and appeal that lurked in her deep, questioning eyes. It seemed almost as if she were pleading for mercy with them.

He thought hard over the situation. The obvious solution came to him: she had been at one time reduced to the necessity of posing, a circumstance evidently known to but few and least of all to Sara Wrandall, from whom the girl plainly meant to keep the truth. This conviction distressed him, but not in the way that might have been expected. He had no scruples about sharing the secret or in keeping it inviolate; his real distress lay in the fear that Mrs. Wrandall might hear of all this from other and perhaps ungentle sources. As for her posing for Hawkright, it meant little or

nothing to him.   In his own experience, two girls of
gentle birth had served as models for pictures of his own
making, and he fully appreciated the exigencies that
had driven them to it.   One had posed in the " altogether."   She was a girl of absolutely irreproachable
character, who afterwards married a chap he knew very
well, and who was fully aware of that short phase in her
life.   That feature of the situation meant nothing to
him.   He was in no doubt concerning Hetty.   She was
what she appeared to be: a gentlewoman.

He began to experience a queer sense of pity for her.
Her eyes haunted him when they were separated; they
dogged him when they were together.   More than once
he was moved to rush over and take her in his arms,
and implore her to tell him all, to trust him with
everything.   At such times the thought of holding the
slim, warm, ineffably feminine body in his arms was
most distracting.   He rather feared for himself.   If
such a thing were to happen,— and it might happen if
the impulse seized him at the psychological moment of
least resistance,— the result in all probability would
be disastrous.   She would turn on him like an injured
animal and rend him!   Alas, for that leveller called
reason!   It spoils many good intentions.

He admitted to himself that he was under the spell
of her.   It was not love, he was able to contend; but
it was a mysterious appeal to something within him
that had never revealed itself before.   He couldn't
quite explain what it was.

In his solitary hours at the cottage on the upper
road, he was wont to take his friend Leslie Wrandall
into consideration.   As a friend, was it not his duty
to go to him with his sordid little tale?   Was it right
to let Wrandall go on with his wooing when there ex-

isted that which might make all the difference in the
world to him?   He invariably brought these delibera-
tions to a close by relaxing into a grim smile of amusement, as much as to say: "Serve him right, anyway.
Trust him to sift her antecedents thoroughly. He's
already done it, and he is quite satisfied with the result.
Serve them all right, for that matter."

But then there was Hetty Glynn. What of her?
Hetty Glynn, real or mythical, was a disturbing factor
in his deductions.   If there was a real Hetty Glynn and
she was Hetty Castleton's double, what then?

On the fifth day of a series of rather prolonged and
tedious sittings, he was obliged to confine his work to
an hour and a half in the forenoon. Mrs. Wrandall
was having a few friends in for auction-bridge immediately after luncheon. She asked him to stay over and
take a hand, but he declined. He did not play bridge.

Leslie was coming out on an evening train. Booth,
in commenting on this, again remarked a sharp change
in Hetty's manner. They had been conversing somewhat buoyantly up to the moment he mentioned Leslie's
impending visit. In a flash her manner changed. A
quick but unmistakable frown succeeded her smiles, and
for some reason she suddenly relapsed into a state of
reserve that was little short of sullen. He was puzzled, as he had been before.

The day was hot. Sara volunteered to take him
home in the motor. An errand in the village was the
excuse she gave for riding over with him. Heretofore
she had sent him over alone with the chauffeur.

She looked very handsome, very tempting, as she
came down to the car.

"By Jove," he said to himself, "she is wonderful!"

He handed her into the car with the grace of a courtier, and she smiled upon him serenely, as a princess might have smiled in the days when knighthood was in flower.

When she sat him down at his little garden gate, he put the question that had been seething in his mind all the way down the shady stretch they had traversed.

"Have you ever seen Hetty Glynn, the English actress?"

Sara was always prepared. She knew the question would come when least expected.

"Oh, yes," she replied, with interest. "Have you noticed the resemblance? They are as like as two peas in a pod. Isn't it extraordinary?"

He was a bit staggered. "I have never seen Hetty Glynn," he replied.

"Oh? You have seen photographs of her?" she inquired casually.

"What has become of her?" he asked, ignoring her question. "Is she still on the stage?"

"Heaven knows," she replied lightly. "Miss Castleton and I were speaking of her last night. We were together the last time I saw her. Who knows? She may have married into the nobility by this time. She was a very poor actress, but the loveliest thing in the world — excepting *our* Hetty, of course."

If he could have seen the troubled look in her eyes as she was whirled off to the village, he might not have gone about the cottage with such a blithesome air. He was happier than he had been in days, and all because of Hetty Glynn!

Leslie Wrandall did not arrive by the evening train. He telephoned late in the afternoon, not to Hetty but to Sara, to say that he was unavoidably detained and would not leave New York until the next morning.

Something in his voice, in his manner of speaking, disturbed her. She went to bed that night with two sources of uneasiness threatening her peace of mind. She scented peril.

The motor met him at the station and Sara was waiting for him in the cool, awning-covered verandah as he drove up. There was a sullen, dissatisfied look in his face. She was stretched out comfortably, lazily, in a great chaise-longue, her black little slippers peeping out at him with perfect abandonment.

"Hello," he said shortly. She gave him her hand. "Sorry I couldn't get out last night." He shook her hand rather ungraciously.

"We missed you," she said. "Pull up a chair. I was never so lazy as now. Dear me, I am afraid I'll get stout and gross."

"Spring fever," he announced. He was plainly out of sorts. "I'll stand, if you don't mind. Beastly tiresome, sitting in a hot, stuffy train."

He took a couple of turns across the porch, his eyes shifting in the eager, annoyed manner of one who seeks for something that, in the correct order of things, ought to be plainly visible.

"Please sit down, Leslie. You make me nervous, tramping about like that. We can't go in for half an hour or more."

"Can't go in?" he demanded, stopping before her. He began to pull at his little moustache.

"No. Hetty's posing. They won't permit even me to disturb them."

He glared. With a final, almost dramatic twist he gave over jerking at his moustache, and grabbed up a chair, which he put down beside her with a vehemence that spoke plainer than words.

"I say," he began, scowling in the direction of the doorway, "how long is he going to be at this silly job?"

"Silly job? Why, it is to be a masterpiece," she cried.

"I asked you how long?"

"Oh, how can I tell? Weeks, perhaps. One can't prod a genius."

"It's all tommy-rot," he growled. "I suppose I'd better take the next train back to town."

"Don't you like talking with me?" she inquired, with a pout.

"Of course I do," he made haste to say. "But do you mean to say they won't let anybody in where — Oh, I say! This is rich!"

"Spectators upset the muse, or words to that effect."

He stared gloomily at his cigarette case for a moment. Then he carefully selected a cigarette and tapped it on the back of his hand.

"See here, Sara, I'm going to get this off my chest," he said bluntly. "I've been thinking it over all week. I don't like this portrait painting nonsense."

"Dear me! Didn't you suggest it?" she inquired innocently, but all the time her heart was beating violent time to the song of triumph.

He was jealous. It was what she wanted, what she had hoped for all along. Her purpose now was to encourage the ugly flame that tortured him, to fan it into fury, to make it unendurable. She knew him well: his supreme egoism could not withstand an attack upon its complacency. Like all the Wrandalls, he had the habit of thinking too well of himself. He possessed a clearly-defined sense of humour, but it did not begin to include self-sacrifice among its endowments. He had never been able to laugh at himself for the excellent reason that some things were truly sacred to him.

She realised this, and promptly laughed at him. He stiffened.

" Don't snicker, Sara," he growled. He took time to light his cigarette, and at the same time to consider his answer to her question. " In a way, yes. I suggested a sort of portrait, of course. A sketchy thing, something like that, you know. But not an all-summer operation."

" But she doesn't mind," explained Sara. " In fact, she is enjoying it. She and Mr. Booth get on famously together."

" She likes him, eh? "

" Certainly. Why shouldn't she like him? He is adorable."

He threw his cigarette over the railing. " Comes here every day, I suppose? "

" My dear Leslie, he is to do me as soon as he has finished with her. I don't like your manner."

" Oh," he said in a dull sort of wonder. No one had ever cut him short in just that way before. " What's up, Sara? Have I done anything out of the way? "

" You are very touchy, it seems to me."

" I'm sore about this confounded portrait monopoly."

" I'm sorry, Leslie. I suppose you will have to give in, however. We are three to one against you,— Hetty, Mr. Booth and I."

" I see," he said, rather blankly. Then he drew his chair closer. " See here, Sara, you know I'm terribly keen about her. I think about her, I dream about her,

I — oh, well, here it is in a nutshell: I'm in love with her. Now do you understand?"

"I don't see how you could help being in love with her," she said calmly. "I believe it is a habit men have where she is concerned."

" You're not surprised?" he cried, himself surprised.

" Not in the least."

" I mean to ask her to marry me," he announced with finality. This was intended to bowl her over completely.

She looked at him for an instant, and then shook her head. " I'd like to be able to wish you good luck."

He stared. " You don't mean to say she'd be fool enough —" he began incredulously, but caught himself up in time. " Of course, I'd have to take my chances," he concluded, with more humility than she had ever seen him display. " Do you know of any one else?"

" No," she said seriously. " She doesn't confide in me to that extent, I fear. I've never asked."

" Do you think there was any one back there in England?" He put it in the past tense, so to speak, as if there could be no question about the present.

" Oh, I dare say."

He was regaining his complacency. " That's neither here nor there," he declared. " The thing I want you to do, Sara, is to rush this confounded portrait. I don't like the idea, not a little bit."

" I don't blame you for being afraid of the attractive Mr. Booth," she said, with a significant lifting of her eyebrows.

" I'm going to have it over with before I go up to town, my dear girl," he announced, in a matter-of-fact way. " I've given the whole situation a deuce of a lot of thought, and I've made up my mind to do it. I'm not the sort, you know, to delay matters once my mind's made up. By Jove, Sara, *you* ought to be pleased. I'm not such a rotten catch, if I do say it who shouldn't."

She was perfectly still for a long time, so still that she did not appear to be breathing. Her eyes grew darker, more mysterious. If he had taken the pains to notice, he would have seen that her fingers were rigid.

"I *am* pleased," she said, very softly, even gently.

She could have shrieked the words.

He showed no elation. Why should he? He took it as a matter of course. Settling back in his chair, he lit another cigarette, first offering the case to her, but she shook her head. Then he lapsed into a satisfied discussion of the situation as it appeared to him. All the while she was regarding him with a thoroughly aroused light in her dark eyes. She was breathing quickly again, and there were moments when she felt a shudder rush through her veins, as of exquisite excitement.

How she hated all these smug Wrandalls!

"I came to the decision yesterday," he went on, tapping the arm of the chair with his finger tips, as if timing his words with care and precision. "Spoke to dad about it at lunch. I was for coming out on the five o'clock, as I'd planned, but he seemed to think I'd better talk it over with the mater first. Not that she would be likely to kick up a row, you know, but — well, for policy's sake. See what I mean? Decent thing to do, you know. She never quite got over the way you and Chal stole a march on her. God knows I'm not like Chal."

Her eyes narrowed again. "No," she said, "you are not like your brother."

"Chal was all right, mind you, in what he did," he added hastily, noting the look. "I would do the same, 'pon my soul I would, if there were any senseless objections raised in my case. But, of course, it *was* right for me to talk it over with her, just the same. So I stayed in and gave them all the chance to say what they thought of me — and, incidentally, of Hetty. Quite the decent thing, don't you think? A fellow's mother is his mother, after all. See what I mean?"

"And she was appeased?" she said, in a dangerously satirical tone.

"Hardly the word, old girl, but we'll let it stand. She *was* appeased. Wanted to be sure, of course, if I knew my own mind, and all that. Just as if I didn't! Ha! Ha! I was considerate enough to ask her if she was satisfied I wasn't marrying beneath the family dignity. 'Gad, she got off a rather neat one at that. Said I might marry under the family tree if I felt like it. Rather good, eh, for mother? I said I preferred a church. Nothing al fresco for me."

"She is quite satisfied, then, that you are not throwing yourself away on Miss Castleton," said Sara, with a deep breath, which he mistook for a sigh.

"Oh, trust mother to nose into things. She knows Miss Castleton's pedigree from the ground up. There's Debrett, you see. What's more, you can't fool her in a pinch. She knows blood when she sees it. Father hasn't the same sense of proportion, however. He says you never can tell."

Sara was startled. "What do you mean?"

"Oh, it's nothing to speak of; only a way he has of grinding mother once in a while. He uses you as an example to prove that you never can tell, and mother has to admit that he's right. You have upset every

one of her pet theories. She sees it now, but — whew!
She couldn't see it in the old days, could she?"

"I fear not," said she in a low voice. Her eyes
smouldered. "It is quite natural that she should not
want you to make the mistake your brother made."

"Oh, please don't put it that way, Sara. You make
me feel like a confounded prig, because that's what it
comes to, with them, don't you know. And yet my attitude has always been clear to them where you're concerned. I was strong for you from the beginning. All
that silly rot about —"

"Please, please!" she burst out, quivering all over.

"I beg your pardon," he stammered. "You — you
know how I mean it, dear girl."

"Please leave me out of it, Leslie," she said, collecting herself. After a moment she went on calmly:
"And so you are going to marry my poor little Hetty,
and they are all pleased with the arrangement."

"If she'll have me," he said with a wink, as if to say
there wasn't any use doubting it. "They're tickled to
death."

"Vivian?"

"Viv's a snob. She says Hetty's much too good
for me, blood and bone. What business, says she, has
a Wrandall aspiring to the descendant of Henry the
Eighth."

"What!"

"The Murgatroyds go back to old Henry, straight
as a plummet. 'Gad, what Vivvy doesn't know about
British aristocracy isn't worth knowing. She looked
it up the time they tried to convince her she ought to
marry the duke. But she's fond of Hetty. She says
she's a darling. She's right: Hetty is too good for
me."

Sara swished her gown about and rose gracefully from the chaise-longue. Extending her hand to him she said, and he was never to forget the deep thrill in her voice:

"Well, I wish you good luck, Leslie. Don't take no for an answer."

"Lord, if she *should* say no," he gasped, confronted by the possibility of such stupidity on Hetty's part. "You don't think she will?"

Her answer was a smile of doubt, the effect of which was to destroy his tranquillity for hours.

"It is time for luncheon. I suppose we'll have to interrupt them. Perhaps it is just as well, for your sake," she said tauntingly.

He grinned, but it was a sickly effort.

"You're the one to spoil anything of that sort," he said, with some ascerbity.

"I?"

"Certainly," he said with so much meaning in the word that she flushed.

"Oh, I see," she mused, with understanding. "Can't you trust Vivian to do that for you?" There was intense irony in the question.

He laughed disdainfully. "Vivvy wouldn't stand a ghost of a chance with you, take it from me." He stopped abruptly at the doorway, a frown of recollection creasing his seamless brow. "Oh, that reminds me, there is something else I want to discuss with you, Sara. After luncheon will be time enough. Remind me of it, will you?"

"Not if it is to be unpleasant," she replied, with a sudden chill in her heart.

"It's this, in a word: Viv would like to have Miss Castleton over to spend a month or so with her after

the — well, after the house is open." He came near
to saying after the engagement was announced.

Sara's decision was made at once. Her face hardened.

"That is quite out of the question, Leslie," she said.

"We can discuss it, can't we?" he demanded loftily.

She did not condescend to reply. They were now in
the wide hallway, and she was a step or two ahead of
him. Voices could be heard in the recess at the lower
end of the hall, beyond the staircase, engaged in what
appeared to be a merry exchange of opinions. He
caught the sound of a low laugh from Booth. There
was something acutely subdued about it, as if a warning had been whispered by some one. Leslie's sensitive
imagination pictured the unseen girl with her finger to
her lips.

He caught up with Sara, and, curiously red in the
face, snapped out with dogged insistence:

"Mother is set on having her come, Sara. Can't
you see the way the land lays? They —"

Hetty and Booth came into view at that instant, and
his lips were closed. The painter was laying a soft,
filmy scarf over the girl's bare shoulders as he followed
close behind her.

"Hello!" he cried, catching sight of Wrandall.
"Train late, old chap? We've been expecting you for
the last hour. How are you?"

He came up with a frank, genuine smile of pleasure
on his lips, his hand extended. Leslie rose to the occasion. His self-esteem was larger than his grievance.
He shook Booth's hand heartily, almost exuberantly.

"Didn't want to disturb you, Brandy," he cried,
cheerily. "Besides, Sara wouldn't let me." He then
passed on to Hetty, who had lagged behind. Bending

low over her hand, he said something commonplace in a very low tone, at the same time looking slyly out of the corner of his eye to see if Booth was taking it all in. Finding that his friend was regarding him rather fixedly, he obeyed a sudden impulse and raised the girl's slim hand to his lips. As suddenly he released her fingers and straightened up with a look of surprise in his eyes; he had distinctly heard the agitated catch in her throat. She was staring at her hand in a stupefied sort of way, holding it rigid before her eyes for a moment before thrusting it behind her back as if it were a thing to be shielded from all scrutiny save her own.

"You must not kiss it again, Mr. Wrandall," she said in a low, intense voice. Then she passed him by and hurried up the stairs, without so much as a glance over her shoulder.

He blinked in astonishment. All of a sudden there swept over him the unique sensation of shyness — most unique in him. He had never been abashed before in all his life. Now he was curiously conscious of having overstepped the bounds, and for the first time to be shown his place by a girl. This to him, who had no scruples about boundary lines!

All through luncheon he was volatile and gay. There was a bright spot in his cheek, however, that betrayed him to Sara, who already suspected the temper of his thoughts. He talked aeroplaning without cessation, directing most of his conversation to Booth, yet thrilled with pleasure each time Hetty laughed at his sallies. He was beginning to feel like a half-baked schoolboy in her presence, a most deplorable state of affairs he had to admit.

"If you hate the trains so much, and your automobile is out of whack, why don't you try volplaning down from the Metropolitan tower?" demanded Booth in response to his lugubrious wail against the beastly luck of having to go about in railway coaches with a lot of red-eyed, nose-blowing people who hadn't got used to their spring underwear as yet.

"Sinister suggestion, I must say," he exclaimed. 'You must be eager to see my life blood scattered all over creation. But, speaking of volplaning, I've had three lessons this week. Next week Bronson says I'll be flying like a gull. 'Gad, it's wonderful. I've had two tumbles, that's all,— little ones, of course,— net result a barked knee and a peeled elbow."

"Watch out you're not flying like an angel before you get through with it, Les," cautioned the painter. "I see that a well-known society leader in Chicago was killed yesterday."

"Oh, I love the danger there is in it," said Wrandall carelessly. "That's what gives zest to the sport."

"I love it, too," said Hetty, her eyes a-gleam. "The glorious feel of the wind as you rush through it! And yet one seems to be standing perfectly still in the air when one is half a mile high and going fifty miles an hour. Oh, it is wonderful, Mr. Wrandall."

"I'll take you out in a week or two, Miss Castleton, if you'll trust yourself with me."

"I will go," she announced promptly.

Booth frowned. "Better wait a bit," he counselled. "Risky business, Miss Castleton, flying about with fledgelings."

"Oh, come now!" expostulated Wrandall with some heat. "Don't be a wet blanket, old man."

"I was merely suggesting she'd better wait till you've got used to your wings."

"Jimmy Van Wickle took his wife with him the third

time up," said Leslie, as if that were the last word in aeroplaning.

"It's common report that she keeps Jimmy level, no matter where she's got him," retorted Booth.

"I dare say Miss Castleton can hold me level," said Leslie, with a profound bow to her. "Can't you, Miss Castleton?"

She smiled. "Oh, as for that, Mr. Wrandall, I think we can all trust you to cling pretty closely to your own level."

"Rather ambiguous, that," he remarked dubiously.

"She means you never get below it, Leslie," said Booth, enjoying himself.

"That's the one great principle in aeroplaning," said Wrandall, quick to recover. "Vivian says I'll break my neck some day, but admits it will be a heroic way of doing it. Much nobler than pitching out of an automobile or catapulting over a horse's head in Central Park." He paused for effect before venturing his next conclusion. "It must be ineffably sublime, being squashed — or is it squshed?— after a drop of a mile or two, isn't it?"

He looked to see Miss Castleton wince, and was somewhat dashed to find that she was looking out of the window, quite oblivious to the peril he was in figuratively for her special consideration.

Booth was acutely reminded that the term "prig" as applied to Leslie was a misnomer; he hated the thought of the other word, which reflectively he rhymed with "pad."

It occurred to him early in the course of this rather one-sided discussion that their hostess was making no effort to take part in it, whether from lack of interest or because of its frivolous nature he was, of course, unable to determine. Later, he was struck by the curious pallor of her face, and the lack-lustre expression of her eyes. She seldom removed her gaze from Wrandall's face, and yet there persisted in the observer's mind the rather uncanny impression that she did not hear a word her brother-in-law was saying. He, in turn, took to watching her covertly. At no time did her expression change. For reasons of his own, he did not attempt to draw her into the conversation, fascinated as he was by the study of that beautiful, emotionless face. Once he had the queer sensation of feeling, rather than seeing, a haunted look in her eyes, but he put it down to fancy on his part. Doubtless, he concluded, the face or voice or manner of her husband's brother recalled tragic memories from which she could not disengage herself. But undoubtedly there was something peculiar in the way she looked at Leslie through those dull, unblinking eyes. It was some time before Booth realised that she made but the slightest pretence of touching the food that was placed before her by the footman.

And Leslie babbled on in blissful ignorance of, not to say disregard for, this strange ghost at the feast, for, to Booth's mind, the ghost of Challis Wrandall was there.

Turning to Miss Castleton with a significant look in his eyes, meant to call her attention to Mrs. Wrandall, he was amazed to find that every vestige of colour had gone from the girl's face. She was listening to Wrandall and replying in monosyllables, but that she was aware of the other woman's abstraction was not for an instant to be doubted. Suddenly, after a quick glance at Sara's face, she looked squarely into Booth's eyes, and he saw in her an expression of actual concern, if not alarm.

Leslie was in the middle of a sentence when Sara laughed aloud, without excuse or reason. The next instant she was looking from one to the other in a dazed sort of way, as if coming out of a dream.

Wrandall turned scarlet. There had been nothing in his remarks to call for a laugh, he was quite sure of that. Flushing slightly, she murmured something about having thought of an amusing story, and begged him to go on, she wouldn't be rude again.

He had little zest for continuing the subject and sullenly disposed of it in a word or two.

"What the devil was there to laugh at, Brandy?" he demanded of his friend after the women had left them together on the porch a few minutes later. Hetty had gone upstairs with Mrs. Wrandall, her arm clasped tightly about the older woman's waist.

"I dare say she was thinking about you falling a mile or two," said Booth pleasantly.

But he was perplexed.

- CHAPTER XI

THE young men cooled their heels for an hour before word was brought down to them that Mrs. Wrandall begged to be excused for the afternoon on account of a severe headache. Miss Castleton was with her, but would be down later on. Meanwhile they were to make themselves at home, and so on and so forth.

Booth took his departure, leaving Leslie in sole possession of the porch. He was restless, nervous, excited; half-afraid to stay there and face Hetty with the proposal he was determined to make, and wholly afraid to forsake the porch and run the risk of missing her altogether if she came down as signified. Several things disturbed him. One was Hetty's deplorable failure to hang on his words as he had fondly expected her to do; and then there was that very disquieting laugh of Sara's. A hundred times over he repeated to himself that sickening question: "What the devil *was* there to laugh at?" and no answer suggested itself. He was decidedly cross about it.

Another hour passed. His heels were quite cool by this time, but his blood was boiling. This was a deuce of a way to treat a fellow who had gone to the trouble to come all the way out in a stuffy train, by Jove, it was! With considerable asperity he rang for a servant and commanded him to fetch a time table, and to be quick about it, as there might be a train leaving before he could get back if it took him as long to find it as it took other people to remember their obligations! His sarcasm failed to impress Murray, who said he thought

187

there was a schedule in Mrs. Wrandall's room, and he'd
get it as soon as the way was clear, if Mr. Wrandall
didn't mind waiting.

"If I minded waiting," snapped Leslie, "I wouldn't
be here now."

"It's the thing most people object to in the country,
sir," said Murray consolingly. "Waiting for trains,
sir."

"And the sunset," added Mr. Wrandall pointedly,
with a westward glare.

"We don't mind that, sir. We rather look forward
to it. It means one day less of waiting for the trains."
It was rather cryptic, but Leslie was too deeply absorbed in self-pity to take account of the pathos in
Murray's philosophy.

"What time is it, Murray?"

"Five-twenty, Mr. Wrandall."

"That's all, Murray."

"Thank you, sir."

As the footman was leaving, Sara's automobile
whirled up to the porte-cochere.

"Who is going out, Murray?" he called in surprise.

"Miss Castleton, sir. For the air, sir."

"The deuce you say!" gasped the harassed Mr.
Wrandall. It *was* a pretty kettle of fish!

Hetty appeared a few minutes later, attired for motoring.

"Oh, there you are," she said, espying him. "I am
going for a spin. Want to come along?"

He swallowed hard. The ends of his moustache described a pair of absolutely horizontal exclamation
points. "If you don't mind being encumbered," he remarked sourly.

"I don't in the least mind," said she sweetly.

"Where are you going?" he asked without much enthusiasm. He wasn't to be caught appearing eager,
not he. Besides, it wasn't anything to be flippant
about.

"Yonder," she said, with a liberal sweep of her arm,
taking in the whole landscape. "And be home in time
to dress for dinner," she added, as if to relieve his
mind.

"Good Lord!" he groaned, "do we have to eat
again?"

"We have to dress for it, at least," she replied.

"I'll go," he exclaimed, and ambled off to secure a
cap and coat.

"Sara has planned for a run to Lenox to-morrow if
it doesn't rain," she informed him on his return.

"Oh," he said, staring. "Booth gets a day off on
the portrait then."

"Being Sunday," she smiled. "We knock off on
Sundays and bank holidays. But, after all, he doesn't
really get a holiday. He is to go with us, poor fellow."

He looked as though he expected nothing. He could
only sit back and wonder what the deuce Sara meant
by behaving like this.

It was not by way of being a profitable excursion, if
we are to judge by the amount of pleasure Leslie derived from the two hours' spin through the cool, leafy
byways of the forest with the object of his heart's desire
on the seat beside him. He tried to screw up his courage to the point of asking her why he shouldn't kiss her
hand, which might have opened the way to more profound interrogations, but somehow he felt unable to
cope with the serenity that confronted him. Moreover,
he had a horrible conviction that the chauffeur was a
brute with abnormally long ears and a correspondingly

short sense of honour.   No, it was not the time or the
place for love-making.   He would have to be content
to bide his time till after dinner, which now began to
lose some of its disadvantages.   There was a most engaging nook, he remembered, in the corner of the garden facing the Sound, where the shadows were deep;
where sentiment could thrive on its own ecstasy; where
no confounded menial dared to show his face — although he had to admit that the chauffeur was most
punctilious in that respect.

And so he was satisfied to sit back in the corner of
the seat and feed his senses on the lovely creature before him.   He had never seen her so beautiful, so utterly worth having as now.   He was conscious of a
great, overwhelming sense of pride, somewhat smother-
ing in its vastness.   She *was* a creature to be proud of!
His heart was very full.

They returned at seven.   Dinner was unusually
merry.   Sara appeared to have recovered from her in-
disposition; there was colour in her cheeks and life in
her smile.   He took it to be an omen of good fortune,
and was immeasurably confident.   The soft cool breezes
of the star-lit night blew visions of impending happiness
across his lively imagination; fanned his impatience
with gentle ardour; filled him with surpressed sighs of
contentment, and made him willing to forego the delight
of conquest that he might live the longer in serene anticipation of its thrills.

Ten o'clock came.   He arose and stretched himself
in a sort of ecstasy.   His heart was thumping loudly,
his senses swam.   Walking to the verandah rail he
looked out across the moonlit Sound, then down at the
selected nook over against the garden wall — spot to be
immortalised!— and actually shivered.   In ten minutes'

time, or even less, she would be down there in his arms!
Exquisite meditations!

He turned to her with an engaging smile, in which
she might have discerned a prophecy, and asked her to
come with him for a stroll along the wall. And so he
cast the die.

Hetty sent a swift, appealing look at Sara's purposely averted face. Leslie observed the act, but misinterpreted its meaning.

"Oh, it is quite warm," he said quickly. "You
won't need a wrap," he added, and in spite of himself
his voice trembled. Of course she wouldn't need a
wrap!

"I have a few notes to write," said Sara, rising.
She deliberately avoided the look in Hetty's eyes.
"You will find me in the library."

She stood in the doorway and watched them descend
to the terrace, a sphinx-like smile on her lips. Hetty
seemed very tall and erect, as one going to meet a sol-
dier's fate.

Then Sara entered the house and sat down to wait.

A long time after a door closed stealthily in a distant part of the house — the sun-parlour door, she knew
by direction.

A few minutes later an upstairs door creaked on
its hinges. Some one had come in from the mellow
night, and some one had been left outside.

Many minutes passed. She sat there at her father's
writing table and waited for the other to come in. At
last quick, heavy footfalls sounded on the tiled floor
outside and then came swiftly down the hall toward the
small, remote room in which she sat. She looked up as
he unceremoniously burst into the room.

He came across and stood over her, an expression of

utter bewilderment in his eyes. There was a ghastly smile on his lips.

"Damn it all, Sara," he said shrilly, "she — she turned me down."

He seemed incapable of comprehension.

She was unmoved. Her eyes narrowed, but that was the only sign of emotion.

"I — I can't believe —" he began querulously. "Oh, what's the use? She won't have me. 'Gad! I'm trembling like a leaf. Where's Watson? Have him get me something to drink. Never mind! I'll get it from the sideboard. I'm — I'm damned!"

He dropped heavily into a chair at the end of the table and looked at her with glazed eyes. As she stared back at him she had the curious feeling that he had shrunk perceptibly, that his clothes hung rather limply on him. His face seemd to have lost all of its smart symmetry; there was a looseness about the mouth and chin that had never been there before. The saucy, arrogant moustache sloped dejectedly.

"I fancy you must have gone about it very badly," she said, pursing her lips.

"Badly?" he gasped. "Why — why, good heavens, Sara, I actually pleaded with her," he went on, quite pathetically. "All but got down on my knees to her. Damn me, if I can understand myself doing it either. I must have lost my head completely. Begged like a love-sick school-boy! And she kept on saying no — no — no! And I, like a blithering ass, kept on telling her I couldn't live without her, that I'd make her happy, that she didn't know what she was saying, and — But, good Lord, she kept on saying no! Nothing but no! Do — do you think she meant to say no? Could it have been hysteria? She said it so often, over and over again, that it might have been hysteria. I never thought of that. I —"

" No, Leslie, it wasn't hysteria, you may be sure of that," she said deliberately. " She meant it, old fellow."

He sagged deeper in the chair.

" I — I can't get it through my head," he muttered.

" As I said before, you did it badly," she said. " You took too much for granted. Isn't that true? "

" God knows I didn't *expect* her to refuse me," he exclaimed, glaring at her. " Would I have been such a fool as to ask her if I thought there was the remotest chance of being —" The very thought of the word caused it to stick in his throat. He swallowed hard.

" You really love her? " she demanded.

" Love her? " There was a sob in his voice. " I adore her, Sara. I can't live without her. And the worst of it is, I love her now more than I did before. Oh, it's appalling! It's horrible! What am I to do, Sara? What *am* I to do? "

" Be a man for a little while, that's all," she said coolly.

" Don't joke with me," he groaned.

" Go to bed, and when you see her in the morning tell her that you understand. Thank her for what she has done for you. Be —"

" Thank her? " he almost shouted.

" Yes; for destroying all that is detestable in you, Leslie,— your self-conceit, your arrogance, your false notions concerning yourself,— in a word, your egotism."

He blinked incredulously. " Do you know what you're saying? " he gasped.

She went on as if she hadn't heard him.

" Assure her that she is to feel no compunction for what she has done, that you are content to be her loyal, devoted friend to the end of your days."

" But, hang it, Sara, I *love* her ! "

" Don't let her suspect that you are humiliated. On the contrary, give her to understand that you are cleansed and glorified."

" What utter tommy —"

" Wait! Believe me, it is your only chance. You will have to learn some time that you can't ride rough-shod among angels. Think it over, old fellow. You have had a good lesson. Profit by it."

" You mean I'm to sit down and twirl my thumbs and let some other chap snap her up under my very nose? Well, I guess not! "

" Not necessarily. If you take it manfully, she may discover a new interest in you. Don't breathe a word of love to her. Go on as if nothing had happened. Don't forget that I told you in the beginning not to take no for an answer."

He drooped once more, biting his lip. " I don't see how I can ever tell mother that she refused —"

" Why tell her? " she inquired, rising.

His eyes brightened. " By Jove, I shan't," he exclaimed.

" I am going up to the poor child now," she went on. " I dare say you have frightened her almost to death. Naturally she is in great distress. I shall try to convince her that her decision does not alter her position in this house. I depend on you to do your part, Leslie. Make it easy for her to stay on with me."

He mellowed to the verge of tears.

" I can't keep on coming out here after this, as I've been doing, Sara."

"Don't be silly! Of course you can. This will blow over."

"Blow over?" he almost gasped.

"I mean the first effects. Try being a martyr for a while, Leslie. It isn't a bad plan, I can assure you. It may interest you to know that Challis proposed to me three times before I accepted him, and yet I — I loved him from the beginning."

"By Jove!" he exclaimed, coming to his feet with a new light in his eyes. The hollows in his cheeks seemed to fill out perceptibly.

"Good-night!"

"I say, Sara dear, you'll — you'll help me a bit, won't you? I mean, you'll talk it over with her and —"

"My sympathy is entirely with Miss Castleton," she said from the doorway. His jaw dropped.

He was still ruminating over the callousness of the world in respect to lovers when she mounted the stairs and tapped firmly on Hetty's door.

His hopes began to revive. A new thought had entered in and lodged securely among them, bracing them up amazingly. "By Jove," he said to himself, staring hard at the floor, "I dare say I *did* go about it badly. Sara was clever enough to see it. I must have taken her off her feet with my confounded earnestness. Girls do lose their heads, bless 'em, if you go at them with a rush. I'm sure she'll look at it differently when she's had time to compose herself." He was perplexed, however, over something he had not revealed to Sara, and his sudden frown proved that it was still disturbing him. "I can't for the life of me understand why she should have been so damned horrified at the idea."

He started for the dining-room, recalling his need of a drink, but changed his mind in the hall. Grabbing up his hat and stick, he darted out of the house and was soon swinging briskly down the moonlit avenue. He had come to the conclusion that a long walk would prove settling; and moreover it wasn't a stupid idea to go over and have his drink with Brandon Booth. The longer he walked, the more springy his stride. Sara was quite right; he *had* gone about it badly. He'd go about it differently next time.

Half way to Booth's cottage his pace slackened. A disconcerting thought struck him, almost like a dash of cold water in the face: Was she in love with Booth? He sat down on the rugged stone fence to ponder. A cold perspiration broke out all over him. When he next resumed his walk, his back was towards Booth's cottage. He attributed the perspiration to the violence of his exercise.

. . . . . .

Hetty Castleton was standing in the middle of her room when Sara entered. From her position, it was evident that she had stopped short in her nervous, excited pacing of the floor. She was very pale but there was a dogged, set expression about her mouth.

"Come in, dear," she said, in a manner that showed she had been expecting the visit. "Have you seen him?"

Sara closed the door, and then stood with her back against it, regarding her agitated friend with serious, compassionate eyes.

"Yes. He is terribly upset. It was a blow to him, Hetty."

"I am sorry for him, Sara. He was so dreadfully in earnest. But, thank God, it is over!" She threw back her head and breathed deeply. "That horrible, horrible nightmare is ended. I suppose it had to be.

But the mockery of it — think of it, Sara! — the damnable mockery of it!"

" Poor Leslie!" sighed the other. " Poor old Leslie."

Hetty's eyes filled with tears. " Oh, I *am* sorry for him. He didn't deserve it. God in heaven, if he really knew everything! If he knew why I could not listen to him, why I almost screamed when he held my hands in his and begged — actually begged me to — Oh, it was ghastly, Sara!"

She covered her face with her hands, and swayed as if about to fall. Sara came quickly to her side. Putting an arm about the quivering shoulders, she led the girl to the broad window seat and threw open the blinds.

" Don't speak of it, dearest,— don't think of *that*. Sit here quietly in the air and pull yourself together. Let me talk to you. Let me tell you how deeply distressed I am, not only on your account, but his."

They were silent for a long time, the girl lying still and almost breathless against the other's shoulders. She was still wearing the delicate blue dinner gown, but in her fingers was the exquisite pearl necklace Sara had given her for Christmas. She had taken it off and had forgotten to drop it in her jewel box.

" I suppose he will go up to the city early," she said monotonously.

" Leslie is a better loser than you think, my dear," said Sara, looking out over the tops of the cedars. " He will not run away."

Hetty looked up in alarm. " You mean he will persist in — in his attentions," she cried.

" Oh, no. I don't believe you will find him to be the bugbear you imagine. He can take defeat like a man. He is devoted to you, he is devoted to me. Your de-

cision no doubt wrecks his fondest hope in life, but it
doesn't make a weakling of him."

" I don't quite understand —"

" He is sustained by the belief that he has paid you
the highest honour a man can pay to a woman.   There
is no reason why he should turn his back on you, as a
sulky boy might do.   No, my dear, I think you may
count on him as your best, most loyal friend from this
night on.   He has just said to me that his greatest
pain lies in the fear that you may not be willing to accept him as a simple, honest, unpresuming friend
since —"

" Oh, Sara, if he will only be that and nothing more ! "
cried the girl wonderingly.

Sara smiled confidently.   " I fancy you haven't much
to fear in that direction, my dear.   It isn't in Leslie
Wrandall's make-up to court a second repulse.   He is
all pride.   The blow it suffered to-night can't be repeated — at least, not by the same person."

" I am so sorry it had to be Leslie," murmured Hetty.

" Be nice to him, Hetty.   He deserves that much of
you, to say the least.   I should miss him if he found
it impossible to come here on account of —"

" I wouldn't have that happen for the world," cried
the girl in distress.   " He is your dearest friend.   Send
me away, Sara, if you must.   Don't let anything stand
in the way of your friendship for Leslie.   You depend
on him for so much, dear.   I can't bear the thought
of —"

" Hush, dearest!   You are first in my love.   Better
for me to lose all the others and still have you."

The girl looked at her in wonder for a long time.
" Oh, I know you mean it, Sara, but — but how can it
be true? "

"Put yourself in my place," was all that Sara said
in reply, and her companion had no means of translat-
ing the sentence.

She could only remain mute and wondering, her eyes
fixed on that other mystery: the cameo face in the
moon that hung high above the sombre forest.

"If it were not for the trip to Lenox," she murmured
plaintively.

"The trip is off," announced Sara. She too was
staring at the cloudless sky. "There will be rain to-
morrow."

"It is very clear to-night, Sara."

"Do you hear that little wail in the trees — as if
a child were whimpering out there? That is the plaint
of the fairies who live in the buds and twigs, in the
flower cups and mosses. They famish, their gods will
hear. Their gods hear when ours is deaf. You will
see. There will be clouds over us to-morrow and we
will breathe the mist."

The girl shivered.

Many minutes afterward she said, as one who mar-
vels: "I hear the promise in the wind, Sara,— the new,
cool wind."

"The gods are whispering. Soon the fairies and
elves will come forth to revel. Ah, what a wonderful
thing the night is!"

"The fairies," mused the girl. "You believe in
them?"

"Resolutely."

"And I too."

"We will never grow old, my dear," said Sara.
"That is what the fairies are for: to keep those who
love them young."

Hetty had relaxed. Her soft young body was warm

again; that ineffably feminine charm was revived in her.

"Poor Leslie," murmured Sara, a long time afterward, a dreamy note in her voice. "I can't put him out of my thoughts. He will never get over it. I have never seen one so stricken and yet so brave. He would have been more than a husband to you, Hetty. It is in him to be a slave to the woman he loves. I know him well, poor boy."

Hetty was silent, brooding. Sara resumed her thoughtful observations.

"Why should you let what happened months ago stand in the way of —"

She got no farther than that. With an exclamation of horror, the girl sprang away from her and glowered at her with dilated eyes.

"My God, Sara!" she whispered hoarsely. "Are you mad?"

The other sighed. "I suppose you must think it of me," she said dismally. "We are made differently, you and I. If I cared for a man, nothing in all this world could stand between me and him. My love would fortify me against the enemy we are prone to call conscience. It would justify me in slaying the thing we call conscience. In your heart, Hetty, you have not wronged Leslie Wrandall by any act of yours. You owe him no reparation. On the contrary, it is not far out of the way to say that he owes you something, but of course it is a claim for recompense and resolves itself into a sentimental debt, so there's really no use discussing it."

Hetty was still staring. "You don't mean to say you would have me marry Challis Wrandall's brother?" she said, in a sort of stupefaction.

Sara shook her head. "I mean this: you would be

justified in permitting Leslie to glorify that which his
brother desecrated; your womanhood, my dear."

" My God, Sara! " again fell in a hoarse whisper from
the girl's lips.

" I simply voice my point of view," explained Sara
calmly. " As I said before, we look at things differently."

" I can't believe you mean what you have said," cried
Hetty. " Why — why, if I loved him with all my heart,
soul and body I could not even think of — Oh, I shudder to think of it! "

" I love you," continued Sara, fixing her mysterious
eyes on those of the girl, " and yet you took from me
something more than a brother. I love you, knowing
everything, and I am paying in full the debt he owes
to you. Leslie, knowing nothing, is no less your debtor.
All this is paradoxical, I know, my dear, but we must
remember that while other people may be indebted to
us, we also owe something to ourselves. We ought to
take pay from ourselves. Please do not conclude that
I am urging or even advising you to look with favour
upon Leslie Wrandall's honourable, sincere proposal of
marriage. I am merely trying to convince you that
you are entitled to all that any man can give you in
this world of ours,— we women all are, for that matter."

" I was sure that you couldn't ask me to marry him.
'I couldn't believe —"

" Forget what I have said, dearest, if it grieves you,"
cried Sara warmly. She arose and drew the girl close
to her. " Kiss me, Hetty." Their lips met. The
girl's eyes were closed, but Sara's were wide open and
gleaming. " It is because I love you," she said softly,
but she did not complete the sentence that burned in her

brain. To herself she repeated: "It is because I love you that I would scourge you with Wrandalls!"

"You are very good to me, Sara," sobbed Hetty.

"You *will* be nice to Leslie?"

"Yes, yes! If he will only let me be his friend."

"He asks no more than that. Now, you must go to bed."

Suddenly, without warning, she held the girl tightly in her arms. Her breathing was quick, as of one moved by some sharp sensation of terror. When Hetty, in no little wonder, opened her eyes Sara's face was turned away, and she was looking over her shoulder as if cause for alarm had come from behind.

"What is it?" cried Hetty anxiously.

She saw the look of dread in her companion's eyes, even as it began to fade.

"I don't know," muttered Sara. "Something, I can't tell what, came over me. I thought some one was stealing up behind me. How silly of me."

"Ah," said Hetty, with an odd smile, "I can understand how you felt."

"Hetty, will you take me in with you to-night?" whispered Sara nervously. "Let me sleep with you. I can't explain it, but I am afraid to be alone to-night." The girl's answer was a glad smile of acquiescence. "Come with me, then, to my bedroom while I change. I have the queerest feeling that some one is, in my room. I don't want to be alone. Are you afraid?"

Hetty held back, her face blanching.

"No, I am not afraid," she cried at once, and started toward the door.

"There *is* some one in this room," said Sara a few moments later, when they were in the big bedroom down the hall.

" I — I wonder," murmured Hetty.

And yet neither of them looked about in search for the intruder!

Far into the night Sara sat in the window of Hetty's dressing-room, her chin sunk low in her hands, staring moodily into the now opaque night, her eyes sombre and unblinking, her body as motionless as death itself. The cooling wind caressed her and whispered warnings into her unheeding ears, but she sat there unprotected against its chill, her night-dress damp with the mist that crept up with sinister stealth from the sea.

In the flats below, a vast army of frogs shrilled in ceaseless chatter; night birds and insects responded to the bedlam challenge; the hoarse monotonous grunts of a fog-horn came up from the Sound. There were people out there, asleep in passage.

A cat mewed piteously somewhere in the garden. She was curiously disturbed by this. She hated cats. There had never been one on the place before.

CHAPTER XII

MR. REDMOND WRANDALL, grey and gaunt and somewhat wistful, rode slowly through the leafy lane, attended some little distance behind by Griggs the groom, who slumped in the saddle and thought only of the sylvan dell to curse it with poetic license. (Ever since Mr. Wrandall had been thrown by his horse in the Park a few years before his wife had insisted on having a groom handy in case he lost his seat again: hence Griggs.) It sometimes got on Mr. Wrandall's nerves, having Griggs lopping along like that, but there didn't seem to be any way out of it, nor was there the remotest likelihood that the groom himself might one day be spilled and broken in many places while engaged in this obnoxious espionage.

Mr. Wrandall was grey because he was old, he was gaunt because he was old, and he usually was somewhat wistful for the same reason. He nourished the lament that he had grown old before his time, despite the sixty odd years that lay behind him. He was always a trifle annoyed with himself for not having demanded more of his youth. Griggs, therefore, was a physical insult, any way you looked at him: his very presence in the road behind was a blatant, house-top sort of proclamation that he, Redmond Wrandall, was in his dotage, and that was something Mr. Wrandall would never have admitted if he had had anything to say about it.

To-day he was riding over to Southlook to visit his daughter-in-law and one whom he looked upon as a prospective daughter-in-law. It was Wednesday and the family had been in the country since Monday. His wife and Vivian had motored over on Tuesday. They were letting no grass grow under their feet, notwithstanding a sudden and unexplained period of procrastination on the part of Leslie, who had gone off for a fortnight's fishing in Maine. Moreover, so far as they knew, he had departed without proposing to Miss Castleton: an oversight which deprived his mother of at least two weeks of activity along obvious lines. Naturally, it was quite impossible to discuss the future with Miss Castleton under the circumstances, and it was equally out of the question to discuss it with security in the very constricted circle that Mrs. Wrandall affected in the country. It really was too bad of Leslie! He should have known better.

Half way to Southlook, Mr. Wrandall, turning a bend in the road, caught sight of two people walking some distance ahead: a man and a woman. They were several hundred yards away, and travelling in the direction he was going. He pulled his horse down to a walk, a circumstance that for the moment escaped the attention of Griggs, who rode alongside before he quite realised what had happened.

" Griggs," said his master, staring at the pedestrians, " when did my son return? "

Griggs grasped the situation at a glance — a rather vague and imperfect glance, however. " This morning, sir," he replied promptly, although he was as much at sea as his master.

" I understood Mrs. Wrandall to say he was not expected before Saturday."

" Yes, sir. He came unexpected, sir."

" Well," said Mr. Wrandall, with an indulgent smile, " we will not ride them down."

"No, indeed, sir," consented Griggs, with a wink that Mr. Wrandall did not see.

The pleased, satisfied smile grew on Redmond Wrandall's gaunt old face: not reminiscent, I am bound to say, yet reflective.

The tall young man and the girl far ahead apparently were not aware of the scrutiny. They appeared to be completely absorbed in each other. At last, coming to a footpath diverging from the macadam, they stopped and parleyed. Then they turned into this narrow, tortuous path over the hillside and were lost to view.

Mr. Wrandall's smile broadened as he touched his horse lightly with the crop. Coming to the obscure little bypath, he shot a surreptitious glance into the fastnesses of the wood, but did not slacken his speed. No one was in sight.

"I dare say the danger is past, Griggs," he said humorously. "They are safe."

"I believe you, sir," said Griggs, also forgetting himself so far as to steal a look over his right shoulder.

It was Mr. Wrandall's design to ride on to Southlook and surprise Leslie and his inamorata at the lodge gates, where he would wait for them. Arriving there, he dismounted and turned his steed over to Griggs, with instructions to ride on. He would join Mr. Leslie and Miss Castleton and walk with them for the remainder of the distance.

He sat down on the rustic bench and lighted a cigar. The lodge-keeper saluted him from the garden below. Later the keeper's small son came up and from the opposite side of the roadway regarded him with the wide, curious gaze of a four-year-old. Mr. Wrandall disliked children. He made no friendly overtures. The child stood his ground, which was in a sense disconcerting, althought he couldn't tell why. He felt like saying " shoo ! " Presently the keeper's collie came up and sniffed his puttees, all the while looking askance. Mr. Wrandall said: " Away with you," and the dog retreated with some dignity to the steps where he laid down and fixed his eyes on the stranger.

Half-an-hour passed. Mr. Wrandall frowned as he looked at his watch. Another quarter of an hour went by. He changed his position, and the dog lifted his head, without wagging his tail.

" 'Pon my soul," said Mr. Wrandall in some annoyance.

Just then the dog and the child deflected their common stare. He was at first grateful, then interested. The child was beaming, the dog's tail was thumping a merry tattoo on the wooden step. Footsteps crunched on the gravel and he turned to look, although it was not the direction from which he expected his son and Miss Castleton.

He came to his feet, plainly perplexed. Miss Castleton approached, but the fellow beside her was not Leslie.

" How are you, Mr. Wrandall? " called out the young man cheerily, crossing the road.

" Good afternoon, Brandon," said Mr. Wrandall, nonplussed. " How do you do, Miss Castleton? Delighted to see you looking so well. Where did you leave my son? "

" Haven't seen him," said Booth. " Is he back? "

Mr. Redmond Wrandall swallowed hard.

" I was so informed," he replied, with an effort.

" Are you not coming up to the house, Mr. Wrandall? " inquired Miss Castleton, and he thought he detected a note of appeal in her voice.

" Certainly," he announced, taking his place beside

her. To himself he was saying: " This young blade has been annoying her, confound him."

" Miss Castleton had a note from Leslie this morning, saying he wouldn't start home till Friday," said Booth, puzzled. " You don't mind my saying so, Miss Castleton? "

" Not at all. I am sure he said Friday."

" I fancy he did say Friday," said Mr. Wrandall. " I think Griggs had been drinking."

" Griggs? " inquired the two in unison.

He volunteered no more than that. He was too busily engaged in wondering what his son could be thinking of, to leave this delightful girl to the tender mercies of a handsome, fascinating chap like Brandon Booth. He didn't relish the look of things. She *was* agitated, suspiciously so; and Booth wasn't what one would describe as perfectly at ease. There was something in the air, concluded Leslie's father.

" I hear you are coming over to spend a fortnight with us, Miss Castleton," said he pleasantly.

Hetty started. " I beg your pardon, Mr. Wrandall," she said, although he had spoken very distinctly.

" Leslie mentioned it a — oh, some time ago, my dear. This is the first time I have seen you, otherwise I should have added my warmest appeal for you to come early and to stay late. Ha-ha! Hope you will find your way to our place, Brandon. You are always a most welcome visitor."

The girl walked on in silence, her lips set with curious firmness. Booth looked at her and indulged in a queer little smile, to which she responded with a painful flush.

" Vivian expects to have a few friends out at the same time — very quietly, you know, and without much of a hurrah. Young ladies you ought to know in New York, my dear Miss Castleton. I dare say you will remember all of them, Brandon."

"I dare say," said Booth, without interest.

"I understand the portrait is finished," went on the old gentleman, blissfully oblivious to the disturbance he had created. "Mrs. Wrandall says it is wonderful, Brandon. You won't mind showing it to me? I am very much interested."

"Glad to have you see it, sir."

"Thanks."

He slackened his pace, an uneasy frown appearing between his eyes.

"I am almost afraid to tell Sara the news we have had from town this morning. She is so opposed to notoriety and all that sort of thing. Poor girl, she's had enough to drive one mad, I fear, with all that wretched business of a year ago."

Hetty stopped in her tracks. She went very white.

"What news, Mr. Wrandall?"

"They say they have stumbled upon a clew,— an absolutely indisputable clew. Smith had me on the wire this morning. He is the chief operative, you understand, Miss Castleton. He informs me that his original theory is quite fully substantiated by this recent discovery. If you remember, he gave it as his opinion a year ago that the woman was not — er — I may say, of the class catalogued as fast. He is coming out to-morrow to see me."

Things went suddenly black before her eyes, but in an instant she regained control of herself.

"They have had many clews, Mr. Wrandall," she complained, shaking her head.

"I know," he replied; "and this one may be as futile

as the rest. Smith appears to be absolutely certain this time, however."

" I understood that Mrs. Wrandall — I mean Mrs. Challis Wrandall — refused to offer a reward," said Booth. " These big detective agencies are not keen about —"

" There is a ten thousand dollar reward still standing, Brandon," said Mr. Wrandall.

Again the girl started.

" That isn't generally known, sir," observed the painter. " Leslie told me there was no reward."

" It was privately arranged," explained Leslie's father.

They came in sight of the house at that moment, and the subject was dropped, for Sara was approaching them in earnest conversation with Mr. Carroll, her lawyer.

They met at the edge of the lower basin, where the waters trickled down from an imposing Italian fountain on the level above, forming a deep, clear pool to which the lofty sky lent unfathomable depths. To the left of the basin there was a small tea-house, snug in the shadow of the cypresses that lined the crest of the hill. A series of rough stone steps wound down to the water's edge and the boathouse.

" Mr. Carroll is the bearer of startling news, Mr. Wrandall," said Sara, after the greetings. There was a trace of the sardonic in her voice.

" Indeed? " said Mr. Wrandall gravely.

" I was not aware, sir," said the old lawyer stiffly, and with a positive glare, " that your detectives were such unmitigated asses as they now appear to be."

" I fail to understand, Mr. Carroll," with considerable loftiness.

"That confounded rascal Smith called to see me this morning, sir. He is a rogue, sir. He —"

"I beg your pardon, Mr. Carroll," protested Mr. Wrandall, in a far from conciliatory manner.

"It seems, in short, that he has been working on a very intimate clew," said Sara, staring fixedly at her father-in-law's face.

"So he informed me over the 'phone this morning," said he, rather taken a-back. "However, he did not go into the details. I am here, Sara, to tell you that he is coming out to-morrow. I want to ask you to come over to my place at —"

"That is out of the question, sir," exclaimed Mr. Carroll vehemently.

"My dear Mr. Carroll —" began Wrandall angrily, but Sara interrupted him to suggest that they talk it over in the tea-house. She would ring for tea.

"If you will excuse me, Mrs. Wrandall, I think I will be off," said Booth.

"Please stay, Mr. Booth," she urged. "I would like to have you here."

She fell behind with Hetty. The girl's eyes were glassy.

"Don't be alarmed," she whispered.

Booth pressed the button for her. "Thank you. You will be surprised, Mr. Wrandall, to hear that the new clew leads to a member of your own family."

Mr. Wrandall was in the act of sitting down. At her words he dropped. His eyes bulged.

"Good God!"

"It appears that Mr. Smith suspects — *me!*" said she coolly.

Her father-in-law's lips moved, but no sound issued. His face was livid.

" The stupid fool ! " hissed the irate Mr. Carroll.

There was deathly silence for a moment following this
outburst. Every face was pale. In Hetty's there was
an expression of utter horror. Her lips too were
moving.

" He has, it seems, put one thing and another to
gether, as if it were a picture puzzle," went on Sara.
" His visit to Mr. Carroll this morning was for the
purpose of ascertaining how much it would be worth
to me if he dropped the case — *now*."

" The infernal blackmailer ! " gasped Mr. Wrandall,
finding his voice. " I will have him kicked off the place
if he comes to me with — My dear, my dear ! You
cannot mean what you say."

He was in a shocking state of bewilderment.

" I'd advise you to call off your infernal blackmailer,
Mr. Redmond Wrandall," snarled Mr. Carroll, pacing
back and forth.

" My dear sir," stammered the other, " I — I — do
you mean to imply that I know anything about this
infamous business ? "

" He is your dog, not ours," declared the lawyer,
pacing the brick floor.

" Peace, gentlemen," admonished Sara. " Let us discuss it calmly."

" Calmly ? " gasped Mr. Wrandall.

" Calmly ! " snapped the lawyer.

" At least deliberately. It appears, Mr. Wrandall,
that Smith has been working on the theory all along that
it was I who went to the inn with Challis. You recall the description given of the woman ? She was of
my size and figure, they said at the time. Well, he
has —"

" It is infamous ! " shouted Mr. Wrandall, springing to his feet. "He shall hear from me to-night. I shall have him lodged in jail before —"

"You will do nothing of the sort," interrupted Sara firmly. "I think you will do well to hear his side of the story. And remember, sir, that it would be very difficult for me to establish an alibi."

"Bless me!" groaned the old man. Then his eyes brightened. "But Miss Castleton can prove that for you, my dear. Don't forget Miss Castleton."

"Miss Castleton did not come to me, you should remember, until after the — the trouble. It occurred the second night after my arrival from Europe. Mr. Smith has discovered that I was not in my rooms at the hotel that night."

"You were not?" fell from Mr. Wrandall's lips. "Where were you?"

"I spent the night in our apartment — alone." She shivered as with a chill as she uttered these words.

"What!"

"Leslie met me at the dock. He said that Challis had gone away from town for a day or two. The next day I telephoned to the garage and asked them to send the big car to me as I wanted to make some calls. They said that Mr. Wrandall had discharged the chauffeur a week or two before and had been using my little French runabout for a few days, driving it himself. I then instructed them to send the runabout around with one of their own drivers. You can imagine my surprise when I was told that Mr. Wrandall had taken the car out that morning and had not returned with it."

"I see," said Mr. Wrandall, beads of perspiration standing on his forehead.

"He had not left town. I will not try to describe

my feelings. Late in the afternoon, I called them up again. He had not returned. It was then that I thought of going to the apartment, which had been closed all winter. Watson and his wife were to go in the next day by my instructions. Challis had been living at a club, I believe. Somehow, I had the feeling that during the night my husband would come to the apartment — perhaps not alone. You understand. I went there and waited all night. That is the story. Of course, it is known that I did not spend the night at the hotel. Mr. Smith evidently has learned as much. It is on this circumstance that he bases his belief."

Booth was leaning forward, breathless with interest.

"May I enquire, Mr. Carroll, how the clever Mr. Smith accounts for the secrecy observed by Mr. Wrandall and his companion, if, as he proclaims, you were the woman? Is it probable that husband and wife would have been so mysterious?"

Mr. Carroll answered. "He is rather ingenious as to that, Mr. Booth. You must understand that he does not specifically charge my cli — Mrs. Wrandall with the murder of her husband. He merely arranges his theories so that they may be applied to her with a reasonable degree of assurance. He only goes this far in his deductions: If, as he has gleaned, Challis Wrandall was engaged in an illicit — er — we'll say distraction — with some one unknown to Sara his wife, what could be more spectacular than her discovery of the fact and the subsequently inspired decision to lay a trap for him? Of course, it is perfect nonsense, but it is the way he goes about it. It has been established beyond a doubt that Wrandall met the woman at a station four miles down the line from Burton's Inn.

She came out on one of the local trains, got off at this station as prearranged, and found him waiting for her. Two men, you will recall, testified to that effect at the inquest sixteen months ago. She was heavily veiled. She got in the motor and drove off with him. This was at half past eight o'clock in the evening. Smith makes this astounding guess; the woman instead of being the person expected, was in reality his wife, who had by some means intercepted a letter. Our speculative friend Smith is not prepared to suggest an arrest on these flimsy claims, but he believes it to be worth Mrs. Wrandall's while to have the case permanently closed, rather than allow these nasty conclusions to get abroad. They would spread like wildfire. Do you see what I mean?"

"It is abominable!" cried Hetty, standing before them with flashing eyes. "I *know* she did not —"

"Hetty, my dear!" cried Sara sharply.

The girl looked at her for a moment in a frenzied way, and then turned aside, biting her lips to keep back the actual confession that had rushed up to them.

"It is blackmail," repeated Mr. Wrandall miserably.

"In the most diabolical form," augmented Carroll. "The worst of it is, Wrandall, we can't stop his tongue unless we fairly choke him with greenbacks. All he has to do is to give the confounded yellow journals an inkling of his suspicions, and the job is done. It seems to be pretty well understood that the crime was not committed by a person in the ordinary walks of life, but by one who is secure in the protection of mighty influences. There are those who believe that his companion was one of the well-known and prominent young matrons in the city, many of whom were at one time or another interested in him in a manner not at all compli-

mentary. Smith suggests — mind you, he merely suggests — that the person who was to have met Wrandall
in the country that night was so highly connected that
she does not dare reveal herself, although absolutely
innocent of the crime. Or, it is possible on the other
hand, he says, that she may consider herself extremely
lucky in failing to keep her appointment and thereby
alluring him to take up with another, after she had written the letter breaking off the engagement,— said letter not having been received by him because it had fallen into the hands of his wife. Do you see? It is ingenious, isn't it? "

"What is to be done? " groaned Mr. Wrandall, in a
state of collapse. He was sitting limply back in the
chair, crumpled to the chin.

"The sanest thing, I'd suggest," said Booth sarcastically, " is the capture of the actual perpetrator of
the deed."

"But, confound them," growled Carroll, " they say
they can't."

"I shall withdraw my offer of reward," proclaimed
the unhappy father, struggling to his feet. " I never
dreamed it could come to such a pass as this. You *do*
believe me, don't you, Sara, my child — my daughter?
God hear me, I never —"

"Oh," said she cuttingly, " you, at least, are innocent, Mr. Wrandall."

He looked at her rather sharply.

"The confounded fellow is coming to see me to-
morrow," he went on after a moment of indecision. " I
shall be obliged to telephone to the city for my attorney
to come out also. I don't believe in taking chances
with these scoundrels. They —"

"May I enquire, sir, why you entrusted the matter

to a third rate detective agency when there are such
reputable concerns as the Pinkertons or —" began Mr.
Carroll bitingly.

Mr. Wrandall held up his hand deprecatingly.

"We had an idea that an unheard of agency might
accomplish more than one of the famous organisations."

"Well, you see what has come of it," growled the
other.

"I was opposed to the reward, sir," declared Mr.
Wrandall with some heat. "Not that I was content
to give up the search, but because I felt sure that the
guilty person would eventually reveal herself. They
always do, sir. It is the fundamental principle of
criminology. Soon or late they falter. My son Leslie
is of a like opinion. He has declared all along that
the mystery will be cleared up if we are quiescent. A
guilty conscience takes its own way to relieve itself.
If you keep prodding it with sharp sticks you encourage fear, and stealth, and all that sort of thing,
without really getting anywhere in the end. Give a
murderer a free rope and he'll hang himself, is my belief. Threaten him with that self-same rope, and he'll
pay more attention to dread than to conscience, and
your ends are defeated."

Sara was inwardly nervous. She stole a glance at
the white, emotionless face of the girl across the table,
and was filled with apprehension.

"Can you be sure, Mr. Wrandall," she began earnestly, "that justice isn't the antidote for the posion-
ous thing we call a conscience? Suppose this woman
to have been fully justified in doing what she did, does
it follow that conscience can force her to admit, even
to herself, that she is morally guilty of a crime against
man? I doubt it, sir."

She was prepared for a subtle change in Hetty's countenance and was not surprised to see the light of hope steal back into her eyes.

"Fully justified?" murmured the old gentleman painfully.

"Perhaps we would better not go into that question too intimately," suggested Mr. Carroll.

"My son Leslie has peculiar views along the very line —" began Mr. Wrandall, in great distress of mind. He fell into a reflective mood and did not finish the sentence.

"I shall see this man Smith," announced Sara calmly.

Her father-in-law stood over her, his face working. "My dear," he said, "I promise you this absurd business shall go no farther. Don't let it trouble you in the least. I will attend to Smith. If there is no other way to check his vile insinuations, I will pay his price. You are not to be submitted to these dreadful —"

She interrupted him. "You will do nothing of the kind, Mr. Wrandall," she said levelly. "Do you want to convince him that I *am* guilty?"

"God in heaven, no!"

"Then why pay him the reward you have offered for the person who is guilty?"

"It is an entirely different propo —"

"It amounts to the same thing, sir. He tells you he has discovered the woman you want and you fulfil your part of the bargain by paying him for his services. That closes the transaction, so far as he is concerned. He goes his way fully convinced that he has put his hands on the criminal, and then proceeds to wash them in private instead of in public. No. Let me see this man. I insist."

"He will be at my place to-morrow at eleven," said

Wrandall resignedly. "I wish Leslie were here. He is so level-headed."

Sara laid her hand on his arm. He looked up and found her regarding him rather fixedly.

"It would be just as well as to keep this from Mrs. Wrandall and Vivian," she said meaningly.

"You are right, Sara. It would distress them beyond words."

She smiled faintly. "May I enquire whether Mr. Smith is to report to you or to Mrs. Wrandall?"

He flushed. "My wife — er — made the arrangements with him, Sara," he said, but added quickly: "With my sanction, of course. He reports to me. As a matter of fact, now that I think of it, he advised me to say nothing to my wife until he had talked with me."

"Inasmuch as he has already talked it over with me, through counsel, I don't see any reason why we should betray his gentle confidence, do you?"

"I — I suppose not," said he uncomfortably.

"Then, bring him here at eleven, Mr. Wrandall," said she serenely. "He has already paved the way. I imagine he expects to find me at home. Put the things here, Watson."

Watson had appeared with the tray. It being a very hot day, he did not bring tea.

CHAPTER XIII

MR. WRANDALL PERJURES HIMSELF

SMITH arrived at eleven, somewhat after the fashion of the Hawkshaws of "yellow back" fame, who, if our memory serves us right, were so punctual that their appearance anywhere was described as being in the "nick o' time," only in this instance he was expected and did not "drop from the sky," as the saying goes.

Mr. Wrandall met him at the station and escorted him in a roundabout way to Southlook, carefully avoiding the main village thoroughfare and High street, where the fashionable colony was intrenched. Mr. Smith, being an experienced detective, was not surprised to find (after the introduction), that Mr. Wrandall's attorney had been a fellow-passenger from town. If he was impressed, he did not once betray the fact during the four mile spin to Sara's. On the contrary, he seemed to be entirely absorbed in the scenery.

Mr. Wrandall had said, without shaking hands: "We will repair at once to Mrs. Challis Wrandall's house, Mr. Smith. She is expecting you. I have informed her of your mission."

"I think we'd better discuss the matter between ourselves, Mr. Wrandall, before putting it up to —"

"There is nothing in connection with this unhappy affair, sir, that cannot be discussed first-hand with her," said his employer stiffly.

"Just as you like, sir," said Smith indifferently. "I have talked it over with old man Carroll. He understands."

"I am quite sure he does, Mr. Smith," said the other,

with emphasis. Mr. Smith successfully hid a smile. He took his seat beside the chauffeur.

" I am surprised," he observed to the driver, as a " feeler," " that you haven't changed bodies."

" Mr. Wrandall ordered the limousine, sir," said the chauffeur.

" Oh, I see. Keeps it on hand for rainy days, I suppose."

" It's Mrs. Wrandall's idea," explained the man. " Women are fussy about their hair. We always have a limousine handy."

" It is a handy thing to have about," said Mr. Smith drily, as he looked out of the corner of his eye and remarked the two men behind him. They were in very close conversation.

" The boss usually takes the other car. He likes the wind in his face, he says. I don't know why he ordered the limousine to-day."

" Probably there's something in the wind to-day he doesn't like," remarked Smith, after which he devoted himself assiduously to the road ahead, not being a practiced motorist.

As they were ascending the steps in Sara's exotic garden, Smith ventured a somewhat sinister remark.

" These steps are not good for a man with a weak heart, Mr. Wrandall. I hope yours is sound."

" Quite, Mr. Smith. Have no fear," said Mr. Wrandall, with an acute sense of divination. " You will also find it to be in the right place."

" Umph," said Mr. Smith.

Sara did not keep them waiting long in the morning room. She came in soon after they were announced, followed by Mr. Carroll, who had spent the night at Southlook. Hetty Castleton was not in evidence.

She motioned them to seats after Mr. Wrandall had ceremoniously introduced his lawyer, and as unceremoniously neglected to do as much for Smith.

"This is Mr. Smith, I presume," said she, with a slight uplifting of her eyebrows. She took a chair facing the detective.

"Yes, my dear," said her father-in-law. "Joseph Smith."

"Benjamin, if you please," corrected Mr. Smith.

"I regret to state that my memory for names does not go back to the Old Testament," said Wrandall, with a frosty smile.

"There are no Smiths in the Old Testament," said the detective grimly.

"I understand, Mr. Smith, that you are prepared to charge me with the murder of my husband."

She said it very quietly, very levelly. Smith was a bit staggered.

"Well, I — er — hardly that, Mrs. Wrandall," he said, disconcerted.

"Will you be good enough to come to the point at once?"

"My report in this matter, madam, is to be made to Mr. Wrandall here, as I understand it," said the detective, his jaw stiffening. "We don't, as a rule, report our findings to — well, to the person we suspect. It isn't what you'd call regular. Mr. Wrandall has employed me to make the investigation. He can hardly expect me to reveal my findings to you."

"My dear Sara —" began Mr. Wrandall.

"As this is a rather intimate conference, Mr. Smith," interrupted Sara, with a gracious smile for her father-in-law, "I fancy we have nothing to gain, one way or another, by recriminations. You have already con-

sulted Mr. Carroll, and I have talked it over with Mr.
Wrandall. That was to have been expected, I believe.
As I understand the situation, you are somewhat curious
to know just how much it is worth to me to have the
matter dropped."

Smith eyed her steadily.

" That is the case, precisely," he said briefly.

" Then you are not really interested in having the
guilty person brought to justice? "

" I am not an officer of the law, madam. I am a private individual, working for private ends. It is for
Mr. Wrandall to say whether my discoveries shall be
related in court. I respectfully submit that I am acting within my rights. My deductions have been formed.
That is as far as I can go without his authority. He
has offered a reward, and he has gone farther than that
by engaging us to devote our time, brains and energies
to the case. I am in this position at present: our firm
cannot accept the reward he has offered without deliberately declaring to the world that we can put our
hand on the slayer of his son. As I cannot produce the
actual proof that we have found that person, I am in
honour compelled to submit our findings so far as they
have gone, and then either to withdraw from the matter
or carry it on to the end, as he may elect. Our time is
worth something, madam. We have made a careful and
exhaustive investigation. We have come to the point
where we can go no farther without more or less publicly associating you with our theories. I spoke to Mr.
Carroll yesterday, it is true, and I am here to-day to
lay my facts before Mr. Wrandall — and his attorney,
I see. Mr. Carroll chose to call me a blackmailer. He
may be correct in his legal way of looking at it. But
he is wrong in assuming that *my* motives are criminal.

I submit that they are fair, open and above board."

There was a moment's silence following this astonishingly succinct summing up of his position. The three men had not taken their eyes from his shrewd, frank face during that clever speech. They had nothing to say. It had been agreed among them that Sara was to do the talking. They were to do the watching.

"You put the case very fairly, Mr. Smith," said she seriously. "I think your position is clear enough, assuming of course that you have any real evidence to support your theories, whatever they may be. I am perfectly free to say that you interest me."

"Interest you?" he said, in some exasperation. He had expected her to fly into a passion. "Don't you take me seriously, madam?"

"As far as you have gone, yes."

Mr. Wrandall could hold in no longer. He was most uncomfortable.

"See here, Smith, out with it. Let us have your story. My daughter-in-law is not in the least alarmed. You've been on the wrong track, of course. But that isn't the point. What we want now is to find out just where we stand."

"You put it in a rather compromising way, Mr. Wrandall. The pronoun 'we' is somewhat general, if you will permit me to say so. Do you expect me to discuss my findings in the presence of Mrs. Wrandall and her counsel?"

"Certainly, sir, certainly. You need have no hesitancy on that score. I dare say you came here knowing that what you were to say would go no further than these four walls."

"Would you say that, sir, if I were to submit proof that would make it look so black for Mrs. Wrandall that you couldn't very well doubt her complicity in the crime, even though you saw fit to let it go no further than these four walls?"

Mr. Wrandall hesitated. A heavy frown appeared between his eyes; his fingers worked nervously on the arm of the chair.

"I may say to you, Mr. Smith, that if you produce conclusive proof I shall do my duty as a law-respecting citizen. I would not hesitate on that score."

Sara looked at him through half-closed lids. His jaws were firmly set.

Smith seemed to be reflecting. He did not speak for a long interval.

"In the first place, it struck me as odd that the man's wife did not take more interest in the search that was made immediately after the kill — after the tragedy. Not only that, but it is of record that she deliberately informed the police that she didn't care whether they caught the guilty party or not. Isn't that true?" The question was directed to no one in particular.

It was Sara who answered.

"Quite true, Mr. Smith. And if it will interest you in the least, I repeat that I don't care even now."

"You were asked if you would offer a reward in addition to the small one announced by the authorities. Why didn't you offer a reward?"

"Because I did not care to make it an object for well-meaning detectives to pry into the affairs of indiscreet members of society," she said.

"I see," said he reflectively. "May I be so bold as to ask why you don't want to have the guilty punished?"

She looked at Mr. Wrandall before offering a reply to this direct question.

"I can't answer that question without publicly wounding Mr. Wrandall."

"We understand each other, Sara," said the old man painfully. "I think you would better answer his question."

"Because my husband courted the fate that befell him, Mr. Smith. That is my reply. While I do not know what actually transpired at the inn, I am reasonably certain that my husband's life was taken by some one who had suffered at his hands. I can say no more."

"The eye for an eye principle, eh?" There was deep sarcasm in the way he said it. As she did not respond to the challenge, he abruptly changed tactics. "Where were you on the night of the murder, Mrs. Wrandall?"

She smiled. "I thought you knew, Mr. Smith."

"I have reason to believe that you were at Burton's Inn," he said bluntly.

"But you wouldn't be at all sure about it if I said I wasn't there, would you, Mr. Smith?"

"I don't quite get you, Mrs. Wrandall."

"I mean to say, if I made it worth your while to change your opinion," she said flatly.

He cleared his throat. "You couldn't change my opinion, so there's an end to that. You could stop me right where I am, if that's what you mean. I'm perfectly frank about it, gentlemen. You needn't look as if you'd like to kill me. I'm not anxious to go on with the investigation. I don't know enough up to date to be sure of a conviction, but I guess I could get the proof if it is to be found. This is a family affair, I take it. Mr. Wrandall here doesn't want to —"

Mr. Wrandall struck the arm of his chair a violent blow with his clenched fist.

"You have no authority, sir, to make such a statement!" he exclaimed. "I want it distinctly understood that I would give half of what I possess to have the slayer of my son brought to justice."

"But you don't want this thing to go any further so far as Mrs. Challis Wrandall is concerned," said Smith coolly.

"Of course not, you miserable scoundrel!" cried the other in a rage. "She's no more guilty than I am."

"Don't call names, Mr. Wrandall," said Smith, a steely glitter in his eyes. "I am prepared to lay before you certain facts that I have unravelled, but I am not willing to give them to Mrs. Wrandall."

"My daughter-in-law spent the night at her own apartment, waiting for my son," said Wrandall, regaining control of himself. "That is positively known to me, sir. Positively!"

"How can you be sure of that, Mr. Wrandall?" asked Smith sharply.

The gaunt old face, suddenly very much older than it had been before, took on a stern, defiant expression.

"I spoke with her over the telephone at half past nine o'clock that night," said he steadily.

Smith was not the only one to be surprised by this startling declaration. Sara Wrandall's eyes widened ever so slightly, and one might have detected a sharp catch in her breath.

"She called you up?" asked Smith, after a moment to collect his wits.

Mr. Wrandall was not to be trapped. He had made up his mind to lie for Sara in this hour of need, and he had considered well his methods.

"No. I called up the apartment."

"How did you know she was at her apartment?"

"I did not know it. I called up to speak with my son. She answered the call, Mr. Smith."

He arose from the chair. Smith also came slowly to his feet, the look of astonishment still on his face.

"And now, sir," went on the old man, levelling a bony finger at him, "I think we can dispense with your services. I will give you credit for one thing: you are plain-spoken and above board. You want money and you don't beat about the bush. If you will instruct your office to send to me a bill for services, I will pay it. I engaged you, and I am ready to pay for my stupidity. My car will take you back to the station."

Smith picked up his hat and fumbled with it for a moment, plainly dismayed.

"If I have been on the wrong lead, Mr. Wrandall, I am willing to drop it and start all over again. I suppose your reward still stands. I am sure we can —"

"It does not stand, sir. I shall withdraw it this very day. God knows if I had thought it would lead us to this pass, it should never have been offered. Now, go, sir."

Smith held his ground doggedly. "There are a few points I'd like to —"

"No!"

"For the sake of justice and —"

Sara interrupted the man. She had crossed to Mr. Wrandall's side, a queer light in her eyes. Her hand fell upon his trembling old arm and he felt a thrill pass from her warm, strong fingers into the very core of his body.

"Mr. Smith, will you give me an off-hand estimate of what your services amount to in dollars and cents up to date?"

"You don't owe me anything, Mrs. Wrandall," said Smith, flushing a dull red.

"You came here to give me a chance, Mr. Smith, feeling that I was actually implicated. You had a price fixed in your mind. You still have your doubts, in spite of what Mr. Wrandall says. It occurred to you that it would be worth considerable to me if the investigation went no farther. You realised that you could not have brought this crime home to me, because you could not have found *real*, satisfying evidence. But you could have gone to the newspapers with your suspicions, and you could have made one-half the world believe that an innocent person was guilty of a foul crime. The world loves its sensations. It would have gloated over the little you could have given it, and it would have damned me unheard. I owe you something for sparing me a fate so wretched as that. Your price: What is it?"

"Sara!" cried Mr. Wrandall, aghast.

"My dear Mrs. Wrandall," cried Carroll, blinking his eyes, "you are not thinking of —"

"I am thinking of paying Mr. Smith his price," said Sara calmly.

"Why, damn it all," roared Carroll, "you countenance his ridiculous assertions —"

"No; I do nothing of the sort, Mr. Carroll, and Mr. Smith knows it quite as well as you do. He still has it in his power to set the tongues to wagging. We can't get around that, gentlemen. I want to pay him to drop the case entirely. The reward has been withdrawn. Will it satisfy your cupidity, Mr. Smith, if I agree to pay to you a like amount?"

"Good Lord!" gasped Smith, staggered.

"I cannot permit —" began Mr. Wrandall.

She looked him squarely in the eye and the words died on his lips.

"I prefer to have it my way," she said. "I will not accept favours from Mr. Smith — nor any other man." Wrandall alone caught the significance of the last four words. She would not accept the favour of a lie from him! And yet she would not humiliate by denying him in the presence of others. "Mr. Carroll will attend to this matter for me, Mr. Smith, if you will call at his office at your convenience. I shall make but a single stipulation in addition to the one involved: you are to drop the case altogether. Mr. Wrandall has already dismissed you. You are under no further obligations to him or his family. I respectfully submit to all of you, gentlemen, that when the investigations go so far astray as they have gone in this instance, it isn't safe to let them continue with the possible chance of proving unwholesome to other innocent persons, toward whom, in some justice, attention might be drawn. The young woman now in the far West is a sickening example. I refer to the Ashtley girl. If, by any chance, the right person should be taken, I will do my part, Mr. Wrandall, with the same purpose if not the same spirit that actuates you, but I am opposed to baring skeletons to gratify the morbid curiosity of a public that despises all of us because, unhappily, we are what we are. I trust I make myself plain to you. I loved my husband. I have no desire to know the names of women who were his — we will say — who were in love with him."

Mr. Wrandall bowed his head and said not a word. His attorney, who had been a silent listener from the beginning, spoke for the first time.

"If Mr. Smith will call at my office to-morrow, I will attend to the closing of this matter to his entire

satisfaction. Mr. Wrandall has already authorised me
to settle in full for his time and — patience."

" I don't like to take money in this way —"

" We won't discuss ethics, Mr. Smith."

" Just as you like, then. I'm only too happy to be
off the job. Good morning, madam. Good morning,
gentlemen."

He stalked from the room. Watson was waiting in
the hall.

" This way," he said, indicating the big front door.

Smith grinned sheepishly. " 'Gad, they don't even
think I can find a front door," he said.

Redmond Wrandall turned to the two men after he
heard the door of his automobile slam in the porte-cochere.

" Gentlemen, I believe it is unnecessary to announce
to you that I did not speak over the telephone with my
daughter-in-law on that wretched night," he said slowly.

They nodded their heads.

" I am not a good liar. Do you think the fellow believed me? "

" No," said Sara instantly. " He is accustomed to
better lying than you can supply. But it doesn't in
the least matter. He knows, however, that you spoke
the truth when you said I was in my apartment, even
though you are not sure of it yourself, Mr. Wrandall
I will not presume to thank you for what you did, but
I shall never forget it, sir."

He regarded her rather austerely for a moment. " I
am glad you do not thank me, Sara," he said. " You
are not to feel that you are under the slightest obligation to me."

" I regret that you felt it necessary to perjure
yourself," she said levelly, and then broke into a soft

little laugh as she laid her hand on his arm once more. "Come! Let us have a semi-public view of Hetty's portrait."

He looked up alertly at the mention of the girl's name.

"By the way, where is Miss Castleton?" he asked, drawing a long breath as if the air had suddenly become wholesome.

"She is back yonder in the living-room, having her last sitting to Brandon Booth. Just a few finishing touches, that's all. I hear them laughing. The day's work is done."

She led the way down the long hall, followed by the old gentlemen, who came three abreast, hoary retainers at the heels of youth.

CHAPTER XIV

LATER on Sara, in sober reflection, endorsed what had appeared at the time to be a whimsical, quixotic proceeding on her part. She brought herself completely to the point where she could view her action with complacency. At first, there was an irritating, nagging fear that Mr. Wrandall had been genuinely soul-sacrificing in his effort to defend her; that his decisive falsehood was a sincere declaration of loyalty to her and not the transparent outburst of one actuated by a sort of fanatical selfishness, in that he dreaded the further dragging in the dust of the name of Wrandall, and all that in spite of his positive belief that she was being wrongly, unfairly attacked. She knew that her father-in-law had no doubt in his mind that she could successfully combat any charge Smith might bring against her; that her innocence would prevail even in the opinion of the scheming detective. But behind all this was the Wrandall conclusion that a skin was to be saved, and that skin the one which covered the Wrandall pride.

His lie was not glorifying. She even consented that it might be the first deliberate falsehood this honourable, discriminating gentleman had told in all his life. At the moment, he may have been actuated by a motive that deceived him, but even unknown to him the Wrandall self-interest was at work. He was not lying for her, but for the Wrandalls! And she would have to remain his debtor all her life because of that amiable falsehood!

She intuitively felt the force of that secret motive

almost the instant it found expression, and she resented it even as she applauded it in the first wave of inward enthusiasm. She might have marked it down to his credit, and loved him a little for it, had not his rather distorted integrity impelled him to confess his transgression to the lawyers, whereas it was perfectly plain that they appreciated his distortion of the truth without having it explained to them in so many words. That virtuous little speech of his was all-illuminating; it let in a great light and laid bare the weakness that was too strong for him.

Her abrupt change of front, her suddenly formed resolve to pay the man his price, was the result of a natural opposition to the elder Wrandall. She acted hastily, even ruthlessly, in direct contradiction to her original intentions, but she now felt that she had acted wisely. There could be no doubt in the mind of the keen-witted Smith that Mr. Wrandall had lied; his lips therefore were sealed, not by the declaration, but by her own surprising offer to remunerate.

When she told Hetty what she had done, the girl, who had been tortured by doubts and misgivings, threw herself into her arms and sobbed out her gratitude.

" I could die for you, Sara. I could die a thousand deaths," she cried.

" Oh, I dare say Smith is quite delighted," said Sara carelessly. " He had come up against a brick wall, don't you see. He could go no further. There was but one thing for him to do and he did it. He had no case, but he felt that he ought to be paid just the same. Mr. Wrandall would never have paid him, he was sure of that. His game failed. He thinks better of me now than he ever did before, and I have made a friend of him, strange as it may appear."

"Oh, I hope so."

Sara stroked her cheek gently. "Don't be afraid, Hetty. We are quite safe."

Hetty secretly gloated over that little pronoun 'we.' It spelt security.

"And wasn't it splendid of Mr. Wrandall to say what he did?" she mused, lying back among the cushions with a sigh of relaxation.

Sara did not at once reply. She smiled rather oddly.

"It was," she said succinctly. "I am sure Leslie will go into raptures over his father's decline and fall."

"Must he be told?" in some dismay.

"Certainly. Every son should know his own father," she explained, with a quiet laugh.

The next day but one was overcast. On cloudy, bleak days Hetty Castleton always felt depressed. Shadowless days, when the sun was obscured, filled her with a curious sense of apprehension, as if when the sun came out again he would not find the world as he had left it. She did not mope; it was not in her nature. She was more than ever mentally alert on such days, for the very reason that the world seemed to have lapsed into a state of indifference, with the sun nowhere to be seen. There was a queer sensation of dread in knowing that that great ball of fire was somewhere in the vault above her and yet unlocated in the sinister pall that spread over the skies. Her fancy ofttimes pictured him sailing in the west when he should be in the east, dodging back and forth in impish abandon behind the screen, and she wondered at such times if he would be where he belonged when the clouds lifted.

Leslie was to return from the wilds on the following day. Early in the morning Booth had telephoned to enquire if she did not want to go for a long walk with him before luncheon. The portrait was finished, but he could not afford to miss the morning hour with her. He said as much to her in pressing his invitation.

" To-morrow Leslie will be here and I shan't see as much of you as I'd like," he explained, rather wistfully. " Three is a crowd, you know. I've got so used to having you all to myself, it's hard to break off suddenly."

" I will be ready at eleven," she said, and was instantly surprised to find that her voice rang with new life, new interest. The greyness seemed to lift from the view that stretched beyond the window; she even looked for the sun in her eagerness.

It was then that she knew why the world had been bleaker than usual, even in its cloak of grey.

A little before eleven she set out briskly to intercept him at the gates. Unknown to her, Sara sat in her window, and viewed her departure with gloomy eyes. The world also was grey for her.

They came upon each other unexpectedly at a sharp turn in the avenue. Hetty coloured with a sudden rush of confusion, and had all she could do to meet his eager, happy eyes as he stood over her and proclaimed his pleasure in jerky, awkward sentences. Then they walked on together, a strange shyness attending them. She experienced the faintness of breath that comes when the heart is filled with pleasant alarms. As for Booth, his blood sang. He thrilled with the joy of being near her, of the feel of her all about him, of the delicious feminine appeal that made her so wonderful to him. He wanted to crush her in his arms, to keep her there for ever, to exert all of his brute physical strength so that she might never again be herself but a part of him.

They uttered commonplaces.   The spell was on them.
It would lift, but for the moment they were powerless
to struggle against it.   At length he saw the colour fade
from her cheeks; her eyes were able to meet his without
the look in them that all men love.   Then he seemed
to get his feet on the ground again, and a strange, ineffably sweet sense of calm took possession of him.

"I must paint you all over again," he said, suddenly
breaking in on one of her remarks.   "Just as you are
to-day,— an outdoor girl, a glorious outdoor girl in —"

"In muddy boots," she laughed, drawing her skirt
away to reveal a shapely foot in an American walking
shoe.

He smiled and gave voice to a new thought.   "By
Jove, how much better looking our American shoes are
than the kind they wear in London!"

"Sara insists on American shoes, so long as I am
with her.   I don't think our boots are so villainous, do
you?"

"Just the same, I'm going to paint you again, boots
and all.   You —"

"Oh, how tired you will become of me!"

"Try me!"

"Besides, you are to do Sara at once.   She has consented to sit to you.   She will be wonderful, Mr. Booth,
oh, how wonderful!"

There was no mistaking the sincerity of this rapt
opinion.

"Stunning," was his brief comment.   "By the way,
I've hesitated about asking how she and Mr. Wrandall
came out with the detective chap."

Her face clouded.   "It was so perfectly ridiculous,
Mr. Booth.   The man is satisfied that he was wrong.
The matter is ended."

238 THE HOLLOW OF HER HAND

"Pure blackmail, I'd call it. I hope it isn't ended so far as she is concerned. I'd have him in jail so quick his —"

"She's tender-hearted, and sensitive. No real harm has been done. She refuses to prosecute him."

"You can't mean it."

"If you knew her as I do, you would understand."

"But her lawyer, what had he to say about it? And Mr. Wrandall? I should have thought they —"

"I believe they quite approve of what she has done. Nothing will come of it."

He walked on in silence for a couple of rods. "I have a feeling they will never know who killed Challis Wrandall," he said. "It is a mystery that can't be solved by deduction or theory, and there is nothing else for them to work on, as I understand the case. The earth seems to have been generous enough to swallow her completely. She's safe unless she chooses to confess, and that isn't likely. To be perfectly frank with you, Miss Castleton, I rather hope they never get her. He was something of a beast, you know."

She was looking straight ahead. "You used the word generous, Mr. Booth. Do you mean that she deserves pity?"

"Without knowing all the circumstances, I would say yes. I've had the feeling that she was more sinned against than sinning."

"Would you believe that she acted in self-defence?"

"It is quite possible."

"Then, will you explain why she does not give herself up to the authorities and assert her innocence? There is no proof to the contrary." She spoke hurriedly, with an eagerness which he mistook for doubt.

"For one reason, she may be a good woman who was

indiscreet. She may have some one else to think of
besides herself. A second reason: she may lack moral
courage."

"Moral courage!"

"It is one thing to claim self-defence and another
thing to get people to believe in it. I suppose you
know what Leslie thinks about it?"

"He has not discussed it with me."

"He believes his brother deserved what he got."

"Oh!"

"For that reason he has not taken an active part
in hounding her down."

She was silent for a long time, so long indeed that he
turned to look at her.

"A thoroughly decent, fair-minded chap is Leslie
Wrandall," he pronounced, for want of something better to say. "Still, I'm bound to say, I'm sorry he is
coming home to-morrow."

The red crept into her cheeks again.

"I thought you were such pals," she said nervously.

"I expect to be his best man if he ever marries,"
said he, whacking a stone at the road-side with his walking stick. Then he looked up at her furtively and
added, with a quizzical smile: "Unless something happens."

"What *could* happen?"

"He *might* marry the girl I'm in love with, and, in
that case, I'd have to be excused."

"Where shall we walk to this morning?" she asked
abruptly. He had drawn closer to her in the roadway.

"Is it too far to the old stone mill? That's where
I first saw you, if you remember."

"Yes, let us go there," she said, but her heart sank.
She knew what was coming. Perhaps it were best to

have it over with; to put it away with the things that
were to always be her lost treasures. It would mean the
end of their companionship, the end of a love dream.
She would have to lie to him: to tell him she did not
love him.

One would go many a fruitless day in quest of a
more attractive pair than they as they strode swiftly
down the shady road. They lagged not, for they were
strong and healthy, and walking was a joy to them,
not an exercise. She kept pace beside him, with her
free stride; half a head shorter than he, she did not
demand it of him that he should moderate his stride
to suit hers. He was tall and long-limbed, but not
camel-like in his manner of walking, as so many tall
men are apt to be. His eyes were bright with the excitement that predicted a no uncertain encounter, although he had no definite purpose in mind. There was
something singularly wistful, unfathomable, in her velvety blue eyes that gave him hope, he knew not why.

Coming to the jog in the broad macadam, they were
striking off into the narrow road that led to the quaint
old mill, long since abandoned in the forest glade beyond, when their attention was drawn to a motor-car,
which was slowing down for the turn into Sara's do-
main. A cloud of dust swam in the air far behind the
machine.

A bare-headed man on the seat beside the driver,
waved his hand to them, and two women in the tonneau
bowed gravely. Both Hetty and Booth flushed uncomfortably, and hesitated in their progress up the forest
road.

The man was Leslie Wrandall. His mother and sister were in the back seat of the touring car.

"Why — why, it was Leslie," cried Booth, looking

over his shoulder at the rapidly receding car. "Shall we turn back, Miss Castleton?"

"No," she cried instantly, with something like impatience in her voice. "And spoil our walk?" she added in the next breath, adding a nervous little laugh.

"It seems rather —" he began dubiously.

"Oh, let us have our day," she cried sharply, and led the way into the by-road.

They came, in the course of a quarter-of-an-hour, to the bridge over the mill-race. Beyond, in the mossy shades, stood a dilapidated, centurion structure known as Rangely's Mill, a landmark with a history that included incidents of the revolutionary war, when eager patriots held secret meetings inside its walls and plotted under the very noses of Tory adherents to the crown.

Pausing for a few minutes on the bridge, they leaned on the rail and looked down into the clear, mirror-like water of the race. Their own eyes looked up at them; they smiled into their own faces. And a fleecy white cloud passed over the glittering stream and swept through their faces, off to the bank, and was gone for ever.

Suddenly he looked up from the water and fixed his eyes on her face. He had seen her clear blue eyes fill with tears as he gazed into them from the rail above.

"Oh, my dear!" he cried. "What is it?"

She put her handkerchief to her eyes as she quickly turned away. In another instant, she was smiling up at him, a soft, pleading little smile that went straight to his heart.

"Shall we start back?" she asked, a quaver in her voice.

"No," he exclaimed. "I've got to go on with it

now, Hetty. I didn't intend to, but — come, let us go
up and sit on that familiar old log in the shade of the
mill. You must, dear!"

She suffered him to lead her up the steep bank beyond and through the rocks and rotten timbers to the
great beam that protruded from the shattered founda-
tions of the mill. The rickety old wheel, weather-beaten
and sad, rose above them and threatened to topple over
if they so much as touched its flimsy supports.

He did not release her hand after drawing her up
beside him.

"You must know that I love you," he said simply.

She made no response. Her hand lay limp in his.
She was staring straight before her.

"You *do* know it, don't you?" he went on.

"I — God knows I don't want you to love me. I
never meant that you should —" she was saying, as if
to herself.

"I suppose it's hopeless," he said dumbly, as her
voice trailed off in a whisper.

"Yes, it is utterly hopeless," she said, and she was
white to the lips.

"I — I shan't say anything more," said he. "Of
course, I understand how it is. There's some one else.
Only I want you to know that I love you with all my
soul, Hetty. I — I don't see how I'm going to get on
without you. But I — I won't distress you, dear."

"There isn't any one else, Brandon," she said in a
very low voice. Her fingers tightened on his in a sort
of desperation. "I know what you are thinking. It
isn't Leslie. It never can be Leslie."

"Then,— then —" he stammered, the blood surging
back into his heart —" there may be a chance —"

"No, no!" she cried, almost vehemently. "I can't

let you go on hoping.   It is wrong — so terribly wrong,
You must forget me.   You must —"

He seized her other hand and held them both firmly,
masterfully.

"See here, my — look at me, dearest!   What is
wrong?   Tell me!   You are unhappy.   Don't be afraid
to tell me.   You — you *do* love me? "

She drew a long breath through her half-closed lips.
Her eyes darkened with pain.

"No.   I don't love you.   Oh, I am so sorry to have
given you —"

He was almost radiant.   "Tell me the truth," he
cried triumphantly.   "Don't hold anything back, darling.   If there is anything troubling you, let me shoulder it.   I can — I will do anything in the world for you.
Listen: I know there's a mystery somewhere.   I have
felt it about you always.   I have seen it in your eyes,
I have always sensed it stealing over me when I'm with
you — this strange, bewildering atmosphere of —"

"Hush!   You must not say anything more," she
cried out.   "I cannot love you.   There is nothing
more to be said."

"But I know it now.   You *do* love me.   I could
shout it to —"   The miserable, whipped expression in
her eyes checked this outburst.   He was struck by it.
even dismayed.   "My dearest one, my love," he said,
with infinite tenderness, "what is it?   Tell me! "

He drew her to him.   His arm went about her shoulders.   The final thrill of ecstasy bounded through his
veins.   The feel of her!   The wonderful, subtle, feminine feel of her!   His brain reeled in a new and vast
whirl of intoxication.

She sat there very still and unresisting, her hand to
her lips, uttering no word, scarcely breathing.   He

waited. He gave her time. After a little while her fingers strayed to the crown of her limp, rakish panama. They found the single hat-pin and drew it out. He smiled as he pushed the hat away and then pressed her dark little head against his breast. Her blue eyes were swimming.

"Just this once, just this once," she murmured with a sob in her voice. Her hand stole upward and caressed his brown cheek and throat. Tears of joy started in his eyes — tears of exquisite delight.

"Good God, Hetty, I — I can't do without you," he whispered, shaken by his passion. "Nothing can come between us. I must have you always like this."

"*Che sará, sará,*" she sighed, like the breath of the summer wind as it sings in the trees.

The minutes passed and neither spoke. His rapt gaze hung upon the glossy crown that pressed against him so gently. He could not see her eyes, but somehow he felt they were tightly shut, as if in pain.

"I love you, Hetty. Nothing can matter," he whispered at last. "Tell me what it is."

She lifted her head and gently withdrew herself from his embrace. He did not oppose her, noting the serious, almost sombre look in her eyes as she turned to regard him steadfastly, an unwavering integrity of purpose in their depths.

She had made up her mind to tell him a part of the truth. "Brandon, I am Hetty Glynn."

He started, not so much in surprise as at the abruptness with which she made the announcement.

"I have been sure of it, dear, from the beginning," he said quietly.

Then her tongue was loosed. The words rushed to her lips. "I was Hawkright's model for six months.

I posed for all those studies, and for the big canvas in the academy. It was either that or starvation. Oh, you will hate me — you must hate me."

He laid his hand on her hair, a calm smile on his lips. "I can't love and hate at the same time," he said. "There was nothing wrong in what you did for Hawkright. I am a painter, you know. I understand. Does — does Mrs. Wrandall know all this?"

"Yes — everything. She knows and understands. She is an angel, Brandon, an angel from heaven. But," she burst forth, "I am not altogether a sham. I *am* the daughter of Colonel Castleton, and I *am* the cousin of all the Murgatroyds,— the poor relation. It isn't as if I were the scum of the earth, is it? I *am* a Castleton. My father comes of a noble family. And, Brandon, the only thing I've ever done in my life that I am really ashamed of is the deception I practised on you when you brought that magazine to me and faced me with it. I did not lie to you. I simply let you believe I was not the — the person you thought I was. But I deceived you —"

"No, you did not deceive me," he said gently. "I read the truth in your dear eyes.

"There are other things, too. I shall not speak of them, except to repeat that I have not done anything else in all my life that I should be ashamed of." Her eyes were burning with earnestness. He could not but understand what she meant.

Again he stroked her hair. "I am sure of that," he said.

"My mother was Kitty Glynn, the actress. My father, a younger son, fell in love with her. They were married against the wishes of his father, who cut him off. He was in the service, and he was brave enough to

stick. They went to one of the South African gar-
risons, and I was born there. Then to India. Then
back to London, where an aunt had died, leaving my
father quite a comfortable fortune. But his old friends
would have nothing to do with him. He had lived —
well, he had made life a hell for my mother in those
frontier posts. He deserted us in the end, after he had
squandered the fortune. My mother made no effort to
compel him to provide for her or for me. She was
proud. She was hurt. To-day he is in India, still in
the service, a martinet with a record for bravery on the
field of battle that cannot be taken from him, no matter
what else may befall. I hear from him once or twice a
year. That is all I can tell you about him. My
mother died three years ago, after two years of invalid-
ism. During those years I tried to repay her for the
sacrifice she had made in giving me the education,
the —" She choked up for a second, and then went
bravely on. " Her old manager made a place for me
in one of his companies. I took my mother's name,
Hetty Glynn, and — well, for a season and a half I
was in the chorus. I could not stay there. I *could*
not," she repeated with a shudder. "I gave it up after
my mother's death. I was fairly well equipped for
work as a children's governess, so I engaged myself
to —"

She stopped in dismay for he was laughing.

" And now do you know what I think of you, Miss
Hetty Glynn? " he cried, seizing her hands and regarding her with a serious, steadfast gleam in his eyes.
" You are the pluckiest, sandiest girl I've ever known.
You are the kind that heroines are made of. There is
nothing in what you've told me that could in the least
alter my regard for you, except to increase the love I

thought could not be stronger. Will you marry me, Hetty?"

She jerked her hands away, and held them clenched against her breast.

"No! I cannot. It is impossible, Brandon. If I loved you less than I do, I might say yes, but — no, it is impossible."

His eyes narrowed. A grey shadow crept over his face.

"There can be only one obstacle so serious as all that," he said slowly. "You — you are already married."

"No!" she cried, lifting her pathetic eyes to his. "It isn't that. Oh, please be good to me! Don't ask me to say anything more. Don't make it hard for me, Brandon. I love you — I love you. To be your wife would be the most glorious — No, no! I must not even think of it. I must put it out of my mind. There *is* a barrier, dearest. We cannot surmount it. Don't ask me to tell you, for I cannot. I — I am so happy in knowing that you love me, and that you still love me after I have told you how mean and shameless I was in deceiving —"

He drew her close and kissed her full on the trembling lips. She gasped and closed her eyes, lying like one in a swoon. Soft, moaning sounds came from her lips. He could not help feeling a vast pity for her, she was so gentle, so miserably hurt by something he could not understand, but knew to be monumental in its power to oppress.

"Listen, dearest," he said, after a long silence; "I understand this much, at least: you can't talk about it now. Whatever it is, it hurts, and God knows I don't want to make it worse for you in this hour when I am so

selfishly happy. Time will show us the way. It can't
be insurmountable. Love always triumphs. I only
ask you to repeat those three little words, and I will
be content. Say them."

"I love you," she murmured.

"There! You are mine! Three little words bind
you to me for ever. I will wait until the barrier is
down. Then I will take you."

"The barrier grows stronger every day," she said,
staring out beyond the tree-tops at the scudding clouds.
"It never can be removed."

"Some day you will tell me — everything?"

She hesitated long. "Yes, before God, Brandon, I
will tell you. Not now, but — some day. Then you
will see why — why I cannot —" She could not complete the sentence.

"I don't believe there is anything you can tell me
that will alter my feelings toward you," he said firmly.
"The barrier may be insurmountable, but my love is
everlasting."

"I can only thank you, dear, and — love you with
all my wretched heart."

"You are not pledged to some one else?"

"No."

"That's all I want to know," he said, with a deep
breath. "I thought it might be — Leslie."

"No, no!" she cried out, and he caught a note of
horror in her voice.

"Does — does he know this — this thing you can't
tell me?" he demanded, a harsh note of jealousy in his
voice.

She looked up at him, hurt by his tone. "Sara
knows," she said. "There is no one else. But you
are not to question her. I demand it of you."

"I will wait for you to tell me," he said gently.

CHAPTER XV

SARA had kept the three Wrandalls over for luncheon.

"My dear," said Mrs. Redmond Wrandall, as she stood before Hetty's portrait at the end of the long living-room, "I must say that Brandon has succeeded in catching that lovely little something that makes her so — what shall I say? — so mysterious? Is that what I want? The word is as elusive as the expression."

"Subtle is the word you want, mother," said Vivian, standing beside Leslie, tall, slim and aristocratic, her hands behind her back, her manner one of absolute indifference. Vivian was more than handsome; she was striking.

"There isn't anything subtle about Hetty," said Sara, with a laugh. "She's quite ingenuous."

Leslie was pulling at his moustache, and frowning slightly. The sunburn on his nose and forehead had begun to peel off in chappy little flakes.

"Ripping likeness, though," was his comment.

"Oh, perfect," said his mother. "Really wonderful. It will make Brandon famous."

"She's so healthy-looking," said Vivian.

"English," remarked Leslie, as if that covered everything.

"Nonsense," cried the elder Mrs. Wrandall, lifting her lorgnette again. "Pure, honest, unmixed blood, that's what it is. There is birth in that girl's face."

"You're always talking about birth, mother," said her son sourly, as he turned away.

"It's a good thing to have," said his mother with conviction.

"It's an easy thing to get in America," said he, pulling out his cigarette case. "Have a cigarette, mother? Sara?"

"I'll take one, Les," said Vivian. She selected one and passed the case on to her mother. Sara shook her head.

"No, thanks," she said.

Mrs. Redmond Wrandall laid her cigarette down without attempting to light it, a sudden frostiness in her manner. Vivian and Leslie blew long plumes of smoke from the innermost recesses of their lungs.

"Nerves?" asked Vivian mildly.

"I don't like Leslie's brand," explained Sara.

"They're excellent, I think," said Mrs. Wrandall, and thereupon accepted a light from Leslie.

"Well, let's be off," said he, somewhat irritably. "Tell Miss Castleton we're sorry to have missed her."

It was then that Sara prevailed upon them to stop for luncheon. "She always takes these long walks in the morning, and she will be disappointed if she finds you haven't waited —"

"Oh, as for that —" began Leslie and stopped, but he could not have been more lucid if he had uttered the sentence in full.

"Why didn't you pick her up and bring her home with you?" asked Sara, as they moved off in the direction of the porch.

"She seemed to be taking Brandy out for his morning exercise," said he surlily. "Far be it from me to — Umph!"

Sara repressed the start of surprise. She thought Hetty was alone.

"She will bring him in for luncheon, I suppose," she said carelessly, although there was a slight contraction of the eyelids. "He is a privileged character."

It was long past the luncheon hour when Hetty came in, flushed and warm. She was alone and she had been walking rapidly.

"Oh, I am so sorry to be late," she apologised, darting a look of anxiety at Sara. "We grew careless with time. Am I shockingly late?"

She was shaking hands with Mrs. Redmond Wrandall as she spoke. Leslie and Vivian stood by, rigidly awaiting their turn. Neither appeared to be especially cordial.

"What is the passing of an hour, my dear," said the old lady, "to one who is young and can spare it?"

"I did not expect you — I mean to say, nothing was said about luncheon, was there, Sara?" She was in a pretty state of confusion.

"No," said Leslie, breaking in; "we butted in, that's all. How are you?" He clasped her hand and bent over it. She was regarding him with slightly dilated eyes. He misinterpreted the steady scrutiny. "Oh, it will all peel off in a day or two," he explained, going a shade redder.

"When did you return?" she asked. "I thought to-morrow was —"

"Leslie never has any to-morrows, Miss Castleton," explained Vivian. "He always does to-morrow's work to-day. That's why he never has any troubles ahead of him."

"What rot!" exclaimed Leslie.

"Where is Mr. Booth?" inquired Sara. "Wouldn't he come in, Hetty?"

"I — I didn't think to ask him to stop for luncheon," she replied, and then hurried off to her room to make herself presentable.

"Don't be long," called out Sara.

"We are starving," added Vivian.

"Vivian!" exclaimed her mother, in a shocked voice.

"Well, *I* am," declared her daughter promptly.

"You know you *never* eat anything in the middle of the day," said her mother, frowning. As Sara was paying no attention to their remarks, Mrs. Wrandall was obliged to deliver the supplemental explanation to Leslie, who hadn't the remotest interest in the matter. "She's so silly about getting fat."

Hetty was in a state of nervous excitement during the luncheon. The encounter with Booth had not resulted at all as she had fancied it would. She had betrayed herself in a most disconcerting manner, and now was more deeply involved than ever before. She had been determined at the outset, she had failed, and now he had a claim — an incontestable claim against her. She found it difficult to meet Sara's steady, questioning gaze. She wanted to be alone.

"I suppose you have heard nothing recent from poor Lord Murgatroyd," Mrs. Wrandall was saying to her, in a most sympathetic tone.

Hetty scarcely grasped the importance of the remark. She looked rather blankly at their guest.

Sara stepped into the breach. "What do the morning despatches say, Mrs. Wrandall?"

"He is sinking rapidly, I fear. Of course, his extreme age is against him. How old is he, Miss Castleton?"

"I — I haven't the remotest idea, Mrs. Wrandall,"
said the girl. "He is very, very old."

"Ninety-two, the *Sun* says," supplied Vivian.

There was an unaccountable silence.

"I suppose there is — ah — really no hope," said
Mrs. Redmond Wrandall at last.

"I fear not," said Hetty composedly. "Except
for the heirs-at-law."

Mrs. Wrandall sat up a little straighter in her
chair. "Dear me," she said.

"They've been waiting for a good many years,"
commented Hetty, without emotion. "Of course,
Mrs. Wrandall, you understand that I am not one
of those who will profit by his death. The estate is
entailed. I am quite outside the walls."

"I did not know the — ah —"

"My father may come in for a small interest. He
is in England at present on furlough. But there are
a great many near relatives to be fed before the bowl
of plenty gets to him."

"Dear, dear!" murmured Mrs. Wrandall, quite ap-
palled by her way of putting it. Leslie looked at
her and coughed. "What a delicious dressing you
have for these alligator pears, Sara," she went on,
veering quickly. "You must tell me how it is made."

After luncheon, Leslie drew Sara aside.

"I must say she doesn't seem especially overjoyed
to see me," he growled. "She's as cool as ice."

"What do you expect, Leslie?" she demanded with
some asperity.

"I can't stand this much longer, Sara," he said.
"Don't you see how things are going? She's losing
her heart to Booth."

"I don't see how we can prevent it."

"By gad, I'll have another try at it — to-night. I say, has she said — anything?"

"She pities you," said she, a malicious joy in her soul. "That's akin to something else, you know."

"Confound it all, I don't want to be pitied!"

"Then I'd advise you to defer your 'try' at it," she remarked.

"I'm mad about her, Sara. I can't sleep, I can't think, I can't — yes, I *can* eat, but it doesn't taste right to me. I've just got to have it settled. Why, people are beginning to notice the change in me. They say all sorts of things. About my liver, and all that sort of thing. I'm going to settle it to-night. It's been nearly three weeks now. She's surely had time to think it over; how much better everything will be for her, and all that. She's no fool, Sara. And do you know what Vivian's doing this very instant over there in the corner? She's inviting her to spend a fortnight over at our place. If she comes,— well, that means the engagement will be announced at once."

Sara did not marvel at his assurance in the face of what had gone before. She knew him too well. In spite of the original rebuff, he was thoroughly satisfied in his own mind that Hetty Castleton would not be such a fool as to refuse him the second time.

"It is barely possible, Leslie," she said, "that she may consider Brandon Booth quite as good a catch as you, and infinitely better looking at the present moment."

"It's this beastly sunburn," he lamented, rubbing his nose gently, thinking first of his person. An instant later he was thinking of the other half of the declaration. "That's just what I've been afraid of," he said. "I told you what would happen if that portrait nonsense went on for ever. It's your fault, Sara."

" But I have reason to believe she will not accept him, if it goes so far as that. You are quite safe in that direction."

" 'Gad, I'd hate to risk it," he muttered. " I have a feeling she's in love with him."

Vivian approached. " Sara, you must let me have Miss Castleton for the first two weeks in July," she said serenely.

" I can't do it, Vivian," said the other promptly. " I can't bear the thought of being alone in this big old barn of a place. Nice of you to want her, but —"

" Oh, don't be selfish, Sara," cried Vivian.

" You don't know how much I depend on her," said Sara.

" I'd ask you over, too, dear, if there weren't so many others coming. I don't know where we're going to put them. You understand, don't you? "

" Perfectly," said her sister-in-law, smiling.

" But I've been counting on — Hetty."

" I say, Sara," broke in Leslie, " you *could* go up to Bar Harbour with the Williamsons at that time. Tell her about the invitation, Vivie."

" It isn't necessary," said Sara coldly. " I scarcely know the Williamsons." She hesitated an instant and then went on with sardonic dismay: " They're in trade, you know."

" That's nothing against 'em," protested he. "Awfully jolly people — really ripping. Ain't they, Viv? "

" I don't know them well enough to say," said Vivian, turning away. " I only know we're all snobs of the worst sort."

" Just a minute, Viv," he called out. " What does

Miss Castleton say about coming?" It was an eager question. Much depended on the reply.

"I haven't asked her," said his sister succinctly. "How could I, without first consulting Sara?"

"Then, you don't intend to ask her?"

"Certainly not."

"Oh, I'll fix it up with Sara," said he confidently. "Eh, Sara?"

"I'd suggest that you 'fix it up' with Miss Castleton," said Sara pointedly.

Vivian shot a swift glance over her shoulder at her sister-in-law, and then broke into a good-humoured laugh. She joined Hetty and Mrs. Redmond Wrandall.

"Sometimes I feel that I really like Vivian," observed Sara, as much to herself as to Leslie. "She's above the board, at least."

"Disagreeable as the devil at times, though," said he, biting his lip.

After the Wrandalls had departed, Sara took Hetty off to her room. The girl knew what was coming.

"Hetty," said the older woman, facing her after she had closed the door of her boudoir, "what is going on between you and Brandon Booth? I must have the truth. Are you doing anything foolish?"

"Foolish? Heaven help me, no! It — it is a tragedy," cried Hetty, meeting her gaze with one of utter despair.

"What has happened? Tell me!"

"What am I to do, Sara darling? He — he has told me that he — he —"

"Loves you?"

"Yes."

"And you have told him that his love is returned?"

" I couldn't help it. I was carried away. I did not mean to let him see that I —"

" You are such a novice in the business of love," said Sara sneeringly. " You are in the habit of being carried away, I fear."

" Oh, Sara! "

" You must put a stop to all this at once. How can you think of marrying him, Hetty Glynn? Send him —"

" I do not intend to marry him," said the girl, suddenly calm and dignified.

" I am to draw but one conclusion, I suppose," said the other, regarding the girl intently.

" What do you mean? "

" Is it necessary to ask that question? "

The puzzled expression remained in the girl's eyes for a time, and then slowly gave way to one of absolute horror.

" How dare you suggest such a thing? " she cried, turning pale, then crimson. " How dare you? "

Sara laughed shortly. " Isn't the inference a natural one? You are forgetting yourself."

" I understand," said the girl, through pallid lips. Her eyes were dark with pain and misery. " You think I am altogether bad." She drooped perceptibly.

" You went to Burton's Inn," sententiously.

" But, Sara, you must believe me. I did not know he was — married. For God's sake, do me the justice to —"

" But you went there with him," insisted the other, her eyes hard as steel. " It doesn't matter whether he was married — or free. You *went*."

Hetty threw herself upon her companion's breast and wound her strong young arms about her.

" Sara, Sara, you must let me explain — you must let me tell you everything. Don't stop me! You have refused to hear my plea —"

" And I still refuse!" cried Sara, throwing her off angrily. "Good God, do you think I will listen to you? If you utter another word, I will — strangle you!"

Hetty shrank back, terrified. Slowly she moved backward in the direction of the door, never taking her eyes from the impassioned face of her protector.

" Don't, Sara, please don't!" she begged. "Don't look at me like that! I promise — I promise. Forgive me! I would not give you an instant's pain for all the world. You would suffer, you would —"

Sara suddenly put her hands over her eyes. A single moan escaped her lips — a hoarse gasp of pain.

" Dearest!" cried Hetty, springing to her side.

Sara threw her head up and met her with a cold, repelling look.

" Wait!" she commanded. "The time has come when you should know what is in my mind, and has been for months and months. It concerns you. I expect you to marry Leslie Wrandall."

Hetty stopped short.

" How can you jest with me, Sara?" she cried, suddenly indignant.

" I am not jesting," said Sara levelly.

" You — you — really mean — what you have just said?" The puzzled look gave way to one of revulsion. A great shudder swept over her.

" Leslie Wrandall must pay his brother's debt to you."

" My God!" fell from the girl's stiff lips. "You — you must be going mad — mad!"

Sara laughed softly. "I have meant it almost from the beginning," she said. "It came to my mind the day that Challis was buried. It has never been out of it for an instant since that day. Now you understand."

If she expected Hetty to fall into a fit of weeping, to collapse, to plead with her for mercy, she was soon to find herself mistaken. The girl straightened up suddenly and met her gaze with one in which there was the fierce determination. Her eyes were steady, her bosom heaved.

"And I have loved you so devotedly — so blindly," she said, in low tones of scorn. "You have been hating me all these months while I thought you were loving me. What a fool I have been! I might have known. You *couldn't* love me."

"When Leslie asks you to-night to marry him, you are to say that you will do so," said Sara, betraying no sign of having heard the bitter words.

"I shall refuse, Sara," said Hetty, every vestige of colour gone from her face.

"There is an alternative," announced the other deliberately.

"You will expose me to — him? To his family?"

"I shall turn you over to them, to let them do what they will with you. If you go as his wife, the secret is safe. If not, they may have you as you really are, to destroy, to annihilate. Take your choice, my dear."

"And you, Sara?" asked the girl quietly. "What explanation will you have to offer for all these months of protection?"

Her companion stared. "Has the prospect no terror for you?"

" Not now. Not since I have found you out. The
thing I have feared all along has come to pass. I am
relieved, now that you show me just where I truly
stand. But, I asked: what of you? "

" The world is more likely to applaud than to curse
me, Hetty. It likes a new sensation. My change of
heart will appear quite natural."

" Are you sure that the world will applaud your
real design? You hate the Wrandalls. Will they be
charitable toward you when the truth is given out?
Will Leslie applaud you? Listen, please: I am trying to save you from yourself, Sara. You will fail
in everything you have hoped for. You will be more
accursed than I. The world will pity me, it may even
forgive me. It will listen to my story, which is more
than you will do, and it will believe me. Ah, I am
not afraid now. At first I was in terror. I had no
hope of escape. All that is past. To-day I am
ready to take my chances with the big, generous world.
Men will try me, and men are not made of stone and
steel. They punish but they do not avenge when they
sit in jury boxes. They are not women! Good God,
Sara, is there a man living to-day who could have
planned this thing you have cherished all these
months? Not one! And all men will curse you for
it, even though they send me to prison or to the —
chair. But they will not condemn me. They will hear
my story and they will set me free. And then, what
of you? "

Sara stood perfectly rigid, regarding this earnest
reasoner with growing wonder.

" My dear," she said, " you would better be thinking of yourself, not of me."

" Why, when I tell my story, the world will hate

you, Sara Wrandall. You have helped me, you have been good to me, no matter what sinister motive you may have had in doing so. It is my turn to help you."

"To help me!" cried Sara, astonished in spite of herself.

"Yes. To save you from execration — and even worse."

"There is no moral wrong in marriage with Leslie Wrandall," said Sara, returning to her own project.

"No moral wrong!" cried Hetty, aghast. "No, I suppose not," she went on, a moment later. "It is something much deeper, much blacker than moral wrong. There is no word for it. And if I marry him, what then? Wherein lies your triumph? You can't mean that — God in Heaven! You would not go to them with the truth when it was too late for him to — to cast me off!"

"I am no such fool as that. The secret would be for ever safe in that event. My triumph, as you call it, we will not discuss."

"How you must hate me, to be willing to do such an infamous thing to me!"

"I do not hate you, Hetty."

"In heaven's name, what do you call it?"

"Justification. Listen to me now. I am saying this for your good sense to seize and appreciate. Would it be right in me to allow you to marry any other man, knowing all that I know? There is but one man you can in justice marry: the one who can repair the wreck that his own blood created. Not Brandon Booth, nor any man save Leslie Wrandall. He is the man who must pay."

"I do not intend to marry," said Hetty.

"But Leslie will marry some one, and I intend that it shall be you. He shall marry the ex-chorus girl, the artist's model, the — the prostitute! Wait! Don't fly at me like that! Don't assume that look of virtuous horror! Let me say what I have to say. This much of your story shall they know, and no more. They will be proud of you!"

Hetty's eyes were blazing. "You use that name — you call me *that* — and yet you have kissed me, caressed me — loved me!" she cried hoarse with passion.

"He will ask you to-night for the second time. You will accept him. That is all."

"You must take back what you have just said to me — of me,— Sara Wrandall. You must unsay it! You must beg my pardon for *that!*"

"I draw no line between mistress and prostitute."

"But I —"

"Enough!"

"You wrong me vilely! You must let me —"

"I have an excellent memory, and it serves me well."

Hetty suddenly threw herself upon the couch and buried her face in her arms. Great sobs shook her slender frame.

Sara stood over her and watched for a long time with pitiless eyes. Then a queer, uneasy, wondering light began to develop in those dark, ominous eyes. She leaned forward the better to listen to the choked, inarticulate words that were pouring from the girl's lips. At last, moved by some power she could not have accounted for, she knelt beside the quivering body, and laid her hand, almost timorously, upon the girl's shoulder.

"Hetty,— Hetty, if I have wronged you in — in thinking that of you,— I — I —" she began brokenly.

Then she lifted her eyes, and the harsh light tried to steal back into them. "No, no! What am I saying? What a fool I am to give way —"

"You have wronged me — terribly, terribly!" came in smothered tones from the cushions. "I did not dream you thought that of me."

"What was I to think?"

Hetty lifted her head and cried out: "You would not let me speak! You refused to hear my story. You have been thinking this of me all along, holding it against me, damning me with it, and I have been closer to you than — My God, what manner of woman are you?"

Sara seized her hands and held them in a fierce, tense grip. Her eyes were glowing with a strange fire.

"Tell me — tell me now, on your soul, Hetty;—I were you — were you —"

"No! No! On my soul, no!"

"Look into my eyes!"

The girl's eyes did not falter. She met the dark, penetrating gaze of the other and, though dimmed by tears, her blue eyes were steadfast and resolute. Sara seemed to be searching the very soul of her, the soul that laid itself bare, denuded of every vestige of guile.

"I — I think I believe you," came slowly from the lips of the searcher. "You are looking the truth. I can see it. Hetty, Hetty, I — I don't understand myself. It is so — so overwhelming, so tremendous. It is so incredible. Am I really believing you? Is it possible that I have been wrong in —"

"Let me tell you everything," cried the girl, suddenly throwing her arms about her.

"Not now! Wait! Give me time to think. Go away now. I want to be alone." She arose and

pushed the girl toward the door. Her eyes were fixed
on her in a wondering, puzzled sort of way, and she
was shaking her head as if trying to discredit the
new emotion that had come to displace the one created ages ago.

Slowly Hetty Castleton retreated toward the door.
With her hand on the knob, she paused.

"After what has happened, Sara, you must not expect me to stay with you any longer. I cannot. You
may give me up to the law, but —"

Some one was tapping gently on the door.

"Shall I see who it is?" asked the girl, after a
long period of silence.

"Yes."

It was Murray. "Mr. Leslie has returned, Miss
Castleton, and asks if he may see you at once. He
says it is very important."

"Tell him I will be down in a few minutes, Murray."

After the door closed, she waited until the footman's
steps died away on the stairs.

"I shall say no to him, Sara, and I shall say to
him that you will tell him why I cannot be his wife.
Do you understand? Are you listening to me?"

Sara turned away without a word or look of response.

Hetty quietly opened the door and went out.

CHAPTER XVI

Booth trudged rapidly homeward after leaving Hetty at the lodge. He was throbbing all over with the love of her. The thrill of conquest was in his blood. She had raised a mysterious barrier; all the more zest to the inevitable victory that would be his. He would delight in overcoming obstacles — the bigger the better,— for his heart was valiant and the prize no smaller than those which the ancient knights went out to battle for in the lists of love. He had held her in his arms, he had kissed her, he had breathed of her fragrant hair, he had felt the beating of her frightened heart against his body. With the memory of all this to lift him to the heights of divine exaltation, he was unable to conjure up a finer triumph than the winning of her after the manner of the knights of old, to whom opposition was life, denial a boon.

It was enough for the present to know that she loved him.

What if she were Hetty Glynn? What if she had been an artist's model? The look he had had into the soul of her through those pure blue eyes was all-convincing. She was worthy of the noblest love.

After luncheon — served with some exasperation by Patrick an hour and a half later than usual — he smoked his pipe on the porch and stared reminiscently at the shifting clouds above the tree-tops, and with a tenderness about the lips that must have surprised and gratified the stubby, ill-used brier, inanimate confederate in many a lofty plot. He recalled

all she had said to him in that sylvan confessional,
and was content. His family? Pooh! He had a soul
of his own. It needed its mate.

He did not see the Wrandall motor at his garden
gate until a lusty voice brought him down from the
clouds into the range of earthly sounds. Then he
dashed out to the gate, bareheaded and coatless, forgetting that he had been sitting in the obscurity of
trailing vines and purple blossoms the while he thought
of her.

Leslie was sitting on the wide seat between his
mother and sister.

"Glad to see you back, old man," said Booth; reaching in to shake hands with him. "Day early, aren't
you? Good-afternoon, Mrs. Wrandall. Won't you
come in?"

He looked at Vivian as he gave the invitation.

"No, thanks," she replied. "Won't you come to
dinner this evening?"

He hesitated. "I'm not quite sure whether I can,
Vivian. I've got a half-way sort of —"

"Oh, do, old chap," cut in Leslie, more as a command than an entreaty. "Sorry I can't be there myself, but you'll fare quite as well without me. I'm
dining at Sara's. Wants my private ear about one
thing and another — see what I mean?"

"We shall expect you, Brandon," said Mrs. Wran
dall, fixing him with her lorgnette.

"I'll come, thank you," said he.

He felt disgustingly transparent under that inquisi-
tive glass.

Wrandall stepped out of the car. "I'll stop off for
a chat with Brandy, mother."

"Shall I send the car back, dear?"

"Never mind. I'll walk down."

The two men turned in at the gate as the car sped away.

"Well," said Booth, "it's good to see you. Pat!" He called through a basement window. "Come up and take the gentleman's order."

"No drink for me, Brandy. I've been in the temperance State of Maine for two weeks. One week more of it and I'd have been completely pickled. I shall always remember Maine." He dropped into a broad wicker chair and felt tenderly of his nose. "'Gad, I'm not quite sure that the sun did it, old man. It was dreadful."

Booth grinned. "Do any fishing?"

"Yes. The first day. Oh, you needn't look at me like that. I'm back in the narrow path." After a moment of painful reflection, he added, "We didn't see water after the first day. I'm just beginning to get used to the taste of it again."

"Never mind, Pat," said Booth, as the servant appeared in the doorway. "Mr. Wrandall is not suffering."

"You know I'm not a drinking man," declared Leslie, a pathetic note of appeal in his voice. "I hate the stuff."

"It is a good thing to let alone."

"And don't I let it alone? You never saw me tight in your life."

Booth sat down on the porch rail, hooked his toes in the supports and proceeded to fill his pipe. Then he struck a match and applied it, Leslie watching him with moody eyes.

"How do you like the portrait, old man?" he inquired between punctuating puffs.

"It's bully. Sargent never did anything finer. Ripping."

"I owe it all to you, Les."

"To me?"

"You induced her to sit to me."

"So I did," said Leslie sourly. "I was Mr. Fix-it sure enough." He allowed a short interval to elapse before taking the plunge. "I suppose, old chap, if I should happen to need your valuable services as best man in the near future, you'd not disappoint me?"

Booth eyed him quizzically. "I trust you're not throwing yourself away, Les," he said drily. "I mean to say, on some one — well, some one not quite up to the mark."

Leslie regarded him with some severity. "Of course not, old chap. What the devil put that into your head?"

"I thought that possibly you'd been making a chump of yourself up in the Maine woods."

"Piffle! Don't be an ass. What's the sense pretending you don't know who she is?"

"I suppose it's Hetty Castleton," said Booth, puffing away at his pipe.

"Who else?"

"Think she'll have you, old man?" asked Booth, after a moment.

"I don't know," replied the other, a bit dashed. "You might wish me luck, though."

Booth knocked the burnt tobacco from the bowl of his pipe. A serious line appeared between his eyes. He was a fair-minded fellow, without guile, without a single treacherous instinct.

"I can't wish you luck, Les," he said slowly. "You see I'm — I'm in love with her myself."

"The devil!" Leslie sat bolt upright and glared at him. "I might have known! And — and is *she* in love with you?"

"My dear fellow, you reveal considerable lack of tact in asking that question."

"What I want to know is this," exclaimed Wrandall, very pale but very hot: "is she going to marry you?"

Booth smiled. "I'll be perfectly frank with you. She says she won't."

Leslie gulped. "So you've asked her?"

"Obviously."

"And she said she wouldn't? She refused you? Turned you down?" His little moustache shot up at the ends and a joyous, triumphant laugh broke from his lips. "Oh, this is rich! Ha, ha! Turned you down, eh? Poor old Brandy! You're my best friend, and dammit I'm sorry. I mean to say," he went on in some embarrassment, "I'm sorry for you. Of course, you can hardly expect me to — er —"

"Certainly not," accepted Booth amiably. "I quite understand."

"Then, since she's refused you, you might wish *me* better luck."

"That would mean giving up hope."

"Hope?" exclaimed Leslie quickly. "You don't mean to say you'll annoy her with your —"

"No, I shall not annoy her," replied his friend, shaking his head.

"Well, I should hope not," said Leslie with a scowl. "Turned you down, eh? 'Pon my soul!" He appeared to be relishing the idea of it. "Sorry, old chap, but I suppose you understand just what that means."

Booth's lips hardened for an instant, then relaxed into a queer, almost pitying smile.

"And you want me to be your best man?" he said reflectively.

Leslie arose. His chest seemed to swell a little; assuredly he was breathing much easier. He assumed an air of compassion.

"I shan't insist, old fellow, if you feel you'd rather not — er — See what I mean?" It then occurred to him to utter a word or two of kindly advice. "I shouldn't go on hoping if I were you, Brandy. 'Pon my soul, I shouldn't. Take it like a man. I know it hurts but — Pooh! What's the use aggravating the pain by butting against a stone wall?"

His companion looked out over the tree-tops, his hands in his trouser pockets, and it must be confessed that his manner was not that of one who is oppressed by despair.

"I think I'm taking it like a man, Les," he said. "I only hope you'll take it as nicely if she says nay to you."

An uneasy look leaped into Leslie's face. He seemed noticeably less corpulent about the chest. He wondered if Booth knew anything about his initial venture. A question rose to his lips, but he thought quickly and held it back. Instead, he glanced at his watch.

"I must be off. See you to-morrow, I hope."

"So long," said Booth, stopping at the top of the steps while his visitor skipped down to the gate with a nimbleness that suggested the formation of a sudden resolve.

Leslie did not waste time in parting inanities; he strode off briskly in the direction of home, but not without a furtive glance out of the tail of his eye as he disappeared beyond the hedge-row at the end of Booth's garden. That gentleman was standing where he had left him, and was filling his pipe once more.

The day was warm, and Leslie was in a dripping perspiration when he reached home. He did not enter the house but made his way direct to the garage.

"Get out the car at once, Brown," was his order.

Three minutes later he was being driven over the lower road toward Southlook, taking good care to avoid Booth's place by the matter of a mile or more. He was in a fever of hope and eagerness. It was very plain to him why she had refused to marry Booth. The iron was hot. He didn't intend to lose any time in striking.

And now we know why he came again to Sara's in the middle of a blazing afternoon, instead of waiting until the more seductive shades of night had fallen, when the moon sat serene in the seat of the Mighty.

.   .   .   .   .   .

He didn't have to wait long for Hetty. Up to the instant of her appearance in the door, he had revelled in the thought that the way was now paved with roses. But with her entrance, he felt his confidence and courage slipping. Perhaps that may explain the abruptness with which he proceeded to go about the business in hand.

"I couldn't wait till to-night," he explained as she came slowly across the room toward him. She was half way to him before he awoke to the fact that he was standing perfectly still. Then he started forward, somehow impelled to meet her at least halfway. "You'll forgive me, Hetty, if I have disturbed you."

"I was not lying down, Mr. Wrandall," she said quietly. There was nothing ominous in the words, but he experienced a sudden sensation of cold. "Won't you sit down? Or would you rather go out to the terrace?"

"It's much more comfortable here, if you don't mind. I — I suppose you know what it is I want to say to you. You —"

"Yes," she interrupted wearily; "and knowing as much, Mr. Wrandall, it would not be fair of me to let you go on."

"Not fair?" he said, in honest amazement. "But, my dear, I —"

"Please, Mr. Wrandall," she exclaimed, with a pleading little smile that would have touched the heart of any one but Leslie. "Please don't go on. It is quite as impossible now as it was before. I have not changed."

He could only say, mechanically: "You haven't?"

"No. I am sorry if you have thought that I might come to —"

"Think, for heaven's sake, think what you are doing!" he cried, feeling for the edge of the table with a support-seeking hand. "I — I had Sara's word that you were not —"

"Unfortunately Sara cannot speak for me in a matter of this kind. Thank you for the honour you would —"

"Honour be hanged!" he blurted out, losing his temper. "I love you! It's a purely selfish thing with me, and I'm blowed if I consider it an honour to be refused by any woman. I —"

"Mr. Wrandall!" she cried, fixing him with her flashing, indignant eyes. "You are forgetting yourself." She was standing very straight and slim and imperious before him.

He quailed. " I — I beg your pardon. I — I —"

" There is nothing more to be said," she went on icily. " Good-bye."

" Would you mind telling me whether there is any one else? " he asked, as he turned toward the door.

" Do you really feel that you have the right to ask that question, Mr. Wrandall? "

He wet his lips with his tongue. " Then, there *is* some one!" he cried, rapping the table with his knuckles. He didn't realise till afterward how vigorously he rapped. " Some confounded English nobody, I suppose."

She smiled, not unkindly. " There is no English nobody, if that answers your question."

" Then, will you be kind enough to offer a reason for not giving me a fair chance in a clear field? I think it's due —"

" Can't you see how you are distressing me? Must I again go through that horrid scene in the garden? Can't you take a plain no for an answer? "

" Good Lord! " he gasped, and in those two words he revealed the complete overturning of a life-long estimate of himself. It seemed to take more than his breath away.

" Good-bye," she said with finality.

He stared at the door through which she disappeared, his hopes, his conceit, his self-regard trailing after her with shameless disloyalty to the standards he had set for them, and then, with a rather ghastly smile of self-commiseration on his lips, he slipped out of the house, jumped into the motor car, and gave a brief but explicit command to the chauffeur, who lost

no time in assisting his master to turn tail in igno-
minious flight.

Hetty was gloomily but resolutely employed in laying out certain of her personal belongings, prepara-
tory to packing them for departure, when Sara entered
her room.

They regarded each other steadily, questioningly
for a short space of time.

"Leslie has just called up to ask 'what the devil' I
meant by letting him make a fool of himself," said
Sara, with a peculiar little twisted smile on her lips.

Hetty offered no comment, but after a moment
gravely and rather wistfully called attention to her
present occupation by a significant flaunt of her hand
and a saddened smile.

"I see," said Sara, without emotion. "If you
choose to go, Hetty, I shall not oppose you."

"My position here is a false one, Sara. I prefer
to go."

"This morning I should have held a sword over
your head."

"It is very difficult for me to realise all that has
happened."

"You are free to depart. You are free in every
sense of the word. Your future rests with yourself,
my dear."

"It hurts me more than I can tell to feel that you
have been hating me all these months."

"It hurts me — now."

Hetty walked to the window and looked out.

"What are your plans?" Sara inquired, after an
interval.

"I shall seek employment — and wait for you to
act."

" I? You mean? "

" I shall not run away, Sara. Nor do I intend to reveal myself to the authorities. I am not morally guilty of crime. A year ago I feared the consequences of my deed, but I have learned much since then. I was a stranger in a new world. In England we have been led to believe that you lynch women here as readily as you lynch men. I now know better than that. From you alone I learned my greatest lesson. You revealed to me the true meaning of human kindness. You shielded me who should not. Even now I believe that your first impulse was a tender one. I shall not forget it, Sara. You will live to regret the baser thought that came later on. I have loved you — yes, almost as a good dog loves his master. It is not for me to tell the story of that night and all these months to the world. I would not be betraying myself, but you. You would be called upon to explain, not I. And you would be the one to suffer. When you met me on the road that night I was on my way back to the inn to give myself into custody. You have made it impossible for me to do so now. My lips are sealed. It rests with you, Sara."

Sara joined her in the broad window. There was a strangely exalted look in her face. A gilded birdcage hung suspended in the casement. Without a word, she threw open the window screen. The gay little canary in the gilded cage cocked his head and watched her with alert eyes. Then she reached up and gently removed the cage from its fastenings. Putting it down upon the window sill, she opened the tiny door. The bird hopped about his prison in a state of great excitement.

Hetty looked on, fascinated.

At last a yellow streak shot out through the open door and an instant later resolved itself into the bobbing, fluttering dicky-bird that had lived in a cage all its life without an hour of freedom. For a few seconds it circled over the tree-tops and then alighted on one of the branches. One might well have imagined that he could hear its tiny heart beating with terror. Its wings were half-raised and fluttering, its head jerking from side to side in wild perturbation. Taking courage, Master Dicky hopped timorously to a nearby twig, and then ventured a flight to a tree-top nearer the window casement. Perched in its topmost branches he cheeped shrilly, as if there was fear in his little breast.

In silence the two women in the window watched the agitated movements of the bird. The same thought was in the mind of each, the same question, the same intense wish.

A brown thrush sped through the air, close by the timid canary. Like a flash it dropped to the twigs lower down, its wings palpitating in violent alarm.

"Dicky!" called Sara Wrandall, and then cheeped between her teeth.

A moment later Dicky was fluttering about the eaves; his circles grew smaller, his winging less rhythmic, till at last with a nervous little flutter he perched on the top of the window shutter, so near that they might have reached to him with their hands. He sat there with his head cocked to one side.

"Dicky!" called Sara again. This time she held out her finger. For some time he regarded it with indifference, not to say disfavour. Then he took one more flight, but much shorter than the first, bringing up again at the shutter-top. A second later he hopped down and his little talons gripped Sara's finger with an earnestness that left no room for doubt.

She lowered her hand until it was even with the open door of the gilded cage. He shot inside with a whir that suggested a scramble. With his wings folded, he sat on his little trapeze and cheeped. She closed and fastened the door, and then turned to Hetty.

"My symbol," she said softly.

There were tears in Hetty's eyes.

.   .   .   .   .   .

Leslie did not turn up at his father's place in the High Street that night until Booth was safely out of the way. He spent a dismal evening at the boat club.

His father and mother were in the library when he came in at half-past ten. From a dark corner of the garden he had witnessed Booth's early departure. Vivian had gone down to the gate in the low-lying hedge with her visitor. She came in a moment after Leslie's entrance.

"Hello, Les," she said, bending an inquiring eye upon him. "Isn't this early for you?"

Her brother was standing near the fireplace.

"There's a heavy dew falling, Mater," he said gruffly. "Shan't I touch a match to the kindling?"

His mother came over to him quickly, and laid her hand on his arm.

"Your coat is damp," she said anxiously. "Yes, light the fire."

"It's very warm in this room," said Mr. Wrandall, looking up from his book. They were always doing something for Leslie's comfort.

No one seemed to notice him. Leslie knelt and struck a match.

"Well?" said Vivian.

"Well what?" he demanded without looking up.

His sister took a moment for thought. "Is Hetty coming to stay with us in July?"

He stood erect, first rubbing his knee to dislodge the dust,— then his palms.

"No, she isn't coming," he said. He drew a very long breath — the first in several hours — and then expelled it vocally. "She has refused to marry me."

Mr. Wrandall turned a leaf in his book; it sounded like the crack of doom, so still had the room become.

Vivian had the forethought to push a chair toward her mother. It was a most timely act on her part, for Mrs. Wrandall sat down very abruptly and very limply.

"She — *what?*" gasped Leslie's mother.

"Turned me down — cold," said Leslie briefly.

Mr. Wrandall laid his book on the table without thinking to put the bookmark in place. Then he arose and removed his glasses, fumbling for the case.

"She — she — *what?*" he demanded.

"Sacked me," replied his son.

"Please do not jest with me, Leslie," said his mother, trying to smile.

"He isn't joking, mother," said Vivian, with a shrug of her fine shoulders.

"He — he *must* be," cried Mrs. Wrandall impatiently. "What did she *really* say, Leslie?"

"The only thing I remember was ' good-bye,'" said he, and then blew his nose violently.

"Poor old Les!" said Vivian, with real feeling.

"It was Sara Gooch's doing!" exclaimed Mrs. Wrandall, getting her breath at last.

"Nonsense," said Mr. Wrandall, picking up his book once more and turning to the place where the bookmark lay, after which he proceeded to re-read four or five pages before discovering his error.

No one spoke for a matter of five minutes or more. Then Mrs. Wrandall got up, went over to the library table and closed with a snap the bulky blue book with the limp leather cover, saying as she held it up to let him see that it was the privately printed history of the Murgatroyd family:

"It came by post this evening from London. She is merely a fourth cousin, my son."

He looked up with a gleam of interest in his eye.

CHAPTER XVII

CROSSING THE CHANNEL

BOOTH, restless with a vague uneasiness that had come over him during the night, keeping him awake until nearly dawn, was hard put during the early hours of the forenoon to find occupation for his interest until a seasonable time arrived for appearing at South-look. He was unable to account for this feeling of uncertainty and irritation.

At nine he set out to walk over to Southlook, realising that he should have to spend an hour in profitless gossip with the lodge-keeper before presenting himself at the villa, but somehow relishing the thought that even so he would be nearer to Hetty than if he remained in his own door-yard.

Half-way there he was overtaken by Sara's big French machine returning from the village. The car came to a standstill as he stepped aside to let it pass, and Sara herself leaned over and cordially invited him to get in and ride home with her.

"What an early bird you are," he exclaimed as he took his seat beside her.

She was not in a mood for airy persiflage, as he soon discovered.

"Miss Castleton has gone up to town, Mr. Booth," she said rather lifelessly. "I have just taken her to the station. She caught the eight-thirty."

He was at once solicitous. "No bad news, I hope?" There was no thought in his mind that her absence was other than temporary.

"She is not coming back, Brandon." She had not addressed him as Brandon before.

He stared. "You — you mean —" The words died on his lips.

"She is not coming back," she repeated.

An accusing gleam leaped into his eyes.

"What has happened, Mrs. Wrandall?" he asked. She was quick to perceive the change in his voice and manner.

"She prefers to live apart from me. That is all."

"When was this decision reached?"

"But yesterday. Soon after she came in from her walk with you."

"Do — do you mean to imply that *that* had anything to do with her leaving your home?" he demanded, with a flush on his cheek.

She met his look without flinching. "It was the beginning."

"You — you criticised her? You took her to task —"

"I notified her that she was to marry Leslie Wrandall, if she marries any one at all," she said in a perfectly level tone.

"Good Lord, Mrs. Wrandall!"

"But she is not going to marry Leslie."

"I know it — I knew it yesterday," he cried triumphantly. "She loves me, Sara. Didn't she say as much to you?"

"Yes, Brandon, she loves you. But she will not be your wife."

"What is all this mystery? Why can't she be my wife? What is there to prevent?"

She regarded him with dark, inscrutable eyes. Many seconds passed before she spoke.

"Would you want her for your wife if you knew she had belonged to another man?"

He turned very cold. The palms of his hands were wet, as with ice-water. Something dark seemed to flit before his eyes.

"I will not believe that of her," he said, shaking his head with an air of finality.

"That is not an answer to my question."

"Yes, I would still want her," he declared steadily.

"I merely meant to put you to the harshest test," she said, and there was relief in her voice. "She is a good girl, she is pure. I asked my question because until yesterday I had reason to doubt her."

"Good heavens, how could you doubt those honest, guiltless eyes of —"

She shook her head sadly. "To answer you I would have to reveal the secret that makes it impossible for her to become your wife, and that I cannot, will not do."

"Is it fair to me?"

"Perhaps not, but it is fair to her, and that is why I must remain silent."

"Before God, I shall know the truth,— from her, if not from you,— and —"

"If you love her, if you will be kind to her, you will let her go her way in peace."

He was struck by the somewhat sinister earnestness of her words.

"Tell me where I may find her," he said, setting his jaw.

"It will not be difficult for you to find her," she said, frowning, "if you insist on pursuing her."

"You drive her away from your house, Sara Wrandall, and yet expect me to believe that your motives are friendly. Why should I accept your word as final? "

" I did not drive her away, nor did I ask her to stay."

He stared hard at her.

" Good Lord, what is the meaning of all this? " he cried in perplexity. " What am I to understand? "

The car had come to a stop under the porte cochere. She laid her hand on his arm.

" If you will come in with me, Brandon, I will try to make some things clear to you."

He left in half-an-hour, walking rapidly down the drive, his coat buttoned closely, although the morning was hot and breathless. He held in his hand a small scrap of paper on which was written: " If I loved you less, I would come to you now and lie to you. If you love me, Brandon, you will let me go my way. It is the only course. Sara is my friend, and she is yours. Be guided by her, and believe in my love for you. Hetty."

.   .   .   .   .   .

And now, as things go in fairy stories, we should prepare ourselves to see Hetty pass through a season in drudgery and hardship, with the ultimate quintessence of joy as the reward for her trials and tribulations. Happily, this is not a fairy tale. There are some things more fantastic than fairy tales, if they are not spoiled in the telling. Hetty did not go forth to encounter drudgery, disdain and obloquy. By no manner of means! She went with a well-filled purse, a definite purpose ahead and a determined factor behind.

In a manner befitting her station as the intimate friend of Mrs. Challis Wrandall, as the cousin of the

Murgatroyds, as the daughter of Colonel Castleton of the Indian Corps, as a person supposed to be possessed of independent means withal, she went, with none to question, none to cavil.

Sara had insisted on this, as much for her own sake as for Hetty's; she argued, and she had prevailed in the end. What would the world think, what would their acquaintances think, and above all what would the high and mighty Wrandalls think if she went with meek and lowly mien?

Why should they make it possible for any one to look askance?

And so it was that she departed in state, with a dozen trunks and boxes; an obsequiously attended seat in the parlour-car was hers; a telegram in her bag assured her that rooms were being reserved for herself and maid at the Ritz-Carlton; alongside it reposed a letter to Mr. Carroll, instructing him to provide her with sufficient funds to carry out the plan agreed upon; and in the seat behind sat the lady's maid who had served her for a twelve-month and more.

The timely demise of the venerable Lord Murgatroyd afforded the most natural excuse for her trip to England. The old nobleman gave up the ghost, allowing for difference in time, at the very moment when Mrs. Redmond Wrandall was undoing a certain package from London, which turned out to be a complete history of what his forebears had done in the way of propagation since the fourteenth century.

Hetty did not find it easy to accommodate her pride to the plan which was to give her a fresh and rather imposing start in the world. She was to have a full year in which to determine whether she should accept toil and poverty as her lot, or emulate the symbolic

example of Dicky the canary bird. At the end of the
year, unless she did as Dicky had done, her source of
supplies would be automatically cut off and she would
be entirely dependent upon her own wits and resources. In the interim, she was a probationary person of leisure. It had required hours of persuasion
on the part of Sara Wrandall to bring her into line
with these arrangements.

"But I am able and willing to work for my living,"
had been Hetty's stubborn retort to all the arguments
brought to bear upon her.

"Then let me put it in another light. It is vital to
me, of course, that you should keep up the show of
affluence for a while at least. I think I have made
that clear to you. But here is another side to the matter; the question of recompense."

"Recompense?" cried Hetty sharply.

"Without your knowing it, I have virtually held
you a prisoner all these months, condemned in my own
judgment if not in the sight of the law. I have taken
the law unto myself. You were not convicted of murder in this unitarian court of mine, but of another sin.
For fifteen months you have been living under the
shadow of a crime you did not commit. I was reserv-
ing complete punishment for you in the shape of an
ignoble marriage, which was to have served two bitter
ends. Well, I have had the truth from you. I believe you to be absolutely innocent of the charge I
held over you, for which I condemned you without a
hearing. Then, why should I not employ my own
means of making restitution?"

"You have condescended to believe in me. That
is all I ask."

"True, that is all you ask. But is it altogether

the fair way out of it? To illustrate: our criminal laws are less kind to the innocent than to the guilty. Our law courts find a man guilty and he is sent to prison. Later on, he is found to be innocent — absolutely innocent. What does the State do in the premises? It issues a formal pardon,— a mockery, pure and simple,— and the man is set free. It all comes to a curt, belated apology for an error on the part of justice. No substantial recompense is offered. He is merely pardoned for something he didn't do. The State, which has wronged him, condescends to pardon him! Think of it! It is the same as if a man knocked another down and then said, before he removed his foot from the victim's neck: 'I pardon you freely.' My father was opposed to the system we have — that all countries have — of pardoning men who have been unjustly condemned. The innocent victim is pardoned in the same manner as the guilty one who comes in for clemency. I accept my father's contention that an innocent man should not be shamed and humiliated by a *pardon*. The court which tried him should reopen the case and honourably *acquit* him of the crime. Then the State should pay to this innocent man, dollar for dollar, all that he might have earned during his term of imprisonment, with an additional amount for the suffering he has endured. Not long ago in an adjoining State a man, who had served seventeen years of a life sentence for murder, was found to be wholly innocent. What happened? A *pardon* was handed to him and he walked out of prison, broken in spirit, health and purse. His small fortune had been wiped out in the futile effort to prove his innocence. He gave up seventeen years of his life and then was *pardoned* for the sacrifice. He should have been paid for every day spent in prison. That was the very least they could have done."

"I see now what you mean," mused Hetty. "I have never thought of it in that way before."

"Well, it comes to this in our case, Hetty: I have tried you all over again in my own little court and I have acquitted you of the charge I had against you. I do not offer you a silly pardon. You must allow me to have my way in this matter, to choose my own means of compensating you for —"

"You saved my life," protested Hetty, shaking her head obstinately.

"My dear, I appreciate the fact that you are English," said Sara, with a weary smile, "but won't you *please* see the point?"

Then Hetty smiled too, and the way was easier after that for Sara. She gained her quixotic point, and Hetty went away from Southlook feeling that no woman in all the world was so bewildering as Sara Wrandall.

When she sailed for England, two days later, the newspapers announced that the beautiful and attractive Miss Castleton was returning to her native land on account of the death of Lord Murgatroyd, and would spend the year on the Continent, where probably she would be joined later on by Mrs. Wrandall, whose period of mourning and distress had been softened by the constant and loyal friendship of "this exquisite Englishwoman."

Four hundred miles out at sea, she was overtaken by wireless messages from three persons.

Brandon Booth's message said: "I am sailing tomorrow on a faster ship than yours. You will find me waiting for you on the landing stage." Her heart gave a leap to dizzy heights, and, try as she would, she could not crush it back to the depths in which it had dwelt for days.

The second bit of pale green paper contained a cry from a most unexpected source: "Cable your London address. S. refuses to give it to me. I think I understand the situation. We want to make amends for what you have had to put up with during the year. She has shown her true nature at last." It was signed "Leslie."

From Sara came these cryptic words: "For each year of famine there will come seven years of plenty."

All the way across the Atlantic she lived in a state of subdued excitement. Conflicting emotions absorbed her waking hours but her dreams were all of one complexion: rosy and warm and full of a joyousness that distressed her vastly when she recalled them to mind in the early morning hours. During the day she intermittently hoped and feared that he would be on the landing stage. In any event, she was bound to find unhappiness. If he were there her joy would be short-lived and blighting; if he were not there, her disappointment would be equally hard to bear.

He was there. She saw him from the deck of the tender as they edged up to the landing. His tall figure loomed in the front rank against the rail that held back the crowd; his sun-bronzed face wore a look of eager expectancy; from her obscured position in the shadow of the deck building, purposely chosen for reasons only too obvious, she could even detect the alert, swift-moving scrutiny that he fastened upon the crowd.

Later on, he stood looking down into her serious blue eyes; her hands were lying limp in his. His own eyes were dark with earnestness, with the restraint that had fastened itself upon him. Behind her stood the respectful but immeasurably awed maid, who could not, for the life of her, understand how a man could be on both sides of the Atlantic at one and the same time.

"Thank the Lord, Hetty, say I, for the five day boats," he was saying.

"You should not have come, Brandon," she cried softly, and the look of misery in her eyes was tinged with a glow she could not suppress. "It only makes everything harder for me. I — I — Oh, I wish you had not come!"

"But isn't it wonderful?" he cried, "that I should be here and waiting for you! It is almost inconceivable. And you were in the act of running away from me, too. Oh, I have that much of the tale from Sara, so don't look so hurt about it."

"I am so sorry you came," she repeated, her lip trembling.

Noting her emotion, he gave her hands a fierce, encouraging pressure and immediately released them.

"Come," he said gently; "I have booked for London. Everything is arranged. I shall see to your luggage. Let me put you in the carriage first."

As she sat in the railway carriage, waiting for him to return, she tried in a hundred ways to devise a means of escape, and yet she had never loved him so much as now. Her heart was sore, her desolation never so complete as now.

He came back at last and took his seat beside her in the compartment, fanning himself with his hat. The maid very discreetly stared out of the window at the hurrying throng of travellers on the platform. One other person occupied the compartment with them,

a crabbed Englishman who seemed to resent the fact
that his seat was not next the window, and that maids
should be encouraged to travel first class.

"Isn't it really wonderful?" whispered Booth once
more, quite as if he couldn't believe it himself. She
smiled rather doubtfully. He was sitting quite close
to her and leaning forward.

The Englishman got up and went into the corridor
to consult the conductor. One might have heard him
say he'd very much prefer going into another compartment where it wouldn't be necessary for him to
annoy a beastly American bride and groom — her
maid and perhaps later on his man — all the way up
to London.

"How I love you. Hetty — how I adore you!"
Booth whispered passionately.

"Oh, Brandon!"

"And I don't mean to give you up," he added, his
lean jaw setting hard.

"You must — oh, you must," she cried miserably.
"I mean it, Brandon —"

The Englishman came back and took his seat. He
glared at Booth through his eye-glass, and that young
gentleman sat up in sudden embarrassment.

"What are your plans?" asked he, turning his back
on their fellow-passenger.

"Please don't ask me," she pleaded. "You must
give it up, Brandon. Let me go my own way."

"Not until I have the whole story from you. You
see, I am not easily thwarted, once I set my heart on
a thing. I gathered this much from Sara: the obstacle is *not* insurmountable."

"She — said — that?"

"In effect, yes," he qualified.

"What did she tell you?" demanded Hetty, laying her hand on his arm.

"I will confess she didn't reveal the secret that you consider a barrier, but she went so far as to say that it was very dark and dreadful," he said lightly.   They were speaking in very low tones.   "When I pinned her down to it, she added that it did not in any sense bear upon your honour.   But there is time enough to talk about this later on.   For the present, let's not discuss the past.   I know enough of your history from your own lips as well as what little I could get out of Sara, to feel sure that you are, in a way, drifting.   I intend to look after you, at least until you find yourself.   Your sudden break with Sara has been explained to me.   Leslie Wrandall is at the back of it. Sara told me that she tried to force you to marry him. I think you did quite right in going away as you did, but, on the other hand, was it quite fair to me?"

"Yes, it was most fair," she said, compressing her lips.

He frowned.

"We can't possibly be of the same opinion," he said seriously.

"You wouldn't say that if you knew everything."

"How long do you intend to stay in London?"

"I don't know.   When does this train arrive there?"

"At four o'clock, I think.   Will you go to an hotel or to friends?"   He put the question very delicately.

She smiled faintly.   "You mean the Murgatroyds?"   .

"Your father is here, I am informed.   And you must have other friends or relatives who —"

"I shall go to a small hotel I know near Trafalgar

Square," she interrupted quietly. "You must not come there to see me, Brandon."

"I shall expect you to dine with me at — say Prince's this evening," was his response to this.

She shook her head and then turned to look out of the window. He sat back in his seat and for many miles, with deep perplexity in his eyes, studied her half-averted face. The old uneasiness returned. Was this obstacle, after all, so great that it could not be overcome?

They lunched together, but were singularly reserved all through the meal. A plan was growing in her brain, a cruel but effective plan that made her despise herself and yet contained the only means of escape from an even more cruel situation.

He drove with her from the station to the small hotel off Trafalgar Square. There were no rooms to be had. It was the week of Ascot and the city was still crowded with people who awaited only the royal sign to break the fetters that bound them to London. Somewhat perturbed, she allowed him to escort her to several hotels of a like character. Failing in each case, she was in despair. At last she plucked up the courage to say to him, not without constraint and embarrassment:

"I think, Brandon, if you were to allow me to apply *alone* to one of these places I could get in without much trouble."

"Good Lord!" he gasped, going very red with dismay. "What a fool I —"

"I'll try the Savoy," she said quickly, and then laughed at him. His face was the picture of distress.

"I shall come for you at eight," he said, stopping the taxi at once. "Good-bye till then."

He got out and gave directions to the chauffeur. Then he did a very strange thing. He hailed another taxi and, climbing in, started off in the wake of the two women. From a point of vantage near the corridor leading to the "American bar," he saw Hetty sign her slips and move off toward the lift. Whereupon, seeing that she was quite out of the way, he approached the manager's office and asked for accommodations.

"Nothing left, sir."

"Not a thing?"

"Everything has been taken for weeks, sir. I'm sorry."

"Sorry, too. I had hoped you might have something left for a friend who expects to stop here — a Miss Castleton."

"Miss Castleton has just applied. We could not give her anything."

"Eh?"

"Fortunately we could let her have rooms until eight this evening. We were more than pleased to offer them to her for a few hours, although they are reserved for parties coming down from Liverpool to-night."

Booth tried the Cecil and got a most undesirable room. Calling up the Savoy on the telephone, he got her room. The maid answered. She informed him that Miss Castleton had just that instant gone out and would not return before seven o'clock.

"I suppose she will not remove her trunks from the station until she finds a permanent place to lodge," he inquired. "Can I be of any service?"

"I think not, sir. She left no word, sir."

He hung up the receiver and straightway dashed

over to the Savoy, hoping to catch her before she left
the hotel.   Just inside the door he came to an abrupt
stop.   She was at the news and ticket booth in the
lobby, closely engaged in conversation with the clerk.
Presently the latter took up the telephone, and after
a brief conversation with some one at the other end,
turned to Hetty and nodded his head.   Whereupon
she nodded her own adorable head and began the
search for her purse.   Booth edged around to an obscure spot and saw her pay for and receive something
in return.

"By Jove!" he said to himself, amazed.

She passed near him, without seeing him, and went
out into the court.   He watched her turn into the
Strand.

When the night boat from Dover to Calais slipped
away from her moorings that evening, Hetty Castleton and her maid were on board, with all their bags
and trunks, and Brandon Booth was supposed to be
completely at sea in the heart of that glittering London-
town.

The night was fog-laden and dripping, and the
crossing promised to be unpleasant.   Wrapped in a
thick sea-ulster Hetty sat huddled up in the lea of
the deck-house, sick at heart and miserable.   She re-
proached herself for the scurvy trick she was playing
on him, reviled herself and yet pitied herself.   After
all, she was doing him a good turn in forcing him to
despise her for the shameless way in which she treated
his devotion, his fairness, his loyalty.   He would be
happier in the end for the brief spasm of pain and disgust he was to experience in this second revelation of
her unworthiness.

Crouching there in the shadow, with the foghorn

chortling hoarsely over the shabby trick,— so it seemed to her,—she stared back at the misty glow of the pier and tried to pierce the distance that lay between her and the lights o' London, so many leagues away. *He* was there, in the glitter and glamour of it all, but black with disappointment and wonder. Oh, it was a detestable thing she had done! Her poor heart ached for him. She could almost see the despair, the bewilderment in his honest eyes as he sat in his room, hours after the discovery of her flight, defeated, betrayed, disillusioned.

There were but few people crossing. Sailors stood by the rail, peering into the fog, but it seemed to her that no one else was afoot on board the steamer. Already the boat was beginning to show signs of the uneasy trip ahead. Many foghorns, far and near, were barking their lugubrious warnings; the choppy waves were slashing against the vessel with a steady beat; the bobbling of the ship increased as it plunged deeper into the cross-seas. But she had no thought of the ship, the channel or the perils that surrounded her. Her mind was back in London with her heart, and there was nothing ahead of her save the dread of tomorrow's sunlight.

She was a good sailor. A dozen times, perhaps, she had crossed the English Channel, in fair weather and foul, and never with discomfort. Her maid, she knew, was in for a wretched brawl with the waves, but Hetty was too wise a sailor to think of trying to comfort the unhappy creature. Misery does not always love company.

A tall man came shambling down the narrow space along the rail and stopped directly in front of her. She started in alarm as he reached out his hand to support himself against the deck house. As he leaned forward, he laughed.

"You were thinking of me, Hetty," said the man.

For a long time she stared at him, transfixed, and then, with a low moan, covered her eyes with her hands.

"Is it true — is it a dream?" she sobbed.

He dropped down beside her and gathered her in his strong, eager arms.

"You *were* thinking of me, weren't you? And reproaching yourself, and hating yourself for running away like this? I thought so. Well, you might just as well try to dodge the smartest detective in the world as to give me the slip now, darling."

"You — you spied on me?" she cried, in muffled tones. She lay very limp in his arms.

"I did," he confessed, without shame. "'Gad, when I think of what I might be doing at this moment if I hadn't found you out in time! Think of me back there in London, racing about like a madman, searching for you in every —"

"Please, please!" she implored.

"But luck was with me. You can't get away, Hetty. I shan't let you out of my sight again. I'll camp in front of your door and you'll see me wither and die of sleeplessness, for one or the other of my eyes will always be open."

"Oh, I am so tired, so miserable," she murmured.

"Poor little sweetheart!"

"I wish you would hate me."

"Lie where you are, dearest, and — forget!"

"If I only could — forget!"

"Rest. I will hold you tight and keep you warm. We're in for a nasty crossing, but it is paradise for me. I am mad with the delight of having you here, holding you close to me, feeling you in my arms. The wilder the night the better, for I am wild with the joy of it all. I love you! I love you!" He strained her closer to him in a sort of paroxysm.

She was quiet for a long time. Then she breathed into his ear:

"You will never know how much I was longing for you, just as you are now, Brandon, and in the midst of it all you came. It is like a fairy story, and oh, I shall always believe in fairies."

All about them were the sinister sounds of the fog — the hoots, the growls and groans of lost things in the swirl of the North Sea current, creeping blindly through the guideless mist. To both of them, the night had a strangely symbolic significance: whither were they drifting and where lay the unseen port?

A huge liner from one of the German ports slipped across their bows with hoarse blasts of warning. They saw the misty glow of her lights for an instant, and even as they drew the sharp breath of fear, the night resumed its mantle and their own little vessel seemed to come to life again after the shock of alarm and its engines throbbed the faster, just as the heart-beats quicken when reaction sets in.

A long time afterward the throbbing ceased, bell-buoys whistled and clanged about them; the sea suddenly grew calm and lifeless; they slid over it as if it were a quavering sheet of ice; and lights sneaked out of the fog and approached with stealthy swiftness. Bells rang below and above them, sailors sprang up from everywhere and calls were heard below; the rattling of chains and the thumping of heavy luggage took the place of that steady, monotonous beat of the engines. People began to infest the deck, limp and groaning, harassed but voiceless. A mighty sigh seemed to envelop the whole ship — a sigh of relief.

Then it was that these two arose stiffly from their sheltered bench and gave heed to the things that were about them.

The Channel was behind them.

CHAPTER XVIII

THEY journeyed to Paris by the night mail. He was waiting for her on the platform when she descended from the *wagon lit* in the Gare du Nord. Sleepy passengers crowded with them into the customs department. She, alone among them all, was smiling brightly, as if the world could be sweet at an hour when, by all odds, it should be sleepiest.

" I was up and on the lookout for you at Amiens," he declared, as they walked off together. " You might have got off there, you know," with a wry grin.

" I shall not run away from you again, Brandon," she said earnestly. " I promise, on my honour."

" By Jove," he cried, " that's a relief! " Then he broke into a happy laugh.

" I shall go to the Ritz," she said, after her effects had been examined and were ready for release.

" I thought so," he announced calmly. " I wired for rooms before I left London."

" Really, this is ridic —"

" Don't frown like that, Hetty," he pleaded.

As they rattled and bounced over the cobble-stones in a taxi-metre on the way to the Place Vendome, he devoted the whole of his conversation to the delicious breakfast they were to have, expatiating glibly on the wonderful berries that would come first in that always-to-be-remembered meal. She was ravenously hungry by the time they reached the hotel, just from listening to his dissertation on chops and rolls and coffee as they are served in Paris, to say nothing of waffles and honey and the marmalade that no Englishman can do without.

Alone in his room, however, he was quite another person. His calm assurance took flight the instant he closed the door and moodily began to prepare for his bath. Resolution was undiminished, but the facts in the case were most desolating. Whatever it was that stood between them, there was no gainsaying its power to influence their lives. It was no trifle that caused her to take this second flight, and the sooner he came to realise the seriousness of opposition the better.

He made up his mind on one point in that half-hour before breakfast: if she asked him again to let her go her way in peace, it was only fair to her and right that he should submit to the inevitable. She loved him, he was sure of it. Then there must be a very good reason for her perplexing attitude toward him. He would make one more attempt to have the truth from her. Failing in that, he would accept the situation as hopeless, for the time being at least. She should know that he loved her deeply enough for that.

She joined him in the little open-air café, and they sat down at a table in a remote corner. There were few people breakfasting. In her tender blue eyes there was a look of sadness that haunted him, even as she smiled and called him beloved.

"Hetty, darling," he said, leaning forward and laying his hand on hers, "can't you tell me what it is?"

She was prepared for the question. In her heart she knew the time had come when she must be fair with him. He observed the pallor that stole into her warm, smooth cheeks as she regarded him fixedly for a long time before replying.

" There is only one person in the world who can tell you, Brandon. It is for her to decide. I mean Sara Wrandall."

He felt a queer, sickening sensation of uneasiness sneak into existence. In the back of his mind, a hateful fear began to shape itself. For a long time he looked into her sombre eyes, and as he looked the fear that was hateful took on something of a definite shape.

" Did you know her husband? " he asked, and somehow he knew what the answer would be.

" Yes," she replied, after a moment. She was startled. Her lips remained parted.

He watched her closely. " Has this — this secret anything to do with Challis Wrandall? "

" It has," said she, meeting his gaze steadily.

His hands clutched the edge of the table in a grip that turned the knuckles white.

" Hetty! " he cried, in a hoarse whisper. " You — can't mean that you —"

" You must go to Sara," she cried hurriedly. " Haven't I told you that she is the one —"

" Were you in love with that infernal scoundrel? " he demanded fiercely.

" Sara knows everything. She will tell you —"

" Were you carrying on an affair with him while professing to be the friend of his wife? Tell me that! Did she find you out and —"

" Oh, Brandon, why will you persist? " she cried, her eyes aflame. " I can tell you no more. Why do you glare at me as if I were the meanest thing on earth? Is this love? Is this your idea of greatness? Isn't it enough for you to know that Sara is my loyal, devoted friend; that she —"

" Wait! " he commanded darkly. " Is it possible

that she did not discover your secret until the day
you left her house so abruptly? Does that explain
your sudden departure? "

"I can answer that," she said quietly. " She has
known everything from the day I met her. I have not
said anything, Brandon, to lead you to believe that I
was in love with Challis Wrandall, have I? "

His eyes softened. "No, you haven't. I — I hop
you will forget what I said. You see, I knew Wrandall's reputation. He had no sense of honour.
He —"

" Well, I *have!* " she said levelly.

He flushed. " I am a beast! I'll put it in this way,
then: Was he in love with you? "

" You are still unfair. I shall not answer."

He was silent for a long time. " And Sara's lips
are sealed," he mused, still possessed of doubts and
fears.

" Until she elects to tell the story, dearest love, my
lips are also sealed. I love you better than anything
else in all this world. I could willingly offer up my
life for you, but — well, my life does not belong to me.
It is Sara's."

" For heaven's sake, Hetty, what is all this? " he
cried in desperation.

" I can say no more. It is useless to insist, Brandon. If you can wrest the story from her, all well
and good. You will hate me then, dear love. But it
cannot be helped. I am prepared."

" Tell me this much: when you refused to marry
Leslie, was your course inspired by what had happened
in — in connection with Challis Wrandall? "

" You forget that it is *you* that I love," she responded simply.

"But why should Sara urge you to marry Leslie if there is anything —"

"Hush! Here is the waiter. Come to my sitting-room after breakfast. I have something to say to you. We must come to a definite understanding. This cannot go on."

He was with her for an hour in that pinched little sitting-room, and left her there without a vestige of rancour in his soul. She would not give an inch in the stand she had taken, but something immeasurably great in his make-up rose to the occasion and he went forth with the conviction that he had no right to demand more of her than she was ready to give. He was satisfied to abide by her decision. The spell of her was over him more completely than ever before.

Two days later he saw her off at the Gare de Lyons, bound for Interlaken. There was a complete understanding between them. She wanted to be quite alone in the Alpine town; he was not to follow her there. She had reserved rooms at the Schweitzerhof, and the windows of her sitting-room looked straight up the valley to the snow-covered crest of the Jungfrau. She remembered these rooms; as a young girl she had occupied them with her father and mother. By some hook or crook, Booth arranged by wire for her to have them again, not an easy matter at that season of the year. Later she was to go on to Lucerne, and then to Venice.

The slightest shred of hope was left for Booth. Even though he might accomplish the task he had set unto himself — the conquest of Sara in respect to the untold story — he still had Hetty's dismal prophecy that after he learned the truth he would come to see why they could not be married. But he would not despair.

"We'll see," was all that he said in response to her forlorn cry that they were parting for ever. There was a grimness in the way he said it that gave her something to cherish during the months to come; the hope that he *would* come back and take her in spite of herself.

He sailed from Cherbourg on the first steamship calling there. Awake, he thought of her; asleep, he dreamed of Challis Wrandall. There was something uncanny in the persistence with which that ruthless despoiler of peace forced his way into his dreams, to the absolute exclusion of all else. The voyage home was made horrid by these nightly reminders of a man he scarcely knew, yet dreaded. He became more or less obsessed by the idea that an evil spell had descended upon him in the shape of a ghostly influence.

The weeks passed slowly for Hetty. There were no letters from Sara, but an occasional line or so from Mr. Carroll. She had made Brandon Booth promise that he would not write to her, nor was he to expect anything from her. If her intention was to cut herself off entirely from her recent world and its people, as she might have done in another way by pursuing the time-honoured and rather cowardly plan of entering a convent, she was soon to discover that success in the undertaking brought a deeper sense of exile than she could have imagined herself able to endure at the outset. She found herself more utterly alone and friendless than at any time in her life. The chance companions she formed at Interlaken,— despite a well-meant reserve,— served only to increase her feeling of loneliness and despair. The very natural attentions of men, young and old, depressed her, instead of encouraging that essentially feminine thing called vanity. She lived as one without an aim, without a single purpose except to close one day that she might begin the next.

After a time, she went on to Lucerne. Here the life on the surface was gayer, and she was roused from her state of lethargy in spite of herself. Once, from her little balcony in the National, she saw two of her old acquaintances in the chorus at the Gaiety. They were wearing many pearls. Another time, she met them in the street. She was rather quietly dressed. They did not notice her. But the prosperous Hebraic gentlemen who attended them were not so careless.

One day a card was brought to her rooms. For the next two weeks she had a true and unavoidable friend in Lucerne. It would appear that Mrs. Rowe-Martin had not been apprised of the rift in the Wrandall lute. She had no reason to consider the exclusive Miss Castleton as anything but the most desirable of companions. Mrs. Rowe-Martin was not long in finding out (though how she did it, heaven knows!), that Lord Murgatroyd's grandniece was no longer the intimate of that impossible person, Sara Gooch. She couldn't think of Sara without thinking of Gooch.

But at last Mrs. Rowe-Martin departed, much to Hetty's secret relief, but not before she had increased the girl's burthens by introducing her into a cold-nosed cosmopolitan set from which there were but three ways of escape. She refused to marry one of them, denied another the privilege of making love to her, and declined to play auction bridge with all of them. They were not long in dropping her, although it must be said there was real regret among the men.

From Mrs. Rowe-Martin and others she heard that

Mrs. Redmond Wrandall and Vivian were to be in
Scotland in October, for somebody-or-other's christen-
ing, and that Leslie had been doing some really wonderful flying at Pau.

"I am *so* glad, my dear," said Mrs. Rowe-Martin,
"that you refused to marry Leslie. He is a cad.
Besides, you would have been in a perpetual state of
nerves over his flying."

Of Sara, there was no news, as might have been expected. Mrs. Rowe-Martin made it very clear that
Sara was a respectable person,—but heavens!

The chill days of autumn came and the crowd began
to dwindle. Hetty made preparations to join in the
exodus. As the days grew short and bleak, she found
herself thinking more and more of the happy-hearted,
symbolic dicky-bird on a faraway window ledge. His
life was neither a travesty nor a tragedy; hers was
both of these.

Something told her too that Brandon Booth had
wormed the truth out of Sara, and that she would
never see him again. It hurt her to think that while
Sara believed in her, the man who loved her did not.
It is a way men have.

On the eve of her departure, an event transpired
that was to alter the whole course of her life; or,
more properly speaking, it was destined to put her
back into an old groove.

She was walking along the quay, in the dusk of
early evening, her mind full of the next day's journey over the mountains to Milan. The wind was cold;
about her neck there was a boa of white ostrich
feathers, one end of which fluttered gaily over her
shoulder. She was continually turning half-way about
against the wind to reclaim the truant end of the boa.

It was in the act of doing so on one occasion that her attention was drawn to two men who sauntered across the avenue from the approach to the Schweitzerhof.

She stopped still in her tracks, petrified by amazement — and alarm, if we may anticipate the sensation by a second or two.

One of the men was Leslie Wrandall, the other — her own father!

In a flash came the impulse to avoid them, to fly before they recognised her. But even as she turned and started off with a sudden acceleration of speed, a shout assailed her ears, and then came the swift rush of footsteps over the hard pavement.

"Hetty! As I live!" cried Leslie, planting himself in front of her. His astonishment alone kept him from laying hands upon her, to make sure that she was really there. "Well, of all the —"

She extended her hand. "This *is* a surprise," she said, with admirable control. "I hadn't the faintest notion you were in Lucerne."

"By Jove!" he mumbled, shaking hands with her but still dazed and uncertain. He suddenly remembered his companion. Turning with a shout, he brought the soldierly, middle-aged gentleman about-face with scant ceremony. "Hey! Colonel Castleton! See who's here! Doesn't this bowl you over completely? "

Colonel Castleton, sallow, ascetic, deliberate in his movements, raised his glass to his eye as he came toward them.

"'Pon my soul!" burst from his astonished lips a second afterward. He stopped short and his jaw dropped in a most unmilitary fashion. "'Pon my soul! It *can't* be my daughter!" He seemed to be having difficulty not only with his head but with his feet; neither appeared to be operating intelligently. As a matter of fact, he stood for an instant on his toes and then on his heels. He was perilously near to being bowled over completely and literally.

Hetty was the first to recover. She advanced with a fair assumption of warmth in her manner. Her heart, belying her, was as cold as ice.

"Father!" she cried, holding out her hands.

He grasped them, and looked wildly about.

"Kiss me!" she whispered imperatively.

He stooped and brushed her cheek with his long moustache.

"Good God!" he muttered, still incredulous.

She turned to the excited Leslie with a quavering smile on her lips.

"We haven't seen each other in twelve years, Mr. Wrandall," she said.

"'Pon my soul!" added her father for the third time, thereby reaching the limit of emphasis, having placed it differently each time.

Leslie surprised himself by rising to the occasion. It occurred to him that they would like to be alone for a little while at least.

"Then, I'll stroll on, Colonel," he said. "By Jove!" The mild expletive was a tribute to Providence.

Not a word was spoken by father or daughter until Wrandall was many rods away.

"Where did you meet Leslie Wrandall?" she demanded, showing which way her thoughts ran. They were far from filial.

"Aviation field — somewhere," said he in a vague sort of way. "Pau, I dare say. What are you doing here? I hear you've cut loose from Wrandall's sister-in-law. Was that a sensible thing to do?"

" I fancy you've been misinformed," said she in an emotionless voice, but offered no further word of explanation.

" Shan't we sit down here on this bench, my dear?" suggested the Colonel, distinctly ill at ease.

" For the sake of appearances, yes," she assented.

Leslie, looking over his shoulder from a distance, saw them sitting together on one of the outer benches.

" By Jove! " he said to himself once more, this time with accumulative perplexity.

" See here, Hetty, my child," began the Colonel nervously, " it's all nonsense your taking the stand you do toward me. I am your father. I repeat, it's all nonsense — damned nonsense. You've got to —"

" Has it taken you all these years to find out that it's nonsense?" she demanded, her eyes flashing. " It's no good arguing, father. I don't like you. There is a very good reason why I should despise you. We won't go into it. After this meeting, we go our separate ways again. This, it seems, was unavoidable. I shan't ask anything of you, and I advise you to ask nothing of me."

"My God, that a child should utter such words to a father! " he groaned.

" A father! " she cried so scornfully that he must have shrivelled had he been any one else but Colonel Castleton of the Indian Corps. As it was, he had the grace to turn a very bright red. " A noble father you have been! And what a splendid, self-sacrificing husband you were. No! I can't forget how my mother lived and died. You call it nonsense. Well, I call it something else. You took a most effective way to punish my poor mother for having the temerity to marry an English gentleman. Thank God, I have my mother to look back to for my own ideas of gentility."

"You never understood the way things went wrong between your mother and me," he said harshly. "She wasn't all you may be pleased to think she was. She —"

"How dare you insinuate —"

"She chucked me. That's the sum and sub —"

"Oh, I was old enough to know that she left you — chucked you, if you will — and to know why she did it. I — I suppose you are looked upon by — these people here — Leslie Wrandall and every one else, as a fine English gentleman, a cousin of the great Lord Murgatroyd. Are you?"

"Confound you, Hetty, how dare you use such a tone in speaking to me?" he exclaimed.

"They *think* you are a gentleman, do they?"

"*Think?* Why, dammit, I am a gentleman. The only ungentlemanly thing I ever did in my life was to —" He checked the angry words, biting his lips to keep them down.

"Was to desert your wife," she supplied scathingly.

"No! To marry her!" He blurted it out in his rage.

"Oh!" she cried, shrinking farther away from him, cut to the quick.

He regarded her with cold, fishy eyes. She was uncommonly pretty, he was bound to admit that. Her mother's eyes, her mother's exquisite skin, but singularly like certain Castleton portraits that he knew. It somehow galled him to find that there was quite as much of the blue-blooded Castleton in her as there was commonplace Glynn; galled him more particularly because she was his own flesh and blood after all and, in spite of that, could taunt him with it.

"I didn't mean to hurt you, Hetty," he said, to his own surprise. The touch of tenderness had a brief life. He scowled an instant later. "We won't discuss the past, if you please. God knows I don't want to dig up rotten bones. You are against your own father. That's enough for me. I shan't impose myself upon you. You—"

"Why couldn't you have treated her with—" began Hetty hotly.

"Sh! No more of that, I say. I will not be upbraided by my own child. Now, see here, what do you mean by letting a chance like that get away from you?" He jerked his head in the direction Leslie had taken.

"Chance?"

"Yes. This Wrandall fellow. 'Gad, I've known him less than a fortnight and he's told me every secret he ever knew. Why don't you marry him? He's not a bad sort."

"That is my affair," said she coldly.

"I'd take him like a shot if I was a gel in your shoes."

"He told you I had refused to marry him?"

"A hundred times."

"Did you reward his confidence by relating the *whole* history of the Castleton family?"

He stared at her. "Good Lord, do you think I'm an ass?"

"What have you told him?"

"Nothing. I permitted him to do all the telling. He gave me a highly commendable account of myself, of you, of the fine old family of Glynns and—God

knows what all. He restored my pride, 'pon my soul
he did." The Colonel laughed as he twisted his moustache with ironic fondness.

She was quite still for a minute or two. "I heard
you were in England," she said, changing the subject.

"It may interest you to know that the old man overlooked us completely," he said, striking the calf of his
leg with his thin walking-stick.

"Why should he leave anything to you?"

"And why not, curse him?" he growled. "Am I
not his brother's son? What do you mean by asking
a question like that?"

"I think I will say good-bye to you now, father,"
she said deliberately. "We may never see each other
again." She arose and stood before him, cold and
proud, without a spark of emotion in her eyes.

He sat still, looking up at her in surprise. "Do
you think you're doing the right thing, Hetty?" he
asked, annoyed in spite of himself. "Remember that
I am your father. I can and will overlook all you
have said and done —"

"If you will go to her grave and kneel there and
ask her pardon, I may think differently of you because, after all, I am your daughter. You will not
find her buried among the stately Castletons, but in a
poor little spot far, far away from them. I can tell
you how to find it. You have never inquired, I suppose?"

His eyes narrowed. "By Jove, you are a mean little beggar!"

"Mean?" she cried, clenching her hands. Then she
laughed suddenly, shrilly. "Oh, if my mother could
hear you say that to me!"

"Damme!" he exclaimed, coming to his feet in con-

siderable agitation. "Do you want people to hear
us ragging each other? Don't go into hysterics,
Hetty! See here, do you forget that I have written
to you — loving letters they were — from the heart
— written, I say, over and over again and what do I
get in return? Not a single stroke of the pen from
you, except the note a year ago telling me where you
were and —"

"And that was merely to relieve your anxiety when
you found I'd given up my work on the stage and
might become a burden on you. Oh, I read between
your lines."

"Nothing of the sort. I never wanted you to go
on the stage. Why have you persistently refused to
answer my subsequent letters?"

"Because I read between the lines in all of them,"
she said levelly.

"You have no right to say that I expected you to
get money out of that bally Wrandall woman — the
goods merchant's daughter. That's downright insult-
ing in you. I shan't let it go undefend —"

"You knew I couldn't lend you a thousand pounds,
father," said she, very slowly and distinctly.

He coughed, perhaps in apology to her but more
than likely to himself.

"You are at liberty," she went on, "to tell Mr.
Leslie Wrandall all there is to tell about me. He
doesn't know, but it won't matter much if he does
have the truth concerning me. Tell him all if you
like."

"My child," said he, with a fine display of wounded
dignity, "I am not quite the rotter you think I am."

He did not feel called upon to explain to her that
he had already borrowed a thousand pounds from her

disappointed suitor, and was setting his nets for another thousand or two.

"It really won't matter," she said wearily. "Good-bye. I am leaving at nine to-morrow for Italy."

"See you at dinner? Or afterward, just for a —"

"I think not. I do not care to see Mr. Wrandall."

"Think it over again, Hetty. Don't —"

"Oh, father! How can you say such things to me?" she cried, a break in her voice.

"Good God, my dear, isn't it natural for a father to want to see his daughter well provided for?"

She turned away.

"I am contemplating a visit to the States shortly," he remarked, following after her.

She whirled on him. "What!"

"Young Wrandall has asked me over for a month or two about the first of the year. His people are in Scotland now, I hear."

"Are you *through* with India?" she asked in a very low voice.

"Resigned," said he succinctly.

"*T'ruly?*"

He flushed and muttered an oath. She understood. He had been "kicked out!"

"Hello!" called out a sprightly voice from the gathering darkness, and the next moment Leslie joined them. "Have dinner with us to-night, Hetty? Just the three of us. Please do."

"No, thank you, Mr. Wrandall. I am getting ready to leave to-morrow. Packing and all that sort of thing."

"Did Colonel Castleton tell you that I'm off for New York on Saturday? Mother and Viv are to get the boat at Southampton. I thought you'd be interested to know what's just turned up over there?"

"What has happened?" she cried quickly.

Leslie hesitated. A curious gleam stole into his eyes. Was it of triumph?

"Father's got rather old-fashioned ideas about certain things," he observed, by way of preface. "He writes that Sara is contemplating a second venture into the state of wedded bliss."

Hetty stared at him. "I — I don't believe it," she said flatly. "How can it be possible? She sees no one."

He laughed. "You're wrong there," said he mendaciously. "She's been seeing a great deal of a certain mutual friend of ours — all summer long."

"You mean?"

"Brandon Booth. Father says that rumour has it they are to be married after the holidays. I fancy he needed consolation, after what happened to him earlier in the year. He was pretty hard hit, believe me." After a moment, he went on boldly: "I ought to be in a position to sympathise with him, I suppose, but I don't. It isn't in me to —"

"You say they are to be married?" cried Hetty, dazed and bewildered.

They had fallen behind Colonel Castleton, who walked on stiffly ahead of them.

Leslie treated her to his most engaging smile.

"Looks very Goochy, doesn't it? I'm coming to believe more than ever that blood will tell. Sara knew what she was doing when she cleared her decks for action a few months ago. 'Gad, I understand now why she was so eager to bring off the — well, another match we know about. Pretty canny, eh?"

" It is incredible," said she, with unnecessary vehemence.

" Not in the least. Clever person, Sara is. Sets her heart on a thing, and — woof! she gets it, whether or no. Now, don't misunderstand me. I'm fond of Brandon Booth. We all are. We don't object to him as a sort of family attachment. But if she's going to marry him, we want to know where we stand in a business way. You see, he will not only step into my brother Chal's shoes at home, but at the office. And, heaven knows, Brandy is not a good business man. He's great on portraits, but — I beg pardon! "

" I must leave you here, Mr. Wrandall. Goodbye! "

" Oh, I say, can't we see something of —"

" I am afraid not."

He kept pace with her through the hall.

" I suppose your father told you that I — I haven't altogether given up hope of — you."

" He spoke of going to America with you, if that's what you mean," she said coldly, and left him at the foot of the staircase.

Leslie's hand trembled as it went up to his moustache. " I can't understand her beastly obstinacy," he said to himself.

CHAPTER XIX

CHIEF among Booth's virtues was his undeviating loyalty to a set purpose. He went back to America with
the firm intention to clear up the mystery surrounding
Hetty Castleton, no matter how irksome the delay in
achieving his aim or how vigorous the methods he
would have to employ. Sara Wrandall, to all pur-
poses, held the key; his object in life now was to
induce her to turn it in the lock and throw open the
door so that he might enter in and become a sharer in
the secrets beyond.

A certain amount of optimistic courage attended
him in his campaign against what had been described
to him as the impossible. He could see no clear reason why she should withhold the secret under the new
conditions, when so much in the shape of happiness
was at stake. It was in this spirit of confidence that
he prepared to confront her on his arrival in New
York, and it was the same unbounded faith in the belief that nothing evil could result from a perfectly
just and honourable motive that gave him the needed
courage.

He stayed over night in New York, and the next
morning saw him on his way to Southlook. There
was something truly ingenuous in his desire to get to
the bottom of the matter without fear or apprehension.
At the very worst, he maintained, there could be nothing more reprehensible than a passing infatuation,
long since dispelled, or perhaps a mildly sinister epi-
sode in which virtue had been triumphant and vice

defeated with unpleasant results to at least one person, and that person the husband of Sara Wrandall.

Pat met him at the station and drove him to the
little cottage on the upper road.

"Ye didn't stay long," said he reflectively, after
he had put the bag up in front. He took up the reins.

"Not very," replied his master.

After a dozen rods or more, Pat tried again.

"Just siventeen days, I make it."

"Seems longer."

"Perhaps you'll be after going back soon."

"Why should you think that, Patrick?"

"Because you don't seem to be takin' much interest
in your surroundin's here," said Pat loftily. He delivered a smart smack on the crupper with his stubby
whip, and pursed his lips for the companionship to
be derived from whistling.

"I suppose you know why I went to Europe," said
Booth, laying his hand affectionately on the man's
arm.

"Sure I do," said Pat, forgetting to whistle.
"And was it bad luck you had, sor?"

"A temporary case of it, I'm afraid."

"Well," said the Irishman, looking up at his employer with the most profound encouragement in his
wink, "if it's anny help to you, sor, I'll say that I've
niver found bad luck to be annything but timporary.
And, believe *me*, I've had plinty of it. Mary was
dom near three years makin' up her mind to say yis
to me."

"And since then you've had no bad luck?" said
Booth, with a smile.

"Plinty of it, begob, but I've had some one besides
meself to blame for it. There's a lot in that, Mr.

Brandon. Whin a man marries, he simply divides his luck into two parts, good and bad, and if he's like most men he puts the bulk av the bad luck on his wife and kapes to himself all he can av the good for a rainy day. That's what makes him a strong man and able to meet trouble when it comes. The beauty av the arrangement is that bad luck is only timporary and a woman enjoys talking about it, while good luck is wid us nine-tinths of the time, whether we know it or not, and we don't have to talk about it."

This was fine philosophy, but Booth discerned the underlying motive.

" Have you been quarrelling? "

"I have *not*," said Pat wrathfully. " But I won't say as much for Mary. The point av me argument is that I have all the good luck in havin' married her, and she claims to have had all the bad luck in marryin' me. Still, as I said before, 'tis but timporary. The good luck lasts and the bad don't. She'll be after tellin' me so before sundown. That's like all women. You'll find it out for yourself wan o' these days, Mr. Brandon, and ye'll be dom proud ye're a man and can enjoy your good luck when ye get it. The bad luck's always fallin' behind ye, and ye can always look forward to the good luck. So don't be down-hearted. She'll take you, or me name's not what it ought to be."

Booth was inclined to accept this unique discourse as a fair-weather sign.

" Take these bags upstairs, Pat," said he on their arrival at the cottage, " and then come down and drive me over to Mrs. Wrandall's."

" Will ye be after stayin' for lunch with her, Mr. Brandon? " inquired Pat, climbing over the wheel.

" I can't answer that question now."

"Hiven help both av us if Mary's good luncheon goes to waste," said Pat ominously. "That's all I have to say. She'll take it out av both av us."

"Tell her I'll be here for lunch," said Booth, with alacrity. From which it may be perceived that master and man were of one mind when it came to considering the importance of Mary.

Pat studied his watch for a moment with a calculating eye.

"It's half-past eliven now, sor," he announced. "D'ye think ye can make it?"

Booth reflected. "I think not," he said. "I'll have luncheon first." Whereupon he leaped from the trap and went in to tell Mary how happy he was to be where he could enjoy home-cooking.

At four he was delivered at Sara's door by the astute Patrick, announced by the sedate Watson and interrogated by the intelligent Murray, who seemed surprised to hear that he would *not* have anything cool to drink. Sara sent word that she would be down in fifteen minutes, but, as a matter of fact, appeared in less than three.

She came directly to the point.

"Well," she said, with her mysterious smile, "she sent you back to me, I see." He was still clasping her hand.

"Have you heard from her?" he asked quickly.

"No. But I knew just what would happen. I told you it would prove to be a wild goose chase. Where is she?"

He sat down beside her on the cool, white covered couch.

"In Switzerland. I put her on the train the night before I sailed. Yes, she did send me back to you.

Now I'm here, I want the whole story, Sara. What is it that stands between us?"

For an hour he pleaded with her, all to no purpose. She steadfastly refused to divulge the secret. Not even his blunt reference to Challis Wrandall's connection with the affair found a vulnerable spot in her armour.

"I shan't give it up, Sara," he said, at the end of his earnest harangue against the palpably unfair stand both she and Hetty were taking. "I mean to harass you, if you please, until I get what I'm after. It is of the most vital importance to me. Quite as much so, I am sure, as it appears to be to you. If Hetty will say the word, I'll take her gladly, just as she is, without knowing what all this is about. But, you see, she won't consent. There must be some way to override her. You both admit there is no legal barrier. You tell me to-day that there is no insanity in her family, and a lot of other things that I've been able to bring out by questioning, so I am more than ever certain that the obstacle is not so serious as you would have me believe. Therefore, I mean to pester you until you give in, my dear Sara."

"Very well," she said resignedly. "When may I expect a renewal of the conflict?"

"Would to-morrow be convenient?" he asked quaintly.

She returned his smile. "Come to luncheon."

"Have I your permission to start the portrait?"

"Yes. As soon as you like."

He left her without feeling that he had gained an inch along the road to success. That night, in the gloaming of his star-lit porch, he smoked many a pipeful and derived therefrom a profound estimate of the value of tact and discretion as opposed to bold and impulsive measures in the handling of a determined woman. He would make haste slowly, as the saying goes. Many an unexpected victory is gained by dilatory tactics, provided the blow is struck at the psychological moment of least resistance.

The weeks slipped by. He was with her almost daily. Other people came to her house, some for rather protracted visits, others in quest of pillage at the nightly bridge table, but he was seldom missing. There were times when he thought he detected a tendency to waver, but each cunning attempt on his part to encourage the impulse invariably brought a certain mocking light into her eyes and he veered off in defeat. Something kept telling him, however, that the hour was bound to come when she would falter in her resolution; when frankness would meet frankness, and the veil be lifted.

A rather impossible relative in the person of an aunt came to spend the month of August with Sara — her father's sister. She was a true, unvarnished Gooch. Booth shuddered at times when she emerged flat-foot from the background and revelled in the Goochiness that would not stay put, no matter how hard she tried to subdue it. She was a good soul,— much too good, in fact,—and her efforts to live up to requirements were not only ludicrous but exasperating. Sara was quite serene about her, however. She made no excuses for the old lady; in fact, she appeared to be quite devoted to her. Booth was beginning to appreciate something of the horror the Wrandalls must have felt when Challis took unto himself a Gooch. He berated himself in secret for his snobbishness and in public made atonement by being expansively polite to

Mrs. Coburn. The good lady had the habit of telling every one what a wonderful person Sebastian Gooch had been, sometimes comparing him not unfavourably with Napoleon Bonaparte and George Washington: he was like the Corsican in getting the better of his adversaries, no matter how he had to go about it, but like the Father of his Country in the matter of veracity. So far as she knew, Sebastian had never told a lie. To Mrs. Coburn, Sebastian was Saint Sebastian.

The portrait was finished before Mrs. Coburn left. She liked everything about it except the gown, the drapery and — yes, the hands. They were too long and tapering. No Gooch ever had a hand like that. The Gooch hands were broad and strong: like her own. All this, notwithstanding the fact that Sara's hand lay exposed all the time she was speaking, a physical contradiction to her assertion.

She stayed the month and then re-entered Yonkers.

There were no letters from Hetty, no word of any description. If Sara knew anything of the girl's movements she did not take Booth into her confidence.

Leslie Wrandall went abroad in August, ostensibly to attend the aviation meets in France and England. His mother and sister sailed in September, but not before the entire colony of which they were a part had begun to discuss Sara and Booth with a relish that was obviously distasteful to the Wrandalls.

Where there is smoke there is fire, said all the gossips, and forthwith proceeded to carry fagots.

A week or so before sailing, Mrs. Redmond Wrandall had Booth in for dinner. I think she said *en famille*. At any rate, Sara was not asked, which is proof enough that she was bent on making it a family affair.

After dinner, Booth sat in the screened upper balcony with Vivian. He liked her. She was a keen-witted, plain-spoken young woman, with few false ideals and no subtlety. She was less snobbish than arrogant. Of all the Wrandalls, she was the least self-centred. Leslie never quite understood her for the paradoxical reason that she thoroughly understood him.

"You know, Brandon," she said, after a long silence between them, "they've been setting my cap for you for a long, long time." She blew a thin stream of cigarette smoke toward the moon.

He started. It was a bolt from a clear sky. "The deuce!"

"Yes," she went on in the most casual tone, "mother's had her heart set on it for months. You were supposed to be mine at first sight, I believe. Please don't look so uneasy. I'm not going to propose to you." She laughed her little ironic laugh.

"So that is the way things stood, eh?" he said, still a little amazed by her candour.

"Yes. And what is more to the point, I am quite sure I should have said yes if you had asked me. Sounds odd, doesn't it? Rather amusing, too, being able to discuss it so unreservedly, isn't it?"

"Good heavens, Viv!" he cried uncomfortably. "I —I had no idea you cared —"

"Cared!" she cried, as he paused. "I don't care two pins for you in that way. But I would have married you, just the same, because you are worth marrying. I'd very much rather have you for a husband than any man I know, but as for loving you! Pooh! I'd love you in just the way mother loves father, and I wouldn't have been a bit more trouble to you than she is to him."

" 'Gad, you don't mind what you say!"

" Failing to nab you, Brandy, I dare say I'll have to
come down to a duke or, who knows? maybe a mere
prince. It isn't very enterprising, is it? And certainly it isn't a gay prospect. Really, I had hoped
you would have me. I flatter myself, I suppose, but,
honestly now, we would have made a rather nice looking couple, wouldn't we? "

" You flatter me," he said.

" But," she resumed, calmly exhaling, " you very
foolishly fell in love with some one else, and it wasn't
necessary for me to pretend that I was in love with
you — which I should have done, believe me, if you
had given me the chance. You fell in love, first with
Hetty Castleton."

" First? " he cried, frowning.

" And now you are heels over head in love with my
beautiful sister-in-law. Which all goes to prove that
I would have made just the kind of wife you need,
considering your tendency to fluctuate. But how
dreadful it would have been for a sentimental, loving
girl like Hetty!"

He sat bolt upright and stared hard at her.

" See here, Viv, what the dickens are you driving
at? I'm not in love with Sara — not in the least,—
and —" He checked himself sharply. " What an ass
I am! You're guying me."

" In any event, I am right about Hetty," she said,
leaning forward, her manner quite serious.

" If it will ease your mind," he said stiffly, " I plead
guilty with all my heart."

She favoured him with a slight frown of annoyance.

" And you deny the fluctuating charge? "

" Most positively. I can afford to be honest with

you, Viv. You are a corker. I love Hetty Castleton
with all my soul."

She leaned back in her chair. "Then why don't
you dignify your soul by being honest with *her?*"

"What do you mean?"

For a half-minute she was silent. "Are you and
I of the same stripe, after all? Would you marry
Sara without loving her, as I would have done by
you? It doesn't seem like you, Brandon."

"Good heaven, I'm not going to marry Sara!"
he blurted out. "It's never entered my head."

"Perhaps it has entered hers."

"Nonsense! She isn't going to marry anybody.
And she knows how I feel toward Hetty. If it came
to the point where I decided to marry without love,
'pon my soul, Viv, I believe I'd pick you out as the
victim."

"Wonderful combination!" she said with a frank
laugh. "The quintessence of 'no love lost.' But to
resume! Do you know that people are saying you
are to be married before the winter is over?"

"Let 'em say it," he said gruffly.

"Oh, well," she said, despatching it all with a gesture, "if that's the way you feel about it, there's no
more to be said."

He was ashamed. "I beg your pardon, I shouldn't
have said that."

"You see," she went on, reverting to the original
topic, "people who know Sara are likely to credit
her with motives you appear to be totally ignorant
of. She set her heart on my brother Challis, when
she was a great deal younger than she is now, and she
got him. If age and experience count for anything,
how capable she must be by this time."

He was too wise to venture an opinion. "I assure you she has no designs on me."

"Perhaps not. But I fancy that even you could not escape as St. Anthony did. She is most alluring."

"You don't like her."

"Obviously. And yet I don't dislike her. She has the virtue of consistency, if one may use the expression. She loved my brother. Leslie says she should have hated him. We have tried to like her. I think I have come nearer to it than any of the others, not excepting Leslie, who has always been her champion. I suppose you know that he was your rival at one time."

"He mentioned it," said Booth drily.

"I should have been very much disappointed in her if she had accepted him."

"Indeed?"

"I sometimes wonder if Sara spiked Leslie's guns for him."

"I can tell you something you don't know, Vivian," said he. "Sara was rather keen about making a match there."

Vivian's smile was slow but triumphant. "That is just what I thought. There you are! Doesn't that explain Sara?"

"In a measure, yes. But, you see, it developed that Hetty cared for some one else, and that put a stop to everything."

"Am I to take it that you are the some one else?"

"Yes," said he soberly.

"Then, may I ask why she went away so suddenly?"

"You may ask but I can't answer."

"Do you want my opinion? She went away because Sara, failing in her plan to marry her off to Leslie,

decided that it would be fatal to a certain project of
her own if she remained on the field of action. Do
I make myself clear?"

"Oh, you are away off in your conclusions, Viv."

"Time will tell," was her cabalistic rejoinder.

Her father appeared on the lawn below and called
up to them.

"You are wanted at the telephone, Brandon. I've
just been talking to Sara."

"Did she call you up, father?" asked Vivian, leaning over the rail.

"Yes. About nothing in particular, however."

She turned upon Booth with a mocking smile. He
felt the colour rush to his face, and was angry with
himself.

He went in to the telephone. Almost her first words
were these:

"What has Vivian been telling you about me, Brandon?"

He actually gasped. "Good heavens, Sara!"

He heard her low laugh. "So she *has* been saying
things, has she?" she asked. "I thought so. I've
had it in my bones to-night."

He was at a loss for words. It was positively uncanny. As he stood there, trying to think of a trivial
remark, her laugh came to him again over the wire,
followed by a drawling "good-night," and then the
soughing of the wind over the "open" wire.

The next day he called her up on the telephone quite
early. He knew her habits. She would be abroad in
her gardens by eight o'clock. He remembered well that
Leslie, in commenting on her absurdly early hours, had
once said that her "early bird" habit was hereditary:
she got it from Sebastian.

"What put it into your head, Sara, that Vivian was saying anything unpleasant about you last night?"

"Magic," she replied succinctly.

"Rubbish!"

"I have a magic tapestry that transports me, hither and thither, and by night I always carry Aladdin's 'amp. So, you see, I see and hear everything."

"Be sensible."

"Very well. I will be sensible. If you intend to be influenced by what Vivian or her mother said to you last night, I think you'd be wise to avoid me from this time on."

Prepared though he was, he blinked his eyes and said something she didn't quite catch.

She went on: "Moreover, in addition to my attainments in the black art, I am quite as clever as Mr. Sherlock Holmes in some respects. I really do some splendid deducing. In the first place, you were asked there and I was not. Why? Because I was to be discussed. You see —"

"Marvellous!" he interrupted loudly.

"You were to be told that I have cruel designs upon you."

"Go on, please."

"And all that sort of thing," she said sweepingly, and he could almost see the inclusive gesture with her free hand. He laughed but still marvelled at the shrewdness of her perceptions.

"I'll come over this afternoon and show you wherein you are wrong," he began, but she interrupted him with a laugh.

"I am starting for the city before noon, by motor, to be gone at least a fortnight."

"What! This is the first I've heard of it."

Again she laughed. "To be perfectly frank with you, I hadn't heard of it myself until just now. I think I shall go down to the Homestead with the Carrolls."

"Hot Springs?"

"Virginia," she added explicitly.

"I say, Sara, what does all this mean? You—"

"And if you should follow me there, Vivian's estimate of us will not be so far out of the way as we'd like to make it."

True to her word, she was gone when he drove over later on in the day. Somehow, he experienced a queer feeling of relief. Not that he was oppressed by the rather vivacious opinions of Vivian and her ilk, but because something told him that Sara was wavering in her determination to withhold the secret from him and fled for perfectly obvious reasons.

He had two commissions among the rich summer colonists. One, a full length portrait of young Beardsley in shooting togs, was nearly finished. The other was to be a half-length of Mrs. Ravenscroft, who wanted one just like Hetty Castleton's, except for the eyes, which she admitted would have to be different. Nothing was said of the seventeen years' difference in their ages. Vivian had put off posing until Lent.

The Wrandalls departed for Scotland, and other friends of his began to desert the country for the city. The fortnight passed and another week besides. Mrs. Ravenscroft decided to go to Europe when the picture was half-finished.

"You can finish it when I come back in December, Mr. Booth," she said. "I'll have several new gowns to choose from, too."

"I shall be busy all winter, Mrs. Ravenscroft," he said coldly.

"How annoying," she said calmly, and that was the end of it all. She had made the unpleasant discovery that it *wasn't* going to be in the least like Hetty Castleton's, so why bother about it?

Booth waited until Sara came out to superintend the closing of her house for the winter. He called at Southlook on the day of her arrival. He was struck at once by the curious change in her appearance and manner. There was something bleak and desolate in the vividly brilliant face: the tired, wistful, harassed look of one who has begun to quail and yet fights on.

"Will you go out with me to-morrow, Brandon, for an all-day trip in the car?" she asked, as they stood together before the open fireplace on this late November afternoon. Her eyes were moody, her voice rather lifeless.

"Certainly," he said, watching her closely. Was the break about to come?

"I will stop for you at nine." After a short pause, she looked up and said: "I suppose you would like to know where I am taking you."

"It doesn't matter, Sara."

"I want you to go with me to Burton's Inn."

"Burton's Inn?"

"That is the place where my husband was killed," she said, quite steadily.

He started. "Oh! But — do you think it best, Sara, to open old wounds by —"

"I have thought it all out, Brandon. I want to go there — just once. I want to go into that room again."

CHAPTER XX

AGAIN Sara Wrandall found herself in that never-to-be-forgotten room at Burton's Inn. On that grim night in March, she had entered without fear or trembling because she knew what was there. Now she quaked with a mighty chill of terror, for she knew not what was there in the quiet, now sequestered room. Burton had told them on their arrival after a long drive across country that patrons of the inn invariably asked which room it was that had been the scene of the tragedy, and, on finding out, refused point-blank to occupy it. In consequence, he had been obliged to transform it into a sort of store and baggage room.

Sara stood in the middle of the murky room, for the shutters had long been closed to the light of day, and looked about her in awe at the heterogeneous mass of boxes, trunks, bundles and rubbish, scattered over the floor without care or system. She had closed the door behind her and was quite alone. Light sneaked in through the cracks in the shutters, but so meagrely that it only served to increase the gloom. A dismantled bedstead stood heaped up in the corner. She did not have to be told what bed it was. The mattress was there too, rolled up and tied with a thick garden rope. She knew there were dull, ugly blood-stains upon it. Why the thrifty Burton had persevered in keeping this useless article of furniture, she could only surmise. Perhaps it was held as an inducement to the

morbidly curious who always seek out the gruesome
and gloat even as they shudder.

For a long time she stood immovable just inside
the door, recalling the horrid picture of another day.
She tried to imagine the scene that had been enacted
there with gentle, lovable Hetty Glynn and her whilom
husband as the principal characters. The girl had
told the whole story of that ugly night. Sara tried
to see it as it actually had transpired. For months
this present enterprise had been in her mind: the desire
to see the place again, to go there with old impressions
which she could leave behind when ready to emerge in
a new frame of mind. It was here that she meant to
shake off the shackles of a horrid dream, to purge herself of the last vestige of bitterness, to cleanse her
mind of certain thoughts and memories.

Downstairs Booth waited for her. He heard the
story of the tragedy from the surly inn-keeper, who
crossly maintained that his business had been ruined.
Booth was vaguely impressed, he knew not why, by
Burton's description of the missing woman. "I'd say
she was about the size of Mrs. Wrandall herself, and
much the same figger," he said, as he had said a thousand times before. "My wife noticed it the minute
she saw Mrs. Wrandall. Same height and everything."

A bell rang sharply and Burton glanced over his
shoulder at the indicator on the wall behind the desk.
He gave a great start and his jaw sagged.

"Great Scott!" he gasped. A curious greyness
stole over his face. "It's — it's the bell in that very
room. My soul, what can —"

"Mrs. Wrandall is up there, isn't she?" demanded
Booth.

"It ain't rung since the night he pushed the button for — Oh, gee! You're right. She *is* up there. My, what a scare it gave me." He wiped his brow. Turning to a boy, he commanded him to answer the bell. The boy went slowly, and as he went he removed his hands from his pockets. He came back an instant later, more swiftly than he went, with the word that "the lady up there" wanted Mr. Booth to come upstairs.

She was waiting for him in the open doorway. A shaft of bright sunlight from a window at the end of the hall fell upon her. Her face was colourless, haggard. He paused for an instant to contrast her as she stood there in the pitiless light with the vivid creature he had put upon canvas so recently.

She beckoned to him and turned back into the room. He followed.

"This is the room, Brandon, where my husband met the death he deserved," she said quietly.

"Deserved? Good heavens, Sara, are you —"

"I want you to look about you and try to picture how this place looked on the night of the murder. You have a vivid imagination. None of this rubbish was here. Just a bed, a table and two chairs. There was a carpet on the floor. There were two people here, a man and a woman. The woman had trusted the man. She trusted him until the hour in which he died. Then she found him out. She had come to this place, believing it was to be her wedding night. She found no minister here. The man laughed at her and scoffed. Then she knew. In horror, shame, desperation she tried to break away from him. He was strong. She was a good woman; a virtuous, honourable woman. She saved herself."

He was staring at her with dilated eyes. Slowly the truth was being borne in upon him.

" The woman was — Hetty? " came hoarsely from his stiffening lips. " My God, Sara! "

She came close to him and spoke in a half-whisper. " Now you know the secret. Is it safe with you? "

He opened his lips to speak, but no words came forth. Paralysis seemed to have gripped not only his throat but his senses. He reeled. She grasped his arm in a tense, fierce way, and whispered:

" Be careful! No one must hear what we are say-ing." She shot a glance down the deserted hall. " No one is near. I made sure of that. Don't speak! Think first — think well, Brandon Booth. It is what you have been seeking for months: — the truth. You share the secret with us now. Again I ask, is it safe with you? "

" My God! " he muttered again, and passed his hand over his eyes. His brow was wet. He looked at his fingers dumbly as if expecting to find them covered with blood.

" Is it safe with you? " for the third time.

" Safe? Safe? " he whispered, following her exam-ple without knowing that he did so. " I — I can't believe you, Sara. It can't be true."

" It *is* true."

" You have known — all the time? "

" From that night when I stood where we are stand-ing now."

" And — and — *she?* "

" I had never seen her until that night. I saved her."

He dropped suddenly upon the trunk that stood behind him, and buried his face in his hands. For a long time she stood over him, her interest divided between him and the hall, wherein lay their present peril.

"Come," she said at last. "Pull yourself together. We must leave this place. If you are not careful, they will suspect something downstairs."

He looked up with haggard eyes, studying her face with curious intentness.

"What manner of woman are you, Sara?" he questioned, slowly, wonderingly.

"I have just discovered that I am very much like other women, after all," she said. "For awhile I thought I was different, that I was stronger than my sex. But I am just as weak, just as much to be pitied, just as much to be scorned as any one of my sisters. I have spoiled a great act by stooping to do a mean one. God will bear witness that my thoughts were noble at the outset; my heart was soft. But, come! There is much more to tell that cannot be told here. You shall know everything."

They went downstairs and out into the crisp autumn air. She gave directions to her chauffeur. They were to traverse for some distance the same road she had taken on that ill-fated night a year and a half before. In course of time the motor approached a well-remembered railway crossing.

"Slow down, Cole," she said. "This is a mean place — a very mean place." Turning to Booth, who had been sitting grim and silent beside her for miles, she said, lowering her voice: "I remember that crossing yonder. There is a sharp curve beyond. This is the place. Midway between the two crossings, I should say. Please remember this part of the road, Brandon, when I come to the telling of that night's ride to town. Try to picture this spot — this smooth,

For a long time she stood over him, her interest divided
between him and the hall

straight road as it might be on a dark, freezing night
in the very thick of a screaming blizzard, with all the
world abed save — two women."

In his mind he began to draw the picture, and to
place the two women in the centre of it, without knowing the circumstances. There was something fascinating in the study he was making, something gruesome
and full of sinister possibilities for the hand of a virile
painter. He wondered how near his imagination was
to placing the central figures in the picture as they
actually appeared on that secret night.

.   .   .   .   .   .

At sunset they went together to the little pavilion
at the end of the pier which extended far out into
the Sound. Here they were safe from the ears of
eavesdroppers. The boats had been stowed away for
the winter. The wind that blew through the open
pavilion, now shorn of all its comforts and luxuries,
was cold, raw and repelling. No one would disturb
them here.

With her face set toward the sinking east, she leaned
against one of the thick posts, and, in a dull, emotionless voice, laid bare the whole story of that dreadful
night and the days that followed. She spared no details, she spared not herself in the narration.

He did not once interrupt her. All the time she
was speaking he was studying the profile of her face
as if fascinated by its strange immobility. For the
matter of a full half-hour he sat on the rail, his back
against a post, his arms folded across the breast of
the thick ulster he wore, staring at her, drinking in
every word of the story she told. A look of surprise
crept into his face when she came to the point where
the thought of marrying Hetty to the brother of

her victim first began to manifest itself in her designs.
For a time the look of incredulity remained, to be succeeded by utter scorn as she went on with the recital.
Her reasons, her excuses, her explanations for this
master-stroke in the way of compensation for all that
she had endured at the hands of the scornful Wrandalls, all of whom were hateful to her without exception, stirred him deeply. He began to understand the
forces that compelled her to resort to this Machiavel-
lian plan for revenge on them. She admitted everything: her readiness to blight Hetty's life for ever; her
utter callousness in laying down these ugly plans; her
surpassing vindictiveness; her reflections on the triumph
she was to enjoy when her aims were fully attained.
She confessed to a genuine pity for Hetty Castleton
from the beginning, but it was outweighed by that
thing she could only describe as an obsession! . . .
How she hated the Wrandalls! . . . Then came
the real awakening: when the truth came to her as a
revelation from God. Hetty had not been to blame.
The girl was innocent of the one sin that called for
vengeance so far as she was concerned. The slaying
of Challis Wrandall was justified! All these months
she had been harbouring a woman she believed to have
been his mistress as well as his murderess. It was not
so much the murderess that she would have foisted
upon the Wrandalls as a daughter, but the mistress! . . . She loved the girl, she had loved her
from that first night. Back of it all, therefore, lay
the stern, unsuspected truth: from the very beginning
she instinctively had known this girl to be innocent of
guile. . . . Her house of cards fell down. There
was nothing left of the plans on which it had been
constructed. It had all been swept away, even as she

strove to protect it against destruction, and the
ground was strewn with the ashes of fires burnt
out. . . . She was shocked to find that she had
even built upon the evil spot! . . . Almost word
for word she repeated Hetty's own story of her meeting with Challis Wrandall, and how she went, step
by step and blindly, to the last scene in the tragedy,
when his vileness, his true nature was revealed to her.
The girl had told her everything. She had thought
herself to be in love with Wrandall. She was carried
away by his protestations. She was infatuated.
(Sara smiled to herself as she spoke of this. She
knew Challis Wrandall's charm!) The girl believed
in him implicitly. When he took her to Burton's Inn
it was to make her his wife, as she supposed. He had
arranged everything. Then came the truth. She de-
fended herself. . . .

"I came upon her in the road on that wild night,
Brandon, at the place I pointed out. Can you picture
her as I have described her? Can you picture her
despair, her hopelessness, her misery? I have told you
everything, from beginning to end. You know how
she came to me, how I prepared her for the sacrifice,
how she left me. I have not written to her. I cannot. She must hate me with all her soul, just as I
have hated the Wrandalls, but with greater reason, I
confess. She would have given herself up to the law
long ago, if it had not been for exposing me to the
world as her defender, her protector. She knew she
was not morally guilty of the crime of murder. In
the beginning she was afraid. She did not know our
land, our laws. In time she came to understand that
she was in no real peril, but then it was too late. A
confession would have placed me in an impossible po-

sition. You see, she thought of me all this time. She loved me as no woman ever loved another. Was not I the wife of the man she had killed, and was not I the noblest of all women in her eyes? God! And to think of what I had planned for her!"

This was the end of the story.

The words died away in a sort of whimpering wail, falling in with the wind to be lost to his straining ears. Her head drooped, her arms hung limply at her side.

For a long time he sat there in silence, looking out over the darkening water, unwilling, unable indeed, to speak. His heart was full of compassion for her, mingling strangely with what was left of scorn and horror. What could he say to her?

At last she turned to him. "Now you know all that I can tell you of Hetty Castleton,— of Hetty Glynn. You could not have forced this from me, Brandon. She *would* not tell you. It was left for me to do in my own good time. Well, I have spoken. What have you to say?"

"I can only say, Sara, that I thank God for *everything*," he said slowly.

"For everything?"

"I thank God for you, for her and for everything. I thank God that she found him out in time, that she killed him, that you shielded her, that you failed to carry out your devilish scheme, and that your heart is very sore to-day."

"You do not despise me?"

"No. I am sorry for you."

Her eyes narrowed. "I don't want you to feel sorry for me."

"You don't understand. I am sorry for you because you have found yourself out and must be despising yourself."

"You have guessed the truth. I despise myself. But what could be expected of me?" she asked ironically. "As the Wrandalls would say, 'blood will tell.'"

"Nonsense! Don't talk like that! It is quite unworthy of you. In spite of everything, Sara, you are wonderful. The very thing you tried to do, the way you went about it, the way you surrender, makes for greatness in you. If you had gone on with it and succeeded, that fact alone would have put you in the class with the great, strong, virile women of history. It —"

"With the Medicis, the Borgias and —" she began bitterly.

"Yes, with them. But they were great women, just the same. You are greater, for you have more than they possessed: a conscience. I wish I could tell you just what I feel. I haven't the words. I —"

"I only want you to tell me the truth. Do you despise me?"

"Again I say that I do not. I can only say that I regard you with — yes, with *awe*."

"As one might think of a deadly serpent."

"Hardly that," he said, smiling for the first time. He crossed over and laid his hand on her shoulder. "Don't think too meanly of yourself. I understand it all. You lived for months without a heart, that's all."

"You put it very gently."

"I think I'm right. Now, you've got it back, and it's hungry for the sweet, good things of life. You want to be happy. You want to love again and to be loved. You don't want to be pitied. I understand.

It's the return of a heart that went away long months ago and left an empty place that you filled with gall. The bitterness is gone. There is something sweet in its place. Am I not right?"

She hesitated. "If you mean that I want to be loved by my enemies, Brandon, you are wrong," she said clearly. "I have not been chastened in that par-\ ticular."

"You mean the Wrandalls?"

"It is not in my nature to love my enemies. We stand on the same footing as before, and always shall. They understand me, I understand them. I am glad that my project failed, not for their sake, but for my own."

He was silent. This woman was beyond him. He could not understand a nature like this.

"You say nothing. Well, I can't ask you to understand. We will not discuss my enemies, but my friends. What do you intend to do in respect to Hetty?"

"I am going to make her my wife," he said levelly.

She turned away. It was now quite dark. He could not see the expression on her face.

"What you have heard does not weaken your love for her?"

"No. It strengthens it."

"You know what she has done. She has taken a life with her own hands. Can you take her to your bosom, can you make her the mother of your own children? Remember, there is blood on her hands."

"Ah, but her heart is clean!"

"True," she said moodily, "her heart is clean."

"No cleaner than yours is now, Sara."

She uttered a short, mocking laugh. "It isn't necessary to say a thing like that to me."

"I beg your pardon."

Her manner changed abruptly. She turned to him, intense and serious.

"She is so far away, Brandon. On the other side of the world, and she is full of loathing for me. How am I to regain what I have lost? How am I to make her understand? She went away with that last ugly thought of me, with the thought of me as I appeared to her on that last, enlightening day. All these months it has been growing more horrible to her. It has been beside her all the time. All these months she has known that I pretended to love her as —"

"I don't believe you know Hetty as well as you think you do," he broke in. "You forget that she loved you with all her soul. You can't kill love so easily as all that. It will be all right, Sara. You must write and ask her to come back. It —"

"Ah, but you don't know!" Then she related the story of the liberated canary bird. "Hetty understands. The cage door is open. She may return when she chooses, but — don't you see? — she must come of her own free will."

"You will not ask her to come?"

"No. It is the test. She will know that I have told you everything. You will go to her. Then she may understand. If she forgives she will come back. There is nothing else to say, nothing else to consider."

"I shall go to her at once," he said resolutely.

She gave him a quick, searching glance.

"She may refuse to marry you, even now, Brandon."

"She can't!" he cried. An instant later his face fell. "By Jove, I — I suppose the law will have to be considered now. She will at least have to go through the form of a trial."

She whirled on him angrily. "The law? What has the law to do with it? Don't be a fool!"

"She ought to be legally exonerated," he said.

Her fingers gripped his arm fiercely. "I want you to understand one thing, Brandon. The story I have told you was for your ears alone. The secret lives with us and dies with us."

He looked his relief. "Right! It must go no farther. It is not a matter for the law to decide. You may trust me."

"I am cold," she said. He heard her teeth chatter distinctly as she pulled the thick mantle closer about her throat and shoulders. "It is very raw and wet down here. Come!"

As she started off along the long, narrow pier, he sprang after her, grasping her arm. She leaned rather heavily against him for a few steps and then drew herself up. Her teeth still chattered, her arm trembled in his clasp.

"By Jove, Sara, this is bad," he cried, in distress. "You're chilled to the marrow."

"Nerves," she retorted, and he somehow felt that her lips were set and drawn.

"You must get to bed right away. Hot bath, mustard, and all that. I'll not stop for dinner. Thanks just the same. I will be over in the morning."

"When will you sail?" she asked, after a moment.

"I can't go for ten days, at least. My mother goes into the hospital next week for an operation, as I've told you. I can't leave until after that's over. Nothing serious, but — well, I can't go away. I shall write to Hetty to-night, and cable her to-morrow. By the way, I — I don't know just where to find her. You see, we were not to write to each other. It was in the bargain. I suppose you don't know how I can —"

"Yes, I can tell you precisely where she is. She is in Venice, but leaves there to-morrow for Rome, by the Express."

"Then you have been hearing from her?" he cried sharply.

"Not directly. But I will say this much: there has not been a day since she landed in England that I have not received news of her. I have not been out of touch with her, Brandon, not even for an hour."

"Good heaven, Sara! You don't mean to say you've had her shadowed by — by detectives," he exclaimed, aghast.

"Her maid is a very faithful servant," was her ambiguous rejoinder.

CHAPTER XXI

He walked home swiftly through the early night, his
brain seething with tumultuous thoughts. The revelations of the day were staggering; the whole universe
seemed to have turned topsy-turvy since that devas-
tating hour at Burton's Inn. Somehow he was not
able to confine his thoughts to Hetty Castleton alone.
She seemed to sink into the background, despite the
absolution he had been so ready, so eager to grant
her on hearing the story from Sara's lips. Not that
his resolve to search her out and claim her in spite of
everything was likely to weaken, but that the absorb-
ing figure of Sara Wrandall stood out most clearly in
his reflections.

What an amazing creature she was! He could not
drive her out of his thoughts, even when he tried to
concentrate them on the one person who was dearest
to him of all in all the world, his warm-hearted, adorable Hetty. Strange contrasts suggested themselves
to him as he strode along, head bent and shoulders
hunched. He could not help contrasting the two
women. He loved Hetty; he would always love her, of
that he was positive. She was Sara's superior in every
respect, infinitely so, he argued. And yet there was
something in Sara that could crowd this adored one,
this perfect one out of his thoughts for the time being. He found it difficult to concentrate his thoughts
on Hetty Castleton.

How white and ill Sara had looked when she said
good-night to him at the door! The memory of her

dark, mysterious eyes haunted him; he could see them in the night about him. They had been full of pain; there were torrents of tears behind them. They had glistened as if burnished by the fires of fever.

Even as he wrote his long, triumphant letter to Hetty Castleton, the picture of Sara Wrandall encroached upon his mental vision. He could not drive it out. He thought of her as she had appeared to him early in the spring; through all the varying stages of their growing intimacy; through the interesting days when he vainly tried to translate her matchless beauty by means of wretched pigments; up to this present hour in which she was revealed, and yet not revealed, to him. Her vivid face was always before him, between his eyes and the thin white paper on which he scribbled so eagerly. Her feverish eyes were looking into his; she was reading what he wrote before it appeared on the surface of the sheet!

His letter to Hetty was a triumph of skill and diplomacy, achieved after many attempts. He found it hard not to say too much, and quite as difficult not to say too little. He spent hours over this all-important missive. At last it was finished. He read and re-read it, searching for the slightest flaw: a fatal word or suggestion that might create in her mind the slightest doubt as to his sincerity. She was sure to read this letter a great many times, and always with the view to finding something between the lines: such as pity, resignation, an enforced conception of loyalty, or even faith! He meant that she should find nothing there but love. It was full of tenderness, full of hope, full of promise. He was coming to her with a steadfast, enduring love in his heart, he wanted her now more than ever before.

There was no mention of Challis Wrandall, and but once was Sara's name used. There was nothing in the letter that could have betrayed their joint secret to the most acute outsider, and yet she would understand that he had wrung everything from Sara's lips. Her secret was his.

He decided that it would not be safe to anticipate the letter by a cablegram. It was not likely that any message he could send would have the desired effect. Instead of reassuring her, in all probability it would create fresh alarm.

Sleep did not come to him until after three o'clock. At two he got up and deliberately added a postscript to the letter he had written. It was in the nature of a poignant plea for Sara Wrandall. Even as he penned the lines, he shuddered at the thought of what she had planned to do to Hetty Castleton. Staring hard at the black window before him, the pen still in his hand, he allowed his thoughts to dwell so intimately on the subject of his well-meant postcript that her ashen face with its burning eyes seemed to take shape in the night beyond. It was a long time before he could get rid of the illusion. Afterwards he tried to conjure up Hetty's face and to drive out the likeness of the other woman, and found that he could not recall a single feature in the face of the girl he loved!

When he reached Southlook in the morning, he found that nearly all of the doors and windows were boarded up. Wagons were standing in the stable-yard, laden with trunks and crates. Servants without livery were scurrying about the halls. There was an air of finality about their movements. The place was being desolated.

"Yes, sir," said Watson, in reply to his question,

"we *are* in a rush. Mrs. Wrandall expects to close the 'ouse this evening, sir. We all go up this after-noon. I suppose you know, sir, we 'ave taken a new apartment in town."

" No!" exclaimed Booth.

"Yes, sir, we 'ave, sir. They've been decorating it for the pawst two weeks. Seems like she didn't care for the old one we 'ad. As a matter of fact, I didn't care much for it, either. She's taken one of them hexpensive ones looking out over the Park, sir. You know we used to look out over Madison Avenue, sir, and God knows it wasn't hinspirin'. Yes, sir, we go up this afternoon. Mrs. Wrandall will be down in a second, thank you, sir."

Booth actually was startled by her appearance when she entered the room a few minutes later. She looked positively ill.

" My dear Sara," he cried anxiously, " this is too bad. You are making yourself ill. Come, come, this won't do."

" I shall be all right in a day or two," she said, with a weary little gesture. " I have been nervous. The strain was too great, Brandon. This is the re-action, the relaxation you might say."

" Your hand is hot, your eyes look feverish. You'd better see your doctor as soon as you get to town. An ounce of prevention, you know."

" Well," she said, with a searching look into his eyes, " have you written to her? "

" Yes. Posted it at seven o'clock this morning."

" I trust you did not go so far as to — well, to volunteer a word in my behalf. You were not to do that, you know."

He looked uncomfortable. " I'm afraid I did take

your name in vain," he equivocated. "You are a —
a wonderful woman, Sara," he went on, moved to the
remark by a curious influence that he could not have
explained any more than he could have accounted for
the sudden gush of emotion that took possession of him.

She ignored the tribute. "You will persuade her
to come to New York with you?"

"For your sake, Sara, if she won't come for mine."

"She knows the cage is open," was her way of dismissing the subject. "I am glad you came over. I
have a letter from Leslie. It came this morning. You
may be interested in what he has to say of Hetty —
and of yourself." She smiled faintly. "He is determined that you shall not be without a friend while
he is alive."

"Les isn't such a rotter, Sara. He's spoiled, but
he is hardly to be blamed for that."

"I will read his letter to you," she said, and there
was no little significance in the way she put it. She
held the letter in her hand, but he had failed to notice
it before. Now he saw that it was a crumpled ball of
paper. He was obliged to wait for a minute or two
while she restored it to a readable condition. "He
was in London when this was written," she explained,
turning to the window for light. She glanced swiftly
over the first page until she found the place where
she meant to begin. "'I suppose Hetty Castleton has
written that we met in Lucerne two weeks ago,'" she
read. "'Curious coincidence in connexion with it, too.
I was with her father, Col. Braid Castleton, when we
came upon her most unexpectedly. I ran across him
in Paris just before the aviation meet, and got to
know him rather well. He's a fine chap, don't you
think? I confess I was somewhat surprised to learn

that he didn't know she'd left America. He explained
it quite naturally, however. He'd been ill in the north
of Ireland and must have missed her letters. Hetty
was on the point of leaving for Italy. We didn't see
much of her. But, by Jove, Sara, I am more completely gone on her than ever. She is adorable. Now
that I've met her father, who had the beastly misfortune to miss old Murgatroyd's funeral, I can readily
see wherein the saying " blood will tell " applies to
her. He is a prince. He came over to London with
me the day after we left Hetty in Lucerne, and I had
him in to meet mother and Vivian at Clarridge's. They
like him immensely. He set us straight on a good
many points concerning the Glynn and Castleton families. Of course, I knew they were among the best
over here, but I didn't know how fine they were until
we prevailed on him to talk a little about himself. You
will be glad to hear that he is coming over with us
on the *Mauretania*. She sails the 27th. We'll be on
the water by the time you get this letter. It had been
our intention to sail last week, but the Colonel had to
go to Ireland for a few days to settle some beastly
squabbles among the tenants. Next year he wants me
to come over for the shooting. He isn't going back
to India for two years, you may be interested to hear.
Two years' leave. Lots of influence, believe me!
We've been expecting him back in London since day
before yesterday. I dare say he found matters worse
than he suspected and has been delayed. He has been
negotiating for the sale of some of his property in
Belfast — factory sites, I believe. He is particularly
anxious to close the deal before he leaves England.
Had to lift a mortgage on the property, however, before he could think of making the sale. I staked him

to four thousand pounds, to tide him over. Of course, he is eager to make the sale. 'Gad, I almost had to beg him to take the money. Terribly proud and haughty, as the butler would say. He said he wouldn't sleep well until he has returned the filthy lucre. We are looking for him back any hour now. But if he shouldn't get here by Friday, we will sail without him. He said he would follow by the next boat, in case anything happened that he didn't catch the *Mauretania.*' "

Sara interrupted herself to offer an ironic observation: " If Hetty did not despise her father so heartily, I should advise you to look farther for a father-in-law, Brandon. The Colonel is a bad lot. Estates in the north of Ireland! Poor Leslie! " She laughed softly.

" He'll not show up, eh? "

" Not a bit of it," she said. " He may be charged to profit and loss in Leslie's books. This part of the letter will interest you," she went on, as if all that had gone before was of no importance to him. " ' I hear interesting news concerning you, my dear girl. My heartiest congratulations if it is all true. Brandy is one in a million. I have hoped all along to have him as a full-fledged brother-in-law, but I'm satisfied to have him as a sort of step-brother-in-law, if that's the way you'd put it. Father writes that every one is talking about it, and saying what a fine thing it is. He has a feeling of delicacy about approaching you in the matter, and I fancy it's just as well until everything is settled. I wish you'd let me make a suggestion, however. Wouldn't it be wise to let us all get together and talk over the business end of the game? Brandy's a fine chap, a corker, in fact, but the question is: has he got it in him to take Challis's place in the firm? You've got to consider the future as well as the present, my dear. We all do. With his artistic temperament he might play hob with your interests, and ours too, for that matter. Wouldn't it be wise for me to sound him a bit before we take him into the firm? Forgive me for suggesting this, but, as you know, your interests are mine, and I'm terribly keen about seeing you get the best of everything. By the way, wasn't he a bit gone on Hetty? Passing fancy, of course, and not deep enough to hurt anybody. Good old Brandy!'"

"There is more, Brandon, but it's of no consequence," she said, tossing the letter upon the table. "You see how the land lays."

Booth was pale with annoyance. "By Jove, Sara, what an insufferable ass he is!"

"The shoe pinches?"

"Oh, it's such perfect rot! I'm sorry on your account. Have you ever heard of such gall?"

"Oh, he is merely acting as the family spokesman. I can see them now in solemn conclave. They think it their indisputable right to select a husband for me, to pass upon him, to accept or decline him as they see fit, to say whether he is a proper man to hang up his hat and coat in the offices of Wrandall & Co."

"Do you mean to say —"

"Let's not talk about it, Brandon. It is too silly."

They fell to discussing her plans for the immediate future, although the minds of both were at work with something else.

"Now that I have served my purpose, I suppose you will not care to see so much of me," she said, as he prepared to take leave of her.

"Served your purpose? What do you mean?"

"I should have put it differently. You have been most assiduous in your efforts to force the secret from me. It has been accomplished. Now do you understand?"

"That isn't fair, Sara," he protested. "If you'll let me come to see you, in spite of what the gossips and Mr. Redmond Wrandall predict, you may be sure I will be as much in evidence as ever. I suppose I have been a bit of a nuisance, hanging on as I have."

"I admire your perseverance. More than that, I admire your courage in accepting the situation as you have. I only hope you may win her over to your way of thinking, Brandon. Good-bye."

"I shall go up to town to-morrow, kit and bag. When shall I see you? We have a great deal left to talk about before I sail."

"Come when you like."

"You really want me to come?"

"Certainly."

He studied her pale, tired face for a moment, and then shook his head. "You must take care of yourself," he said. "You are unstrung. Get a good rest and — and forget certain things if you can. Everything will come out all right in the end."

"It depends on what one is willing to accept as the end," she said.

The next morning she received an expected visitor at her apartment. Expecting him, she made a desperate effort to appear as strong and unconcerned as she had been on the occasion of a former meeting. There was little in her appearance to suggest worry, illness or alarm when she entered the rather unsettled little library and confronted the redoubtable Mr. Smith.

The detective had dropped her a line earlier in the

week asking for an audience at the earliest possible
moment.

"You are worried, madam," he said, after he had
carefully closed the door leading to the hall, "and so
am I."

"What do you want now?" she demanded. "You
have received your money. There is nothing else
that we —"

"Beg pardon, Mrs. Wrandall, but there is something else. I'm not after more money, as you may suspect. The size of the matter is, I'm here to put you
wise to what's going on without your knowing anything about it. Right or wrong, I'm still interested
in this case of yours. Understand me, I haven't lifted
a finger since that day in the country. I've quit cold,
just as I said I would. The trouble is, other people
are still nosing around."

"Sit down, Mr. Smith. Now, tell me what you are
here for."

Smith followed her example and sat down, drawing
a chair quite close to hers. He lowered his voice.

"Well, I've got next to something I think you ought
to know. Maybe old man Wrandall is back of it, but
I don't think he is. You see, so far as outsiders are
concerned, that reward still stands. A murder's a
murder and that's all there is to it. There are men
in this business who are going to hunt for that woman
until they get her. See what I mean?"

"Please go on. I suppose some one else suspects
me, and may have to be bought off," she said so significantly that he turned a bright red.

"Now don't think that of me, Mrs. Wrandall. I
am not in on this, I swear. You paid me of your own
free will and I laid down on the job. I don't deny

that I expected you to do it. I'm not what you'd call
a model of virtue and integrity. I served time in the
pen a good many years ago. They say it takes a
thief to catch a thief. That's not true. A detective
has to be dead honest or the thief catches him. I
think most of the men in my business are honest.
They have to be. You may not agree with me, but I
thought I was doing the square thing by you last summer. I had a theory and I was honest in believing it
was the right one. I thought you'd pay me to drop
the matter. I'm now dead sure I was wrong in sus-
pecting you for a minute. I'm no fool. I —"

Sara interrupted him.

"Will you be good enough to come to the point, Mr.
Smith?" she said coldly.

"Well," he said, leaning forward and speaking
very deliberately, "I've come here to tell you that the
police haven't quit on the job. They're about to make
a worse mistake than I made."

She felt herself turn pale. It required a great effort of the will to suppress the start that might have
betrayed her to the keen-eyed observer.

"That would be impossible, Mr. Smith," she said,
shaking her head and smiling.

"They've been watching that Ashtley girl you sent
out West just after the — er — thing happened. The
show-girl, you'll remember."

He must have observed the swift look of relief that
leaped into her eyes.

"What arrant stupidity," she cried, unable to
choose her words. "Why, that unhappy girl is dying
a slow and awful death. Surely they can't be hounding her now. Her innocence was clearly established
at the time. That is why I felt it to be my duty to

help her. She went out to her old home, to die or to get well. They must be fools."

"I'm just telling you, Mrs. Wrandall, that's all. Maybe you can call 'em off, if you know for a certainty that she's innocent." There was something accusing in his manner.

She became very cautious. "My opinion was formed upon the girl's story, and by what the police said after investigating it thoroughly."

"It's a way the police have, madam. They were not satisfied at the time. They simply gave her the rope, that's all. All this time they've had men watching her, day by day, out there in Montana. They say they've got new evidence, a lot of it."

"It is perfectly ridiculous," she cried, very much distressed. "And it must be stopped. I shall see the authorities at once."

"You may be too late. I heard last night that she is to be re-arrested out there and put through a fierce examination. They believe she's weakening and will confess if they go after her hard enough."

"Confess? How can she confess when she knows she is innocent?" she said sharply.

"You don't know much about the third degree, Mrs. Wrandall. I've known innocent people to confess under the bullying—"

"It must be stopped! Do you hear me? This thing cannot go on." She began to pace the floor in her agitation. "Yes, I have heard of those third degree atrocities. You are right, they may brow-beat the poor, sick thing into a confession. Does she know they have been watching her?"

"Sure. That's part of the game. They make it a point to get on the nerves. Something is bound to give, sooner or later. They've got her scared to death. She knows they're simply waiting for a chance to catch her unawares and trip her up. I tell you, it's a fearful strain. Strong men go down under it time and again. What must it be to this half-dead girl, who hasn't much to be proud of in life at the very best?"

"Tell me what to do," she cried, sitting down again, her eyes suddenly filling with tears.

"I don't know, ma'am. You see, if we had a grain of proof to work on, we might be able to turn 'em back, but there's the rub. We can't say they're wrong without having something up our sleeves to show that we are right. See what I mean?"

"But I tell you she is innocent!"

"Can you swear to that, Mrs. Wrandall?"

"I — I believe I can," she said, and then experienced a sharp sense of dismay. What possessed her to say it? "That is, I could stake my —"

"All that won't count for anything, if they get a signed confession out of her. Now we both know she is innocent. I'm willing to do what I can to help you. Turn about is fair play. If you want to send me out there, I'll try to spike their guns. Maybe I can get there in time to put fresh heart in the girl. She's safe if she doesn't go to pieces and say something she oughtn't to say."

"Oh, this is dreadful," she cried, harassed beyond words.

"It sure is. You see, the police work on the theory that some one's just got to be guilty of that crime. If it ain't the girl out yonder, then who is it? They know her private history. She said enough when she was in custody last year to show that she might have

had a pretty good reason for going after your husband — begging your pardon. You remember she
said he'd given her the go-by not more than two days
before he was killed. They'd been good friends up to
then. All of a sudden he chucks her, without ceremony. She admits she was sore about it. She says
she would have done him dirt if she had had the chance.
Well, that's against her. She did prove an alibi, as
you remember, but they're easy to frame up if necessary. I don't think she was clever enough to do the
job and get away as slick as the real one did. She
was a booze-fighter in those days. They always mess
things up. A mighty smooth party did that job.
Some one with a good deal more at stake than that
poor, reckless girl who didn't care much what became
of her. But the trouble is here: they've got her half
crazy with fear. First thing we know, she'll go clear
off her head and *believe* she did it. Then the law will
be satisfied. She's so far gone, I hear, that she won't
live to be brought to trial, of course. There's some
consolation in that."

"Consolation!" cried Sara bitterly. "She is bad,
as bad as a woman can be, I know, but I can't feel
anything but pity for her now."

"I guess your husband made her what she was,"
said Smith deliberately. "I don't suppose you ever
dreamed what was going on."

She regarded him with a fixed stare. "You are
mistaken, Mr. Smith," she said, and it was his turn to
stare. "Come back this evening at six. I must consult Mr. Carroll. We will decide what action to take."

"I'd advise you to be quick about it, Mrs. Wrandall. Something's bound to happen soon. The time
is ripe. I know for a positive fact that they're expect-

ing news from out there every day. It'd be a God's
blessing if the poor wretch could die before they get a
chance at her."

She started. " A God's blessing," she repeated
dully.

" Pretty hard lines, though," he mused, fumbling
with his hat near the door. " Even death wouldn't
clear her of the suspicion. Pretty tough to be branded
a murderess, no matter whether you're in the grave or
out of it. I'll be back at six."

She stood perfectly still, and, although her lips
were parted, she allowed him to go without a word in
response to his sombre declaration.

Half an hour later Mr. Carroll was on his way to
her apartment, vastly perturbed by the call that had
come to him over the telephone.

While waiting for him to appear, Sara Wrandall
deliberately set herself to the task of concocting a
likely and plausible excuse for intervention in behalf
of the wretched show-girl. She prepared herself for
his argument that the police might be right after all,
and that it would be the better part of wisdom to
shift the burden to their shoulders. She knew she
would be called upon to discount some very sensible
advice from the faithful old lawyer. Her reasons
would have to be good ones, not mere whims. He was
not likely to be moved by sentimentality. Moreover,
he had once expressed doubt as to the girl's innocence.

It did not once occur to her that it was Mr. Carroll's
business to respect the secrets of his clients.

CHAPTER XXII

To her secret amazement, the old lawyer did not offer a single protest when she repeated her convictions that the girl was innocent and should be protected against herself as well as against the police. There was something very disquieting in the way he acquiesced. She began to experience a vague, uneasy sense of wonder and apprehension.

"I am beginning to agree with that amiable scoundrel, Smith," he said, fixing his inscrutable gaze on the snapping coals in the fireplace. "A cleverer woman than this Miss — er — What's-Her-Name managed that affair at Burton's Inn."

She watched his face closely. Somehow she felt that he was about to mention the name of the woman he suspected, and it seemed to her that her heart stood still during the moment of suspense.

He lifted his eyes to her face. She saw something in them that set her to trembling.

"Why not be fair with me, Sara?" he asked calmly. She stared at him, transfixed. "Who killed Challis Wrandall?"

She opened her lips to protest against this startling question, but something rushed up from within to completely change the whole course of her conduct; something she could not explain but which swept away every vestige of strength, and left her weak and trembling, open-mouthed and pallid, with the liberated truth surging up from its prison to give itself into

the keeping of this staunch, loyal old friend and coun-
sellor.

Carroll heard her through to the very end of the
story without an interruption. Then he crossed over
and laid his hands on her shoulders; there was a gleam
of relief and satisfaction in his eyes.

"I am sorry you did not come to me with all this
in the beginning, Sara. A few words from me,—
kindly words, my dear,— would have shown you the
error of your ways and you would have cast out the
ugly devils that beset you. You would not have
planned the thing you are so ashamed of now. Together we could have protected Hetty and she would
not be your accuser now. You began nobly. I am
sorry you have the other part of it to look back upon.
But you may rest assured of one thing: you and Miss
Castleton have nothing to fear. We will keep the secret, if needs be, but if it should come to the worst no
harm would result to her through the law. The main
thing now is to protect that unhappy girl out West
against the inquisition."

She sat with bowed head.

When Smith returned at six o'clock, he found not
only Mr. Carroll waiting for him but Brandon Booth
as well. His instructions were clearly defined and con-
cise. He was to proceed without delay to Montana,
where he was to bolster up the frail girl's courage and
prevent if possible the disaster. Moreover, he was to
assure her that Challis Wrandall's wife forgave her
and would contest every effort made by the police to
lay the crime at her door. He was empowered to en-
gage legal counsel on his arrival in the Western town
and to fight every move of the police, not only in behalf of the girl herself, but of Sara Wrandall, who

thus publicly pronounced her faith in the young woman's innocence.

It was all very cleverly thought out, and Smith went away without being much wiser than when he came. Before departing he offered this rather sinister conclusion for Sara's benefit:

"Of course, Mrs. Wrandall, you understand that the police will wonder why you take such an interest in this girl. They're bound to think, and so will every one else, that you know a good deal more about the case than you've given out. See what I mean?"

"They are at liberty to think what they like, Mr. Smith," said she.

After Smith had gone, the three discussed the advisability of acquainting Hetty with the deplorable conditions that had arisen.

"I don't believe it would be wise to tell her," said Booth reflectively. "She'd be sure to sacrifice herself rather than let harm come to this girl. We couldn't stop her."

"No, she must not be told," said Sara, with finality.

"She is almost sure to find this out for herself some time," said the lawyer dubiously. "I think we'd better take her into our confidence. It is only right and just, you know."

"Not at present, not at present," said Sara irritably. "It would ruin everything."

Booth appreciated her reasons for delay much more clearly than they appeared to the matter-of-fact lawyer.

"The girl may die at any time," he explained, addressing Mr. Carroll, but not without a queer thrill of shame.

"That is not what I meant, Brandon," she exclaimed. "I want Hetty to come back with but one motive in her heart. Can't you see?"

As Booth and the lawyer walked down Fifth Avenue toward the club where they were to dine together, the latter, after a long silence, made a remark that disturbed the young man vastly.

"She's going all to pieces, Booth. Bound to collapse. That's the way with these strong-minded, secret, pent-up natures. She has brooded all these months and she's been living a lie. Well, the break has come. She's told you and me. Now, do you know what I'm afraid will happen?"

"I think I know what's in your mind," said the younger man seriously. "You are afraid she'll tell others?"

The lawyer tapped his forehead significantly. "It may result in *that.*"

"Never!" cried the other emphatically. "It will never be that way with her, Mr. Carroll. Her head is as clear as —"

"Brain fever," interrupted Carroll, with a gloomy shake of his head. "Delirium and all that sort of thing. Haven't you noticed how ill she looks? Feverish, nervous, irritable? Well, there you are."

"It is a dreadful state of affairs," groaned Booth.

"Not especially pleasant for you, my friend."

"God knows it isn't!"

"I believe, if I were in your place, I'd rather have the truth told broadcast than to live for ever with that peril hanging over me. It would be better for Miss Castleton, too."

"I am not worrying over that, sir," said the other earnestly. "I shall be able and ready to defend her, no matter what happens. To be perfectly honest with

you, I don't believe she's accountable to any one but
God in this matter. The law has no claim against
her, except in a perfunctory way. I don't deny that
it is only right and just that Wrandall's family should
know the truth, if she chooses to reveal it to them.
If she doesn't, I shall be the last to suggest it to her."

"On that point I thoroughly agree with you. The
Wrandall family should know the truth. It is —
well, I came near to using the word diabolical — to
keep them in ignorance. There is something owing
to the Wrandalls, if not to the law."

"Of course they would make a merciless effort to
prosecute her," said Booth, feeling the cold sweat start
on his brow.

"I am not so sure of that, my friend," was the
rather hopeful opinion of the old man. He appeared
to be weighing something in his mind, for as they
walked along he shook his head from time to time and
muttered under his breath, the while his companion
maintained a gloomy silence.

The perceptions of the astute old lawyer were not
far out of the way, as developments of the next day
were to prove. When Booth called in the afternoon
at Sara's apartment, he was met by the news that she
was quite ill and could see no one,— not even him.
The doctor had been summoned during the night and
had returned in the morning, to find that she had a
very high temperature. The butler could not enlighten Booth further than this, except to add that a
nurse was coming in to take charge of Mrs. Wrandall, more for the purpose of watching her symptoms
than for anything else, he believed. At least, so the
doctor had said.

Two days passed before the distressed young man

could get any definite news concerning her condition.
He unconsciously began to think of it as a *malady*, not
a mere illness, due of course to the remark Carroll had
dropped. It was Carroll himself who gave a definite
report of Sara. He met the lawyer coming away
from the apartment when he called to inquire.

" She isn't out of her head, or anything like that,"
said Carroll uneasily, " but she's in a bad way, Booth.
She is worrying over that girl out West, of course,
but I'll tell you what I think is troubling her more
than anything else. Down in her heart she realises
that Hetty Castleton has got to be brought face to
face with the Wrandalls."

" The deuce you say! "

" To-day I saw her for the first time. Almost immediately she asked me if I thought the Wrandalls
would treat Hetty fairly if they ever found out the
truth about her. I said I thought they would. I
didn't have the heart to tell her that their grievance
undoubtedly would be shifted from Hetty to her, and
that they wouldn't be likely to forgive her for the
stand she'd taken. She doesn't seem to care, however,
what the Wrandalls think of her. By the way, have
you any influence over Hetty Castleton? "

" I wish I were sure that I had," said Booth.

" Do you think she would come if you sent her a
cablegram? "

" I am going over —"

" She will have your letter in a couple of days, according to Sara, who seems to have a very faithful
correspondent in the person of that maid. I shudder
to think of the cable tolls in the past few months! I
sometimes wonder if the maid suspects anything more
than a loving interest in Miss Castleton. What I was

about to suggest is this: Couldn't you cable her on
Friday saying that Sara is very ill? This is Tuesday. We'll be having word from Smith to-morrow, I
should think."

" I will cable, of course, but Sara must not know that
I've done it."

" Can you come to my office to-morrow afternoon? "

" Yes. To-morrow night I shall go over to Philadelphia, to be gone till Friday. I hope it will not be
necessary for me to stay longer. You never can tell
about these operations."

" I trust everything will go well, Brandon."

.   .   .   .   .   .

Several things of note transpired before noon on
Friday.

The Wrandalls arrived from Europe, without the re-
calcitrant Colonel. Mr. Redmond Wrandall, who met
them at the dock, heaved a sigh of relief.

" He will be over on the *Lusitania*, next sailing,"
said Leslie, who for some reason best known to himself
wore a troubled look.

Mr. Wrandall's face fell. " I hope not," he said,
much to the indignation of his wife and the secret uneasiness of his son. " These predatory connections of
the British nobility —"

" Predatory! " gasped Mrs. Wrandall.

"— are a blood-sucking lot," went on the old gentleman firmly. " If he comes to New York, Leslie, I'll
stake my head he won't be long in borrowing a few
thousand dollars from each of us. And he'll not seek
to humiliate us by attempting to pay it back. Oh, I
know them."

Leslie swallowed rather hard. " What's the news
here, Dad? " he asked hastily. " Anybody dead? "

"Sara is quite ill, I hear. Slow fever of some sort, Carroll tells me."

"Is she going to marry Brandy Booth?" asked his son.

Mr. Wrandall's face stiffened. "I fear I was a little hasty in my conclusions. Brandon came to the office a few days ago and informed me in rather plain words that there is absolutely nothing in the report."

"The deuce you say! 'Gad, I wrote her a rather intimate letter —" Leslie got no farther than this. He was somewhat stunned and bewildered by his private reflections.

Mr. Wrandall was lost in study for some minutes, paying no attention to the remarks of the other occupants of the motor that whirled them across town.

"By the way, my dear," he said to his wife, a trifle irrelevantly, "don't you think it would be right for you and Vivian to drop in this afternoon and see Sara? just to let her know that she isn't without —"

"It's out of the question, Redmond," said his wife, a shocked expression in her face as much as to say that he must be quite out of his head to suggest such a thing. "We shall be dreadfully busy for several days, unpacking and — well, doing all sorts of *necessary* things."

"She is pretty sick, I hear," mumbled he.

"Hasn't she got a nurse?" demanded his wife.

"I merely offered the suggestion in order —"

"Well, we'll see her next week. Any other news?"

"Mrs. Booth, Brandon's mother, was operated on for something or other day before yesterday."

"Oh, dear! The poor thing! Where?"

"Philadelphia, of course."

"I wonder if — let me see, Leslie, isn't there a good

train to Philadelphia at four o'clock? I could go —"

" Really, my dear," said her husband sharply.

" You forget how busy we are, mother," said Vivian, without a smile.

" Nonsense!" said Mrs. Wrandall, in considerable confusion. " Was it a serious operation, Redmond?"

" They cut a bone out of her nose, that's all. Brandon says her heart is weak. They were afraid of the ether. She's all right, Carroll says."

" Goodness!" cried Mrs. Wrandall. One might have suspected a note of disappointment in her voice.

" I shall go up to see Sara this afternoon," said Vivian calmly. " What's the number of her new apartment?"

" *You* have been up to see her, of course," said Mrs. Wrandall acidly.

He fidgetted. " I didn't hear of her illness until yesterday."

" I'll go up with you, Viv," said Leslie.

" No, you won't," said his sister flatly. " I'm going to apologise to her for something I said to Brandon Booth. You needn't tag along, Les."

At half-past five in the afternoon, the Wrandall limousine stopped in front of the tall apartment building near the Park, a footman jerked open the door, and Miss Wrandall stepped out. At the same moment a telegraph messenger boy paused on the sidewalk to compute the artistic but puzzling numerals on the imposing grilled doors of the building.

Miss Wrandall had herself announced by the obsequious doorman, and stood by in patience to wait for the absurd rule of the house to be carried out: " No one could get in without being announced from below," said the doorman.

"I c'n get in all right, all right," said the messenger boy, "I got a tellygram for de loidy."

"Go to the rear!" exclaimed the doorman, with
some energy.

While Miss Wrandall waited in Sara's reception hall
on the tenth floor, the messenger, having traversed a
more devious route, arrived with his message.

Watson took the envelope and told him to wait.
Five minutes passed. Miss Wrandall grew very uncomfortable under the persistent though complimen-
tary gaze of the street urchin. He stared at her,
wide-eyed and admiring, his tribute to the glorious.
She stared back occasionally, narrow-eyed and reprov-
ing, *her* tribute to the grotesque.

"Will you please step into the drawing-room, Miss
Wrandall," said Watson, returning. He led her
across the small foyer and threw open a door. She
passed into the room beyond.

Then he turned to the boy who stood beside the hall
seat, making change for a quarter as he approached.
"Here," he said, handing him the receipt book and a
dime, "that's for you." He dropped the quarter into
his own pocket, where it mingled with coins that were
strangers to it up to that instant, and imperiously
closed the door behind the boy who failed to say
"thank you." Every man to his trade!

There was a woman in the drawing-room when
Vivian entered, standing well over against the windows with her back to the light. The visitor stopped
short in surprise. She had expected to find her sister-
in-law in bed, attended by a politely superior person
in pure white.

"Why, Sara," she began, "I am *so* glad to see you
are up and—"

The other woman came forward. " But I am not Sara, Miss Wrandall," she said, in a well-remembered voice. " How do you do? "

Vivian found herself looking into the face of Hetty Castleton. Instantly she extended her hand.

" This *is* a surprise! " she exclaimed. " When did you return? Leslie told me your plans were quite settled when he saw you in Lucerne. Oh, I see! Of course! How stupid of me. Sara sent for you."

" She has been quite ill," said Hetty, non-committally. " We got in yesterday. I thought my place was here, naturally."

" Naturally," repeated Vivian, in a detached sort of way. " How is she to-day? May I see her? "

" She is very much better. In fact, she is sitting up in her room." A warm flush suffused her face, a shy smile appeared in her eyes. " She is receiving two gentlemen visitors, to be perfectly honest, Miss Wrandall, her lawyer, Mr. Carroll, and — Mr. Booth."

They were seated side by side on the uncomfortable Louis Seize divan in the middle of the room.

" Perhaps she won't care to see me, after an audience so fatiguing," said Miss Wrandall sweetly. " And so exasperating," she added, with a smile.

Hetty looked her perplexity.

" But she will see you, Miss Wrandall — if you don't mind waiting. It is a business conference they're having."

An ironic gleam appeared in the corner of Vivian's eye. " Oh," she said, and waited. Hetty smiled uncertainly. All at once the tall American girl was impressed by the wistful, almost humble look in the Englishwoman's eyes, an appealing look that caused her to wonder not a little. Like a flash she jumped at an obvious conclusion, and almost caught her breath. This girl loved Booth and was losing him! Vivian exulted for a moment and then, with an impulse she could not quite catalogue, laid her hand on the other's slim fingers, and murmured somewhat hazily: "Never mind, never mind!"

"Oh, you *must* wait," cried Hetty, not at all in touch with the other's mood. "Sara expects to see you. The men will be out in a few minutes."

"I think I will run in to-morrow morning," said Vivian hastily. She arose almost immediately and again extended her hand. "So glad to see you back again, Miss Castleton. Come and see me. Give my love to Sara."

She took her departure in some haste, and in her heart she was rejoicing that she had not succeeded in making a fool of herself by confessing to Sara that she had said unkind things about her to Brandon Booth.

Hetty resumed her seat in the broad French window and stared out over the barren tree-tops in the Park. A frightened, pathetic droop returned to her lips. It had been there most of the day.

In Sara's boudoir, the doors of which were carefully closed, three persons were in close, even repressed conference. The young mistress of the house sat propped up in a luxurious chaise-longue, wan but intense. Confronting her were the two men, leaning forward in their chairs. Mr. Carroll held in his hand a number of papers, prominent among them being three or four telegrams. Booth's face was radiant despite the serious matter that occupied his mind. He had reached town early in the morning in response to a telephone message from Carroll announcing the sudden, unan-

nounced appearance of Hetty Castleton at his offices
on the previous afternoon. The girl's arrival had
been most unexpected. She walked in on Mr. Carroll, accompanied by her maid, who had a distinctly
sheepish look in her eyes and seemed eager to explain
something but could not find the opportunity.

With some firmness, Miss Castleton had asked Mr.
Carroll to explain why the woman had been set to spy
upon her every movement, a demand the worthy lawyer could not very well meet for the good and sufficient
reason that he wasn't very clear about it himself.
Then Hetty broke down and cried, confessing that she
was eager to go to Mrs. Wrandall, at the same time
sobbing out something about a symbolic dicky-bird,
much to Mr. Carroll's wonder and perplexity.

He sent the maid from the room, and retired with
Miss Castleton to the innermost of his private offices,
where without much preamble he informed her that he
knew everything. Moreover, Mr. Booth was in possession of all the facts and was even then on the point
of starting for Europe to see her. Of course, his letter had failed to reach her in time. There was quite
a tragic scene in the seclusion of that remote little
office, during which Mr. Carroll wiped his eyes and
blew his nose more than once, after which he took it
upon himself to despatch a messenger to Sara with the
word that he and Miss Castleton would present themselves within half an hour after his note had been delivered.

A telegram already had come from Smith in the
far-away Montana town, transmitting news that disturbed him more than he cared to admit. The show-
girl was lying at the point of death, and he was having a very hard time of it trying to keep the resolute

authorities from swooping down upon her for the ante-mortem statement they desired. It would appear that he arrived just in time to put courage into the girl. He would see to it that any statement she made would be the truth! But Mr. Carroll was not so sure of Smith's ability to avert disaster. He knew something of the terrors of the third degree. The police would fight hard for vindication.

The meeting between Sara and Hetty was affecting. . . . Almost immediately the former began to show the most singular signs of improvement. She laughed and cried and joyously announced to the pro-testing nurse that she was feeling quite well again! And, in truth, she got up from the couch on which she reclined and insisted on being dressed for dinner. In another room the amazed nurse was frantically appeal-ing to Mr. Carroll to let her send for the doctor, only to be confounded by his urbane announcement that Mrs. Wrandall was as " right as a string " and, please God, she wouldn't need the services of doctor or nurse again for years to come. Then he asked the nurse if she had ever heard of a disease called " nostalgia."

She said she had heard of " home-sickness."

" Well, that's what ailed Mrs. Wrandall," he said. " Miss Castleton is the *cure*."

Booth came the next morning. . . . Even as she lay passive in his arms, Hetty denied him. Her arms were around his neck as she miserably whispered that she could not, would not be his wife, notwithstand-ing her love for him and his readiness to accept her as she was. She was obdurate, lovingly, tenderly ob-durate. He would have despaired but for Sara, to whom he afterwards appealed.

" Wait," was all that Sara had said, but he took

heart. He was beginning to look upon her as a sorceress. A week ago he had felt sorry for her; his heart had been touched by her transparent misery. To-day he saw her in another light altogether; as the determined, resourceful, calculating woman who, having failed to attain a certain end, was now intensely, keenly interested in the development of another of a totally different nature. He could not feel sorry for her to-day.

Hetty deliberately had placed herself in their hands, withdrawing from the conference shortly before Vivian's arrival to give herself over to gloomy conjectures as to the future, not only for herself, but for the man she loved and the woman she worshipped with something of the fidelity of a beaten dog.

.   .   .   .   .   .

Carroll had in his hand the second telegram from Smith, just received.

"This relieves the situation somewhat," he observed, with a deep sigh. "She's dead, and she didn't give in, thanks to Smith. Rather clever of him to get a signed statement, however, witnessed by the prosecuting attorney and the chief of police. It puts an end to everything so far as she is concerned."

"Read again, Mr. Carroll, what she had to say about me," said Sara, a slight tremour of emotion in her voice.

He read from the lengthy telegram: "'She wants me to thank Mrs. Wrandall for all she has done to make her last few months happy ones, such as they were. She appreciates her kindness all the more because she realises that her benefactress must have known everything. Almost the last words she spoke were in the nature of a sort of prayer that God would

forgive her for what she had done to Mrs. Wrandall.' "

" Poor girl! She could not have known that it was
justice, not sentiment that moved me to provide for
her," said Sara.

" Well, she is off our minds, at any rate," said the
matter-of-fact lawyer. " Now are you both willing
to give serious consideration to the plan I propose?
Take time to think it over. No harm will come to
Miss Castleton, I am confident. There will be a nine
days' sensation, but, after all, it is the best thing for
everybody. You propose living abroad, Booth, so
what are the odds if —"

" I shan't live abroad unless Hetty reconsiders her
decision to not marry me," said the young man dismally. " 'Gad, Sara, you must convince her that I
love her better than —"

" I think she knows all that, Brandon. As I said
before, wait! And now, Mr. Carroll, I have this to
say to your suggestion: I for one am relentlessly opposed to the plan you advocate. There is no occasion
for this matter to go to the public. A trial, you say,
would be a mere formality. I am not so sure of that.
Why put poor Hetty's head in the lion's mouth at this
late stage, after I have protected her so carefully all
these months? Why take the risk? We know she is
innocent. Isn't it enough that we acquit her in our
hearts? No, I cannot consent, and I hold both of you
to your promises."

" There is nothing more I can say, my dear Sara,"
said Carroll, shaking his head gloomily, " except to
urge you to think it over very seriously. Remember,
it may mean a great deal to her — and to our eager
young friend here. Years from now, like a bolt from

the sky, the truth may come out in some way. Think
of what it would mean then."

Sara regarded him steadily. "There are but four
people who know the truth," she said slowly. "It
isn't likely that Hetty or Brandon will tell the story.
Professional honour forbids your doing so. That
leaves me as the sole peril. Is that what you would
imply, my dear friend?"

"Not at all," he cried hastily, "not at all. I —"

"That's all tommy-rot, Sara," cried Booth earnestly. "We just *couldn't* have anything to fear
from you."

With curious inconsistency, she shook her head and
remarked: "Of course, you never could be quite easy
in your minds. There would always be the feeling of
unrest. Am I to be trusted, after all? I have proved
myself to be a vindictive schemer. What assurance
can you and Hetty have that I will not turn against
one or the other of you some time and crush you to satisfy a personal grievance? How do you know, Brandon, that I am not in love with you at this very —"

"Good heavens, Sara!" he cried, agape.

"— at this very moment?" she continued. "It
would not be so very strange, would it? I am very
human. The power to love is not denied me. Oh, I
am merely philosophising. Don't look so serious.
We will suppose that I continued along my career as
the woman scorned. You have seen how I smart under the lash. Well?"

"But all that is impossible," said Booth, his face
clearing. "You're not in love with me, and never
can be. That! for your philosophy!"

At the same instant he became aware of the singular gleam in her eyes; a liquid, Oriental glow that

seemed to reflect light on her lower lids as she sat there with her face in the shadow. Once or twice before he had been conscious of the mysterious, seductive appeal. He stared back at her, almost defensively, but her gaze did not waver. It was he who first looked away, curiously uncomfortable.

"Still," she said slowly, "I think you would be wise to consider all possible contingencies."

"I'll take chances, Sara," he said, with an odd buoyancy in his voice that, for the life of him, he could not explain, even to himself.

"Even admitting that such should turn out to be the case," said Mr. Carroll judicially, "I don't believe you'd go so far as to put your loyal friends in jeopardy, Sara. So we will dismiss the thought. Don't forget, however, that you hold them in the hollow of your hand. My original contention was based on the time-honoured saying, 'murder will out.' We never can tell what may turn up. The best laid plans of men and mice oft —"

Sara settled back among the cushions with a peremptory wave of her hand. The loose, flowing sleeve fell away, revealing her white, exquisitely modelled arm almost to the shoulder. For some strange, unaccountable reason Booth's eyes fell.

"I am tired, wretchedly tired. It has been a most exhausting day," she said, with a sudden note of weariness in her voice. Both men started up apologetically. "I will think seriously of your plan, Mr. Carroll. There is no hurry, I'm sure. Please send Miss Wrandall in to me, will you? Perhaps you would better tell Hetty to come in as soon as Vivian leaves. Come back to-morrow afternoon, Brandon. I shall be much more cheerful. By the way, have you noticed that Dicky,

out in the library, has been singing all afternoon as
if his little throat would split? It is very curious, but
to-day is the first time he has uttered a note in nearly
five months. Just listen to him! He is fairly riotous
with song."

Booth leaned over and kissed the hand she lifted to
him. "He is like the rest of us, Sara, inordinately
happy." A slight shiver ran through her arm. He
felt it.

"I am so afraid his exuberance of spirit may annoy
Vivian," said she, with a rare smile. "She detests
vulgarity."

The men departed. She lay back in the chaise-
longue, her eyes fixed on the hand he had touched with
his lips.

Watson tapped twice on the door.

"Miss Wrandall could not wait, ma'am," he said,
opening the door softly. "She will call again to-
morrow."

"Thank you, Watson. Will you hand me the
cigarettes?"

Watson hesitated. "The cigarettes, ma'am?"

"Yes."

"But the doctor's orders, ma'am, begging your pardon for —"

"I have a new doctor, Watson."

"I beg pardon, ma'am!"

"The celebrated Dr. Folly," she said lightly.

CHAPTER XXIII

WHEN Smith returned from the Far West, a few days after the events narrated in the foregoing chapter, he repaired at once to Sara's apartment, bringing with him not only the signed statement of the Ashtley girl, but the well-worn and apparently cherished prayer-book that had been her solace during the last few months of her life. On the fly-leaf she had written: "I have nothing of God's earthly gifts to leave behind but this. It has brought me riches, but it is a poor thing in itself. I bequeath it, my only earthly possession, to the kind and merciful one who taught me that there is good in this bad world of ours." It was inscribed to "Mrs. Challis Wrandall."

"She made me promise to give it to you with my own hands, Mrs. Wrandall," said Smith, in the library, putting as much emotion into his voice and manner as he thought the occasion and the audience demanded. Miss Castleton and Mr. Booth were also present. "She was a queer girl. I never saw one just like her, believe me. Just after she signed that paper, I had a chance to be alone with her for a minute or two. She asked me to stoop over so's I could hear what she had to say, and she made me promise not to say a word about it until after she was gone. Well, it will surprise you just as much as it did me, what she had to say with her dying breath, so to speak." He paused for the effect.

"What did she say to you?" demanded Sara.

"Well, sir, do you know that that girl knew all

along who it was that went up to Burton's Inn that
evening with your husband? What do you think of
that?"

There was not a sound in the room. Even the coals
in the fireplace seemed to take that instant to hush
their blithe crackling. Smith's listeners might have
been absolutely breathless, they were so rigid. Each
had the grotesque fear that he was about to point his
finger at Hetty Glynn and call upon her to answer to
an accusation from the grave.

The next moment they drew a deep, quivering breath
of relief. The detective went on, almost apologetically. "I tried to bluff her into telling me who she
was, Mrs. Wrandall, but she wouldn't fall for it.
After a little while, I saw it was no use questioning
her. She was as firm as a rock about it. And she
was pretty near gone, I can tell you. As a matter of
fact, her heart went back on her suddenly not ten
minutes later, sort of surprising all of us. But she
did manage to whisper a few things to me while the
others were conversing in the hall. She said that she
saw another girl with Mr. Wrandall about a week
before the murder, a stranger and a very pretty one.
He knew how to pick out the pretty — I — I beg your
pardon, ma'am. That sort of slipped out. You
see —"

"Never mind. I understand. Go on."

"Right after that he told her he was through with
her. Chucked her, that's the sum and substance of it,
for the new one, whoever she was. She raised a row
with him about it, and he laughed at her. For nearly
a week she spied on him, and she saw him out in the
car with the stranger at least half a dozen times.
Now comes the queer part of it, and the thing that

made her keep her lips closed at first, right after the
killing — the murder, I mean. She laid for him in
front of his home on the very day of the murder and
swore she'd do something desperate if he didn't give
the other one up. He took her to a cheap restaurant
on the West Side, and she was sure that several waiters
saw that they were quarrelling. To get her out of
the place, he induced her to get in his car and they
went for a ride out as far as Van Courtlandt Park.
The police never got onto all this. But she lived in
terror for a few days, believing that the waiters might
remember them, although neither of them had ever
been in the place before. When she was taken up for
examination, she still wondered if they would be called
on to identify her. Nothing doing. It was right
then, Mrs. Wrandall, that you stepped in and said
that her alibi was sufficient, and staked her for life
out there in the West. She says she saw the other
girl after the murder, but she wouldn't say where it
was or when. Of course, she couldn't swear that this
girl did the job up there at Burton's, but she was
pretty nearly dead certain she was the one who went
up there with him. She was just on the point of telling the police about this girl, to save herself, when you
helped her out of the fix, and then she got to thinking
strange things, she said. This is what she said to me,
there on her death-bed, and I want to tell you it gave
me an idea of character that I had never come across
before in all my experience. She said that if Mrs.
Wrandall here could be fine enough to befriend her,
knowing all you did, ma'am, about her and your husband, it oughtn't to be hard for her to help another
erring girl by keeping her mouth shut. And that's
just what she did. She kept still. That sort of rea-

soning was new to me. But, when you stop to think
it over, maybe she was right. A word from her might
have sent a fellow creature to the chair. She had had
her lesson in charity from you, Mrs. Wrandall, and,
while you didn't mean it to have that effect, you undoubtedly spoiled the best chance we'll ever have to
get the real woman in the case."

There was a moment of tense silence. Booth was
the first to risk the effort at speech.

"And she wouldn't say a word more? She gave
you no — no clue?"

"Not the faintest idea, sir. She took that girl's
name to the grave with her."

"Her name! She knew her name?" cried Sara,
leaning forward.

"She heard it a day or two after you had her set
free, Mrs. Wrandall. Don't it beat all? Now, don't
you see what might have happened if we'd let the police put the screws on her out there? Why, the
chances are, a hundred to one, she would have broken
down in the end, and told who this other woman is.
There is where we made a fatal mistake. But it's too
late now, confound it."

"Yes, it's too late now," said Sara, relaxing in her
chair.

"I'm telling you this, although maybe I wasn't expected to. She made me promise not to tell the police.
Well, I guess I can keep that promise. You ain't the
police."

"It is a most remarkable story, Mr. Smith," said
Sara, "but I do not see that it leads us anywhere.
We are quite as much in the dark as before."

The detective studied the pattern in the rug at his
feet, a defeated look in his eyes.

"I suppose I *might* have forced her to tell me, Mrs. Wrandall, but I—I didn't have the heart to bully her. I suppose you'll always have it in for me for letting the chance slip?"

"I think I have already told you, Mr. Smith, that I am not at all curious."

With the departure of the detective, the three conspirators fell into an agitated discussion of the revelations he had made; so grave had their peril appeared to be at the opening of his narrative that they were still in a state of perturbation from which they were not to recover for a long time. Their cheeks were white and their eyes were dark with the dread that remained even after the danger was past. Hetty's arms hung limp and nerveless at her sides as she lay back in the chair and stared numbly at her friends.

"Do you really believe she knew that I was the one?" she asked miserably. "Do you think she knew my name?" she shuddered.

"What if she did?" demanded Booth with an assumption of indifference he was not yet able to feel. "She was a brick to keep it to herself. The danger's past, dearest. Don't let it worry you now."

"But just think of it! At any time she could have told this story to the police and— Oh, wasn't it appalling? I thought my heart would never beat again!"

"We never knew till now how close we were to the abyss," said Sara, drawing the thin wrap closer about her shoulders. Suddenly she laughed. "But why contemplate the disaster that didn't occur? We are more secure than ever. This girl was the only one who knew, because no one else could have had the same incentive to spy upon him, Hetty. She is dead.

Your name isn't likely to be shouted from the house-tops, for the simple reason that it is safely locked up in a grave." She hesitated for a moment and then added: " In two graves, if it makes you feel more secure."

The others looked at her in open astonishment.

Booth was frowning. Sara glanced at his stern face and her eyes fell. " If that sounded cold and un-feeling, I am sorry, Hetty. It was my unfortunate way of trying to convince you that there is nothing left for you to fear."

She left them a moment later, bending over to kiss Hetty's cheek as she passed by her chair.

" Now, you see what I mean, Brandon, when I in-sist that it would be a mistake for you to marry me," said Hetty in a troubled voice. " We could never be sure of immunity."

" You refer to that remark of hers? "

" She is a strange woman. I sometimes have the feeling that she wants to keep me with her for ever. I feel that she will not let me go."

" That's pure nonsense, Hetty," he said. " She wants you to marry me, I am positive." He may have thought his tone convincing, but something caused her to regard him rather fixedly, as if she were trying to solve an elusive puzzle.

He took her by the arms and raised her to her feet. Holding her quite close, he looked down into her ques-tioning eyes and said very seriously:

" You are suspicious, even of me, dearest. I want you. There is but one way for you to be at peace with yourself: shift your cares over to my shoulders. I will stand between you and everything that may come up to trouble you. We love one another. Why

should we sacrifice our love for the sake of a shadow?
For a week, dearest, I've been pleading with you;
won't you end the suspense to-day — end it now —
and say you will be my wife?"

The appeal was so gentle, so sincere, so full of longing that she wavered. Her tender blue eyes, lately
so full of dread, grew moist with the ineffable sweet-
ness of love, and capitulation was in them. Her
warm, red lips parted in a dear little smile of surrender.

"You know I love you," she said tremulously.

He kissed the lovely, appealing lips, not once but
many times.

"God, how I worship you," he whispered passionately. "I can't go on without you, darling. You
are life to me. I love you! I love you!"

She drew back in his arms, the shadow chasing the
light out of her eyes.

"We are both living in the present, we are both
thinking only of it, Brandon. What of the future?
Can we foresee the future? Dear heart, I am always
thinking of your future, not my own. Is it right for
me to bring you —"

"And I am thinking only of your future," he said
gravely. "The future that shall be mine to shape
and to make glad with the fulfilment of every promise
that love has in store for both of us. Put away the
doubts, drive out the shadows, dearest. Live in the
light for ever. Love is light."

"If I were only sure that my shadows would not
descend upon you, I —"

He drew her close and kissed her again.

"I am not afraid of your shadows. God be my witness, Hetty, I glory in them. They do not reflect

weakness, but strength and nobility. They make you all the more worth having. I thank God that you are what you are, dear heart."

"Give me a few days longer, Brandon," she pleaded. "Let me conquer this strange thing that lies here in my brain. My heart is yours, my soul is yours. But the brain is a rebel. I must triumph over it, or it will always lie in wait for a chance to overthrow this little kingdom of ours. To-day I have been terrified. I am disturbed. Give me a few days longer."

"I would not grant you the respite, were I not so sure of the outcome," he said gently, but there was a thrill of triumph in the tones. Her eyes grew very dark and soft and her lips trembled with the tide of love that surged through her body. "Oh, how adorable you are!" he cried, straining her close in a sudden ecstasy of passion.

The door-bell rang. They drew apart, breathing rapidly, their blood leaping with the contact of opposing passions, their flesh quivering. With a shy, sweet glance at him, she turned toward the door to await the appearance of Watson. He could still feel her in his arms.

A drawling voice came to them from the vestibule, and a moment later Leslie Wrandall entered the library, pulling off his gloves as he came.

"Hello," he said glibly. "I told that fellow down-stairs it wasn't necessary to announce me by telephone. Silly arrangement, I say. Why the deₙₜ should they think everybody's a thief or a book agent or a constable with a subpoena? He knows I'm one of the family. I'm likely to run in any time, I told him, and — Oh, I say, I'm not butting in, am I, Miss Castleton?"

He shook hands with both of them, and then offered his cigarette case to Booth, first selecting one for himself. Hetty assured him that he was not *de trop*, sheer profligacy on her part in view of his readiness to concede the point without a word from her.

"Nipping wind," he said, taking his stand before the fireplace. "Where is Sara? Never mind, don't bother her. I've got all the time in the world. By the way, Miss Castleton, what is the latest news from your father?"

"I dare say you have later news than I," she said, a trace of annoyance in her manner.

"I thought perhaps he had written you about his plans."

"My father does not know that I have returned to New York."

"Oh, I see. Of course. Um — um! By the way, I think the Colonel is a corker. One of the most amiable thoroughbreds I've ever come across. Ripping. He's never said anything to me about your antipathy toward him, but I can see with half an eye that he is terribly depressed about it. Can't you get together some way on —"

"Really, Mr. Wrandall, you are encouraging your imagination to a point where words ultimately must fail you," she said very positively. Booth could hardly repress a chuckle.

"It's not imagination on my part," said Leslie with conviction, failing utterly to recognise the obvious. "I suppose you know that he is coming over to visit me for six weeks or so. We became rattling good friends before we parted. By Jove, you should hear him on old Lord Murgatroyd's will! The quintessence of wit! I couldn't take it as he does. Expectations

and all that sort of thing, you know, going up like a
hot air balloon and bursting in plain view. But he
never squeaked. Laughed it off. A British attribute,
I dare say. I suppose you know that he is obliged to
sell his estate in Ireland."

Hetty started. She could not conceal the look of
shame that leaped into her eyes.

" I — I did not know," she murmured.

" Must be quite a shock to you. Sit down, Brandy.
You look very picturesque standing, but chairs were
made to sit upon — or in, whichever is proper."

Booth shrugged his shoulders.

" I think I'll stand, if you don't mind, Les."

" I merely suggested it, old chap, fearing you might
have overlooked the possibilities. Yes, Miss Castleton, he left us in London to go up to Belfast on this
dismal business." There was something in the back
of his mind that he was trying to get at in a tactful
manner. " By the way, is this property entailed? "

" I know nothing at all about it, Mr. Wrandall,"
said she, with a pleading glance at her lover, as if to
inquire what stand she should take in this distressing
situation.

" If it is entailed he can't sell it," said Booth quietly.

" That's true," said Leslie, somewhat dubiously.
Then, with a magnanimity that covered a multitude of
doubts he added: " Of course, I am only interested in
seeing that you are properly protected, Miss Castleton. I've no doubt you hold an interest in the estates."

" I can't very well discuss a thing I know absolutely
nothing about," she said succinctly.

" Most of it is in building lots and factories in Belfast, of course." It was more in the nature of a ques-

tion than a declaration. "The old family castle isn't very much of an asset, I take it."

"I fancy you can trust Colonel Castleton to make the best possible deal in the premises," said Booth drily.

"I suppose so," said the other resignedly. "He is a shrewd beggar, I'm convinced of that. Strange, however, that I haven't heard a word from him since he left us in London. I've been expecting a cablegram from him every day for nearly a fortnight, letting me know when to expect him."

Hetty had gone over to the window and was looking out over the darkening park.

"Perhaps he means to surprise you, old man," said Booth, with a smile that Leslie did not in the least interpret.

With a furtive glance at the girl, whose back was toward them, he got up from his chair and came quite close to Booth, frowning slightly as he plucked at his moustache with nervous fingers. Lowering his voice to a cautious half-whisper, he inquired:

"I say, Brandy, what do you know about him? Is he on the level, or is he a damned old rascal?"

"Did you lend him any money?" asked Booth, with a malicious grin.

Leslie gulped. A fine perspiration broke out on his forehead. "Yes, I did," he replied, and, on reflection, slyly kicked himself on the ankle, making sure however that Hetty was still looking the other way. "Go on! Break it rudely. He's no good, eh? A shark, eh?"

"Believe me, I don't know anything about him, Les," said Booth, with a sudden feeling of loyalty to the Colonel's daughter. "He may pay up."

Leslie snapped his fingers while they were on the

way to his upper lip, and almost missed his moustache
by the digression. At any rate, he seemed to be fumbling for it.

"I did it on her account," he explained, nodding his
head in Hetty's direction. He thought hard for a
moment. "Of course, he won't be such a blithering
fool as to come over here, will he?"

"I shouldn't, if I had been able to get what I wanted
at home, as he very obviously did," said Booth piti-
lessly. "How much was it?"

Leslie waved his hand disdainfully. "Oh, a few
hundred pounds, that's all. No harm done."

"Are you going to California this winter for the
flying?" asked Hetty, coming toward them.

Sara entered at that juncture, and they all sat down
to listen for half an hour to Leslie's harangue on the
way the California meet was being mismanaged, at the
end of which he departed.

He took Booth away with him, much to that young
man's disgust.

"Do you know, Brandy, old fellow," said he as they
walked down Fifth Avenue in the gathering dusk of the
early winter evening, "ever since I've begun to suspect that damned old humbug of a father of hers, I've
been congratulating myself that there isn't the remotest chance of his ever becoming my father-in-law.
And, by George, you'll never know how near I was to
leaping blindly into the brambles. What a close call
I had!"

Booth's sarcastic smile was hidden by the dusk. He
made no pretence of openly resenting the meanness of
spirit that moved Leslie to these caddish remarks. He
merely announced in a dry, cutting voice:

"I think Miss Castleton is to be congratulated that

her injury is no greater than Nature made it in the beginning."

"What do you mean by 'nature'?"

"Nature gave her a father, didn't it?"

"Obviously."

"Well, why add insult to injury?"

"By Jove! Oh, I *say*, old man!"

They parted at the next corner. As Booth started to cross over to the Plaza, Leslie called out after him:

"I say, Brandy, just a second, please. Are you going to marry Miss Castleton?"

"I am."

"Then, I retract the scurvy things I said back there. I asked her to marry me three times and she refused me three times. What I said about the brambles was rotten. I'd ask her again if I thought she'd have me. There you are, old fellow. I'm a rotten cad, but I apologise to you just the same."

"You're learning, Leslie," said Booth, taking the hand the other held out to him.

While the painter was dining at his club later on in the evening, he was called to the telephone. Watson was on the wire. He said that Mrs. Wrandall would like to know if Mr. Booth could drop in on her for a few minutes after dinner, "to discuss a very important matter, if you please, sir." At nine o'clock, Booth was in Sara's library, trying to grasp a new and remarkable phase in the character of that amazing woman.

He found Hetty waiting for him when he arrived.

"I don't know what it all means, Brandon," she said hurriedly, looking over her shoulder as she spoke. "Sara says that she has come to a decision of some sort. She wants us to hear her plan before making it final. I — I don't understand her at all to-night."

" It can't be anything serious, dearest," he said, but
something cold and nameless oppressed him just the
same.

" She asked me if I had finally decided to — to be
your wife, Brandon. I said I had asked you for two
or three days more in which to decide. It seemed to
depress her. She said she didn't see how she could
give me up, even to you. She wants to be near me
always. It is — it is really tragic, Brandon."

He took he hands in his.

" We can fix that," said he confidently. " Sara
can live with us if she feels that way about it. Our
home shall be hers when she likes, and as long as she
chooses. It will be open to her all the time, to come
and go or to stay, just as she elects. Isn't that the
way to put it? "

" I suggested something of the sort, but she wasn't
very much impressed. Indeed, she appeared to be
somewhat — yes, I could not have been mistaken,—
somewhat harsh and terrified when I spoke of it.
Afterwards she was more reasonable. She thanked me
and — there were tears in her eyes at the time — and
said she would think it over. All she asks is that I
may be happy and free and untroubled all the rest of
my life. This was before dinner. At dinner she appeared to be brooding over something. When we left
the table she took me to her room and said that she
had come to an important decision. Then she instructed Watson to find you if possible."

" 'Gad, it's all very upsetting," he said, shaking his
head.

" I think her conscience is troubling her. She hates
the Wrandalls, but I — I don't know why I should

feel as I do about it,— but I believe she wants them
to know!"

He stared for a moment, and then his face brightened. "And so do I, Hetty, so do I! They ought
to know!"

"I should feel so much easier if the whole world
knew," said she earnestly.

Sara heard the girl's words as she stood in the door.
She came forward with a strange,— even abashed,—
smile, after closing the door behind her.

"I don't agree with you, dearest, when you say that
the world should know, but I have come to the conclusion that you should be tried and acquitted by a
jury made up of Challis Wrandall's own flesh and
blood. The Wrandalls must know the truth."

CHAPTER XXIV

THE Wrandalls sat waiting and wondering. They had been sent for and they had deigned to respond, much to their own surprise. Redmond Wrandall occupied a place at the head of the library table. At his right sat his wife. Vivian and Leslie, by direction, took seats at the side of the long table, which had been cleared of its mass of books and magazines. Lawyer Carroll was at the other end of the table, perceptibly nervous and anxious. Hetty sat a little apart from the others, a rather forlorn, detached member of the conclave. Brandon Booth, pale-faced and alert, drew up a chair alongside Carroll, facing Sara who alone remained standing, directly opposite the four Wrandalls.

Not one of the Wrandalls knew why they, as a family, were there. They had not the slightest premonition of what was to come.

The strong glare of an electric chandelier, seldom used in this quiet, subdued little library, threw its light down upon the group, outlining every feature with a sharpness that almost created shadows. It was a trying light. No play of the emotions could be lost under its convicting glow. A clock struck nine. Outside the first savage storm of the winter was raging.

The Wrandalls had been routed from their comfortable fireside — for what? They were asking the question of themselves and they were waiting stonily for the answer.

"It is very stuffy in here," Vivian had said with

a glance at the closed doors after Sara had successfully placed her jury in the box.

"Keep still, Viv," whispered Leslie, with a fine assumption of awe. "It's a spiritualistic meeting.
You'll scare the spooks away."

It was at this juncture that Sara rose from her
chair and faced them, as calmly, as complacently as
if she were about to ask them to proceed to the dining-
room instead of to throw a bomb into their midst that
would shatter their smug serenity for all time to come.
With a glance at Mr. Carroll she began, clearly, firmly
and without a prefatory apology for what was to
follow.

"I have asked you to come here to-night to be my
judges. I am on trial. You are about to hear the
story of my unspeakable perfidy. I only require of
you that you hear me to the end before passing judgment."

At her words, Hetty and Booth started perceptibly;
a quick glance passed between them, as if each was inquiring whether the other had caught the extraordinary words of self-indictment. A puzzled frown appeared on Hetty's brow.

"Perfidy?" interposed Mr. Wrandall. His wife's
expression changed from one of bored indifference to
sharp inquiry. Leslie paused in the act of lighting
a cigarette.

"It is the mildest term I can command," said Sara.
"I shall be as brief as possible in stating the case, Mr.
Wrandall. You will be surprised to hear that I have
taken it upon myself, as the wife of Challis Wrandall
and, as I regard it, the one *most* vitally concerned if
not interested in the discovery and punishment of the
person who took his life,—I say I have taken it upon

myself to shield, protect and defend the unhappy
young woman who accompanied him to Burton's Inn
on that night in March. She has had my constant,
my personal protection for more than twenty months."

The Wrandalls leaned forward in their chairs.
The match burned Leslie's fingers, and he dropped it
without appearing to notice the pain.

"What is this you are saying?" demanded Redmond Wrandall.

"When I left the inn that night, after seeing my
husband's body in the little upstairs room, I said to
myself that the one who took his life had unwittingly
done me a service. He was my husband; I loved him,
I adored him. To the end of my days I could have
gone on loving him in spite of the cruel return he gave
for my love and loyalty. I shall not attempt to tell
you of the countless lapses of fidelity on his part. You
would not believe me. But he always came back to
me with the pitiful love he had for me, and I forgave
him his transgressions. These things you know. He
confessed many things to you, Mr. Wrandall. He
humbled himself to me. Perhaps you will recall that
I never complained to you of him. What rancour I
had was always directed toward you, his family, who
would see no wrong in your king but looked upon me
as dirt beneath his feet. There were moments when I
could have slain him with my own hands, but my heart
rebelled. There were times when he said to me that I
ought to kill him for the things he had done. You
may now understand what I mean when I say that the
girl who went to Burton's Inn with him did me a service. I will not say that I considered her guiltless at
the time. On the contrary, I looked upon her in quite
a different way. I had no means of knowing then

that she was as pure as snow and that he would have despoiled her of everything that was sweet and sacred to her. She took his life in order to save that which was dearer to her than her own life, and she was on her way to pay for her deed with her life if necessary when I came upon her and intervened."

"You — you know who she is?" said Mr. Wrandall, in a low, incredulous voice.

"I have known almost from the beginning. Presently you will hear her story, from her own lips."

Involuntarily four pairs of eyes shifted. They looked blankly at Hetty Castleton.

Speaking swiftly, Sara depicted the scenes and sensations experienced during that memorable motor journey to New York City.

"I could not believe that she was a vicious creature, even then. Something told me that she was a tender, gentle thing who had fallen into evil hands and had struck because she was unevil. I did not doubt that she had been my husband's mistress, but I could not destroy the conviction that somehow she had been justified in doing the thing she had done. My gravest mistake was in refusing to hear her story in all of its details. I only permitted her to acknowledge that she had killed him, no more. I did not want to hear the thing which I assumed to be true. Therein lies my deepest fault. For months and months I misjudged her in my heart, yet secretly loved her. Now I understand why I loved her. It was because she was innocent of the only crime I could lay at her feet. Now I come to the crime of which I stand self-accused. I must have been mad all these months. I have no other defence to offer. You may take it as you see it for yourselves. I do not ask for pardon. After I de-

liberately had set about to shield this unhappy girl,—
to cheat the law, if you please,— to cheat you, perhaps,
— I conceived the horrible thought to avenge myself
for *all* the indignities I had sustained at the hands of
you Wrandalls, and at the same time to even my account with the one woman whom I could put my finger
upon as having robbed me of my husband's love. You
see I put it mildly. I have hated all of you, Mrs.
Wrandall, even as you have hated me. To-day,—
now,— I do not feel as I did in other days toward you.
I do not love you, still I do not hate you. I do not
forgive you, and yet I think I have come to see things
from your point of view. I can only repeat that I
do not hate you as I once did."

She paused. The Wrandalls were too deeply submerged in horror to speak. They merely stared at
her as if stupefied; as breathless, as motionless as
stones.

"There came a day when I observed that Leslie was
attracted by the guest in my house. On that day the
plan took root in my brain. I —"

"Good God!" fell from Leslie's lips. "You — you
had *that* in mind?"

"It became a fixed, inflexible purpose, Leslie. Not
that I hated you as I hated the rest, for you tried to
be considerate. The one grudge I held against you
was that in seeking to sustain me you defamed your
own brother. You came to me with stories of his misdeeds; you said that he was a scoundrel and that you
would not blame me for 'showing him up.' Do you
not remember? And so my plot involved you; you
were the only one through whom I could strike. There
were times when I faltered. I could not bear the
thought of sacrificing Hetty Castleton, nor was it

easy to thoroughly appease my conscience in respect
to you. Still, if I could have had my way a few
months ago, if coercion had been of any avail, you
would now be the husband of your brother's slayer.
Then I came to know that she was not what I had
thought she was. She was honest. My bubble burst.
I came out of the maze in which I had been living and
saw clearly that what I had contemplated was the
most atrocious —"

"Atrocious?" cried Mrs. Redmond Wrandall between her set teeth. "Diabolical! Diabolical! My
God, Sara, what a devil you —" She did not complete
the sentence, but sank back in her chair and stared
with wide, horror-struck eyes at her rigid daughter-
in-law.

Her husband, his hand shaking as if with palsy,
pointed a finger at Hetty. "And so *you* are the one
we have been hunting for all these months, Miss Castleton! You are the one we want! You who have sat
at our table, you who have smiled in our faces —"

"Stop, Mr. Wrandall!" commanded Sara, noting
the ashen face of the girl. "Don't let the fact escape
you that I am the guilty person. Don't forget that
she owed her freedom, if not her life to me. I alone
kept her from giving herself up to the law. All that
has transpired since that night in March must be
placed to my account. Hetty Castleton has been my
prisoner. She has rebelled a thousand times and I
have conquered — not by threats but by *love!* Do
you understand? Because of her love for me, and because she believed that I loved her, she submitted.
You are not to accuse her, Mr. Wrandall. Accuse
me! I am on trial here. Hetty Castleton is a witness against me, if you choose to call upon her as

such. If not, I shall ask her to speak in my defence, if she can do so."

"This is lunacy!" cried Mr. Wrandall, coming to his feet. "I don't care what your motives may have been. They do not make her any the less a murderess. She —"

"We must give her over to the police —" began his wife, struggling to her feet. She staggered. It was Booth who stepped quickly to her side to support her. Leslie was staring at Hetty.

Vivian touched her father's arm. She was very pale but vastly more composed than the others.

"Father, listen to me," she said. Her voice trembled in spite of her effort to control it. "We are condemning Miss Castleton unheard. Let us hear everything before we —"

"Good God, Vivian! Do you mean to —"

"How can we place any reliance on what she may say?" cried Mrs. Wrandall.

"Nevertheless," said Vivian firmly, "I for one shall not condemn her unheard. I mean to be as fair to her as Sara has been. It shall not be said that *all* the Wrandalls are smaller than Sara Gooch!"

"My child —" began her father incredulously. His jaw dropped suddenly. His daughter's shot had landed squarely in the heart of the Wrandall pride.

"If she has anything to say,"—said Mrs. Wrandall, waving Booth aside and sinking stiffly into her chair. Her husband sat down. Their jaws set hard.

"Thank you, Vivian," said Sara, surprised in spite of herself. "You are nobler than I —"

"Please don't thank me, Sara," said Vivian icily. "I was speaking for Miss Castleton."

Sara flushed. "I suppose it is useless to ask you

to be fair to Sara Gooch, as you choose to call me."

"Do you feel in your heart that we still owe you anything?"

"Enough of this, Vivian," spoke up her father harshly. "If Miss Castleton desires to speak we will listen to her. I must advise you, Miss Castleton, that the extraordinary disclosures made by my daughter-in-law do not lessen your culpability. We do not insist on this confession from you. You deliver it at your own risk. I want to be fair with you. If Mr. Carroll is your counsel, he may advise you now to refuse to make a statement."

Mr. Carroll bowed slightly in the general direction of the Wrandalls. "I have already advised Miss Castleton to state the case fully and completely to you, Mr. Wrandall. It was I who originally suggested this — well, what you might call a private trial for her. I am firmly convinced that when you have heard her story, you, as her judges, will acquit her of the charge of murder. Moreover, you will be content to let your own verdict end the matter, sparing yourselves the shame and ignominy of having her story told in a criminal court for the delectation of an eager but somewhat implacable world."

"Your language is extremely unpleasant, Mr. Carroll," said Mr. Wrandall coldly.

"I meant to speak kindly, sir."

"Do you mean, sir, that we will let the matter rest after hearing the —"

"That is precisely what I mean, Mr. Wrandall. You will not consider her guilty of a crime. Please bear in mind this fact: but for Sara and Miss Castleton you would not have known the truth. Miss Castleton could not be convicted in a court of justice,

Nor will she be convicted here this evening, in this
little court of ours."

"Miss Castleton is not on trial," interposed Sara
calmly. "I am the offender. She has already been
tried and proved innocent."

Leslie, in his impatience, tapped sharply on the table with his seal ring.

"Please let her tell the story. Permit me to say,
Miss Castleton, that you will not find the Wrandalls
as harsh and vindictive as you may have been led to
believe."

Mrs. Wrandall passed her hand over her eyes. "To
think that we have been friendly to this girl all
these —"

"Calm yourself, my dear," said her husband, after
a glance at his son and daughter, a glance of unspeakable helplessness. He could not understand them.

As Hetty arose, Mrs. Wrandall senior lowered her
eyes and not once did she look up during the recital
that followed. Her hands were lying limply in her
lap, and she breathed heavily, almost stertoriously.
The younger Wrandalls leaned forward with their
clear, unwavering gaze fixed on the earnest face of the
young Englishwoman who had slain their brother.

"You have heard Sara accuse herself," said the
girl slowly, dispassionately. "The shock was no
greater to you than it was to me. All that she has
said is true, and yet I — I would so much rather she
had left herself unarraigned. We were agreed that I
should throw myself on your mercy. Mr. Carroll said
that you were fair and just people, that you would
not condemn me under the circumstances. But that
Sara should seek to take the blame is —"

"Alas, my dear, I *am* to blame," said Sara, shaking

her head. " But for me your story would have been
told months ago, the courts would have cleared you,
and all the world would have execrated my husband
for the thing *he* did — my husband and your son, Mrs.
Wrandall,— whom we both loved. God believe me, I
think I loved him more than all of you put together! "

She sat down abruptly and buried her face in her
arms on the edge of the table.

" If I could only induce you to forgive her," began
Hetty, throwing out her hands to the Wrandalls, only
to be met by a gesture of repugnance from the grim
old man.

" Your story, Miss Castleton," he said hoarsely.

" From the beginning, if you please," added the lawyer quietly. " Leave out nothing."

Clearly, steadily and with the utmost sincerity in
her voice and manner, the girl began the story of her
life. She passed hastily over the earlier periods,
frankly exposing the unhappy conditions attending her
home life, her subsequent activities as a performer on
the London stage after Colonel Castleton's defection ; the few months devoted to posing for Hawkright
the painter, and later on her engagement as governess in the wealthy Budlong family. She devoted
some time and definiteness to her first encounter
with Challis Wrandall on board the westbound steamer,
an incident that came to pass in a perfectly natural
way. Her deck chair stood next to his, and he was
not slow in making himself agreeable. It did not occur to her till long afterwards that he deliberately had
traded positions with an elderly gentleman who occupied the chair on the first day out. Before the end
of the voyage they were very good friends. . . .

" When we landed in New York, he assisted me in

many ways. Afterwards, on learning that I was not to go California, I called him up on the telephone to explain my predicament. He urged me to stay in New York; he guaranteed that there would be no difficulty in securing a splendid position in the East. I had no means of knowing that he was married. I accepted him for what I thought him to be: a genuine American gentleman. They are supposed to be particularly considerate with women. His conduct toward me was beyond reproach. I have never known a man who was so courteous, so gentle. To me, he was the most fascinating man in the world. No woman could have resisted him, I am sure of that."

She shot a quick, appealing glance at Booth's hard-set face. Her lip trembled for a second.

"I fell madly in love with him," she went on resolutely. "I dreamed of him, I could hardly wait for the time to come when I was to see him. He never came to the wretched little lodging house I have told you about. I — I met him outside. One night he told me that he loved me, loved me passionately. I — I said that I would be his wife. Somehow it seemed to me that he regarded me very curiously for a moment or two. He seemed to be surprised, uncertain. I remember that he laughed rather queerly. It did not occur to me to doubt him. One day he came for me, saying that he wanted me to see the little apartment he had taken, where we were to live after we were married. I went with him. He said that if I liked it, I could move in at once, but I would not consent to such an arrangement. For the first time I began to feel that everything was not as it should be. I — I remained in the apartment but a few minutes. The next day he came to me, greatly excited and more

demonstrative than ever before, to say that he had
arranged for a quiet, jolly little wedding up in the
country. Strangely enough I experienced a queer
feeling that all was not as it should be, but his eagerness, his persistence dispelled the small doubt that
had begun even then to shape itself. I consented to go
with him on the next night to an inn out in the country, where a college friend who was a minister of the
gospel would meet us, driving over from his parish a
few miles away. I said that I preferred to be married
in a church. He laughed and said it could be arranged when we got to the inn and had talked it over
with the minister. Still uneasy, I asked why it was
necessary to employ secrecy. He told me that his
family were in Europe and that he wanted to surprise
them by giving them a daughter who was actually related to an English nobleman. The family had been
urging him to marry a stupid but rich New York girl
and he — oh, well, he uttered a great deal of nonsense
about my beauty, my charm, and all that sort of
thing —"

She paused for a moment. No one spoke. Her
audience of judges, with the exception of the elder
Mrs. Wrandall, watched her as if fascinated. Their
faces were almost expressionless. With a perceptible
effort, she resumed her story, narrating events that
carried it up to the hour when she walked into the little upstairs room at Burton's Inn with the man who
was to be her husband.

"I did not see the register at the inn. I did not
know till afterwards that we were not booked. Once
upstairs, I refused to remove my hat or my veil or my
coat until he brought his friend to me. He pretended
to be very angry over his friend's failure to be there

beforehand, as he had promised. He ordered a supper served in the room. I did not eat anything. Somehow I was beginning to understand, vaguely of course, but surely — and bitterly, Mr. Wrandall. Suddenly he threw off the mask.

"He coolly informed me that he knew the kind of girl I was. I had been on the stage. He said it was no use trying to work the marriage game on him. He was too old a bird and too wise to fall for that. Those were his words. I was horrified, stunned. When I began to cry out in my fury, he laughed at me but swore he would marry me even at that if it were not for the fact that he already was married. . . . I tried to leave the room. He held me. He kissed me a hundred times before I could break away. I — I tried to scream. . . . A little later on, when I was absolutely desperate, I — I snatched up the knife. There was nothing else left for me to do. I struck at him. He fell back on the bed. . . . I stole out of the house — oh, hours and hours afterward it seemed to me. I cannot tell you how long I stood there watching him. . . . I was crazed by fear. I — I —"

Redmond Wrandall held up his hand.

"We will spare you the rest, Miss Castleton," he said, his voice hoarse and unnatural. "There is no need to say more."

"You — you understand? You *do* believe me?" she cried.

He looked down at his wife's bowed head, and received no sign from her; then at the white, drawn faces of his children. They met his gaze and he read something in their eyes.

"I — I think your story is so convincing that we —

we could not endure the shame of having it repeated to the world."

" I — I cannot ask you to forgive me, sir. I only ask you to believe me," she murmured brokenly. " I — I am sorry it had to be. God is my witness that there was no other way."

Mr. Carroll came to his feet. There were tears in his eyes.

" I think, Mr. Wrandall, you will now appreciate my motives in —"

" Pardon me, Mr. Carroll, if I suggest that Miss Castleton does not require any defence at present," said Mr. Wrandall stiffly. " Your motives were doubtless good. Will you be so good as to conduct us to a room where we may — may be alone for a short while? "

There was something tragic in the man's face. His son and daughter arose as if moved by an instinctive realisation of a duty, and perhaps for the first time in their lives were submissive to an influence they had never quite recognised before: a father's unalterable right to command. For once in their lives they were meek in his presence. They stepped to his side and stood waiting, and neither of them spoke.

Mr. Wrandall laid his hand heavily on his wife's shoulder. She started, looked up rather vacantly, and then arose without assistance. He did not make the mistake of offering to assist her. He knew too well that to question her strength now would be but to invite weakness. She was strong. He knew her well.

She stood straight and firm for a few seconds, transfixing Hetty with a look that seemed to bore into the very soul of her, and then spoke.

" You ask us to be your judges? "

"I ask you to judge not me alone but — your son as well," said Hetty, meeting her look steadily. "You cannot pronounce me innocent without pronouncing him guilty. It will be hard."

Sara raised her head from her arms.

"You know the way into my sitting-room, Leslie," she said, with singular directness. Then she arose and drew her figure to its full height. "Please remember that it is I who am to be judged. Judge me as I have judged you. I am not asking for mercy."

Hetty impulsively threw her arms about the rigid figure, and swept a pleading look from one to the other of the four stony-faced Wrandalls.

They turned away without a word or a revealing look, and slowly moved off in the direction of the boudoir. They who remained behind stood still, motionless as statues. It was Vivian who opened the library door. She closed it after the others had passed through, and did not look behind.

.   .   .   .   .   .

Half an hour passed. Then the door was opened and the tall old man advanced into the room.

"We have found against my son, Miss Castleton," he said, his lips twitching. "He is not here to speak for himself, but he has already been judged. We, his family, apologise to you for what you have suffered from the conduct of one of us. Not one but all of us believe the story you have told. It must never be retold. We ask this of all of you. It is not in our hearts to thank Sara for shielding you, for her hand is still raised against us. We are fair and just. If you had come to *us* on that wretched night and told the story of my son's infamy, *we*, the Wrandalls, would have stood between you and the law. The law

could not have touched you then; it shall not touch
you now. Our verdict, if you choose to call it that,
is sealed. No man shall ever hear from the lips of a
Wrandall the smallest part of what has transpired
here to-night. Mr. Carroll, you were right. We
thank you for the counsel that led this unhappy girl
to place herself in our hands."

"Oh, God, I thank thee — I thank thee!" burst
from the lips of Sara Wrandall. She strained Hetty
to her breast.

"It is not for us to judge you, Sara," said Redmond Wrandall, speaking with difficulty. "You are
your own judge, and a harsh one you will find yourself. As for ourselves, we can only look upon your
unspeakable design as the working of a temporarily
deranged mind. You could never have carried it out.
You are an honest woman. At the last you would
have revolted, even with victory assured. Perhaps
Leslie is the only one who has a real grievance against
you in this matter. I am convinced that he loved Miss
Castleton deeply. The worst hurt is his, and he has
been your most devoted advocate during all the years
of bitterness that has existed between you and us.
You thought to play him a foul trick. You could not
have carried it to the end. We leave you to pass judgment on yourself."

"I have already done so, Mr. Wrandall," said Sara.
"Have I not accused myself before you? Have I not
confessed to the only crime that has been committed?
I am not proud of myself, sir."

"You have hated us well."

"And you have hated me. The crime you hold me
guilty of was committed years ago. It was when I
robbed you of your son. To this day I am the leper

in your path. I may be forgiven for all else, but not
for allowing Challis Wrandall to become the husband
of Sebastian Gooch's daughter. That is the unpar-
donable sin."

Mr. Wrandall was silent for a moment.

"You still are Sebastian Gooch's daughter," he
said distinctly. "You can never be anything else."

She paled. "This last transaction proves it, you
would say?"

"This last transaction, yes."

She looked about her with troubled, questioning eyes.

"I — I wonder if *that* can be true," she murmured,
rather piteously. "Am I so different from the rest
of you? Is the blood to blame?"

"Nonsense!" exclaimed Mr. Carroll nervously.
"Don't be silly, Sara, my child. That is not what
Mr. Wrandall means."

Wrandall turned his face away.

"You loved as deeply as you hate, Sara," he said,
with a curious twitching of his chin. "My son was
your god. We are not insensible to that. Perhaps
we have never realised until now the depth and breadth
of your love for him. Love is a bitter judge of its
enemies. It knows no mercy, it knows no reason.
Hate may be conquered by love, but love cannot be
conquered by hate. You had reason to hate my son.
Instead you persisted in your love for him. We — we
owe you something for that, Sara. We owe you a
great deal more than I find myself able to express in
words."

Leslie entered the room at this instant. He had
his overcoat on and carried his gloves and hat in his
hand.

"We are ready, father," he said thickly.

After a moment's hesitation, he crossed over to Hetty, who stood beside Sara.

"I — I can now understand why you refused to marry me, Miss Castleton," he said, in a queer, jerky manner. "Won't you let me say that I wish you all the happiness still to be found in this rather uneven world of ours?"

The crowning testimonial to an absolutely sincere ego!

CHAPTER XXV

ON the third day after the singular trial of Hetty Castleton in Sara's library, young Mrs. Wrandall's motor drew up in front of a lofty office building in lower Broadway; its owner stepped down from the limousine and entered the building. A few moments later she walked briskly into the splendid offices of Wrandall & Co., private bankers and steamship-owners. The clerks in the outer offices stared for a moment in significant surprise, and then bowed respectfully to the beautiful silent partner in the great concern.

It was the first time she had been seen in the offices since the tragic event that had served to make her a member of the firm. A boy at the information desk, somewhat impressed by her beauty and the trim elegance of her long black broad-tail coat, to say nothing of the dark eyes that shone through the narrow veil, forgot the dignity of his office and went so far as to politely ask her who she wanted to see and "what name, please."

The senior clerk rushed forward and transfixed the new boy with a glare.

"A new boy, Mrs. Wrandall," he made haste to explain. To the new boy's surprise, the visitor was conducted with much bowing and scraping into the private offices, where no one ventured except by special edict of the powers.

"Who was it?" he asked, in some awe, of a veteran stenographer who came up and sneered at him.

"Mrs. Challis Wrandall, you little simpleton," said she, and for once he failed to snap back.

It is of record that for nearly two whole days, he was polite to every visitor who approached him and was generally worth his salt.

Sara found herself in the close little room that once had been her husband's, but was now scrupulously held in reserve for her own use. Rather a waste of space, she felt as she looked about the office. The clerk dusted an easy chair and threw open the long unused desk near the window.

"We are very glad to see you here, madam," he said. "This room hasn't been used much, as you may observe. Is there anything I can do for you?"

She continued her critical survey of the room. Nothing had been changed since the days when she used to visit her husband here on occasions of rare social importance: such as calling to take him out to luncheon, or to see that he got safely home on rainy afternoons. The big picture of a steamship still hung on the wall across the room. Her own photograph, in a silver frame, stood in one of the recesses of the desk. She observed that there was a clean white blotter there, too; but the ink wells appeared to be empty, if she was to judge by the look of chagrin on the clerk's face as he inspected them. Photographs of polo scenes in which Wrandall was a prominent figure, hung about the walls, with two or three pictures of his favourite ponies, and one of a ragged gipsy girl with wonderful eyes, carrying a monkey in a crude wooden cage strapped to her back. On closer observation one would have recognised Sara's peculiarly gipsy-like features in the face of the girl, and then one would have noticed the caption written in red ink at the bottom of the photograph: "*The Trumbell's Fancy Dress Ball, January* 10, '07. *Sara as Gipsy Mab.*"

With a start, Sara came out of her painful reverie. She passed her hand over her eyes, and seemed thereby to put the polite senior clerk back into the picture once more.

"No, thank you. Is Mr. Redmond Wrandall down this afternoon?"

"He came in not ten minutes ago. Mr. Leslie Wrandall is also here. Shall I tell Mr. Wrandall you wish to see him?"

"You may tell him that I am here, if you please," she said.

"I am very sorry about the ink wells, madam," murmured the clerk. "We — we were not expecting —"

"Pray don't let it disturb you, Mr. Bancroft. I shall not use them to-day."

"They will be properly filled by to-morrow."

"Thank you."

He disappeared. She relaxed in the familiar, comfortable old leather-cushioned chair, and closed her eyes. There was a sharp little line between them, but it was hidden by the veil.

The door opened slowly and Redmond Wrandall came into the room. She arose at once.

"This is — er — an unexpected pleasure, Sara," he said, perplexed and ill-at-ease. He stopped just inside the door he had been careful to close behind him, and did not offer her his hand.

"I came down to attend to some business, Mr. Wrandall," she said.

"Business?" he repeated, staring.

She took note of the tired, haggard look in his eyes, and the tightly compressed lips.

"I intend to dispose of my entire interest in Wrandall & Co.," she announced calmly.

He took a step forward, plainly startled by the declaration.

"What's this?" he demanded sharply.

"We may as well speak plainly, Mr. Wrandall," she said. "You do not care to have me remain a member of the firm, nor do I blame you for feeling as you do about it. A year ago you offered to buy me out — or off, as I took it to be at the time. I had reasons then for not selling out to you. To-day I am ready either to buy or to sell."

"You — you amaze me," he exclaimed.

"Does your offer of last December still stand?"

"I — I think we would better have Leslie in, Sara. This is most unexpected. I don't quite feel up to —"

"Have Leslie in by all means," she said, resuming her seat.

He hesitated a moment, opened his lips as if to speak, and then abruptly left the room.

Sara smiled.

Many minutes passed before the two Wrandalls put in an appearance. She understood the delay. They were telephoning to certain legal advisers.

"What's this I hear, Sara?" demanded Leslie, extending his hand after a second's hesitation.

She shook hands with him, not listlessly but with the vigour born of nervousness.

"I don't know what you've heard," she said pointedly.

His slim fingers went searching for the end of his moustache.

"Why,— why, about selling out to us," he stammered.

"I am willing to retire from the firm of Wrandall
& Co.," she said.

"Father says the business is as good as it was a
year ago, but I don't agree with him," said the son,
trying to look lugubrious.

"Then you don't care to repeat your original proposition?"

"Well, the way business has been falling off —"

"Perhaps you would prefer to sell out to me," she
remarked quietly.

"Not at all!" he said quickly, with a surprised
glance at his father. "We couldn't think of letting
the business pass out of the Wrandall name."

"You forget that *my* name is Wrandall," she rejoined. "There would be no occasion to change the
firm's name; merely its membership."

"Our original offer stands," said the senior Wrandall stiffly. "We prefer to buy."

"And I to sell. Mr. Carroll will meet you to-morrow, gentlemen. He will represent me as usual. Our
business as well as social relations are about to end, I
suppose. My only regret is that I cannot further
accommodate you by changing my name. Still you
may live in hope that time may work even that wonder for you."

She arose. The two men regarded her in an ag-
grieved way for a moment.

"I have no real feeling of hostility toward you,
Sara," said Leslie nervously, "in spite of all that you
said the other night."

"I am afraid you don't mean that, deep down in
your heart, Leslie," she said, with a queer little smile.

"But I do," he protested. "Hang it all, we — we live in a glass house ourselves, Sara. I dare say, in a way, I was quite as unpleasant as the rest of the family. You see, we just can't help being snobs. It's in us, that's all there is to it."

Mr. Wrandall looked up from the floor, his gaze having dropped at the first outburst from his son's lips.

"We — we prefer to be friendly, Sara, if you will allow us —"

She laughed and the old gentleman stopped in the middle of his sentence.

"We can't be friends, Mr. Wrandall," she said, suddenly serious. "The pretence would be a mockery. We are all better off if we allow our paths, our interests to diverge to-day."

"Perhaps you are right," said he, compressing his lips.

"I believe that Vivian and I could — but no! I won't go so far as to say that either. There is something genuine about her. Strange to say, I have never disliked her."

"If you had made the slightest effort to like us, no doubt we could have —"

"My dear Mr. Wrandall," she interrupted quickly, "I credit *you* with the desire to be fair and just to me. You have tried to like me. You have even deceived yourself at times. I — but why these gentle recriminations? We merely prolong an unfortunate contest between antagonistic natures, with no hope of genuine peace being established. I do not regret that I am your daughter-in-law, nor do I believe that you would regret it if I had not been the daughter of Sebastian Gooch."

"Your father was as little impressed with my son as I was with his daughter," said Redmond Wrandall drily. "I am forced to confess that he was the better judge. We had the better of the bargain."

"I believe you mean it, Mr. Wrandall," she said, a note of gratitude in her voice. "Good-bye. Mr. Carroll will see you to-morrow." She glanced quickly about the room. "I shall send for — for certain articles that are no longer required in conducting the business of Wrandall & Co."

With a quaint little smile, she indicated the two photographs of herself.

"By Jove, Sara," burst out Leslie abruptly. "I wish you'd let *me* have that Gipsy Mab picture. I've always been dotty over it, don't you know. Ripping study."

Her lip curled slightly.

"As a matter of fact," he explained conclusively, "Chal often said he'd leave it to me when he died. In a joking way, of course, but I'm sure he meant it."

"You may have it, Leslie," she said slowly. It is doubtful if he correctly interpreted the movement of her head as she uttered the words.

"Thanks," said he. "I'll hang it in my den, if you don't object."

"We shall expect Mr. Carroll to-morrow, Sara," said his father, with an air of finality. "Good-bye. May I ask what plans you are making for the winter?"

"They are very indefinite."

"I say, Sara, why don't you get married?" asked Leslie, surveying the Gipsy Mab photograph with undisguised admiration as he held it at arm's length. "Ripping!" This to the picture.

She paused near the door to stare at him for a moment, unutterable scorn in her eyes.

"I've had a notion you were pretty keen about Brandy Booth," he went on amiably.

She caught her breath. There was an instant's hesitation on her part before she replied.

"You have never been very smart at making love guesses, Leslie," she said. "It's a trick you haven't acquired."

He laughed uncomfortably. "Neat stroke, that."

Following her into the corridor outside the offices, he pushed the elevator bell for her.

"I meant what I said, Sara," he remarked, somewhat doggedly. "You ought to get married. Chal didn't leave much for you to cherish. There's no reason why you should go on like this, living alone and all that sort of thing. You're young and beautiful and —"

"Oh, thank you, Leslie," she cried out sharply.

"You see, it's going to be this way: Hetty will probably marry Booth. That's *on dit*, I take it. You're depending on her for companionship. Well, she'll quit you cold after she's married. She will —"

She interrupted him peremptorily.

"If Challis did nothing else for me, Leslie, he at least gave me you to cherish. Once more, good-bye."

The elevator stopped for her. He strolled back to his office with a puzzled frown on his face. She certainly was inexplicable!

The angry red faded from her cheeks as she sped homeward in the automobile. Her thoughts were no longer of Leslie but of another. . . . She sighed and closed her eyes, and her cheeks were pale.

Workmen from a picture dealer's establishment were

engaged in hanging a full length portrait in the long living-room of her apartment when she reached home. She had sent to the country for Booth's picture of Hetty, and was having it hung in a conspicuous place. For a long time she stood in the middle of the room, studying the canvas. Hetty's Irish blue eyes seemed to return the scrutiny, a questioning look in their painted depths. The warm, half smiling lips appeared to be on the point of putting into words the eager question that lay in her wondering eyes.

Passing the open library door, Sara paused for an instant to peer within. Then she went on down the hall to her own sitting-room. The canary was singing glibly in his cage by the window-side.

She threw aside her furs, and, without removing her hat, passed into the bed-chamber at the left of the cosy little boudoir. This was Hetty's room. Her own was directly opposite. On the girl's dressing-table, leaning against the broad, low mirror, stood the unframed photograph of a man. With a furtive glance over her shoulder, Sara crossed to the table and took up the picture in her gloved hand. For a long time she stood there gazing into the frank, good-looking face of Brandon Booth. She breathed faster; her hand shook; her eyes were strained as if by an inward suggestion of pain.

She shook her head slowly, as if in final renunciation of a secret hope or the banishment of an unwelcome desire, and resolutely replaced the photograph. Her lips were almost white as she turned away and re-entered the room beyond.

" He belongs to her," she said, unconsciously speaking aloud; " and he is like all men. She must not be unhappy."

Presently she entered the library. She had exchanged her tailor-suit for a dainty house-gown. Hetty was still seated in the big lounging chair, before the snapping fire, apparently not having moved since she looked in on passing a quarter of an hour before. One of the girl's legs was curled up under her, the other swung loose; an elbow rested on the arm of the chair, and her cheek was in her hand.

Coming softly up from behind, Sara leaned over the back of the chair and put her hands under her friend's chin, tenderly, lovingly. Hetty started and shivered.

"Oh, Sara, how cold your hands are!"

She grasped them in her own and fondly stroked them, as if to restore warmth to the long, slim fingers which gave the lie to Mrs. Coburn's declarations.

"I've been thinking all morning of what you and Brandon proposed to me last night, dear," said Sara, looking straight over the girl's head, the dark, languorous, mysterious glow filling her eyes. "It is good of you both to want me, but —"

"Now don't say 'but,' Sara," cried Hetty. "We mean it, and you must let us have our way."

"It would be splendid to be near you all the time, dear; it would be wonderful to live with you as you so generously propose, but I cannot do it. I must decline."

"And may I ask why you decline to live with me?" demanded Hetty resentfully.

"Because I love you so dearly," said Sara.

THE END